BENEATH A NAVAJO MOON

Lisa Carter

Other books by Lisa Carter

Carolina Reckoning
Aloha Rose

Beneath a Navajo Moon

Copyright © 2014 by Lisa Carter

ISBN-13: 978-1-4267-5799-0

Published by Abingdon Press, P.O. Box 801, Nashville, TN 37202

www.abingdonpress.com

Published in association with the Steve Laube Agency

The persons and events portrayed in this work of fiction
are the creations of the author, and any resemblance
to persons living or dead is purely coincidental.

Scripture quotations are from the Common English Bible.
Copyright © 2011 by the Common English Bible. All rights reserved.
Used by permission. www.CommonEnglishBible.com.

Library of Congress Cataloging-in-Publication Data

Carter, Lisa, 1964-
  Beneath a Navajo moon / Lisa Carter.
    pages cm
  ISBN 978-1-4267-5799-0 (binding: soft black, adhesive : alk. paper) 1. Women anthropologists—Fiction. 2. Navajo Indians—Fiction. 3. Indian reservation police—Fiction. 4. Drug
traffic—Fiction. I. Title.
  PS3603.A77757B46 2014
  813'.6—dc23

                                                                    2013031608

Printed in the United States of America

1 2 3 4 5 6 7 8 9 10 / 18 17 16 15 14

To Corinne—At the beginning of life's greatest adventure—the journey of faith—may you always walk in beauty, harmony, and in the truest of all loves, Jesus Christ. BTW, you rocked the Navajo bun.

For those who've wrestled with faith and surrender, struggled with God's will, yearned for a place to truly belong, walked the road of sacrifice in a "long obedience" in faith, like Abraham, for the hope yet unseen. Hang in there. And may you receive mercy and find grace in the time of your greatest need.

Hold on to the confession since we have a great high priest who passed through the heavens, who is Jesus, God's Son; because we don't have a high priest who can't sympathize with our weaknesses but instead one who was tempted in every way that we are, except without sin.

Finally, let's draw near to the throne of favor with confidence, so that we can receive mercy and find grace when we need help.
Hebrews 4:14-16

A Note from the Author

The Navajo Reservation is a vast area that encompasses rugged and isolated portions of Arizona, New Mexico, and Utah. The Navajo cops are contemporary warrior heroes who deal on a daily basis with modern-day problems such as gangs, murder, drugs, and human trafficking. With too little manpower and resources to patrol the largest Indian reservation in the United States, Navajo Nation police officers are often spread thin. I took the liberty of creating a substation in the fictional town of Cedar Canyon, Arizona.

Acknowledgments

David, Corinne, and Kathryn—Thanks for helping me not forget to live life while writing about life. Thanks, too, for all the technical support that runs the gamut from the computer to the washing machine.

Sue Carter Stout—Your hospitality enabled me to share my vision of *Beneath a Navajo Moon* with Abingdon. I'm here in large part because of your friendship. You are a blessing to me.

My mother, Carolyn Fulghum, for always being my first reader.

Sonny Boyer—retired from the Norfolk Police Department, bond-servant of Jesus—thanks for reading through the manuscript. He wonders how such a proper Southern lady could write such scenes of mayhem. Don't we all wonder?

Hope Dougherty—You have been such a blessing as a friend and critique partner on this stretch of my faith journey.

Patricia Cargill Carter—For recounting to me the vivid story of the long-ago battle on the grassy hillside outside your home on top of the mesa. Where once Anglo settlers, the American army, and Indian warriors fought for supremacy over the land.

Tamela Hancock Murray—You are the best agent in the world. I'm blessed to be represented by you.

Ramona Richards—Editor extraordinaire. This is the story that first drew us together based upon our mutual interests. Thank you for the vision to dream dreams with me.

Teri—For your insightful edits in making this book better.

Cat Hoort, Mark Yeh, Susan Cornell, and the Abingdon marketing, sales, and production teams—Thanks so much for your behind-the-scenes work in making this book the best it can be.

The Anderson Design Group—I can't express how much I love this cover—all the evocative covers you've designed for my books. You are incredible. I'm awestruck at your creativity.

My Precepts class—For the year we spent studying and finding out what it really means to live out Hebrews. Thank you for sharing your lives and hearts with me.

Readers—It is my prayer that as you follow the Lord's leading in every area of life, you will walk in beauty because of God's best gift to us, His Son, Jesus Christ.

Jesus—I come, as must all, humble and broken to the foot of the cross, in gratitude that because of Your sacrifice, I may boldly approach Abba Father's throne. Thank you for the mercy and unmerited grace throughout all the dark hours of my need.

1

Late September 1906

"With the first pink streaks of light piercing the sky, they came . . ."

Olivia Thornton rose early, stuffing her Bible and journal into the pocket of her pinafore. Sneaking out her bedroom window, she hiked down the gently sloping hill at the back of the Cedar Canyon Mission School toward the creek. The hem of her lavender blue calico trailed in the early morning dew beading the buffalo grass. Over her shoulder, she shot a quick, nervous glance at the reddening sky.

Was it her guilty conscience or did the air vibrate with some unspoken tension? Her daddy, back home in Carolina, used to say, "Red sky at morning, sailor take warning." But aside from her fellow teachers at the mission school, not another human being dwelled for miles.

The desolate badlands stretched as far as the eye could see, only red rock canyons and sage. Yet to Olivia's appreciative eyes, the land also contained a harsh beauty. Out of habit, she cocked her head to listen for the comical squawks of the Stellar jay that often greeted her each morning. But today, only an eerie silence.

If the Director caught her out here, she'd be in big trouble. Not that she wasn't already in big trouble with him. She'd

11

gone and plopped herself in one big cow patty. But she needed time alone under God's creation.

Time to think and pray about what she'd do now. Coming to Navajo-land had been a mistake. She didn't belong here. Question was, where *did* she belong?

Crouching underneath a stand of cottonwoods, she cupped her hands in the water, splashing herself awake. Removing her hands from her face, she first noticed leaves floating past her reflection in the water. She'd remember those dead, brown leaves.

Later.

Her scalp prickled. And he lunged. She screamed . . .

Present-day, April

Cupping her hands around the piping hot coffee mug, Erin Dawson stood at the kitchen sink, watching the tall prairie grass on the mesa quiver in the early morning breeze. A red sky morning, like Olivia's final morning. A tingle of excitement and a slight foreboding teased at Erin's mind. Funny, how after all these years dreaming of finding Olivia or at least the rest of her story—the research in dusty library carrels across the country, Internet searches, phone calls—and lots of prayer—she was here.

Here in the spot where it began. What luck—no, she didn't believe in luck. This was God, despite what her family chose to believe. God had enabled her to rent one of the few homes available on the reservation. The flat-roofed, one-story adobe located on the former remains of Olivia's plundered Cedar Canyon Mission School. The place where Olivia's adventure had truly begun and . . . where Erin prayed her own future destiny might be revealed.

She'd dreamed last night of Olivia as she must have appeared that fateful morning in 1906. Having read her journal entries many times, she'd all but memorized each passage. In ways she didn't understand, Olivia's mysterious journey and her own yet undiscovered path were inexplicably linked. If she could solve the ultimate riddle of Olivia's quest, perhaps she'd also find a place to belong.

Rinsing her cup, Erin glanced at her watch. By the time she drove to the foot of the mesa and into town, the workday would be upon her. Her first day on a new job, an internship meant to further her research and, on the side, answer lingering questions regarding Olivia's fate.

Placing the journal into her handbag, she rushed out the door to her car. Turning the key in the ignition, she breathed a sigh of relief when the engine sputtered to life. Graduate students working on doctoral dissertations didn't exactly have spare cash floating around for car repairs. She was just thankful the old Camry, green like her eyes, had successfully made the cross-country trip.

Easing onto the blacktop, she rotated the wheel to avoid hitting a prairie dog. Peaceful up here, but isolated and lonely. She shivered at the mournful howl of the wind through the Ponderosa pines, the crying of the wind a constant companion on top of the mesa. The Navajo refused to live here, preferring their ranches and farms surrounding the small village of Cedar Canyon or the traditional clan sheep-camps in the high country. *Chindis*, they believed dwelled in the ruins of the old school, ghosts of the dead come back to haunt the living—the cries of the souls lost in the raid on that long ago day in 1906.

Goose bumps prickled on her arms. But she shook the cobwebs from her mind as she steered the curving road toward Cedar Canyon. Remember to Whom you belong, she reminded herself.

Someone far stronger than any *chindi*. Someone Who came to set all peoples free from fear. That day in 1906, this day—

each a day of new beginnings. For Olivia and for her, too, God willing.

Adam's eyes narrowed at the sight of the *bilágaana* occupying the receptionist's chair at the Information Center, her eyes scouring a map she'd spread over the counter space. At the whooshing sound of the door closing behind him, her head snapped up.

He stepped away from the entrance, his hand extended. In the two seconds it took him to reach the desk, he inspected every inch of her, the cop in him taking mental notes. Shoulder length brown hair caught up in a side ponytail, large eyes. Medium height. Mid- to late-twenties, within a few years of his age.

The palest of the skin of her people. The lush, luminous glow of women he remembered from his days at Fort Bragg. Women who'd spent their lives in the moisture-rich South, not the bone dry places the women of his tribe inhabited on the Rez of the Navajo Nation.

Serious-minded etched across a perfect oval face. Three-quarter length mauve shirt. Nothing to write home about.

His gaze returning to her face, he stiffened as those green eyes of hers examined him just as intently. And found him wanting?

Did she know the Diné—the Navajo—considered eye-to-eye contact confrontational? He pursed his lips. She flushed at his scrutiny, but she didn't blink or waver. Good for her. Perhaps his carefully wrought reputation preceded him.

He leaned over the counter. "I'm Adam." He flashed his most winsome smile—for which he was renowned—a tool in his arsenal of weapons. "You're new, aren't you?"

She lifted her chin a fraction and didn't take his hand. "You must be Debra's boyfriend. She'll be right—"

"Adam, you tease, you're five minutes early." Debra, the blonde assistant director of the Center, emerged from a back room, her hips swaying provocatively. Her ruffled cream silk blouse revealed her thin, swanlike neck and lots of carefully calculated cleavage.

He dropped his hand still hanging in the air and fastened his smile on Debra. "Couldn't stay away from you any longer, babe."

Debra smiled, running her tongue over her carmine-tipped bottom lip.

He shifted his attention to the other woman and frowned. She'd turned her back on him, her head bent this time over a computer screen. He wasn't used to being so summarily dismissed.

Debra linked her arm through his. "Come on, Adam. I only have an hour for lunch. We'll be at Taqueros," she called over her shoulder. "Can we bring you something? The blue corn enchiladas are to die for."

"No, thanks," came the muffled voice, her face hidden in the folds of the map again. "I brought my lunch today. Have fun." She waved an absentminded hand. "Take your time. I'll man the fort. Inventory to check . . ."

Debra teetered to an abrupt stop on the threshold. A tight crevasse formed between her plucked brows, a distracted look in her ice blue eyes. And . . . fleeting displeasure. So fleeting, if it hadn't been his job to monitor every move Debra made, he might have missed the emotion or discounted it.

Something was going down between these two. Something perhaps the brunette wasn't even cognizant of yet. Something he needed to check out later.

Debra tugged his sleeve, pulling him out the door. With her face smooth once more, she planted a quick kiss on a spot above the collar of his khaki-beige uniform.

He forced himself to relax, to breathe. Per habit, he assessed the street as they strolled down the sidewalk. "Who's your new friend?"

A predatory gleam in her glacial eyes, Debra snuggled into the curve of his arm. "Part of your job with the tribal police to check out newcomers? Or your roving eye wandering again?" She squeezed his arm as if in warning. "Anyway, she's definitely not your type. She's a graduate student from one of those Carolina states—I get them mixed up . . ."

He took care to make sure she didn't catch him in the act of rolling his eyes.

". . . got a grant to study tribal customs for her doctoral dissertation."

He extricated himself from her clutch. "Not my type?"

Debra stroked his arm, her hand abrasive and cold, not unlike the sensation he'd once felt when a horny toad skittered over his bare skin. "I know you think anything in a skirt is your type, but believe me, this girl really isn't. She's the kind, according to your own words"—she jabbed a finger into the buttons on his shirt—"that scares you silly."

He stopped and faced her on the sidewalk.

Reaching, she smoothed away a frown forming between his brows. "Your words," she reminded him, "and I quote 'one of those do-gooder Christians come to ease their conscience and make life better for the poor savages on the reservation.' End quote."

She wrapped her arms around his middle. "Not like me, mind you, who appreciates everything you have to offer." She gave a low-voiced purr. "Maybe I could interest you in something besides lunch today, Officer."

He fought the urge to grimace. He needed more info if he was going to run a check on the brunette. "Her name?" He grazed his lips against hers.

She sighed and lowered her eyelashes. "Erin. Erin Dawson. Now can we forget about the boring anthropologist and get back to more exciting things like . . ."

Fixing a smile in place, he swung her toward the diner. "Like sopapillas for dessert?"

Debra gave a throaty chuckle. "Like me." Grabbing fistfuls of his lapels, she hauled him toward her mouth.

They'd owe him combat pay for this.

His cell phone chirped. Saved—he glanced at the caller ID—by Tulley Singer, his best friend and second-in-command to the Chief of Police. "What's up?" He tilted his head to listen.

Debra, with a deliberate look at her Rolex, crossed her arms over her chest and tapped one Gucci stiletto-clad foot on the pavement.

"Nia's working dispatch today and alerted me Chief Navarro's gone missing." Tulley's resonant bass filled Adam's ear. "She wasn't able to reach him at home, either. Bridger spotted the Chief's car, abandoned, while on patrol a few minutes ago."

Adam glanced sideways at Debra. "Where?"

She straightened, a concerned look on her face. Did he read surprise there?

Or not?

Tulley's voice boomed. "Two miles outside of town. Nia's sending you the coordinates."

"I'm on my way."

He gave a brief, apologetic wave to Debra, heading for his patrol vehicle parked at the curb. Official business, he mouthed, the phone pressed to his ear. The disgruntled look on his come-lately girlfriend could have stopped a bullet.

"Oh, and Adam?" Tulley added.

Adam hit the button on his keychain, springing the locks on his car. "Yes?"

"We're treating this as a crime scene. We found bloodstains on the headrest."

Ten minutes later, Adam turned off the paved surface after sighting the bevy of parked patrol cars dwarfed by the scale of the surrounding canyon walls. The tail end of Navarro's burgundy Chrysler poked out from behind a red sandstone monolith at the entrance to what the People called Echo Canyon. Rolling to a stop, he donned latex gloves before ducking under the yellow Mylar crime scene tape fellow officer Ortiz strung along the perimeter. Manny Ortiz, of mixed blood—Hispanic and Navajo—jerked his head toward the boulder at Adam's questioning look. Everett Atcitty, in the driver's seat of his cruiser, advised Nia, via the radio, regarding their investigation.

Sidestepping clusters of prickly cactus, Adam assessed the scene, noting first the sandblasted windshield of the Chief's car. No telling how long the car had been exposed to the elements. With the wind this time of year, vehicles tended to look as if they'd been in a sandstorm five minutes after being washed. The crime scene kit spread out, Tulley had his head halfway inside the abandoned car, Roland Bridger taking the notes he shouted out.

Tulley straightened, all 6'4" of him, at the sound of Adam's work boots crunching on the gravelly red sand. One hand clamped his Smokey the Bear hat in place as he extracted himself out of the open window. "See for yourself." He gestured.

Removing his regulation hat, Adam stuck his head inside. As his eyes adjusted to the muted glare, his attention fastened on the blood spatter pattern on the worn, upholstered headrest. Averting his gaze, he surveyed the abundance of fast food wrappers littering the floorboards, the half-filled container of sluggish coffee in the cup holder, and the upended official black attaché case of the Navajo Nation Police hitherto practically grafted to the Chief's wrist.

Backing out, his nose caught the subtle, cloying scent of a woman's perfume mixed with the metallic, rusty iron smell of blood. "You noticed the perfume?"

Tulley frowned, a quizzical look on his lean, chiseled face. "Reminds me of somebody." He shook his head. "Can't put my finger on it right now, but it'll come to me." He leaned to inspect Bridger's notes. "Coffee's from Mamacita's Diner. Check to see when he was there last, Roland."

Bridger nodded, making a notation.

"Anything missing from his vehicle?" Adam employed a studied, impersonal tone.

Bridger snorted. "Just his body."

Tulley fixed Bridger with a not-so-friendly look, his feet planted in a wide stance. "He meant from the briefcase."

"Signs of his body?" Adam couldn't bring himself to say his former mentor's name.

His grandfather said names had power. No need to wear them out. Especially if the Chief was . . . He cleared his throat, uncomfortable with his grandfather's traditional beliefs.

Bridger glanced up from his notes, pushing his black sunglasses farther up his wide nose. "Not so far. Nor tracks of any kind—human or another vehicle."

"The food wrappers?" Adam twisted his mouth in a wry grimace. "Didn't remember the Chief being such a food connoisseur."

"Betty, his wife," Bridger sighed. "She was sick a long time with the breast cancer. After she died last month . . ."

"Yeah." Tulley gazed off into the barren expanse. "Easier for a single, lonely man to eat out."

Adam pointed his lips at the steep canyon walls. "Desolate place to—"

Tulley growled. "He's not dead until we find his body." He shuffled his size thirteen feet in the red sand, scuffling pebbles. "Until then," he jabbed a finger at the other two men. "We're treating this as a Missing Persons case, you hear?"

He eyeballed Tulley. "Lot of blood to be a missing person."

Tulley moved away toward his own car. "Crime scene techs will be here soon to dust for fingerprints. I'm headed over to his residence to check for any clues to his whereabouts."

Adam resisted the urge to salute. "Whatever you say. Guess you're the acting Chief of Police for now."

Tulley halted in his tracks. Bridger coughed and retreated a safe distance. Tulley's black eyes narrowed as he pivoted to face Adam. "Only until we find the Chief. Or the tribal council picks his replacement. That's their call." He fixed Adam with a searching gaze, his brows constricting together. "Why are you acting like—?"

His jaw set, Adam's hand clenched onto his gun belt.

An imperceptible emotion flickered across Tulley's face and an uneasy silence. "You . . ." He swallowed. Tulley's arm swept toward the arroyo and the immensity of the landscape. "We have work to do until we find the Chief. Dead or alive."

2

Early September 1906, Before the Raid

Oʟɪᴠɪᴀ ʜᴀᴅ ʙᴇᴇɴ ʜᴏʀʀɪꜰɪᴇᴅ ᴛᴏ ʟᴇᴀʀɴ ᴛʜᴀᴛ ᴛʜᴇ ʙᴏʏꜱ ᴀɴᴅ ɢɪʀʟꜱ ᴀᴛ ᴛʜᴇ mission school were not by any stretch of the imagination voluntary enrollees. Under the willow tree out by the creek, a flush mounted as she recalled her naiveté. Mildred, the reverend's wife, had tried to explain the school would help civilize the Indians, convert them from their barbarous ways.

Fingering the cuff of her sleeve, Olivia gazed far to the south, past the small village of Cedar Canyon to where an early snow glistened on the mountain peaks. Over those mountains, an army outpost. The reverend had told her that education, voluntary or forced, would result in more civilized behavior from the local tribes.

Civilized? she'd asked him. What's so civilized about kidnapping innocent children from their parents and the only way of life they've ever known?

Reverend Walker had threatened to put her on the next train headed east. The rest of the staff had been forbidden to speak with her. Her breath caught. Walker had actually called her an "Injun lover." As if Christ weren't, too. She plucked a small purple aster, absentmindedly beheading it petal by petal.

And when the children from the Hopi mesas and Navajo farms had arrived in the army wagon? Olivia shuddered. She closed her eyes, remembering the indignities perpetrated upon the little ones.

Mr. Walker and the male teachers restrained the most resistant pupils, while Mildred and the women cut short their beautiful long hair. She'd protested. Vehemently. Mr. Walker had her dragged away and locked in her room.

But she'd watched from the window, tears streaming down her cheeks at the soul-hurting humiliation reflected in their coffee-bean eyes. To add insult to injury, the army rounded up a group of the Navajo and Hopi men and forced them to watch the obscene spectacle reaped upon the heads of their sons.

Still furious at the memory weeks later, Olivia threw down the shredded flower. Her hand shook as she wrote in her journal, *"The Navajo seem docile enough, but the Hopi? I spotted a gleam in their obsidian eyes, wild and unpredictable, like the way a wolf measures a flock of sheep. If looks could've killed, we—they call us* bilágaana—*would be rotting in our graves even now . . ."*

Present-day, April

Making peanut butter and jelly sandwiches for the Wednesday night supper at Cedar Canyon Community Church, Erin's toes curled at the memory of the policeman she'd met a week ago. Or, sort of met.

Tall and broad-shouldered. His arrow straight, raven locks cut short on the sides and back like the state troopers in North Carolina. Those high-planed cheekbones. The color of his skin the way she preferred her coffee.

She gulped.

Blushing at her thoughts, she cast a quick look around her at the assembly line of food preparation in the tiny church kitchen. An ancient harvest gold stove and refrigerator. The equally ancient Navajo women. The middle-aged plump mamas. Their pimply-faced teen offspring eager to snitch bits of ham off the tray. Erin gave one olive-skinned girl a wink and caught the eye of Iris, her new friend and Pastor Johnny's wife. As Erin spooned a glob of jam onto one of the slices of bread, Iris surreptitiously palmed several pieces of ham and extended them through the cutout to the girl.

"Shoo," Iris whispered. "Scram, till Pastor Johnny rings the bell." With a giggle, the girl pocketed her prize and motioning for her friends, stepped outside into the fiery orange glow of the setting sun.

Iris slipped Erin a piece and stuffed a smaller bit between her own lips. Iris darted her eyes right and left, her eyebrows raised, an index finger to her chewing mouth. Erin gave in to the grin struggling to break free. Iris Silverhorn was a hoot.

And Erin was glad her pastor back home in North Carolina had recommended she look up his old seminary friend, Johnny Silverhorn, when she took up her internship in Arizona. At Cedar Canyon Community, Johnny pastored his own people on the reservation in a small white-framed church built on top of the ruins of a seventeenth-century Jesuit church at the far end of Main Street. The history geek in her—she wasn't ashamed to admit it—was amazed by the silver cross topped by the sterling crown of thorns in the sanctuary.

The *Diné*, or *the People* as they called themselves, were a source of endless fascination to her, the former missionary kid turned cultural anthropologist who'd majored in Native American Studies. Her research indicated the majority of so-called Native Americans preferred the appellation American Indian. As Pastor Johnny had told her when he handed her the keys to the rental home he managed for a relative, "What's *native* mean anyway? Anybody born in America is native."

Iris extended a platter of ham sandwiches. "Would you mind setting these on the buffet and checking the paper products?"

"Sure thing." Erin held the platter high over her head, weaving her way between the busy church ladies.

"You do that, Erin," called one of the wrinkled old ones, in the singsong English Erin had begun to associate with the older generation. The old one fingered the three-stranded cord of dangling turquoise stones, known as the *heishi*, lying against her brown, three-quarter length shirt. "Maybe keep Iris from eating the rest of our dinner."

The remaining old ones, in their support hose and tan, sensible shoes, tittered. Iris flashed her a smile. A warm glow permeated Erin at the sense of belonging and acceptance she'd found. An acceptance she'd not expected due to the prejudice—duly earned over the centuries—with which the Diné regarded any outsider, especially the *bilágaanas*, the whites.

Bustling out of the kitchen and into the small fellowship hall, she set out the platter, restocked the cutlery, and returned to find the kitchen deserted except for Iris.

"Everybody's gone to round up their young'uns." Tinkling bells jingled above the door as Iris turned to go. "I'm going to get a bag of ice out of the chest freezer, if you want to finish these pb and j's."

Out the window over the chipped kitchen sink, Erin noticed the neat rows of white headstones marching uphill from the cemetery. Maybe one day soon she'd get a chance to explore the cemetery. The history geek in her loved making charcoal renderings of tombstones.

Her thoughts drifted to her encounter with the handsome policeman—as they'd been wont to do these last few days—she smiled. Wont? Such an old-fashioned word. She was starting to sound like Olivia, too.

What had Good-Looking said his name was? Maybe she'd call him that—in her head, that is. The traditional Navajo were especially fond of nicknames based on their beliefs about not using up a person's given name. Her brow wrinkled as she slathered peanut butter on bread.

The cop—definitely something to write home about. But she grimaced, thinking about the latest e-mail from her vagabond, missionary parents. Home? Where was her home these days?

Shuttled from one jungle outpost to another all her life, part of her longed to find a place to belong, to put down roots and invest her life for the kingdom of God. Trouble was, her parents believed that place should be where they were—Papua New Guinea. Arizona didn't register on their missionary world map. But once she found Olivia . . . Erin hoped to come to a decision regarding her place of belonging as well.

Erin shook herself like one of her grandfather's wet bird dogs. Little flecks of strawberry jam landed on the counter. Happier thoughts were called for. Her mind traveled back to Good-Looking.

Good-looking didn't begin to describe the vision that had walked in her—make that the Cultural Center's—front door. But she hadn't liked the look he'd given her. An invasive probe as if seeking hidden flaws. A stare as intense and subtle as the full body X-ray machines in airports. A very unNavajo-like scrutiny from one whose people taught their children not to hurry, to speak quietly, and to be considerate.

Add to that the arrogance, not to mention the conceit, which rolled in palpable waves off him. Erin had been taught not to judge by appearance, but she'd bet money—if she hadn't been raised not to gamble—this Navajo GQ probably didn't possess a brain in his head. At least, her usual experience with handsome men.

Okay, in her limited church girl experience. She knew the type, though. She watched TV—every woman was fair game, a potential conquest in his macho, egocentric worldview.

As if she cared. Or, as if a man like that would ever give her a second glance. Yeah, he'd given her the once-over, probably force of habit or instinctual as per his gender, but as soon as Debra returned . . . Erin had realized at the age of sixteen how the world viewed girls like her, the brainy not-so-attractive girls versus the blue-eyed, statuesque blondes like her new colleague, Debra Bartelli.

She shrugged. At twenty-six, what else did she expect? It was the way of the world. She wasn't ugly, but she was also honest enough to admit though beauty was only skin deep, most men never took the time to see further.

And that was okay. More than okay with her. She had her life—all right, she amended—she had this *obsession*, her brother and sister called it. She had her studies, which she excelled at. Her professors had hinted if this research—known as her wild goose chase by her father—ever panned out, an assistant teaching position awaited her at her alma mater. A good life. A fulfilling life.

Dad always said a person needed three things to make a happy life. Something to look forward to—she looked forward to volunteering at the teen center the church sponsored. Good work to do—finishing her dissertation and finding Olivia. And the third?

Erin frowned. The third—someone to love.

She loved God and she longed to serve Him. Only her way of serving Him didn't match up to her parents' lofty visions of what a "true" calling entailed. But once she found Olivia, she'd be willing to reconsider full-time Christian service overseas. And knowing Mom, she probably already had a position waiting at the field station in Papua New Guinea. Or a tech spot at

Todd's missionary clinic in the Sudan. Or maybe a counselor job at the orphanage Jill and her husband operated in Peru.

Biting her lip, Erin slapped the two pieces of bread together. Jam dribbled out the sides. She blew out a breath. Hopeless. Like her.

She couldn't even make a decent peanut butter and jelly sandwich much less fill the large shoes destiny—or those giant missionary Dawson forebears of her adoptive parents—had consigned her.

Bells jingled above the door.

"Just about done, Iris. I'll help you with those glas—" She swung around, the butter knife raised and glistening red.

Good-looking-what's-his-name retreated a step, a bag of ice bulky in his arms.

Tongue-tied, her eyes hopscotched from the knife in her hand to his amused face.

His lips tilted at the corners and revealed a set of strong white teeth.

Erin's breath hitched, dazzled at their brilliance. She swallowed. Once a geek, always a geek. Why was she always such an idiot?

What's-his-name grinned. "Death by strawberry jam."

He cocked an eye at the knife in her hand. "What a way to go."

"What are you doing here?" Her voice rose. She lowered the knife. A tad.

"Do you mean what am I doing with ice in the kitchen?" Adam shifted the bag. "Do you mean what in the blazes am I doing inside a church?"

She flushed.

Good. His persona was holding up. He'd have bet money that's what she was thinking.

"Or more existentially what am I or any of us doing here on this planet?"

She clamped her lips shut.

Great. He'd made her mad. Why he'd felt the need to make her mad, he couldn't say.

Those cheeks of hers did turn a nice shade of pink, though. Very becoming to her *bilágaana* skin. He'd been unaware there were any *bilágaana* women who still blushed.

She slammed two slices of bread together.

Maybe her rendition of what she'd like to do to him? Temper, temper.

His lips twitched. "Aunt Iris said I had to work if I wanted to eat."

"Iris is your aunt?"

He eased out of the kitchen and toward the table where plastic cups stood stacked and awaiting ice. "Johnny's my mother's brother. Can't believe a reprobate like me has such esteemed Christian relatives, can you?"

"You and me both."

"Reprobate?" He frowned, ripping open the top of the bag. "What kind of reprobate are you? Erin Dawson—the up-and-coming big brain anthropologist who tutors Diné children after school, visits the elderly, makes cakes for new mothers—and I'd like to get in on some of that cake action myself—completely impressing my unimpressionable Uncle Johnny in the space of seven days."

She grabbed an empty cup, swooshing it through the ice and dumping the contents into another cup. "I don't believe I told you my name the other day."

He joined her in filling the cups. "I'm with the tribal police. I have skills, too."

"Why did you bother?"

He invaded her personal space, inches from her nose. "I make it my business when someone tries to infiltrate my family circle to use them like guinea pigs in some sort of anthropological experiment."

Erin Dawson leaned in closer, her breath hot on his cheek. He detected something . . . something resembling vanilla on her person. Something delicious. He must be hungrier than he'd realized.

Her eyes glinted and she gave him glare for glare. "You have no idea what you're talking about. You don't even know the topic of my dissertation. I'm grateful to have found a place to worship on the reservation and new friends."

Adam sneered. "You got agenda written all over you, babe."

"You can save the babe for the bimbos." She pursed her lips, a purplish tint.

Almost against his will—must be that iron-trap cop mind of his—he noticed the plum-colored, V-necked blouse and the stone-washed denim jeans hugging her hips.

She jutted one of those hips. "What did you say your name was?"

His eyes widened. Since when did any one female not remember his name? What was with this girl?

Bells jingled again. "Have you two young people introduced yourselves?"

He and Erin sprang back from each other like scalded cats at the sound of his uncle's voice.

Johnny leaned through the cutout, his long dark hair tied with a leather band. His black eyes, merry, danced from Adam and over to Erin, a beatific smile chiseled across his deep-jowled face. "Adam Silverhorn, my sister Hannah's boy, meet our new friend, Erin Dawson. Sent by God to turn the hearts of our Diné children back to their Father here at our tiny mission church."

Later outside the fellowship hall, Tulley caught Adam as he headed for his truck and home. "We need to talk." He laid a restraining hand on Adam's blue chambray sleeve.

Adam shrugged him off. "Been a long day. I'm not on duty. Don't feel like getting preached at."

Tulley dropped his hand, exasperation lacing his voice. "What's with the attitude these days, Adam? If something's bothering you, you know you can—"

"Nothing's bothering me." He edged past Tulley.

His hands stuffed in his jean pockets, Tulley followed him over to his Ford F-150. "It's just you always seem so . . ." He stopped at the look on Adam's face. "We never hang out together like we used to, man. Is something wrong?"

Regret and guilt knifed through Adam at the hurt in his best friend's voice. He stifled them, pushing the unwanted emotions far down into his gut. Feelings he couldn't afford to indulge right now. "Got some new friends. We have our own brand of fun."

"Debra Bartelli's high-rolling friends, you mean?"

Adam shot him a suspicious glance. Tulley's eyes probed his, confusion written across his bronzed features. Time to deflect and distract for Tulley's own good.

"Lay off Debra." He stabbed a hard finger into Tulley's chest. Tulley took a step back. "Get your own girlfriend and stop pestering me."

"Just where are you getting the money on a cop's salary for this sudden high lifestyle you find yourself living?"

Adam clenched his jaw and threw open his truck door. "None of your business."

"Maybe doing a little moonlighting?" Tulley pressed like a pit bull with a bone.

Getting into the cab, Adam reached to slam the door in Tulley's face. But Tulley caught the dark blue door and inserted his body between Adam and the doorframe.

"Better not be anything illegal, Silverhorn. And as Acting Chief, you are my business. Your mama and Uncle Johnny'd be heartbroken—"

Adam pounded the steering wheel. "Once and for all stay out of it." He glared at his lanky childhood friend.

Tulley's voice went cold and official. "Mind explaining to me why not just the Bureau and the Feds, but DEA, too, have landed like locusts on wheat in the case of the Chief's disappearance?"

Adam kept his eyes fixed on a remote spot above the hill toward the cemetery.

"Mind explaining to me why the guys in the black suits have officially cleared me but have seized everyone else's laptop at the station as well as any personal handheld devices?" Tulley slapped his hand against the steel door. "Including your other good buddy, Nia's? She came to me this afternoon, tears in her eyes, trembling . . ."

Adam gritted his teeth.

Tulley uncoiled like a diamondback. "Makes me think I've already been investigated prior to the Chief's disappearance."

Silence.

"Therefore, I ask myself, 'Self, how would the Feds have gotten access to my personal records, the hard drive I keep at the house, too? Private passwords?'" Tulley closed the distance between their bodies. "Passwords only my best friend could probably guess?"

He sighed. "I know you, Adam. This?" Tulley held his hands, palm up. "This is not you, my friend. You don't act this way, talk this way, or hang out with those kind of . . ." His mouth pulled as if he'd chomped down on something nasty. ". . . women."

Adam averted his gaze.

"Had myself a chat with one of the Feds, name of Carson Williams." Tulley sniffed. "Carson. An unfortunate name for a man assigned to the FBI field office adjacent to the Navajo Nation."

Typical Anglo insensitivity or ignorance, take your pick. Adam had caught the irony when he'd first had the displeasure of meeting the federal agent when the operation began. Carson being the appellation of the Diné's sworn enemy and bringing to mind—to the elephantine memory of the People—the horrors of the forced march, the infamous Long Walk.

"Carson." Wrinkling his nose, Tulley spat the name like one said *dog poop*. "Said I ought to have a little talk with Adam Silverhorn." He waited a beat. "So talk. Deal me in."

Adam sighed. "Get in." In some ways this would be a relief, to unburden himself to someone he trusted. "I swept the truck free of any bugs this afternoon."

Tulley's brows lifted.

"We need to go for a drive."

Tulley started around to the passenger side. "We'll talk?"

Adam nodded. "We'll talk."

Tulley shut his door as Adam turned the key in the ignition. "Thought you'd want to know. Ortiz discovered Navarro's body in a shallow grave this morning."

Adam winced, putting the truck in motion. "Coyotes get to him first?"

"No, first big break we've had." Tulley grunted. "The body was intact. Got the report from the medical examiner. Navarro died instantly from a gunshot wound at point-blank range."

Adam steered the truck down Main Street and toward his mom's empty house. "Execution-style."

"Dr. Rogers also found strands of long hair." Tulley paused for effect. "Long blonde hair. That bring anyone to your mind, Adam? And by the way, I also remembered where I'd encountered that perfume before."

Adam veered into his mother's driveway, the headlights bouncing across the shuttered curtains.

Tulley sniffed. "But then, I suspect, you already know. Or at least could take a good guess as to the identity of our number one suspect in Navarro's murder. And now it's officially a homicide, as with all serious crimes on the Rez, jurisdiction belongs to the Feds."

Adam shifted the gearstick to Park, angling in the seat. "This is about more than Navarro's murder. You can't move against her yet. No, really," at Tulley's motion of protest. "Navarro was up to his eyeballs in corruption. Bribes to look the other way. To obscure the paper trail."

"What are you talking about?"

"Money Ted desperately needed for Betty's alternative cancer treatments. Treatments not covered by the police force's insurance."

Tulley slumped in the seat. "The Chief? On the take? I can't believe it." He wiped a weary hand across his brow.

"Believe it. And there's more." Adam cocked his head at his friend. "Try rival gangs and drug cartels locked in a turf war to control the distribution of methamphetamines. A meth lab in Cedar Canyon. Whereabouts currently unknown."

Tulley peered at the darkness surrounding them. "In this country, without somebody drawing us a map, we'll be till kingdom come looking for it."

Adam nodded. "That's why we wait. And watch. Let me do my job till Debra leads us to the lab and exposes her partners in crime."

Tulley whistled softly. "That's one undercover assignment I don't envy you. But I'll keep my eyes and ears open. And anytime you feel the need to drop cover for a while and revert back to the Adam we know and love . . ." He squeezed Adam's shoulder. "I'll be praying for you, too."

Adam avoided his gaze. "Whatever works, man. I'm willing to try anything at this point."

3

September 1906, The Raid

Only now, as she struggled to free herself from his iron grip, did Olivia detect the smoke arising from the other side of the hill. Where the school lay and beyond the school, the tiny village of Cedar Canyon with its trading post. The army and help were a distant day's journey. But none of them had ever expected . . . this. The sky burned with red-orange flames.

God, help me.

His hard eyes black-banded with paint, the rest of his face and chest were painted with stark white clay. He tied her hands in front of her body and hauled her face first over the broad back of the palomino horse. Kicking and screaming, she tried to wriggle back to the earth.

But with a sudden leap, he vaulted onto the horse. He grabbed her by her long hair, twisting his hand through her mane. Tears pricked and dribbled down her cheeks as he hoisted her by her hair the rest of the way, positioning her body in front of his paint-smeared bare chest. He muttered something in the tonal language she'd come to associate with the Navajo. One arm wrapped around her waist staking her in place, the other long, sinewy arm grasped the bridle.

His alien scent enveloped her, the musky sweat of a man, not the demon he'd painted himself to resemble. His long black hair, braided and beaded with a gray feather, fluttered in the morning breeze against her cheek.

Making a clicking sound, he urged the horse forward. Rendered temporarily silent, she leaned into the granite strength of her kidnapper at the sudden jolt of the horse. What she beheld at the top of the hill overlooking the school—the stuff of nightmares.

She slammed her eyes shut against the bloodbath taking place below but not before spying her roommate, prostrate on the ground. The director and his wife. The male teachers as they fought for their lives. Terror gripped her heart.

God, where are you?

The warrior shouted to another tall Indian holding the reins of four ponies. Both men bespoke rage, making large sweeping gestures toward the burning school and mayhem. The Navajo students sat astride the ponies, ripping and tearing off their *bilágaana* clothing. Throwing his fist into the air, the second brave let loose a guttural roar. He and the children galloped off into the desert.

Was that a trumpet? *God, have You sent the army to rescue—*

Pulling her hair and forcing her head onto his shoulder, he whispered something menacing into her ear. With a grunt, he tightened his hold on her and spurred his horse into the red rock canyons of the high country.

She swallowed a sob, imagining the fate awaiting her. The pain. The humiliation. She vowed to remain silent and be as brave for as long as she could . . . until death's sweet mercy released her.

"Jesus," she whispered to the wind.

Present-day, Mid-April

Erin shielded her eyes with her hand from the bright glare of the afternoon sun. Shivering inside her hooded purple sweatshirt, which read *Southern and Sassy*, she reflected that spring came late to these parts. She'd be wearing shorts and flip-flops back home in Raleigh by now. But here, despite the fragrant scent of juniper, a cool wind blew in from the desert and the cottonwoods were only now beginning to leaf out in tiny apple-green buds.

Her backside ached on the hard steel bleachers, but when nine-year-old Sani Nakai waved from first base, she gave him a huge smile and forgot about her sore behind. Raised by a devoted grandmother as clueless about new math as Erin was about brain surgery, after only a few weeks of tutoring, Sani's math grades showed a noticeable improvement. She loved working afternoons when she'd finished at the Cultural Center with the handful of students Pastor Johnny had privileged her to tutor. Doli Kee, her teenage friend from Cedar Community, waved at her from another bleacher. Fifteen-year-old Clarence Yazz waved at Doli who blushed.

A smile rounded the corners of Erin's lips. Young love. She turned her gaze back to the game and found Adam Silverhorn's eyes boring a hole into hers. By tacit agreement, they'd managed to avoid each other these last few weeks.

She wasn't sure exactly what he had against her, but she'd discovered not all of the Diné were as friendly as Iris, Johnny, or the good people at Cedar Community. There she'd found safe haven and kindred spirits in the Lord. But as far as she could tell, Adam Silverhorn reveled in his reprobate status, often flaunting, so it seemed, his wild ways in the face of his conservative family.

Erin sniffed, scrunching her nose in Silverhorn's direction on the coaching bench. She had as much right as anybody on the planet to watch her students play ball. It was a free coun-try—a free America and a free Navajo Nation. He didn't like having her around? Well, he could just learn to live with it.

Adam swiveled to the field and adjusted his ball cap farther down over his eyes, calling out instructions to Sani as the next batter made his way to the batter's box. Although basketball was universally embraced by all on the Rez, for the athletic Diné, baseball ran a close second.

She shook her head. Adam was every bit as big of an enigma as her quest for Olivia. A party boy and womanizer on the one hand. A devoted—from all accounts—Little League coach and Big Brother on the other hand. Although what sort of behavior Adam Silverhorn could model, she shuddered to think. But the teens and kids in the Cedar Canyon vicinity worshiped the ground he walked on.

And maybe that was his problem with Erin.

She didn't.

Worship the ground he walked on as did so many of her gender from the giggly, sloe-eyed teens to their wrinkled *shimasanis*, grandmothers.

Slow going, but Erin was beginning to learn a few words in the intricately tonal Navajo language—a language many in the younger generation saw no value in retaining. She let out a trickle of a sigh. Then again, maybe the issue with Adam was her problem. Adam Silverhorn was just too good-looking for his own good. Or did she mean *her* own good?

Her work in solving the mystery of Olivia's ultimate destiny also proceeded slowly. She'd traced the group of Navajo forc-ibly enrolled in Olivia's mission school to within a fifty-mile radius of this area of Arizona. Surnames had come after the clans had been relocated and subdued. How to find the partic-ular group Olivia had mentioned was a riddle Erin had not yet succeeded in unraveling.

The batter swung true and the satisfying thunk of aluminum on leather exploded in the air. Erin—and Adam she noticed—leaped to their feet. The whole crowd wildly cheered little Sani to second then third against their traditional enemies, the Hopi Sun-dancers. Jumping up and down, Erin, surrogate cheerleader for Sani's diabetic, housebound grandmother, screamed his name until she was hoarse. Rounding third toward home, Thommy Tso followed Sani close on his heels.

A double header? A third baseman winged the ball toward home plate. It was going to be tight.

The catcher reached to tag Sani. With a burst of speed, Sani dropped to the ground, dodging the outstretched glove and slid into home. "Safe!" screamed the umpire, waving his arms across his chest. Thommy stopped, panting for breath at third. Adam called for a time-out.

Erin barreled down the bleachers to the dugout. Adam hoisted Sani across his shoulders. Sani's teammates chanted, "Sani, Sani."

Sani grinned at her through the wire fence. "Teacher," he yelled. "Did you see? Did you see?"

Erin slipped her fingers between the rings of the caged enclosure. "I'm so proud, Sani. You did it. You really did it."

Leaning, Sani squeezed her fingers. The smile on his face lit her heart. He bucked atop Adam's shoulders and when Adam lowered him to the ground, Sani scampered over to his teammates.

The look Adam gave her sent a shiver of another kind through her.

"He never knew his mother and father." Adam swallowed. "You've become important to him. Don't let him down the way everyone else has." An inexplicable sadness lined his voice.

She lifted her chin, her fingers still woven through the chain–link fence. "I won't if you won't."

Adam touched her fingertips with his own, as light as an eagle's feather. He sighed. "I'm trying not to, Erin. But—" He raised his eyes, clouded with shadows, to hers.

Her pulse pounded.

Grimacing, he pushed back from the fencing. "Got to keep my head in the game."

"Play to win, Adam." If only the Adam Silverhorns of the world knew what true winning meant.

His black eyes seared her. "I always do."

The engine sputtered and then died.

"No . . ." Erin frowned. "Don't quit on me now."

She put the car in Park and jiggled the key in the ignition. "Come on. Come on," she coaxed as the motor turned over.

But with a final grinding sound, the car shuddered before choking into silence.

She banged her fist on the steering wheel. "No way. Not here. Not now."

Glancing out the window, she surveyed the ever-darkening sky. Out in the desert, darkness arrived in one fell stroke. She was still miles from her house on the mesa and miles from Cedar Canyon. Not yet in the Navajo Nation, either. Sighing, she dug her cell phone out of her purse.

Punching in Iris's number, she hit *Send* and pressed the phone to her ear but heard no reassuring ring. Holding the display screen up to what little light remained, she realized she had no signal here in the middle of nowhere. She thrust open the door and dragged her purse out with her.

There was nothing to be done but to hoof it until she came upon a residence. She wrapped her gray jacket tighter around her as the desert wind kicked up dust devils ahead, thankful she'd had the good sense to wear her running shoes today on her research trip.

She strained at her memory, trying to recall if there were any houses on the road. The only building she remembered was the local honky-tonk, a rowdy establishment by the look of the battered trucks and Harley Davidsons usually parked outside. The deafening volume of the jukebox blared from within every time she drove past on her way to the Northern Arizona University's research facilities in Flagstaff. The sale of alcohol was prohibited within the borders of the Rez, but this gin joint operated just over the boundary line from the Navajo Nation.

Her purse slung over her shoulder, she trudged toward the saloon. A chill rippled along the length of her spine as the ominous yipping of a coyote—or wolf?—echoed across the canyon. "When I am afraid, I will trust in You," she whispered to the black sky overhead.

She glanced at the rising moon and wondered what sorts of predators lurked in the shadows under the piñon trees dotting the side of the road. Her hand tightened on the strap of her purse at the hooting of a horned owl from a nearby branch. The Navajo, she'd read, believed the cry of an owl signaled approaching death. A sound of rocks sliding from behind sent her skittering around the curve and into the safety of the beckoning neon lights of the bar.

Erin wished for once her research hadn't been so extensive. The lurid myths of *yeenaldooshi*—the skinwalker monster of Navajo lore, literally meaning "one who goes on all fours"— flitted through her mind. She shivered at another howl from the night creature, the sound closer this time. The pitch of the animal's baying rose. Not quite running, but at a fast walk, she sped the last remaining yards to the entrance.

Reaching the relative sanctuary of the bar, she hesitated to enter, instead clapping her hands over her ears at the loud music pouring through the walls. The slamming of a car door broke Erin from her reverie, and grasping the door handle, she swung the door wide before stepping inside. It took her eyes several seconds to adjust to the cavernlike darkness of the interior.

She wrinkled her nose at the overwhelming odor of stale beer. Glasses clinked, and as her eyes focused, she noticed every head had swiveled in her direction at the sound of the door opening and shutting behind her. Her eyes stung at the miasma of cigarette smoke hanging in the air.

Diné and *bilágaana* men and women filled the room. Tattoos were rampant along with grungy long johns peeping from threadbare cowboy shirts. The worst sort of native and *bilágaana*, the women's faces hardened and their eyes jaded. Five men perched on barstools nursing beers. Several bedraggled couples thronged the sawdust-strewn dance floor pounding out a two-step.

The overblown laughter and conversation died. Only a tune about love in a pickup truck continued to blare. The five men at the bar rose as one and headed toward her where she stood transfixed on the threshold. Behind her, two late arrivals blocked her retreat. They chuckled, an evil deep-throated blasphemy.

Shivers of fear crawled up her arms. This had been a bad idea. Better to have walked all the way home in the dark with the baying of the animals. Human predators dwelled here. And she was their preferred prey. Encircling her, the men loomed around her, their eyes glittering, their breath sour. Erin retreated until she could go no farther.

At a table in the corner, Adam lolled with two *bilágaana* men. One of Adam's hands curled around a glass, the other rested palm up, receiving what looked like a wad of cash. Catching sight of her, his eyes widened and then went opaque.

He shoved his chair back. It scraped across the floor and crashed against the wall. Stuffing the bills into his jean pocket, he said something over his shoulder to his companions and made his way with a bowlegged swagger across the room to her. The two men behind her slunk into the shadows and disappeared from sight.

Adam shoved the other men aside, reached for her, and yanked her into a tight embrace. The smell of cheap whiskey breached her nostrils before his arms entwined around her torso. "Babe? Did you come to kiss and make up?"

His fingers curled tight around her forearms, her hands captured against his chest, immobilizing her. Smirking, he lowered his face toward hers. His lips parted. She gasped. This wasn't the Adam from Wednesday night suppers or Little League.

This Adam scared her.

"Get your hands off me."

She squirmed, struggling to break free of his hold. He released one of her arms, but placed his hand behind her neck, forcing her mouth to his lips.

Resisting contact, she rotated her head, but he grabbed her chin to redirect. "Don't be difficult, babe. I said I was sorry."

His mouth claimed hers, rough and hard against her lips. She braced, expecting a sourness, but found instead his mouth tasted like peppermint gum. A tingle raced down her spine. Her senses reeled.

For a split-second, she melted into him but, coming to her senses, stamped on his foot.

"Ow!" he howled, dropping his hold.

She dodged him only to be grabbed from behind by one of the men. "Got a kiss for me, little lady?" He leered, planting a wet kiss on her neck. She arched her body, writhing to be free of his hold.

Adam jerked a knife from his boot. The man stilled. "Don't make me cut you, Sam. Give her back," growled Adam.

The other men shuffled their feet. "This one yours, too? Ain't you got enough women already, Silverhorn?"

Another shouted out. "Can't you learn to share? This one looks sweet."

Grunting his displeasure, the man Sam nonetheless shoved her toward Adam. Stumbling forward, she barely avoided being impaled on Adam's blade. Adam caught her, bringing his arm around her neck with her back locked against his chest.

"Stop fighting me, Erin," he whispered into the tangled hair around her ear. "I'm trying to save your virtue, not to mention your life."

The fight leaving her, she sagged against him.

"Now clear out boys." He made a slashing motion. "Just a little misunderstanding between me and the missus. No need for you to get involved."

He jabbed the knife in the air for emphasis. "Maybe you guys need to sober up before you try to come between a man and his woman."

Rage pockmarked Sam's face, his fists clenched and unclenched at his sides. Another man tugged his sleeve. "C'mon, Sam. Not our business." Sam shrugged free.

Sam's friend raised his hands palm up to Adam. "Didn't know she belonged to you. Sorry, dude."

Never lowering his gaze from Sam's face, Adam leaned and put the knife away. "No harm done, Sam. How 'bout the next round for everybody's on me?"

Sparks continued to shoot from his rattlesnake eyes, but Sam swallowed, then pursed his lips. "Sure, Silverhorn. No harm done, like you say." He allowed the other men to lead him away this time, reclaiming their spots at the bar.

"Show's over, folks." Adam slurred his words. She darted a look at his face, a frown pulling at the corners of her mouth.

The women wheeled to their partners as they returned to their off-kilter version of the two-step. Conversation and laughter resumed.

"Adam . . ."

"Don't talk," he hissed between clenched teeth. "Don't say a word till we get to my truck." Not releasing his stranglehold on her for one moment, he dragged her outside and across the gravel parking lot to a dark blue truck. He dug a key out of his jean pocket and pressed a button to release the locking mechanism.

He threw open the passenger side door. "Get in."

Adam released her so suddenly, her knees buckled. He grabbed her arm before she hit the dirt. She hung onto his flannel-clad arm for stability, raking in great gulps of fresh air.

"Erin, please . . ." An urgency lent a thread of fear to his voice.

She shot a glance over his shoulder to find Sam, nursing a beer, standing stock-still on the porch watching their every move. She scrambled into the seat, sliding over far enough for Adam to shut the door. Entering from the driver's side, he thrust his key into the ignition.

Gunning the motor and with a spray of gravel, he high-tailed it out of the parking lot. For several silent minutes while she endeavored to control her ragged breathing, he monitored the rearview mirror. At last, apparently satisfied they weren't being followed, he slowed the truck to a more legal and sedate pace.

"What in the blue blazes possessed you to come into a place like The Wagon Wheel, Erin Dawson?" His eyes burned hot in her direction.

"My car." She gestured to the road behind them. "Broke down and I couldn't get a signal for my phone."

She pivoted. "Why were *you* in a place like that, Adam Silverhorn? Your Uncle Johnny would be so-so—" She bit her lip.

He bristled, gripping the steering until his knuckles whitened. "Don't bring my family into this. And keep your nose out of my business."

"Your business?" She snorted. "Like that wad of cash you pocketed back there? What's that all about?"

Slamming on the brakes in the middle of the deserted mesa road, he jerked the gearshift into Park. She snaked out a hand, stopping her forward momentum—and her noggin—from hitting the dashboard head-on. She peered out the side mirror. No traffic coming or going. Could she have broken down in a more isolated stretch of road?

He twisted in the seat. "I mean it, Erin. Stay out of it. Don't ask questions I can't answer. Questions could get you, me, and others hurt." He scowled.

"Questions like why you're pretending to be drunk?" She fanned her face. "And btw, you stink. What'd you do? Pour a bottle of whiskey over yourself?"

Adam leaned against the upholstery, the glow of the dashboard lighting his face. He licked his lips but not before she saw them twitch with amusement. "Actually, yes. Here." He unbuttoned the front of his red flannel shirt. "If it offends you so much."

He shrugged out of it. Her eyebrows arched.

Well.

He wadded the garment into a ball. She scooted over and he lobbed it at the floorboard. "There. Any better?" He pushed up the sleeves of his white Henley and laid one arm along the backrest.

She folded her arms. "Not going to tell me why you poured a bottle of liquor over yourself though, are you?"

He smoldered, a glint in his eye. "You ever consider a career as an interrogator? Can't leave well enough alone, can you? If I told you, I'd have to kill you."

She studied him, unsure after the knife fight if he was serious or not. "I had you figured more as a lover than a fighter." She jerked her chin in the direction of the road. "Where are you taking me?"

He throttled the wheel with both hands. His teeth gleamed in the moonlight.

"Home, Erin Dawson. Home where you belong on nights of the full moon when the *yeenaldooshi* roam."

"Stop trying to scare me with your werewolf stories." But she inched over to the middle, closer to his side.

His shoulders shook with suppressed laughter. Probably, she realized, where he'd intended her to end up all along.

She punched him in the muscle of his bicep.

"Ow-www. Again." Removing one hand from the wheel, he rubbed his arm. "You really know how to hurt a guy."

"You scared me at the bar."

He darted a glance at her. A strange look flitted across his face. "You scared five years off my life when I watched you stroll into that den of iniquity."

"Iniquity? What a thoroughly accurate word coming from you." She jutted her chin. "A topic on which, I gather, you excel."

He tensed and fixed his eyes on the road. "I warned you already I was a reprobate."

At her silence, he jerked his head and caught her eye. A muscle ticked in his cheek. They shared a long, measuring look. Her heart thudded.

He broke eye contact first, the truck jolting over a pothole.

She tilted her head. "But I've learned over the years, that things are not always as they appear."

He cut his eyes to her.

"That maybe you're more than you appear."

"I-I appreciate that." He swallowed before turning his attention to the highway. "Your trusting me."

She shrugged. "Trust has to be earned. And you did save my life back there." She flitted a hand.

He grunted and clamped his mouth shut, going all cigar store Indian on her.

She sighed.

Adam Silverhorn wasn't like anyone she'd ever known. Something dangerous emanated from him. Something forbidden beckoned. And something about him compelled her, made her not care about anything but this moment.

She wondered with a sudden chill at what point in her captivity Olivia had begun feeling the same way.

4

September 1906, Captive

SHE SQUEEZED HER LEGS INTO THE PALOMINO AS THE HORSE STRAINED UPHILL on a trail meant only for mountain goats. Lurching forward, Olivia struggled to balance and maintain her seat on the horse. Her captor's arm snaked tighter around her waist, preventing her just in time from sliding off the horse's back and onto the jagged rocks below.

Now, her arms wrapped around her thin cotton calico, she huddled close to the fire at the mouth of a cave halfway up the side of a sheer canyon wall. With soft nickers and chomping teeth, the palomino grazed on the feed the Navajo had provided in the corner of the large cavernous space. For the first time in hours, she was alone. The Indian had left the cave holding a canteen, muttering the Spanish word, *agua*, for water. He probably figured she was too cowed to move from the spot where he'd unceremoniously dumped her on the dirt floor of the chamber.

Once he returned, she knew what would happen to captives like her. She had to get out of here and away from him. Fast. Before he came back or else . . . She shuddered.

It was now or never. The sky had darkened. During the last several hours, she'd watched the storm clouds build over the distant horizon. And even if she couldn't find her way in the dark or if she perished in the elements, it'd be better than what she'd seen them do to her roommate, Gladys . . .

Pushing against the solid, red walls, she forced herself to stand and commanded her feet to move. Sticking her head outside the cave entrance, she scoped left and right for any sign of the returning warrior. Holding her breath and the hem of her long skirt, she wended her way around the curve of the ledge. If she could get off the cliff face and to the canyon floor below, she might have a chance to, if not outrun him, at least hide until either the army arrived or he gave up the search.

And if he caught her?

Olivia reckoned she'd as soon die out in the open as die in the dark grave of the subterranean chamber.

She picked her way, wincing each time her footfalls sent off a chain of cascading pebbles. Ten yards. Five. Three—

He rose so abruptly from behind the boulder, she screamed. Whirling, she leaped the last two feet to the sandy bottom of the canyon floor. Her ankle turned as she came down hard on the uneven ground. She slipped, her booted foot catching and ripping out the hem of her dress. But panicked, she regained her balance and stumbled on.

She couldn't stop. She dared not stop. Hobbling, she raced forward as fast as her ankle allowed.

Behind her, his ragged breaths matched in rhythm with her own. Her feet pounded the ground, but he was gaining. A muscle in her leg spasmed. Pain like a lance speared her side. She'd never outrun him . . .

His hand brushed the fabric of her bonnet, pushed back from her head. She dodged, attempting to elude his reach. But his fist seized a handful of calico. Jerking, yanking, compelling her backward . . .

The bonnet strings dug into her throat, cutting off her breath. They snapped. She surged forward, momentarily free.

With a sudden burst of speed, his body slammed hers into the red dust. He wrestled her to the ground where she landed with a brain-jarring jolt onto her back. Straddling her, he spread-eagled her arms above her head, immobilizing her.

She writhed to buck him off. His hair, as long as her own, swung into her eyes blinding her. But not before she noted he'd cleaned the paint off his face.

And his face? Angry. Bronzed, scowling, teeth bared. Despite her resolution, she cried out.

His mouth inches from her own, he panted with exertion. "You stay with me, woman. I not hurt you." Flakes of pure, white snow drifted from the leaden sky. "What name do your people call you?"

Gasping, she ceased struggling, going limp. "You speak English?"

Present-day, Mid-April

"Got enough books?" Adam sipped from the ceramic coffee mug in Erin's tiny rented kitchenette. He'd done a thorough check on Erin Dawson. She was exactly who she claimed to be.

Adopted daughter of Dr. Rick and Susan Dawson, from a long and distinguished line of foreign missionaries. Carolina-bred and educated with enough degrees to scare the average man silly.

He glanced into the living area, the thick, white-washed adobe walls lined with floor to ceiling bookshelves. A librarian's dream. "Good coffee." He took another sip. "Do I taste . . . ?" He inhaled a whiff of the nutty aroma.

She turned off the stove and joined him at the table. "All the books I could carry in my car. I left most of them at home."

She warmed her hands around the mug. "Brought the coffee from home, too. Special blend called Southern Pecan."

"You carted this ton of books in your car all the way from North Carolina to Arizona? No wonder your car died." He shook his head. "And you left more books at home? Never seen anybody love books like you do."

He ambled over, cup in hand, to peruse the titles. *"Pride and Prejudice. The Chronicles of Narnia."* He fingered the blue-covered volume. "I loved that as a child."

Adam stepped back, scanning a three-volume work on the history of mission schools in the American Southwest. "A little light reading before bed?" he teased, balancing the tome in one hand.

"Books are better company and more dependable than a lot of people I've known, including family. Not so demanding."

"Amen to that, sister."

Strolling over to the fridge, she removed a pie container. "Want the last piece of pecan pie I made?"

"Does my uncle preach too long every Sunday?"

"I'll take that as a yes." She smiled. "And no, for the record, I think your uncle preaches just right."

He tapped his finger against the spine of the leather-bound book he'd seen her toting around at the Cultural Center. "What's this?"

She plunked a carton of vanilla on the table. "With ice cream or without?"

He carried the small book into the kitchen. "When you get to know me better, you'll realize the foolishness of that question."

She gave him a look, her eyebrows a question mark. "If," she sniffed. "Not when."

He gave her a smug smile. "Á la mode all the way, babe."

She rolled her eyes. "Stop calling me that."

He grinned, unrepentant. "Ice cream makes everything better or hadn't you noticed?"

She handed him a plate with a huge wedge of the sticky treat topped by two scoops of vanilla. "I thought that was chocolate."

"Not if you're a guy." His eyes crinkled at the corners. "Aren't you impressed this poor native boy from the Rez knows words like 'á la mode'?"

"Stop playing dumb. The Navajo are one of the most educated tribes in America. Your aunt told me how you won a baseball scholarship to Arizona State and then proceeded to dazzle your engineering professors with your intellect. Why aren't you working for NASA or something instead of policing the reservation?"

He scowled.

She fixed him with a puzzled, searching look. "Not that there's anything wrong in being a police officer. It's an honorable occupation."

Honorable? Yeah, he reckoned it was that. Though lately . . .

"Somebody's been telling tales out of school." He sank his teeth into a bite of the pie, goo dripping between the tongs of the fork. He groaned with pleasure.

"It's a Southern specialty. We make it from—"

"I've had it before. My grandmother used to make it. When she could get the pecans." He pronounced it the way Erin had, pee-cans.

"So you like it?" She ducked her head and studied the red-checkered tablecloth. "I never did thank you for coming to my rescue tonight. God sent you at the exact time I needed help."

"Whatever." He broke off, raising his shoulders an inch and letting them drop. He crunched the pecans between his teeth.

Same song he'd heard all his life from his grandparents, uncle, and mother. Different verse coming from a *bilágaana* like her.

He fidgeted. "What do you miss the most about your home?"

She gazed over the rim of her mug, her lips twitching and not the least discomfited at his change of topic. "The greenness. The trees, the grass, the colors of the flowers. The lushness . . ."

He held up a hand, "Okay, okay. I get it. But we have color here, too." A defensiveness threaded his voice.

She ticked off her fingers. "Brown, sand-colored, terra cotta. And did I mention brown?"

"Funny redneck Southern girl, it's Diné brown." He jerked a thumb at his chest. "Like Mother Earth my Begay grandfather says."

He pointed his fork at the ceiling. "Never get that turquoise blue sky back home in Carolina."

She snorted. "No, we get Carolina blue in our skies."

He resisted the urge to smile. A sharp-witted and sometimes sharp-tongued woman. Interesting. Different from the girls around here. Worth getting to know?

Maybe . . .

"I'll show you some of our desert color," he promised. "And I'll get my cousin, Sheridan, to tow your car here. He owns an automotive repair shop. He can take a look at it and give you a fair price."

She grimaced. "Even a fair price is more than this grad student has in her savings account right now."

He set down his cup. "Sheridan owes me a favor. I'll donate my labor if you buy whatever parts need fixing." He lowered his eyes, tracing a groove in the wooden table with his finger.

What was with the Good Samaritan act? What was it about Erin Dawson that brought out the chivalrous gentleman his mother had been trying to bring out in him his whole life?

She reached across the table and clasped his hand. "That's so generous of you to offer your time to someone you barely know. Are you sure your cousin would be willing to do that for me?"

His hand tightened around hers. "Positive." She had the long slim fingers of a pianist. Warm and soft. Not the hands of the outdoorsy girls he'd grown up with.

She frowned and extricated her fingers. She placed them in her lap like a schoolgirl, the barricade she erected with everyone but the children, firmly in place. Sometimes his so-called reputation worked against him.

Definitely not like the other women he knew. Okay, he could do friends. Be sort of interesting to try friendship with a *bilágaana* woman. A first for him.

Between bites, he contemplated the pale pink cotton top she wore tonight. The color kissed her complexion. He liked her best in purple, but this color was nice, too . . . Whoa.

What was the matter with him? When did he start having favorite colors in Erin Dawson's wardrobe?

He cleared his throat. "What's in this book you're always carrying around?"

She grabbed the book from his hand. "Stop waving it around. It's old, and you're going to get pie on it."

"Yes, ma'am." He quirked an eyebrow at her. "What is your interest in the People?"

She opened the book, rustling through the pages until she came to the passage she'd been looking for. She read, "Fire poured from the roof of the mission. Ten or so other black-banded braves had Mildred and the two other female teachers on the ground. The children tossed heaps of their hated school clothes on the raging fire and were led away by other warriors in the opposite direction. Reverend was missing his head and the rest of the male teachers—" She stopped, seeing the hard look cross his face.

"War." He raked a hand through his short-cropped hair. "Bad things done on both sides. Things done to the innocent I'm not particularly proud of in my heritage."

"I know. We Southerners live with post-slavery white guilt all the time. Family legacies are a tricky thing." She gave him a reluctant nod. "This book belonged to the sister of a distant ancestor of my adoptive parents. Dad's great-grandfather Charles's sister, Olivia Thornton. She was a teacher when this massacre occurred here in this very spot."

"The Cedar Canyon massacre?" His brows drew together. "Naturally I've heard of it, but we have our own version. Our version recounts the bravery of warriors rescuing kidnapped children from our enemy."

"September 1906." She turned a few more pages. "When he—she later identifies him as Silver Eagle—takes her captive, she managed to keep hold of her small New Testament and this journal."

Erin glanced at him. "Most people assume the taking of captives ended in the nineteenth century. But according to my research, the conflict continued up to the First World War between the federal government and tribes like the Utes, the Hopi, and the Navajo."

Her face clouded. "Although it's generally been accepted Josephine Meeker was the last white female captive taken in 1879, Olivia may, in fact, have been the last taken in the annals of the American West, and I intend to stake my dissertation on it."

Adam's eyes dropped to the table. He pushed the rest of the pie away. "I'm sorry, Erin. No cultural blinders on me. Things I've read remind me of modern-day police reports dealing with gang rapes or sexual psychopaths. Female captives were usually tortured before, during, and after . . ." He licked dry lips, flustered. Unusual for him.

"Actually, Olivia wasn't." She patted his hand, reassuring his awkward silence. "None of that." She flipped another page looking for a reference.

He placed his hand underneath the table, but it continued to tingle from her touch. His heart rate accelerated. Just friends?

Stay focused, Silverhorn. She has shown you she's clearly not interested in something more.

And if she was?

His mind skittered like a jackrabbit away from that and back to the professorial tone in Erin's voice. He pictured her in front of a classroom of university students. Her element.

"She records he never forced himself on her. An early season snowstorm made it impossible for the army to track the band until spring. During that time, she discovered an affinity for her new 'husband' and the Diné way of life. A field white unto harvest as my dad says."

He cocked his eyebrow. "What does this have to do with you?"

She ignored him. "Silver Eagle was familiar with the teachings of Christianity. According to her account, he became a believer along with several other clan members."

He shook his head. "Don't tell me they fell in love, too?" Erin Dawson was a first class brain and a dreamer. "Stockholm syndrome."

Erin let out a breath in exasperation. "Why do you find it so hard to believe?"

"Sentimental, romantic nonsense."

"You don't believe in love?"

He shrugged and adopted a cavalier tone. "They came from two different cultures. Opposing worlds. Never work."

"Yet I notice you seem to prefer *bilágaana* women." Her eyes narrowed. "Or is it strictly for dating purposes only and not marriage?"

He stabbed his pie with his fork. An interesting and irritating woman. Maybe not friends. "We weren't talking about me."

"Weren't we? And I also notice a predilection for blonde *bilágaanas*, Predilection . . ." She drawled it out syllable by syllable. "You're not the only one who knows big words."

"No doubt a psychologist would have a field day with me." He shot her a disgruntled look. "And I'm sure you have a few theories of your own you could share. But don't."

He speared a chunk of pie. "You seem to have spent a remarkable amount of time observing and asking questions about me."

A rosy flush mounted over the top of her collar. "I haven't been . . . whatever." She fluttered her hand in the air. "Back to Olivia and my quest."

Quest?

"She, like many captives, resisted rescue once the army caught up with her. Olivia was shipped back to her family in North Carolina in disgrace for cohabiting with the enemy."

His lips flattened. "End of story." He placed both hands, palms down, on the table. "I can guess the rest of Olivia's life history. Dirty Injun lovers, to quote the era, were treated as ruined, tainted, fallen women."

"Olivia's brother, Dad's ancestor headed for his first mission trip to China, didn't agree with his sister's evangelism methods." She caught his gaze. "Of melding with a people group to present the gospel instead of forcing them to first adopt Western ways."

"Bet his real problem with his sister was all about having found her true love among the Diné. Miscegenation." His mouth twisted at the memories his grandfather had recounted of mission teachers forbidding the use of any language but English, the native tongue of the People almost eradicated among an entire generation.

"Her younger sister who'd married a local minister tried to defend her. Olivia was adamant about finding Silver Eagle and rejoining her 'people' as his wife. Charles declared if she left the family, she'd be disowned as a heathen, her name never spoken, her memory erased from the family annals."

Love like that didn't exist except between the pages of a book, did it? His conscience stirred, though, at the glimpses he'd seen for himself of the love his aunt and uncle shared, the devotion of his grandparents to each other. But the animosity of his parents' marriage also flitted through his mind.

"Did she?" He gripped the edge of the table. "Leave everything to find him?"

That kind of love was not his experience, for sure. Upon further reflection, he figured he wasn't capable of it. But from the love she showered on her Cedar Canyon charges, he suspected Erin was. And one day, some *bilágaana* doofus was going to be an extraordinarily lucky man . . .

Erin nodded, tears pooling in her eyes. "She set out across the continent alone to search for him. She left this journal with her sister AnnaBeth. They each understood it was good-bye forever in this life until heaven. Imagine searching for one man and a group of people who'd been relocated in the vastness of the Southwest. Everyone suspicious of her motives, the government and army thwarting her every move. The distance, the hardships of travel in the early twentieth century, the lack of communication we take for granted today."

"Did she ever find him?" A wistful note crept into his voice. "Did she make it back to this area?" Some small, boneheaded part of him hoped she had found her true love again.

Erin lifted her chin. "I don't know, but that's what I'm here to find out. To find out the rest of Olivia's story."

"You realize, at the risk of you calling me a cynic, that more than likely she never did reunite with him? That something tragic probably ended her life?"

She sighed. "That's what my parents, brother Todd, and sister Jill have told me ever since I discovered the journal in an old trunk in my grandmother's attic, the family home-place where AnnaBeth spent the rest of her life. But something inside me has to know. I don't know why, but I think of it as a calling."

Fumbling with the napkin in her lap, she twisted the paper between her fingers. "My family is big on calling. The legacy of Dad's great-grandfather Charles. Mom and Dad's calling to Papua New Guinea. My brother Todd's medical mission to Sudan. Jill and her family's calling to Peru. My parents consider my 'calling' a blasphemy, a spiritual rebelliousness in contrast to the lives of devotion and service for which generations of the Dawson family have been renowned. So, yeah, that's why I'm the reprobate." Her eyes flickered. "Me, the adopted one, their biggest project failure."

Adam swallowed. "You haven't met my mother. She's in Houston with my sister Lydia who's on bed rest due to pre-eclampsia awaiting the birth of her second child. I don't measure up to her standards. Neither did my dad. She knew who he was when she married him, son of a tribal leader, devoted to the old ways."

He tensed. "What did she think he was going to do? Renounce everything his family stood for because they were in love?" He snorted. "That's what love will do for you. Makes you blind and stupid."

Why was he telling her this? He didn't ever talk about that bad time when he was a boy. What was it with Erin Dawson that lowered his guard?

"Your mother's Hannah Silverhorn, the famous silversmith, isn't she?"

The old bitterness stirred inside him. "She took up the family trade and changed all our names back to her maiden name Silverhorn after she walked out on my father with Lydia and me in tow. He tried to drink himself to death first and then decided alcoholism was too slow a suicide."

"Oh, Adam. I'm sorry. How hard that must have been for you. It explains the deep compassion I see you give to the boys on your Little League team."

Something in his chest tightened. Staggering to his feet, he shoved the chair under the table. "Don't know 'bout that. Dad hung himself when I was eleven." He, like his grandfather Begay had taught him, avoided the use of his dead father's personal name.

Erin stepped around the table. He backed away from her outstretched hand, sensing her intent. He stuffed the memories of that sad, lonely time to the far reaches of his mind, though it had actually felt good to let them see the light of day for once. But why he'd gone down this road with Erin Dawson . . . ?

Rattled, he headed for the door. Kindness undid him. A kindness he wasn't used to seeing in the *bilágaana*. And Erin was one of the kindest women he'd ever known, Diné or *bilágaana*.

Erin Dawson, his *bilágaana* woman friend. Who'd have thunk it?

He rubbed at the five o'clock stubble dotting his jawline. "Sheridan and I will be here bright and early in the morning with your car."

She leaned against the doorjamb, her hair haloed from the light of a reading lamp. "I'll have breakfast ready." She gave a mock salute. "Thanks." She touched his sleeve. "For everything, friend."

Friend?

Then why did his heart feel as if it'd hammer out of his chest at one touch of her hand?

5

September 1906, The Cave

OLIVIA CLUTCHED THE SMALL BOOKS, TAKING COMFORT FROM THE SMOOTH leather bindings of her journal and the tiny New Testament. Somehow, she'd managed to hang on to those.

"Why did you take me?" She gestured around the cavern. "Why did you bring me here?"

The wind howled and the snowstorm raged outside their sanctuary. Huge drifts of snow transformed the sandstone buttes into something out of a fairy tale. But the fairy tale obliterated any tracks the army might attempt to follow. She shivered despite the warmth of the fire, a red and black blanket in jagged geometric zigzags thrown around her shoulders. It smelled strongly, of horse and of him.

On his haunches, the man, Silver Eagle, kept his back to her making broad, sweeping strokes on the wall of the cave. His drawing resembled a sheep, she decided. He continued to ignore her. But she realized now he understood every word she said.

"Why didn't you—?" Her voice quavered. "Why didn't you let them . . . like the others?"

He rose, towering over her. She shrank back, feeling the cold stone against her spine. "We Diné hear of Hopi plan to rescue their children and make revenge." He shook his head, his braids swinging side to side. "Hopi smoke peyote in war council. Believe Great Spirit's power in cactus of peyote." He frowned in an attempt to explain.

"Bad medicine. Make crazy." He thumped his chest. "Hopi change day of attack suddenly. My friend and I not able to save others. He rescue Diné children. I save you."

She gasped. Why her?

"Was it you who alerted the army about the coming raid?"

The man paced the small confines of the chamber. "My wife taught by priest in adobe church beside trading post. She taught me speak." He jabbed a finger in her direction. "She die from disease you bring."

Silver Eagle snatched the testament from her hand. "She believe this tale, told for children." He flung the book at her. She flinched.

"I do not believe. But I listen when she tell me these things. You take the children of my clan. I take you for new wife." He cocked his head. "You call eye for eye?"

Olivia swallowed past the lump blocking her throat. "You took the children back. Why don't you let me go? Did your wife tell you about the loving your enemies part? Doing good to those who—"

Silver Eagle spat into the fire. The flames danced higher, hissing and leaping. "I be good husband to you."

Her heart pounded. "My people will never stop looking for me."

"Maybe. Maybe not." He shrugged. "Horse soldiers can't get through pass till spring. Give children one more year with mothers before they take them to another school."

A slow grin split the wide contours of his face, crinkling his eyes at the corners. "Maybe by spring, you like being Diné woman."

Her eyes widened. "Why me, Silver Eagle?" she whispered, her mouth gone dry.

Something flickered in his flinty eyes. "You kind to our children. You not married. You go to creek every morning and write in that other book."

He'd been watching her . . .

Silver Eagle snatched at the journal in her lap. She made a grab for it. Their fingers overlapped in a brief tug of war.

An electric tingle shot up her arm. He drew back—had he felt something, too?—but he didn't release the journal. His brows constricted.

His breath feathered her cheek. She surrendered her hold on the book.

"You teach me, Ol-liv-vee-a?"

His dark, foreign eyes beckoned her, whispering promises of—She dragged her attention back to his words. "To read and write so my clan not cheated at the trading post."

A muscle in the cheek below his high, contoured cheek-bones leaped. "Please . . ."

Her pulse stirred in response to the current between them. And she realized at that moment she was more afraid of herself than him.

Present-day, Mid-April

At the sound of tires on her gravel drive, balancing the tray of ham biscuits, coffee mugs and thermos with one arm, Erin shouldered open the front door with her hip. A tow truck sporting the moniker "Silverhorn Automotive" maneuvered a three-point turn in her yard before backing her small Camry underneath the flimsy metal carport. A short, compact man with long black hair emerged from the driver's side to begin disengaging her car from the truck. Sheridan, she supposed.

Adam followed the tow truck in his Ford. Rolling to a stop, he jumped out to help release the chains, clad in a Cedar Canyon B-ball cap, an old green T-shirt, and jeans that had seen better decades. A ginormous silver belt buckle gleamed in the morning sunshine.

She waited, tray in hand, while the chains rattled and clanged. Finally, Adam's nose perked, sniffing the air.

"Is that coffee and ham I'm smelling?" He smacked his lips. "The answer to my prayers, if I was a praying man." He scooped up a biscuit. She set the tray on the trunk of her car.

"You ride rodeo?" She nudged her head at his belt buckle that read, *Navajo Nation Rodeo Cowboys Association*. She put a hand to her face as if to shield her eyes. "Kind of blinding."

He grinned. "The small print reads, *Bull Riding Champion*, for your information, Miss Dawson."

She handed him a napkin and a biscuit to Sheridan when he joined them. "No surprise you'd be drawn to the bull, Silverhorn."

He choked, laughter fanning out from his eyes.

Sheridan beat him hard on his back. "See she's got you pegged already."

He swallowed and cleared his throat. "Erin Dawson meet Sheridan Silverhorn." He nodded in Sheridan's direction. "A cousin and usually"—he pursed his lips—"a man of few words."

Sheridan munched on a biscuit. "Better than man of too many. And I am a praying man. Homemade biscuits." He cut his dark eyes at Adam. "Like your grandma used to make on Saturday mornings."

"How early did you get up this morning to fix this?" Adam asked around a mouthful of bread. "Or should I ask what time you got to bed last night?"

She extended a mug to Sheridan. "You like your coffee black or with sugar and cream?"

"This is mighty good, ma'am." The soft-spoken Sheridan in his blue coveralls savored the buttermilk biscuit. "Sugar and cream would be fine."

"And you, Adam?"

Seizing another biscuit, he wolfed down half before answering. "Black's good. I'm sweet enough as it is." He smirked as she rolled her eyes. "At least it's what the ladies hereabouts tell me."

Ignoring him and his ego was probably the wisest course of action, she decided. He was trying to get a rise out of her. Though why, Let's-rile-Erin was such a sport to him she hadn't a clue.

She swiveled toward Sheridan. "Have you had a chance to determine what's wrong with my car?"

"Needs a new starter." Sheridan tossed back a gulp of coffee. "Thanks for the breakfast. I'll head to my shop and get the part ordered. Don't have it in stock. Probably be a week 'fore it arrives and another week before we'll have you up and running again."

She groaned. "So long?"

"'Fraid so. You're on Navajo time on the Rez." Adam wiped the crumbs from his mouth with the back of his hand. "I was going to stay and give the car a once-over and tune-up while I was here. It's not had any maintenance done on it in a long time."

Sheridan set the mug on the tray, turning to go. "I'll give you a call when the part comes in."

Erin walked him over to his truck. "Thanks, Sheridan, for your help."

Sheridan flung open the door and waved at Adam. "No problem. Any friend of family is friend to all of us."

As he drove off, she rejoined Adam, still eating. "Doesn't anybody ever feed you? Or can't you feed yourself?"

"My idea of fending for myself is lunch at Taqueros." He swigged a deep draught of coffee. "Seriously, Erin. Besides tracking long dead ancestors, is cooking a hobby of yours?"

She lowered her eyes, pretending to smooth a wrinkle on her lavender shirt. "When I have a lot on my mind, I like to cook."

He held the mug up to the air. "Well, here's to lots of deep, happy thoughts 'cause I like to eat." He peered into her face. "They were happy thoughts, I hope."

Adam frowned. "Nobody hurt you last night, did they? Touched you or . . . ?"

"Nothing like that," she assured him. "Just wondering if I'll ever find the answers to my questions about Olivia or myself." She rubbed a hand across her eyes. "I received some late-night e-mails from family who think I'm crazy to be here in the first place. Mom's pressuring me to do something useful, as she puts it, in New Guinea. And now with my car out of commission . . ."

"Mothers." Sympathy laced his voice. "Did you have something planned for today?" He popped the hood. Bending over, he fiddled with some wires and switches.

"The director at the Cultural Center told me about an old woman whose mother-in-law had been one of the kidnapped children at the mission school of Olivia's day. He gave me directions to her house in Winslow. I planned to ride out and interview her, see if she remembered seeing Olivia after your people returned to the area."

"What's the old lady's name?"

"Susie Hatathlie."

He craned his neck around the hood. "This time of year, she lives high up in the mountains with her sheep in an old family hogan. I expect she just wants to get away from her children and grandchildren." He yanked a semi-clean handkerchief out of his back pocket and wiped the grease off his hands. "I'll have to take you in my truck."

"Wait a minute." She held one palm up. "You don't have to—"

"If you want to talk to Susie, I will need to come. Susie's ninety if she's a day and doesn't speak much English. She keeps to the old ways, the Navajo Way, and speaks the *diné bizaad*."

He patted the side of the Toyota. "This little grasshopper would never get you there even on a good day. Susie's home is off the beaten track. I'm not talking road—asphalt, blacktop, or concrete. I mean beaten track, beaten by hundreds of sheep over the years."

"Doesn't speak English?" She sighed. "Sometimes I forget all about you being Navajo."

He jerked, bumping his head on the hood. "What exactly do you think of me as being then?"

She shrugged. "Just Adam."

He blinked at her and craned his head over the engine, averting his face.

She handed him a clean cloth. "But I don't want to interrupt your plans."

He straightened. "Feed me lunch and my day is all yours." He smiled, a soft look in his eyes.

Erin's breath hitched. Those teeth could fairly blind a person.

Suppressing a sigh, she wrinkled her brow trying to remember what she had in the fridge. "It'll have to be pimento cheese sandwiches and deviled eggs." She raised her index finger to the air. "But if you give me a few hours, I could probably whip up a couple of pineapple cakes. One for you to take to Sheridan and one for you to take home later."

"Another Southern family recipe?"

She nodded.

He sighed, letting the air trickle out slowly in sheer pleasure. "What we have here, Erin Dawson, is the beginning of a beautiful friendship."

Three hours later with the noonday sun blazing high overhead, Adam steered his truck off the main road and onto a dirt track. Switching off KTNN, the voice of the Navajo Nation, as the radio signal buzzed with static, he glanced over at Erin in the passenger seat. She gazed out the window like a tourist, her eyes gulping in the scenery.

His eyes lingered on her, gulping in as much of her as he could before shifting his attention back to driving. Deeper into the canyon they climbed, the reddish dust of sandstone cliffs coating the truck. The truck bounced along the rutted lane.

"This will take us to Susie's hogan?"

"Eventually." His head bobbed as the truck jostled and rattled over a cattle guard. "It's past time for lunch, and I know a perfect spot for a picnic. Besides," he flashed a smile. "I want to show you something first."

Adam veered to the side of the road and switched off the ignition.

Her eyebrow rose. "Here?"

"Patience." He grabbed the hamper between them. "Look behind the seat and get that blanket."

With the truck door dinging, he exited the vehicle, his brogan boots causing a small dust cloud as they hit the ground. She extricated the black and white geometric blanket from the floorboard.

"You're not going to put this on the ground, Adam Silverhorn." She unfolded the blanket and examined it inch by inch. "This could belong in a museum."

"Naw." He hefted the hamper out of the truck and slammed the door shut. "Grandma made lots of these. This one wasn't up to her trading post standards so she always gave the rejects to family. Grandma had a reputation to maintain she said. Shall we perambulate?"

"Perambulate?" She rolled her eyes. "I continue to be impressed with your command of the English language."

"As well you should be." He motioned for her to follow him as he picked his way through a shallow arroyo. Overhead, cotton white clouds shadowed their path. They trekked past scrub brush around the curve of the canyon wall. "I bring my horse, Buttercup, up here sometimes."

She kept her eyes on her footing. "Buttercup?"

He grimaced. "My sister, Lydia, named him because he's nutty about eating those little yellow weeds and the name stuck. Sisters." He let out an exasperated breath.

Sucking in oxygen behind him, she struggled to keep pace with his long-legged strides across the rocky terrain. "What would you have preferred? Something like Thunder?" She took a quick breath. "Rambo?"

He offered her his hand and hauled Erin up a particularly steep incline. "That's the idea. More in keeping with my image." He puffed out his chest, his shoulders back, matador-style. "Maybe Magnifico."

Erin snorted, brushing her shoulder-length hair from her collar. "Magnificent? Give me a break. If that ego of yours gets any larger, Buttercup will never be able to seat you." Coming within yards of the edge, the rocky cliff dropped to nothingness.

She stumbled into his back and gripped the cotton of his T-shirt to steady herself. Before he could stop himself, he inhaled her sweet fragrance of vanilla and cinnamon. Her brow furrowed, she dropped her hand and retreated a step, as skittish as an unbroken appaloosa.

Just friends, he reminded himself. Chill out, man.

"Color." He flung one arm across the vista that stretched out below in unearthly splendor. Bands of purple layered with mauves, pinks, and stripes of every hue in between. "Desert style." He relished her tiny gasp of wonder.

"What is it?" She tugged at his arm. "It's like the sand art bottles we made at Vacation Bible School as kids."

"A smaller, local version of the famous, much-touristed Painted Desert." He grinned at her appreciation. "Work for you for lunch?"

She looked at him, her eyes shining. "It's beautiful, Adam."

His heart did a strange flip at the sound of his name on her lips.

"The Creator is so awesome and . . . I'm at a loss for words."

"That's a first. Ow!" He protested as she elbowed him in the ribs. A herd of wild pintos thundered away below them.

"How about the Creator is so . . . creative?" He released a deep breath and bent over the hamper to hide his confusion. Now she had him sounding like his Uncle Johnny with her talk of the One the People spoke of as God. "Spread the blanket already. I'm dying of hunger here."

Shaking her head at him as if he amused her, she fluffed out the blanket across the uneven rocky ledge under the scant shade of a lone, wind-crooked piñon tree. "You're always hungry."

Erin handed him a plastic glass of tea as he plopped to the ground. "It's sweet," she warned as he raised it to his lips.

He chugged it down like he'd seen on the TV commercials. He ran his tongue over his lips to capture every drop of its wet goodness. "You got to teach me how to make this."

Silence reigned between them for several minutes as they dived into the lunch she'd prepared. Only the cry of a hawk broke the stillness. The tangy smell of sage permeated the air. He'd never met a woman, *bilágaana* or Diné, until Erin he didn't feel the need to entertain.

A woman friend. What a novel concept. Why had he never thought of it before?

But he and Erin just clicked, understanding each other's silences.

And the beauty of Erin Dawson was that she didn't want a single thing from him. Couldn't even remember he was Diné. Accepted him for himself. Just Adam to her. He swallowed a deviled egg whole.

Her lips twitched. She handed him a napkin. "Breathe and chew, Silverhorn. There's plenty more and nobody's going to take it away from you. You don't have to inhale everything."

Jutting his chin, he seized another egg and popped it into his mouth. Great advantages to this friendship thing.

He swallowed. "You cut some pieces of my cake and packed them?" They'd dropped Sheridan's cake off in route. "Cookies, too?" He probed the basket.

She slapped at his hand. "Not for you. For Susie. Unless . . ." Her brow puckered. "She's not diabetic, is she?"

Many of the People were. He cocked his head. "If I lie and tell you she is, do I get to eat the cookies?"

Erin gave him a long, measured look. "No matter what they say about your playboy ways, nobody's ever said you were a liar."

Squirming, he let that pass and forked a piece of pineapple cake. "If we only had Brunswick Stew like that little place near Goldsboro served."

Erin straightened as he'd expected. "Goldsboro? Seriously? You've been to North Carolina?"

"Hah! Thought you knew all my secrets, didn't you? ROTC at ASU. Enlisted and did training at Fort Bragg before shipping out for my tour in Afghanistan."

"The home-place can't be more than sixty miles from there. Wilbur's, right? In Goldsboro. How long ago were you there? Our paths could have crossed then and we never knew it."

"Small world," he agreed. "Five years ago."

Erin shook her head. "Doing post-grad work in Peru, studying the Incas, and helping out at my sister's orphanage." She fingered the wooden handle of the basket. "Is that where you got interested in law enforcement?"

Adam sighed. True confession time. "I got interested in whatever skill I could use and still live on the Rez. I missed home and all this."

He jerked his head in the direction of the painted vista. "The sky. The sand. The People. In my own way, I want to help my people survive and thrive in this twenty-first-century world. Your white world had nothing that attracted me. Out of balance. No harmony." He leaned forward, his arms across his knees. "No offense but your world is so . . ."

She mirrored his posture. "Empty? Driven? Materialistic? Greedy? You just described every person's life, *bilágaana* or Navajo, without Christ as their center. What about you?"

Her eyes lasered him. "Have you found fulfillment in your calling back home? Are you making a difference?"

Adam lowered his eyes, examining in minute detail the scuffed tip of his boot. "Not like Uncle Johnny. Not yet. But I'm committed to somehow finding a way of restoring harmony to the People. Help them navigate between our world and yours. They're cursed. Lost wandering between our two realities."

He cleared his throat. "How do you plan to get to church tomorrow?"

Erin's mouth turned down at the corners. "I guess I could call Iris or—"

His head snapped up. "Out of the way for them, all the way up the mesa to your house. I'll pick you up in the morning."

"But you don't—"

"I'll have you know I spent most of my childhood on a certain pew in that building, listening to my grandfather preach every Sunday before Uncle Johnny took the pulpit."

Her eyes—the exact color of a willow tree—widened. "I didn't know you came from a family of preachers like me?"

Adam rolled his eyes. "You're not the only one who's a big disappointment to family. Anyway," he leaned back to rest his head on the blanket. "What time?"

"I've got to get there early tomorrow. Eight forty-five?"

He groaned, throwing an arm across his eyes to block out the sunshine. "You're going to be the death of me, Erin Dawson."

"Shouldn't we get going now?"

"What's the hurry, *bilágaana*? Like I said earlier, you're on Navajo time now. We like to move at our own pace and in our own way. And this Diné needs a nap. Too late an evening rescuing damsels in distress and too early a morning trying to resuscitate gallant steeds."

She settled beside him. Close but not quite touching. His heart thumped. Thoughts of sleep fled.

"Would you teach me to speak some Diné, Adam?"

He suppressed a sigh, willing his breathing to even. "Does that brain of yours ever turn off?"

"Please . . . ?"

Why did he have the feeling he could live to regret this? "What do you want to learn to say?"

"How about 'Jesus Loves Me'?"

Adam sat up. "A song? Ambitious, aren't you?"

She smiled, her eyelashes fluttering.

His gut clenched.

Of course, she'd want to sing about God.

He darted a quick look at the turquoise sky.

What was happening to him? To his nice, uncomplicated-by-emotion world?

She'd have him in a church service tomorrow for the first time in a decade *and* she wanted him to sing a song about Jesus? If his Grandma and Grandpa Silverhorn could see him right now, they'd be laughing their heads off.

Her sleeve brushed his shoulder. He bit the inside of his cheek.

"You're not going to let me get any rest, are you?"

She said nothing.

"Pushy, crazy, religious women . . ."

He cut his eyes over to her to see if he'd gotten a rise out of her.

She still said nothing. She tilted her head and smiled again.

No need to say anything, he snorted, when she'd had her way with him.

Fine.

"Jesus loves me," he chanted. "*Jesus ayoo'asho'ní.*"

"Slower this time." Her eyes closed in concentration. "Break it down syllable by syllable."

He raised his eyes to the sky.

What had he gotten himself into?

6

"Auntie," Adam coated his words in the Diné tongue with great respect for one of the elders of his clan. Inside Susie Hatathlie's hexagonal hogan, the light dim, a smell of sheep and wet wool permeated the air. A curing rack hung suspended from the ceiling.

Erin's cinnamon chip cookies lay on the edge of a work-table covered with bright spools of yarn. And the bag of Bluebird flour, highly valued among the traditionalists, that he'd brought along to grease the wheels of the old one's memory. "Do you remember the stories your mother-in-law told you about the time a *bilágaana* woman lived among the People?"

Clad in a long-sleeved teal velveteen blouse and three-tiered pink-sprigged calico skirt, Susie's wrinkled gaze sharpened. She let out a hissing breath. "We do not speak of those gone before." Her hands stilled, resting on the carding paddles of the sheep wool in her lap.

Erin perched cross-legged beside him on the woven rug. "What is she saying?"

"We do not speak of the dead," he explained. "For fear of drawing attention to ourselves and drawing back their spirits."

"Not that I believe their spirits could return, but if they could, would she have reason to be afraid of her mother-in-law?"

He shook his head. "The People believe that upon death all spirits become mischievous and evil."

"Ask her then about the stories she heard of this *bilágaana* woman."

He translated Erin's question to the old one. Her face puckered in thought. She spoke. He listened.

Adam angled his head toward Erin. "She says a woman arrived long ago who told the children fantastic stories about a great flood." He tilted his ear in Susie's direction as she continued to speak. "Young boys who went through fire without burning. Another who faced down giants."

"Bible stories." Excitement tinged Erin's voice. "Noah, Shadrach, Meshach, and Abednego. David." She squeezed his hand. "It must have been Olivia. Ask her what happened to this white woman."

Susie listened as he spoke the words, her head cocked. She swiveled to face Erin, still speaking in the tonal Diné. "Why you not fix your hair for your man in *tsiiéél*—Navajo way?" Susie waved a liver-spotted hand. "I show you."

Adam flushed.

"What did she say? She asked me a question."

"Nothing. Nothing important."

Susie's deep-throated cackle bounced around the room. "And you." She pointed at his chest. "One lovesick man." Her laughter rang against the earthen, pine logged sides of her home.

He gritted his teeth. "No, Auntie. It's not that way."

"What does she want, Adam?" Erin seized him by his shirt cuff. "What's she saying?"

Laying the paddles on the dirt floor beside her chair, Susie plucked a comb missing far too many teeth from the pocket of her skirt. She beckoned to Erin.

Erin wheeled to face him. "What?"

"She wants to fix your hair in a traditional Navajo bun."

Erin reared. "She wants to do *what*?"

"You heard me."

"Why?"

"Come." Susie tugged Erin's arm and hoisted her to her feet. "I tell you what I remember while I fix hair."

His shoulders shook. "She said she'd tell you if you let her fix your hair."

Erin allowed herself to be dragged over to a wooden stool. She settled, stiff-backed, her hands gripping her knees. Susie released the band holding Erin's hair in its ubiquitous side ponytail. Her brown tresses billowed around her face.

She shot him an anxious look as Susie glided the comb through her hair.

"Soft." Susie crooned in the Diné. She flicked a glance over to him. "You like to touch?"

His mouth went dry. He thrust his hands into his jeans pockets, focusing his attention on the American flag and Susie's Remington pump shotgun hanging on the wall behind the old woman.

Susie laughed again.

He laughed when Susie scraped Erin's hair back until her green eyes bulged.

"Adam?" Erin's voice choked.

He licked his lips. "You're going to look beautiful. Remember it's your culture that teaches beauty is painful."

Erin gasped as Susie twisted sections of her shoulder length hair. "I've never been beautiful in my life. Waste of time to try . . . Ow!"

"NO PAIN NO GAIN," Susie chanted in English.

His and Erin's heads snapped up.

"T-V," enunciated Susie.

He and Erin exchanged amused glances.

"She's rolling your hair four times." He attempted to explain. "Four is a sacred number."

Erin tried to nod, wincing with the effort as Susie's iron-fisted grip on her hair never slackened. "The four sacred mountains, I know."

"She'll wrap your hair four times—two times on each side—uh." He shrugged. "Kinda like a burrito."

"Thanks for the word picture."

He laughed at the look on Erin's face. "Where's your sense of adventure? We're cultural anthropologists, remember? Got to fully experience the culture."

Erin grabbed the sides of the stool as Susie continued to twist her locks. "What sort of anthropologist are you, Adam Silverhorn?"

He patted his stomach. "I'm studying the culinary habits of a small—but vocal—tribe of the *bilágaana* known as Southerners."

Erin rolled her eyes.

Susie selected a long strand of yellow yarn from the loom in the corner of the hogan and tied off Erin's hair. After a few more grunts—on Erin's part—Susie stepped back and clapped her hands. She helped Erin stand and whirled Erin to face him.

His mouth lifted at the corners.

Erin put a hand to her face and lowered her eyes to her brown suede hiking boots. "I probably look . . ."

" . . . *Hózhó*," Susie nodded.

"Thank you, Auntie." He gave Susie a small bow. "It is true."

Erin lifted her great big eyes to him, her forehead perplexed.

Why had he never before noticed the delicate line of her jaw?

"She gave you a blessing. She said, 'May you walk in beauty.' It's a traditional prayer for you to walk with your Creator, to embrace the fullness of all that life offers."

"An abundant life?" Erin smiled. "Like we find in Jesus?"

He swallowed and remained silent.

Susie drew Erin over to the looking glass hanging from a cord on one wall. The calendar tacked beside it read March, 1999. The year Susie's beloved husband had died of a stroke, he remembered, noting the wooden framed collage of family photos, too.

Adam rotated his attention back as Susie began a rapid-fire explanation, waving her hands. "She says once when she was a little girl, her grandmother took her far up into the canyons and showed her a cave full of drawings. Drawing of the Diné and a *bilágaana* woman."

He repeated the last Diné word with a quizzical tone to Susie. Susie gave him a short, emphatic nod. "A treasure she says."

"A treasure? Can we go there? Is it permissible for outsiders to visit the cave? Did she tell you how to get there?"

He held up one hand. "Hold your horses, Erin Dawson. It is permissible—and thank you for asking, by the way. No, we cannot go today." He fixed her with a look. "Too far. And yes, she told me how to get there."

Susie ripped a piece of notebook paper out of a spiral notebook. Erin fumbled through her purse for a pen. He jotted down Susie's directions and drew a small map of the route for Susie to approve. She nodded, her twin chins wagging.

He took a quick look out of the hogan, facing east according to Diné custom. "It's getting late, Erin. We'd better call it a day."

"Thank you, Auntie." Erin gathered both of Susie's blue-veined hands in hers. "I have a blessing for you. Adam? Would you translate?"

He nodded.

She peered into Susie's face. "May the good Creator bring rain and green pastures for your herds. And may you always walk in harmony with Him."

At his translation, Susie's face broke into a wide smile. "*Ahe'hee*, Granddaughter," he told Erin when Susie spoke.

Erin hugged her. As he took hold of Erin's arm to return to his truck, Susie tapped him on the shoulder, pointed at Erin and winked.

He hustled Erin out of the hogan. "I hear you, Auntie," he muttered under his breath. "I hear you."

Erin bubbled with excitement. "Drawings." Her eyes shone. "In a cave, Adam. A cave."

The truck cab lurched as it clattered across the narrow wooden bridge over an irrigation canal.

Adam gave her a puzzled look as he brought the truck back to the solid surface of the blacktop. "Yeah? So what?"

"Olivia talks about a cave close to the camp where Silver Eagle brought her after the massacre. She spent her first night as a captive with him in a cave before they travelled on to join the rest of his people."

Erin reached into her bag for the journal and flipped some pages. "Here it is." She read the relevant passage to him, her eyes glued to the page. "What do you want to eat for dinner when we get back to my house?"

Silence.

Her eyes darted to him, his mouth drawn in a grim, straight line. A quick glance at the clock on the dashboard and she clapped a hand to her head. "Oh, Adam. I'm sorry. I didn't realize how late it was and a Saturday night, too. You probably have plans with Debra."

Adam clenched his jaw, keeping his eyes focused on the road.

How stupid of her. Just because she didn't have any life outside Olivia, didn't mean other people didn't. Especially someone like Adam Silverhorn.

Erin swallowed past the sudden lump in her throat. "She may have been trying to reach you all day. Have you checked the messages on your cell phone? Girlfriends like to stay in touch. I'm sure Susie's house was way out of range—"

"Stop babbling, Erin."

He jerked the wheel, narrowly avoiding a pothole.

She closed her mouth like a trap slamming shut. Pivoting, she stared straight ahead, blind to the passing alfalfa and corn-fields as they drew closer to civilization. They'd slipped into such an easy camaraderie, she'd forgotten he . . . that he and she . . . they weren't . . .

Her heart hammered. "I hope Debra won't be mad at you. Tell her you were with me."

She struggled to control the trembling of her lips. "No harm, no foul. She'll understand if you spent your day with me—fixing my car, taking me to interview Susie, eating lunch . . ." she whispered.

"I'd rather—" He banged his hand on the steering wheel.

His eyes bored holes into the side of her head until she felt compelled to meet his gaze. She read confusion, anger, and something she didn't know how to interpret in his expression.

"She's not my girlfriend."

Erin sniffed, angling toward the window. "Better clue her in on that." Hot tears prickled her eyelids. She gripped the handrail of the door.

God, don't let me make a fool out of myself. Not in front of him.

If she could just get through the door of her house.

With undisguised relief, she spotted her little rental house over the next rise of the mesa. "Just like the ungodly amount of dollar bills you pocketed at The Wagon Wheel has nothing to do with . . ." She faltered. "With corruption or drug money or—"

"Stop talking about something you know nothing about," he growled, his hands white-knuckled around the steering wheel.

A sinking feeling wrenched her stomach. How naïve could a girl be? She was an absolute fool. It wasn't like her to be charmed by a handsome face.

Who did she think she was dealing with? His reputation on the Rez alone . . . This man was way beyond the law or anything remotely resembling decency.

Beyond redemption? A voice niggled in her conscience.

Closing down that train of thought, she pointed. "Just drop me at the end of the driveway."

His face set like flint, Adam gunned the truck up the incline of her driveway, jolting her forward. At the edge of her front porch, he slammed on the brakes and threw the vehicle in Park. Reaching across her, he opened her door.

She shrank back.

Temper. Temper.

"I'm picking you up at eight forty-five," he barked, anger radiating off him. "Be ready."

Dragging her purse after her, she clambered out of the vehicle. "I'll find my own way to church, thank you very much."

He jabbed his finger in the air. "If I drive all the way up this mesa and find you've already gone, I'll—I'll . . ."

"You'll what, Adam Silverhorn?"

The look he gave scathed her up and down. She stepped back a pace. His eyes settled on her hair.

Adam smiled as menacing as a Western diamondback. "I'll make you wish you'd waited. Go ahead. Make my day, to quote one of your *bilágaana* folk heroes." His black eyes glinted. "And I promise you'll enjoy the experience."

Her eyes widened, remembering peppermint. Recalling the taste of his mouth on hers. Her breath caught.

Adam feathered his fingers, as lightly as a desert breeze, across the top of her hair. But the heat of his hand scorched her scalp. She gulped, taking a step backward.

He gave her a crooked smile. "Close the door, Erin."

Rattled, she threw the door shut, trying to focus elsewhere, anywhere, other than his lips.

He pressed the button rolling down the passenger side window. "And Erin, I'd consider it a personal favor if you'd keep the bun intact for worship tomorrow morning." He favored her with another knee-buckling smile.

"O-okay," she managed to stammer, unsettled. The power this man had over women—or at least her—was . . . wicked.

The wattage of his white-toothed grin could have kept the entire Navajo Nation supplied with energy for months.

On the porch, she watched him drive away and realized to continue down the path with this man might contain a world of hurt. Might? Try most definitely would. Adam Silverhorn intoxicated and infuriated her.

If only he'd return to the faith of his fathers.

God, help Adam to find You again.

She took a deep breath and blew it out.

And give me the strength to resist this crazy feeling I get every time I'm near him.

Inside, she tossed her purse onto the coffee table. Tomorrow would separate the wheat from the chaff in her mind. A good

Sunday service would set to rights her errant thoughts. The gulf between her belief and his non-belief couldn't—shouldn't—be breached.

Leaning against the door, she squeezed her eyes shut. Images of painted sand, the way his hair glistened like raven's wings in the sun, the laugh lines around his smoky black eyes flitted through her brain.

She groaned. "I'm in big trouble here, God."

Like an addict, she dreaded, and at the same time longed, for her next fix of Adam. She deliberately focused on her first encounter with Adam, Debra clinging like a sandbur to his muscled frame.

No matter what Adam said. If not Debra's guy, certainly never Erin's either.

Friends? What a joke.

On herself.

When he pulled into the parking lot of his apartment building, his spirits sank at the sight of his Grandfather Begay's black Dodge pickup parked next to his space. The old man, a distinguished tribal politician and ranch owner, leaned against the frame of his truck, his booted legs crossed at the ankle, his dark eyes hard, reminding Adam somehow of the vultures that circled the desert sands. A dark blue band wound around his head under his straw hat. Adam sighed, allowing his truck to drift forward to the curb.

Some small part of Adam was a little afraid of his dead father's father, an equal opportunity Anglo and Jesus Way hater. Another part admired his devotion to the traditional Navajo Way. In recent years, Hershal had lost much of his political clout within the tribe due to his right-wing fringe rhetoric.

Cutting the engine, Adam eased his way out of the cab and around to his grandfather. "*Yá'át'ééh*, Grandfather."

Hershal Begay straightened, his body as scrawny as a witch's broom handle. And scowled.

Great.

Another lecture about fulfilling his family legacy. The Begay destiny to lead the People into a new age of Red Power. A charismatic man, Hershal's agenda was half-Messiah complex, the other half Marxist dogma.

"When are you going to ditch those Silverhorn relatives of yours, boy, and take your stand for the People? Someone with your education and training, albeit courtesy of the American imperialist government," Hershal spat, "needs to take a seat on the Council and steer those"—Adam pursed his lips at the foul word his grandfather used to describe the other Council members—"white boot-licking—"

Here we go again.

The wheeling and dealing. Cut-throat tribal politics. Diné style.

He suppressed another sigh, knowing it'd only prolong the tirade by annoying the old man. Hershal, a product in reverse of the rigid mission school mindset and now a radical activist, had long since drifted to another path. A darker path.

"I'm raising up a new generation of Diné warriors, boy. Real Diné men who no longer identify themselves as citizens of the United States of America."

"Much as you'd like to declare a Diné Republic, Grandfather, you can't just decide to leave the Union."

Adam rolled his eyes. "And from where I'm standing right now, doesn't look like any of your so-called warriors are exactly surrendering any of those imperialist American benefits like healthcare and welfare. Or you, your Social Security checks every month."

Hershal grunted. "I intend to reclaim what is rightfully ours. Including the land rights terminated illegally by a racist colonial government."

Adam crossed his arms. "You and your cronies would do far better to work with the Council, within the legal system. Accept the 'hand' the Diné have been dealt by history and work to improve life for the People."

Hershal sneered. "I ain't accepting nothing. I, for one, am no longer willing to accept our oppressed status. And I *am* trying to improve life for the People."

Adam shook his head. "Don't see how your way makes anything better, 'cept for putting both sides at each other's throats. Sure, we've got real grievances, but the future lies in working with Uncle Sam to redress the injustice, not trying to blow him up."

Hershal's eyes narrowed. "Is that what you call what you've been up to lately, boy? Working within the system?"

Adam's gut seized. What had his grandfather heard?

"From where I sit, you excel at collaboration with the Enemy. Seem to prefer their company to the welfare of your own people."

"Not true." At his words, guilt needled through Adam. "That's why I'm on the Navajo Nation police force to—"

"You got some sort of perverse hankering for *bilágaana* women, boy? What's wrong with your own kind? What about that Nia Yow you hung out with in high school?"

Adam gritted his teeth. So this was what had prompted this visit from the old man. "Nia's a friend. Works dispatch at the station. Nothing serious between me and the blonde."

Nor was it any of the old coot's business.

He knew better than to say it, though.

Adam jabbed the Lock mechanism on his key chain. "That all you came by to say?"

Hershal poked a gnarled, arthritic finger into Adam's chest. He flinched. "Not talking 'bout the blonde." He shot a wad of Red Man at the pavement, narrowly or on purpose, just missing Adam's boot.

Something akin to fear needled through his gut. Adam broke out in a cold sweat, the short hair on the back of his neck rising. With his resources, if Hershal set his mind to harassing her . . . living alone on that desolate mesa without protection . . . ?

Adam forced a smile, drawing upon a tactic from the wily old politician's armory of denial and deflection. "You mean the mousy, church-going *bilágaana*?" He snorted. "She's nothing."

Shrugging, he flapped a hand in air. "Something different from the usual banquet. You ought to know by now, I got better taste than that."

Hershal pursed his lips and held his gaze. "Her kind's not for the likes of us." He fingered the buckskin knife pouch on his belt. The old man and his like-minded cohorts had been accused—nothing proven—of using violence to achieve their own militant agenda before.

"Us?" Adam's voice cracked. He swallowed.

"Begays have an obligation to the People to preserve sacred traditions. We must stick to the old ways before what makes us Diné is lost forever. Too many today throw off everything from our heritage like scraping sheep dung from a boot. I'm grooming you, boy, to take my place on the Council one day. No consorting with the enemy of the People."

The old man leaned in closer. Adam could smell his sour, whiskey breath on his cheek. "Me—you—have to point the People back to the true source of Diné power."

A dark power of hate that crossed all ethnic boundaries.

Hershal's lips twisted. "I've got no use for that mealy-mouthed, weak, *bilágaana* excuse for a god—" He uttered an epithet so vile regarding the Savior the entire Silverhorn clan worshiped, Adam cringed.

"Begays and the *bilágaana* religion are like oil and water. Can't mix." Hershal's face darkened, the rage flooding his face like a flash flood in a shallow ravine. "You have a destiny to fulfill. A job to do to help your people."

Adam's fists clenched and unclenched at his side. "I have a job. I *am* helping my people."

The old man smirked. "When you decide to get serious about helping the People, my offer stands waiting." He yanked the door of his Dodge, the hinges groaning open. "You know where to find me. And Adam?"

Hershal slid into the cab. "The girl's nothing but trouble for someone like you. Stay away from her." He slammed the door shut, rattling the chassis. "For her sake, if not your own."

Erin put the potatoes on to boil. She glanced at the clock. Late to be fixing potato salad, but Adam would need feeding if he was going to take her all the way to church tomorrow and bring her back home.

No use trying to get any sleep. Not with her father's latest e-mail, admonishing her for abandoning the family legacy. Nor with her thoughts spiraling of Adam and Debra together . . .

She sliced through the boiled egg on the wooden chopping block, narrowly avoiding splitting open her thumb. She dropped the knife onto the cutting board.

What was the matter with her? Over a man who had trouble with a capital T written all over him. A man who'd made no secret as to where his true loyalties—and appetites—lay.

She sank down at the kitchen table, Olivia's journal and her Bible beside her.

A man whose mind was as razor-sharp as her own. A man who knew how to give as well as get. A man with a strong sense of duty. A man who made her laugh.

She bit her lip.

And, cry.

The lid on the potatoes bounced and rattled as the water boiled. She rose, removing the lid to prevent a boil-over. Nothing worse than cleaning the burners after a pot had boiled over.

Nothing worse than a broken heart, either.

Which was exactly where she was headed if she didn't get a grip on her skyrocketing emotions. She'd thought she could be Adam's friend and nothing more.

Apparently not.

She'd thought God had brought them together for a reason. Adam had rescued her from danger, helped her continue her quest, and had agreed to accompany her to church in the morning.

"Isn't that what You wanted, God?" Her head tilted toward the ceiling. "Adam to find You again? Me to be a part of that?"

The question burned in her soul which one she wanted, if not more, then first. Adam to find God? Or, for Adam to find her?

Uncomfortable at her self-scrutiny, she set the timer for the potatoes and headed for the back door. A little fresh air would clear her mind. Nothing like listening to the croaking of the bullfrogs by the creek. The whisper of the cottonwoods.

Stepping out onto the deck, she shivered and wrapped her arms around herself at the burst of cold air. April here—when would she ever get it through her head?—wasn't like April at home. She should have brought her jacket.

Unwilling to face the blinking computer screen or her troubled thoughts, she decided to brave the cold and the dark night without the protection of her jacket for once. "Thin Southern blood." She tilted her face toward the sky. No matter where her parents roamed, no matter where *she'd* roamed—the rainforest, boarding school, Gram's home-place or here—the stars remained constant.

As did her God. Which was probably more than He could say for Erin Dawson.

What did her parents want from her? What did God want from her? Hadn't she served Him alongside her family her whole life? Served Him wherever she laid her head? What more did He require?

The stars overhead winked. Innumerable. Beyond measure.

Her mind drifted to the patriarch Abraham and what God had required of him. Contemplated how God tested him. Requiring of him one word. The hardest word.

Obedience.

Hard because obedience's conjoined twin was Surrender.

Surrender her hopes and dreams? Her God-given gift of an insatiably curious mind? Her plans to teach at a university some day? Or, work as a museum curator?

Did He require she give up Olivia? Surrender everything . . . including this budding-whatever-you-want-to-call-it relationship with Adam Silverhorn?

She shook her head. "Can't." She licked her dry lips.

"All right, won't. Don't ask me to do it. Please, anything else . . ." she whispered.

Something moved under the cottonwoods by the creek. She stilled, peering into the thick darkness. Not a leaf rustled. No breath of wind, unusual on the mesa. Not a bird or a frog broke the unnatural stillness.

But a red dot glowed. Shadows coalesced. The night suddenly seemed weighted, pressing upon her bones.

The red dot like an eye. Staring out of the blackness at her. Watching her.

She shivered. No, not someone. The position of the eye. Too close to the ground. Not unless the human crouched under the cottonwood.

Like an animal on all fours.

The hair on the back of her neck rose. The sound of the Enemy. Predator coming for prey.

She clutched the silver filigreed cross at her throat. Grasping it, she backed toward the light-filled safety of the house.

The red eye blinked out. Only the wind howled, breaking the silence of the night. Still gripping the cross, she retreated one step at a time until the solid frame of the adobe door grazed her back.

Fumbling behind her, she turned the knob and slipped inside to the warmth of her kitchen. Closing the door tight against the jam, she bolted the lock in place. The timer beeped. She jolted.

Her hand against her racing heart, she moved to the stove and with a twist silenced the noise. Turning off the stovetop, she wrapped a potholder around the handle and carried the pot over to the sink where she poured off the boiling water. She leaned back, avoiding the burning steam rising off the potatoes.

An engine roared to life from the road.

She dropped the pot with a bang into the stainless steel sink and bolted toward the front of the house. Erin shot the lock on the door. Twin headlights bobbed through the picture window, bouncing along the white wall of the living room.

Gasping, she drew aside the curtain in time to see a vehicle, shrouded by the night, disappear over the rim of the road toward the direction of Cedar Canyon. She swallowed, her heart pounding in staccato beats, understanding for the first time why the Diné refused to live up here on the mesa.

Who would be watching her? She remembered the feeling of being stalked on the lonely road outside The Wagon Wheel. Why would someone, anyone, concern themselves with her?

She closed the blinds of every window in the house. Checked and double-checked the lock on every door. Completely isolated. Alone. Not another house or human for miles. Except for the Watcher.

Returning to the kitchen, she retrieved the package Daddy had insisted she carry with her into Arizona. She cut the twine wrapped around the newsprint. Unfolded the paper and laid it on the countertop. Picking up the knife, she diced the potatoes.

She darted her eyes at the shuttered curtain of the window that overlooked her deck. Erin glanced at the Bible lying on the kitchen table. Wiping her hands on a towel, she reached for it. Flipped to Genesis.

Abraham. He knew what it was like to be an alien wherever he went. A stranger.

Longing to belong. A sojourner. A pilgrim, like Erin.

He knew what it was like to be asked to give up everything.

"Not there yet, God." She lifted her face toward the ceiling. "Help me to get there. Please . . ."

The first step to surrender. Time to back off. Time to take her hands off.

Strange forces were at work, she sensed. Forces tugging at her, pulling at Adam and the People.

Time to pray. For all of them.

7

WISHING HE'D WORN HIS SUNDAY, GO-TO-MEETING STRING BOLO TIE WITH the turquoise stone instead, Adam yanked the silk tie with its stranglehold around his neck. Another fine example of cultural imperialism, a *bilágaana* instrument of torture meant to civilize the Diné. "Stop trying to help us," he muttered under his breath.

And what on earth had possessed him to offer to escort Erin to his uncle's church?

From his seat on the pew two-thirds back from the platform, he watched as Erin gave directions to the pianist. He'd also not realized Erin was leading the worship at Cedar Canyon Community today, either. She had a pleasant voice, nice but nothing remarkable.

After a quick warm-up by Erin and the small rhythm band, at his startled look she had smiled, silver loops swaying, as she stashed her purse beside him in the pew. "MK Training 101."

"What in the world is MK Training 101?"

She laughed. "Missionary Kid. MK's should be able, and I quote my father, 'to play, sing, or otherwise lead worship at the drop of a hat.' I sing. Jill accompanied. Todd learned to play a mean percussion or bass guitar as the occasion or available electricity demanded."

He scanned the people filing into the small sanctuary, a congregation established by his grandfather Silverhorn sixty years before. A congregation of thirty faithful made up mostly, despite the years of effort on his family's behalf, of old ones and the very young.

Jesus was a hard sell among the People.

During the opening song, he fumbled through the words to a barely remembered hymn from his childhood, "What a Friend We Have in Jesus."

Friend, huh? If he kept hanging around this Erin person, she'd have him BFF with Jesus before he knew what hit him.

Shooting Erin a suspicious glance over the top of the hymnal, she'd merely smiled as pleasantly remote as the Mona Lisa. She'd kept him at an irritating arm's length ever since he picked her up at eight forty-five on the dot.

But she'd done as he asked. The Navajo bun neat as a pin on the back of her head. He had no clue what had prompted him to ask such a thing of her.

Clarence pounded out a beat on the drum. Doli blew on her flute, making doe eyes at Clarence while Erin led the congregation in a contemporary song of praise his aunt Iris had written about the Creator and Jesus, His Son. Sani and his grandmother, her kerchief knotted under her chin, waved to Adam as Thommy Tso wended his way to the platform to read a passage. Erin gave Adam another smile as she eased down beside him on the pew.

". . . The Lamb of God." Thommy's tremulous voice quavered with nerves. "Who takes away the sin of the world." He cleared his throat.

Adam hid a smile as Thommy's mother gave her son a pointed nod.

"Oh, yeah. John 1:29." Thommy gave a huge sigh of relief, leaping off the raised dais and scooting down the aisle toward his waiting mother in the pew. The congregation chuckled.

Johnny took Thommy's place, gripping the sides of the podium with both hands. "Sheep mean life to our people, the Diné. Spring." He quirked his head in the direction of the arched window along the wall. "Spring among the People is a time we await with great anticipation. Spring is the time of new birth, the lambing season."

He cast a long look over the congregation. "Many of you of a certain age like myself," more laughs, "can remember how on horseback we helped our grandparents herd the lambs during the summer months to water at the high country family hogans."

Johnny winked at Clarence and Doli. "Or by ATV today, as the case may be." Clarence ducked his head, a self-conscious grin on his face.

"Sheep mean everything to us. The wool for our clothes." Johnny smiled at one of the old ones, renowned for her weaving. "Wool fibers for works of art sold at the trading post at the end of summer purchase new shoes for the grandchildren." Many nodded at his words. "Mutton for our bellies."

A stomach growled on cue. Sani clutched his abdomen. His grandmother, her face lined like a leather glove, poked him in the side.

Johnny held up a hand. "I promise. No more mention of food. I'm hungry for Sunday lunch, too."

Amen, reflected Adam. Erin had promised lunch. His mouth already watered. He fidgeted, remembering her words about fried chicken, potato salad . . .

But he resisted the urge to check his wristwatch. Though she'd been dead fifteen years, Adam well remembered his Grandma Silverhorn seizing possession of his watch if he'd been too obvious about his grandfather's long-winded preaching. Beside him, Erin shifted, a wave of vanilla teasing his nostrils.

"We, Diné," Johnny continued, "know the shepherding life. Lambs in our fold represent a balanced, good life between the People and the earth. The Gospel of John also tells us that our Good Shepherd, Jesus, laid down His life for His sheep. He is also the Lamb, my friend Thommy read about, Who takes away our sin and gives instead abundant life."

Something flickered in Adam's heart. But he shifted his mind to his undercover work, refusing to acknowledge the long buried feelings his uncle's words created deep in his soul.

He'd cut his evening short with Debra much to her displeasure. Boring him out of his mind with her inane chitchat, she appeared intent on trapping him into a physical relationship he had no intention of falling into. Strictly a job with her. Nothing more. And would he be glad when this case was over and he could go back to—to what?

Adam darted a look at Erin out of the corner of his eye. Nothing boring about that *bilágaana*. A conversation with Erin Dawson was more like first contact with a hitherto undiscovered species. Not like Debra with her appetites amounting to nothing more than a hankering, as Hershal would've said, for brown sugar.

Unfortunately, he was well acquainted through his university days with the type. A game with many of the sorority girls, hooking up with one of the People, trying to shock conservative parents by their rebellion or for the sheer thrill of bragging rights.

Not like Erin in the least. Not a girl for one-night stands. Not a girl for casual relationships.

He grimaced. Hershal was right. Not a girl for someone like him.

Actions from his past—university and Fort Bragg days—he'd undo and erase if he could. He thanked God—there was a first in a long while—he'd never actually run into Erin while in North Carolina. She'd have never given that Adam the time of day. And why should she?

He flushed, ashamed of the Adam Silverhorn he'd been. The Adam who tried to party and romance his way out of bitter memories of a broken childhood and absent father. He was still vaguely shocked a woman such as Erin chose to count him as her friend.

But was he so different now?

Sure, he was doing something important to help his people, but had he really changed on the inside? For someone as lacking in worldly sophistication as Erin, she'd pegged him right the first time she'd laid eyes on him. A good time, blonde-chasing guy who liked fast cars and fast girls, anything to keep from examining the emptiness that clawed at his heart. An emptiness he tried to drown out with neon lights and lots of noise.

Johnny's eyes grew earnest, recapturing Adam's attention. "For the Christian, Jesus Christ is life. Jesus is everything you will ever need. And I have spent my life proclaiming among you, the People, the incredible gift of our Creator Who sent His Son, the Lamb of God, as a sacrifice for your sin and mine. Jesus desires only for you to draw near to Him to receive this gift of eternal life He offers. Won't you believe, my brothers and sisters? Today?"

His uncle, to give him credit, looked everywhere and at everyone in the sanctuary except for Adam. Never any overt pressure from his uncle to change his heathen ways. He was the son Iris and Johnny had never been able to have. The only pressure from the uncle he'd looked up to since childhood was the kind of pressure the strings of love bring.

Erin made a motion to slide past him out of the pew. His uncle called for Erin to join him on the platform to lead the closing song of worship. As she slipped into the aisle, she smoothed down her long-sleeved midnight blue dress.

He admired the way the fabric hugged her hips and how its V-neckline framed her face. Envisioned how the color of one of his mother's turquoise squash blossom pendants lying against the hollow at the base of Erin's throat would accentuate her fair complexion.

She lifted her face and closed her eyes. The rustling sounds quieted. Erin opened her mouth and Adam's heart quickened as the pure, sweet notes of "Jesus Loves Me" poured from her lips.

"Jesus loves me, this I know . . ."

A loveliness emanated from her being.

"For the Bible tells me so. Little ones to Him belong . . ." Luminosity surrounded her. Beauty and harmony.

When had he decided she was lovely? The beauty of her spirit shone in comparison to the squalor of Debra's. And his own. Her loveliness stung his eyes and his heart ached for the sheer beauty of the Christ in her.

"Yes, Jesus loves me. The Bible tells me so."

She exited the platform and as the last note died away made her way to the bottom level. Lacing her fingers together, she sent Adam a timid look, took a deep breath and then sang, enunciating each syllable carefully, *"Jesus ayoo'asho'ní."*

Jesus loves me.

His head jerked.

Smiles spread across many of the old ones' faces. With a sudden clarity of memory, he remembered echoes of this song in the voices of his grandparents soon after his mother had taken him and Lydia away from their father. He'd hunkered down on his Uncle Johnny's lap, Lydia on Aunt Iris's. Their grown, never-seen-her-cry mother slumped in her own mother's lap, her face pressed against Grandma's bosom, his mother's frame wracked by sobs.

Adam's grandfather had wrapped his arms around them both. Iris and Johnny had taken hold of each of his mother's hands and in that circle of love, his family had sung *Jesus ayoo'asho'ní* until his mother had lifted her tear-streaked face and joined them in song.

How had he forgotten his mother's grief over her broken marriage? How could he have forgotten the healing they'd found in their family's heritage of faith?

Tears winked in his eyes.

"*Binaaltsoos yee shit halne'*." Through His Word He tells me.

Did her Creator take as much pleasure from the sound of Erin's voice as he did?

"*Álchíníigi ánísht'é*," Like a child I am—

"*Doo . . .*" Erin stopped, a frantic look crossing her face. She bit her lip to keep it from trembling.

Her cheeks pinked. She'd forgotten the rest of the song in Navajo.

Adam gripped the back of the pew in front of him. He wouldn't let her fall flat on her face in front of the People. Without stopping to think, he surged to his feet.

"*Doo sidziil da, Ei bidziil*," his rusty baritone rang out.

I'm not strong. Him. He's strong.

Gratitude welling in those lovely eyes, she seized onto his prompt, wrinkling her forehead in an effort to commit the words to the memory of that big scholar brain of hers.

"*Jesus ayóó'ashó'ní*," He loves me. Adam blended his voice to her contralto.

Across the aisle, an old one, Sani's grandmother, creaked to her feet. "*Jesus ayóó'ashó'ní*." Sani rose, weaving his small fingers through his grandmother's hand. Doli and Clarence stood, linking hands, lifting their young faces to the ceiling.

Jesus ayóó'ashó'ní. He loves me.

Iris joined Johnny on the platform. The look Johnny sent Adam's way—of love and pride and joy—pierced Adam's heart. One by one the members of Cedar Canyon Community—*bilágaana* and Diné—joined their voices.

Jesus ayóó'ashó'ní. He loves me.

Adam, too?

For one crazy moment as the song rose heavenward, he imagined the laughing, happy faces of his Grandma and Grandpa Silverhorn smiling down upon them.

"*Bizaad yee shi halne'.*" Through His Word He tells me.

The smile on Erin's face stretched as wide as the distance between Carolina and his homeland. To his surprise, he found tears making a silent trek down his face.

Quiet rang out as the last words of the refrain dissipated into the rafters. A holy stillness settled over the sanctuary.

"Amen," boomed his uncle's voice.

"Amen," thundered the People of Cedar Canyon Community Church.

Erin clutched the armrest of Adam's truck as it lurched and bumped up Cedar Mesa Road to her home. Gripping the steering wheel with eyes fixed straight ahead, Adam wore a funny expression on his face, chagrin, and something she couldn't pinpoint. The smile on her own face could've powered a nuclear generator.

Her cheeks were starting to hurt. Maybe one day both her friends, Jesus and Adam Silverhorn, would be on a first-name basis with each other.

"Don't want to talk about what happened at church," he growled.

Erin's smile dimmed.

He swerved to the left to avoid a kamikaze prairie dog in the middle of the road. "Not ever gonna be an apple."

"A what?"

"Like Uncle Johnny. Like Lydia living in Houston."

"An apple?"

He shot her a look. "Red on the outside. White on the inside."

Erin frowned. "You told me Lydia married one of the People."

"She did. But then they moved to Houston. She's a town Indian now living the *bilágaana* suburban dream of shopping malls and minivans."

Erin blew out her cheeks in exasperation. "She married an oil rig worker. Of course they live in Houston."

Adam stuck out his chin. "She teaches a Bible study, too."

Like it made her some sort of evil Nazi propagandist?

She stiffened, curling her fingers into a tight ball on the armrest. That kind of talk about her friend, Jesus, from someone who ought to know better always got to her. "News flash, Silverhorn. Jesus wasn't a *bilágaana*. He was the Son of God and a Jew. Not a drop of white in those veins He shed for my sins and yours."

As soon as she'd said it, she wished she hadn't. No way to win friends or influence people for Jesus by getting defensive and antagonistic.

But to her surprise, Adam hooted with laughter. "You sound like my Grandpa." He licked his lips around his grin. "Fine. I won't badmouth your friends if you don't badmouth mine." Taking one hand off the wheel, he stuck out the other. "Truce?"

She uncurled her fist and shook his hand. The warmth of his fingers sent a jolt through her spine. Apparently, something jolted Adam as well. The grin disappeared. His black eyes stared out the windshield as they rounded the last hill toward her house.

"Pray for me, though?" he whispered, refusing to meet her gaze again.

"Have been and will continue to do so." To lighten the mood, she gave him a mock salute.

The corners of his full lips tilted up once more. "What's this I hear about you starting an exercise class at the community center? Don't go imposing your perverted, anorexic-thin *bilágaana* notions of beauty on my people." He steered into the driveway.

She arched an eyebrow at him. "It's a nutrition and fitness class for new moms. In case you haven't noticed, the rates of obesity and diabetes on the Rez are horrific."

He shifted the truck to Park, cut the engine, and twisted in the seat. "Healthy is good. But—"

She pushed open the door and slid out. Slowly pirouetting, the hem of her dress billowed. "I'm hardly a poster child for the *bilágaana's* obsession with weight. Though I've wished most of my life for a few more inches and a little less . . ." She fluttered her hands.

"In the Diné culture, we like love handles on our women."

"Well, no wonder I like living here. I go over big and beautiful."

He stepped out of the truck and meandered around to join her. "You certainly don't qualify as big. And as for the beautiful part . . ." He gave her that lopsided smile of his. "I'm glad you like living here. The People also don't mind a little junk in the trunk."

She planted her hands on her hips. "Did you just say I have a big butt?"

Laughing, he held up both hands in surrender. "No, I did not. You are curvy, Erin Dawson. Not big. Just right."

"And what business do you have looking at my butt in the first place?"

A flush started from the edge of his blazer collar. His eyes darted toward the house. "I like your—" The color drained from his face. He reached behind and under his jacket, extracting a gun.

Her eyes went huge. "You carried a gun to church? What are you—?"

"You got your cell phone?" he hissed.

His eyes had gone as opaque and bottomless as a black hole at the bottom of a canyon.

"Yes, but what—?"

"Get in the truck and lock the door. Call 911. The dispatcher will put you through to Tulley Singer. He's on duty today. Tell him I need him to get out here pronto."

"Adam? What's going on?"

He started up the drive. "Get in the truck, I told you," he called over his shoulder. "Someone's broken into your house."

Only then did she notice the front door standing ajar, a strange symbol spray painted red across its surface. Under the carport, the windshield of the Camry smashed.

She gasped. "You're not going in there alone? The intruder could still be in there. You need to wait for your backup."

Adam pivoted. "If he's in there, I mean to catch him."

She extended a hand. "Give me a gun. I'll help."

His eyes widened in disbelief.

"My daddy—"

"This is not MK Training 101, Erin. The thought of my Glock in your inexperienced hands . . ." He shuddered. "You are wasting my time and the opportunity to catch this perp. For once in your life," he said between clenched teeth, "do what you are told to do and Get. In. The. Truck."

Erin stamped her foot. Pebbles flew. No need for this suicidal Lone Ranger act. But she had the sense not to say it out loud noting the I'm-spoiling-for-a-fight look on his face.

She flung open the door and hurled herself into the seat. Refusing to take her eyes off him, she rooted around in her purse until her fingers located her cell phone. Holding it up for him to see, she returned his glare and hit 9-1-1.

Relaying his message, she gave him a curt nod to let him know she'd done as he asked. His lips tightened and he jerked his head toward the truck cab. He mouthed, "Lock the door now."

Frowning, she did as he asked. Inhaling sharply, he placed both hands around his weapon and extended his arms. The cold steel gleamed in the afternoon sun. Sidling to the corner of the house, he dropped to a squatting position and skedaddled in a sideways crablike maneuver under the picture window until he reached the edge of the porch steps.

"Jesus," she whispered, her hands clasped together under her chin.

With a suddenness that took her breath, he vaulted from the bottom to the top step in a single bound. Shoving open the door with his shoulder, he shouted, "Police Officer," before disappearing out of her sight into the confines of the house.

She tolerated the silence about ten seconds. Catching sight of a tire iron wedged under the seat, she made a grab for it and sprang out of the truck. This was her house and Adam was her . . .

Friend?

Right.

Licking her suddenly dry lips, she advanced up the steps before she could change her mind.

Adam, whether he admitted it or not, needed her help. Despite his inflated opinion of himself, no man was an island. Even the Lone Ranger had Tonto. And whether Adam Silverhorn liked it or not, she was going to help him if it killed her.

She swallowed, pausing at the door, her knuckles turning white around the tire iron.

Metaphorically speaking, of course.

8

HE'D WAITED TILL HE HEARD THE DEFINITIVE CLICK OF THE LOCK ON THE truck door before he'd made a move on the house. Erin's safety came before apprehending any criminal. Once inside the house, Adam realized the invaders had come and gone. He gingerly stepped over the piles of books haphazardly tossed from the bookshelves. She'd have a fit when she saw what they'd done to her books.

The crossed spears symbol on the door, the red paint seeming to drip with blood, was all too familiar. Similar graffiti messages littered dumpsters and the sides of buildings across the Rez. The gangs spray painted their turf declarations back as soon as they were removed by the Tribal Council. Gangs were on the rise and an unfortunate aspect of life in the Navajo Nation these days. But why had they targeted a *bilágaana* like Erin?

Unless she'd double-crossed someone in the cartel.

All his earlier suspicions from when he'd first met her rose to the surface. All the inherent doubts and cynicism that came over time with his profession kicked in. He'd checked her out and her records came back as lily white pure as the image she projected. But was she really that clean? Was anybody really that clean?

Or had she just never been caught before?

Couch cushions slashed, their fluffy contents lent a snowy atmosphere to the carpet. In the kitchen, every pan and utensil had been upended onto the linoleum. A butcher knife stuck vertically out of the wall underneath the smashed clock face. The wanton destruction of her bedspread and mattress in the bedroom made him pause. The vandalism wasn't the usual *modus operandi* of the gangs whose violent home invasions tended to be quick-in, quick-out searches for cash to supply the gang members' methamphetamine dependencies.

This . . . brutality smacked of something personal—hatred and fear mixed together. What had Erin done to the RedBloods to invite such hostility? The message scrawled with a tube of Erin's crimson lipstick across the bathroom mirror halted him in his tracks.

Back off b——, it read.

A creak from the living room tensed every muscle in his body. Swiftly, on the balls of his feet, he tiptoed out to the hallway. Spotting a shadow cast by the picture window, he swung into the room, arms extended, finger on the trigger. "Stop!"

Erin screamed, unable to stop the forward, downward momentum of the iron rod in her hand directed at his head. Instinct kicked in and sidestepping, he ducked. The tire iron connected with the wall, burying itself into the sheet rock where he'd stood only seconds before.

"What in the name of all that's holy are you doing in here, Erin Dawson? I told you to stay in the truck. I almost shot you." His heart pounding, he bent over, placing his hands on his knees, trying to control his ragged breaths.

Shaking, she drew her hands to her face and swallowed. "And I almost brained you," she whispered.

He reholstered his gun. "Can't you ever do what somebody— who's been trained to deal with these kind of situations—tells you to do?"

Adam sagged against the wall, the tire iron protruding tomahawk-like. "For all your multiple university degrees, girl you don't have the sense God gave small lizard creatures. You scared the . . ."

Noticing the floor littered with her precious books, Erin, with little whimpering noises, leaned over to retrieve a book.

He seized her hand. "Not just yet. Once Tulley and the crime scene crew get here maybe we'll get lucky and find fingerprints."

"My books." Anguish filled her voice.

She surveyed the room. "The couch." She gasped and strode into the kitchen. "What a mess. Why, Adam? Why me? Who'd do such a thing?" She reached to pull the knife from the wall but giving him a look, she withdrew her hand. "Evidence. I'll try to remember next time."

He accompanied her into the bedroom. He wanted to be there when she read the message. Her face had the tendency to express everything she thought or felt. Not exactly the best kind of face to have if you were a criminal. And he wanted to see how she reacted.

Reading the ugly message, her face blanched chalk white. She clapped a hand over her mouth to stifle another scream. Her green eyes large, she started a rapid descent toward the floor.

Cupping her elbow, he eased her down the rest of the way. She huddled, her knees drawn to her chin, her body wracked with shivers of shock. Despite his best instincts—or maybe because of it—he couldn't help but wrap her in the security of his arms.

"Adam?" Her teeth chattered. "What does it mean? Why would someone—?" She gulped.

No way Erin was lying. She was as shocked and confused by the message as he was. He'd seen her happy and sad, angry and funny.

The memory of her worship in the Diné language rose to his mind. She wasn't that good an actress to pull that off—the reverent, sweet adoration of a child to her Father. He'd seen that look before—genuine—on the faces of his mother and sister and relatives.

She stirred, contemplating the message. "What am I supposed to back off from?"

Not what. Who, he realized with a moment of clarity. Debra had left her gang minions to do her dirty work for her.

She rested her head on his shoulder. "I've been asking a lot of questions about the past. The cave paintings." She straightened. "Is there something in those caves somebody doesn't want me to find?"

Erin and her blasted quest. Leastways, it would keep her from suspecting the truth.

No way could he explain the real reason behind the vandalism and the warning without blowing his cover and jeopardizing an operation a year in the making. The fruition of all his efforts, his reputation-damning deceptions for the sake of the ultimate goal—so close he could taste it. Things were coming to a head. He felt it in his gut, honed through his tour in Afghanistan and police training.

A siren whirred, penetrating the edges of his consciousness. He released Erin and offered her a hand. "Tulley and the cavalry have arrived."

She took a shaky breath, her hand on her throat. "Since when have the People looked forward to the cavalry arriving?" she asked with an attempt at humor.

He towed her out of the bedroom and toward the front of the house. "Since we formed our own cavalry."

The warning was meant for him. He needed to back off. From Erin.

Debra's insecurities and jealousies were getting the best of her. A woman scorned was not just a cliché. If he didn't toe the line, if he did anything to jeopardize Debra's trust in him, Erin's life—not to mention his own—would be in danger.

And, thousands of dollars and man hours lost in bringing down the drug cartel whose tentacles had reached out, ensnaring countless young Diné lives with its deadly web of gang warfare and drug addiction.

He had a job to do. A job he'd been specially recruited for by the DEA, FBI, and Bureau of Indian Affairs from the moment he completed the police academy. No time for friendship, God, or anything else that distracted him from his real purpose.

She leaned against him in the threshold of the door. Her shaking had slowed. Without meaning to, he breathed in the vanilla scent that was all Erin. Closing his eyes against a rush of feeling, he hardened his heart.

"Is that your friend, Tulley Singer? I think I've seen him at church."

He opened his eyes to see Erin pointing at the rangy Navajo. "Yeah."

Tulley unfolded himself, accordionlike, from the tribal police cruiser. Another police vehicle parked on his bumper. A white van sporting the Navajo Nation Tribal Police logo pulled alongside.

His best friend in the entire world tipped his hat back from his eyes as he paused, one foot on the first step. "See you got everything under control, Silverhorn. Don't know why you bothered to call me." A crooked smile belied his words.

Adam jerked his head toward the van. "They got here fast."

Tulley caught sight of Erin behind him. "Ma'am." He nodded. "They were already at the station. Bored. Not much going on for a Sunday. What kind of situation we got here, Adam?"

"I'll give you the grand tour." He stepped past Erin into the living room, Tulley on his heels. "Wait in Tulley's patrol car so the crew can get in here and work, okay?" He gestured out the door. "Tulley will have some questions for the report."

She smoothed her rumpled dress. "Tulley?"

His jaw tightened. "His case now. First responder." He turned his back on her.

"But you—" She stopped when he continued to walk away from her. The longest six feet he'd ever travelled. The air behind him vibrated.

"Sure." But a little-girl-lost note quavered in her voice.

His gut clenched. He willed his feet to keep moving. Away.

Tulley motioned to the crew and glanced around him, his eyes missing nothing. He lowered his voice out of the earshot of the other team members. "RedBloods? Got something to do with your case, I assume."

Adam nodded as fellow members of the department entered the house, setting out their equipment. He waved Tulley into the back of the house. Only Uncle Johnny and now Tulley knew the real reasons behind his cop-on-the-edge routine of the last few months. Corruption was an insidious thing.

"Got Debra and her pals written all over it." He gave a hoarse laugh. "You know Debra's philosophy about loving something and setting it free."

"If it comes back to you . . ." Tulley began.

"And if it doesn't, hunt it down and kill it."

"It meaning you?"

"Or Erin Dawson."

Tulley took stock of the vandalized bedroom and whistled softly at the warning on the mirror. "Been meaning to ask you about the nature of your relationship with newcomer Erin Dawson anyway. Guess this pretty much spells it out, doesn't it?"

He thrust his hands into his pockets. "Just Debra's sick interpretation of things."

Tulley cocked an eyebrow. "So you and Erin Dawson are just friends? Nothing more?"

"Nothing more." He hunched his shoulders, striving to sound matter-of-fact.

"So another guy—say me—wouldn't be tramping on your toes if he asked her out himself?"

His stomach knotted. Tulley Singer—a great all-around guy, youngest elder at Cedar Canyon Community Church, acting chief of police—and Erin Dawson made for each other.

"Go for it, dude. She's out of my league. The whole religion thing, you know."

Tulley planted a hand on his arm. "Relationship, man. God wants a relationship with you."

Adam shrugged off his hand. "Don't start. I've filled my quota for sermons already today." He surveyed the damaged home. "Got fences to mend with Debra. After the crew is done, think you could stick around and help Erin clean up?"

Tulley licked his lips. "Understand she fixes a mean Sunday lunch. You can count on me, old buddy, when sacrifices are called for . . ."

"Ha, ha, ha. Funny Indian." Adam drew his shoulders back. "And she probably shouldn't stay here alone tonight. No telling what the gang might do to drive home their message. Maybe Nia could put her up for a couple of days."

Tulley rubbed his chin. "Sure. We'll swing by the station and hit her up."

Adam made for the door. He wheeled around. "And Tulley?" A menacing tone laced his words.

"If I so much as hear one bad word about you treating her with anything less than the utmost respect . . ."

Tulley's black eyes twinkled. "So that's how it is, man, huh?"

He flushed. A muscle ticked in his cheek. "Just remember we Diné are slow to anger, but we remember our enemies forever."

Tulley laughed low in his throat. "I get it. I'll babysit your *friend* while you nab the bad guys, Silverhorn." He clapped a hand across Adam's back jolting him.

"You just be sure and keep her safe, you hear me?"

"Loud and clear." Tulley laid his hand across his heart. "My word, brother." He couldn't resist one parting shot. "Though if she decides she likes good-looking, tall Diné like myself rather than . . ." His arm swept the room. And Adam.

Adam ground his teeth together. "Gotta watch my so-called friends more than my enemies." Tulley hooted with laughter as he stormed out of the house.

His feet betrayed his intention to go cold turkey on Erin when he came even with Tulley's patrol car and her tear-streaked, forlorn face peering out.

Great. He'd made her cry.

"Tulley's gonna help you clean up," he barked.

She shrank back on the seat.

"The guys will be here a while, though. And then, he thinks it'd be better if you spent a few nights with another old high school buddy of ours, Lavinia Yow. She works as a dispatcher at the station and has an apartment in Cedar Canyon."

Her lips hardened into a straight line. "I don't—"

Adam jabbed a finger through the open window in the direction of her face. "Gangs, Erin. For whatever reason, you've been targeted. Shall I tell you about what one gang in Chinle did to a woman they found asleep during one of their home invasions?"

Fear streaked across her face. He felt like a jerk. But a little fear was not always a bad thing. Especially if it kept you alive.

Scared was way better than dead.

"Okay," she whispered. "Whatever you want."

His eyes constricted. Stupid desert dust. He shoved away from the patrol car and stomped over to his truck.

Want had nothing to do with it. At least not until Debra and the murderous drug cartel rotted behind bars.

"I didn't realize gangs were such a problem on the reservation." Erin reshelved a book. "I guess I think of gangs as more of a big city problem."

With his long dark hair pulled into a ponytail, Tulley bent all six foot plus of himself to the floor, before handing her a heavy volume of anecdotal history on the Southwest. "Used to be. But Diné youth are particularly susceptible to the growing influence of urban Latino and African American gangs."

She smoothed a crinkled page from a book spread-eagled on the carpet. "Why's that?"

"They're caught between two worlds—the *bilágaana* world and the Navajo world—in a clash of cultures. Most come from highly dysfunctional homes. Missing parents or neglectful ones wracked by their own addictions to alcohol."

"Like Sani Nakai's parents. Or Adam's dad?"

Tulley gave her a wry smile. "Yeah." Using a small hand broom and scoop, he swept the cushion fluff from the floor.

"And the grinding Third World poverty. The gangs give the kids a sense of belonging, of family, of mattering to somebody. The possibility of doing something that makes a difference for their homeys."

She sighed. "I don't think most of America understands how hard it is here in their own backyard for our fellow Americans to survive, much less thrive."

He shrugged, putting muscle into scooping up the last shreds of the cushions. Tulley was a wiry fellow. She pictured the skinny teenage kid he'd once been.

She also imagined how he'd come into his own by the time he reached thirty-five. Filled out muscles. The rugged profile. A mountain employed by the tribal police.

"Don't know. Don't care. That way white guilt is easier to ignore. CNN reports of Haiti and Africa and monetary donations to world relief funds make it easier to salve the conscience."

"How about you?"

Tulley yanked the butcher knife from the kitchen wall. "Me? I was blessed with two strict parents."

"Your parents chose to stay on the reservation?"

"My dad's a civil engineer at the mining corporation the Tribal Council oversees. My mom struggles to teach math to the kids at the high school. They chose to return home after college and try to make their corner of the world less bleak."

"So the gangs were not a problem when you and Adam were in school here?"

He bagged the shards of glass and remnants of pillow cushions. "Oh, they'd already made inroads even back then. Adam got pulled in first—"

She dropped the book she was shelving. "Adam was in a gang?"

"Not for long. Once his Uncle Johnny found out about it, he stirred up the community—tribal leaders, teachers and principals, local business owners, parents—and drove the ringleaders out of town temporarily. Kept Sheridan and me and Nia from getting in but not before Adam watched our other friend, Hosteen, die of a drug overdose. There used to be four of us musketeers as the *bilágaana* would say. Nia, Adam, Hosteen, and me. All from Cedar Canyon Community Church."

His face grew grim. "That's why Adam hates the gangs and the drugs so much. He's trained, you know, as our local Native Gang Specialist. That's why he'll do—" He turned his back, twisting the garbage shut with a plastic tie.

She stilled. "That's why he'll do anything, say anything, or pretend anything to put a stop to it."

He stiffened. "That's why he coaches Little League. That's why I coach basketball in the winter and Nia teaches middle grade Sunday School. Prevention goes a long way toward a cure. The gangs recruit them young." Tulley faced her. "And for their sake in the name of God, so do we."

What a fine man Tulley Singer was turning out to be.

Her eyebrows rose. "Adam and God?"

Tulley grinned. "God's working on him. Uncle Johnny told me he had a dream a few months ago—Diné, believers and non-believers, are big on dreams—that a *bilágaana* would bring Adam back to God."

He assessed the house. "Good as we can get it till you have time to go off Rez to Wal-Mart to replace your damaged goods."

She planted her hands on her hips. "A *bilágaana* and Adam?"

"A *bilágaana* woman. God does love His little jokes. Adam will never see it coming."

She backed up a step. "And you guys think I . . . Me?" She pointed at herself.

"Well, you did get him to come to church today. First time he's been since he got back from Afghanistan. Three years at least. Maybe more if you count since his mother stopped being able to force his stubborn backside onto a church pew."

Tulley heaved the trash bag toward the door. "We better head to the station if you've finished packing your overnight case. We'll stop off first at Changing Woman Cafe for an early supper since you and I both missed out on lunch. Touristy place but 'bout the only place open on a Sunday afternoon."

"Aren't you on duty?"

He smiled, his dark eyes lighting. "Clocked out at two. Told the crew to officially clock me out at the station. I'm all yours now." He patted his belly. "And this growing boy needs fuel."

She gave him a playful punch in the belly. "Is food all you Diné boys ever think about?"

He gave her a cheeky grin as he held open the door. "Not quite, Miss Dawson. Not quite. Sorry about the perp wrecking your home-cooked lunch. But I'd like to request a raincheck on that fabulous Southern cooking I've heard so much about."

"You got it." She dusted her hands off and grabbed her duffle. "Fried chicken. Potato salad."

"Don't forget dessert."

Tulley waited in his vehicle, while she checked to make sure the vandals hadn't found the package from her dad. Spotting it in the cubbyhole she'd discovered in the kitchen, she breathed a sigh of relief. She slipped it into her purse.

Riding down the mesa and through town, Tulley waved to a few old men seated on aluminum folding chairs in the front of the local trading post/gas station sipping on colas. "Code talkers."

She swiveled, straining her neck to get a backhand look at the old gentlemen.

"Not many left. My grandfather and Adam's were both code talkers in the Pacific, island-hopping before his grandfather answered the call to preach, and mine to higher education courtesy of the G. I. Bill. Our families go back a long ways."

He squinted his eyes, glancing in the rearview mirror. "Family legend says both families were warriors in the days when the white man, Spaniard and Anglo, first came to the Navajo homeland, the Dinétah. Before the Long Walk."

Tulley inclined his head out the window in the direction of the wooden stalls displaying wool products and silver jewelry lining the road. "Before we became domesticated."

She eyed him. "Adam never said anything about a family history like that."

Tulley snorted. "Adam loved his grandfather Silverhorn but has never cared an iguana's tail for ancient history."

He gave her a long, slow smile, mischief sparking in his eyes. "Now me? I'm a veritable storehouse of knowledge on Navajo history and culture."

She smiled. "Oh, really? Well, in that case Mr. Singer . . ." She spent the next ten minutes giving Tulley the low-down on her search for Olivia.

Driving past the church and the small cemetery on the hill, Tulley steered the car into the crowded parking lot of the cafe lined with blue spruce and silver aspens. He parked the car and rubbed his chin. "Interesting. I've never heard of this white woman captive, but I'll ask around. The old people like me. They love to talk and I love to listen. Got to listen cause one day their wisdom will be gone. Plenty of captives grafted into most Diné family trees anyway."

Tulley nodded at her surprised look. "Captives were traded as slaves between the tribes in the Southwest. Most came from Mexico and eventually were engrafted into the Diné through marriage. That's why you'll encounter names like Manuelito and Navarro all over the Rez."

He pointed at a silver Chevy. "Nia's here. Save us a trip to the station. You'll like her. Known her since she strong-armed my crayons away from me in preschool."

Erin's lips twitched. This Nia sounded like a character. Tulley held the door open and waited for her to step through.

The noisy drone of conversation and the clinking of utensils greeted them. The attention-grabbing smells of grease perfumed the air. Smelled like home—her Carolina home.

"Got good pie here. But I'm as serious as a heart attack about that pig-picking cake I hear you made one Wednesday night." Tulley let the door swing shut behind them.

She nudged him with her hip. "Sure thing. As soon as you guys let me back into my own home."

He draped an arm across her shoulders. "How 'bout I repair the sheetrock and you do a little cooking while I work?"

She smiled. "I'll—"

"Oh, Adam. That's wonderful news."

Erin's head rotated and Tulley froze on the threshold at the sound of the voice. At the mention of Adam's name, she lasered in on the image across the width of the restaurant of a petite, sloe-eyed Navajo woman throwing her arms around Adam. He leaned down to accommodate her slight stature, a grin on his face. The young woman closed her eyes, a wide smile on her beautiful face.

And—noting the woman's trim form clad in a hot pink T-shirt and the circular turquoise discs of squash blossoms topping her hip-hugging blue jeans—no love handles anywhere in sight.

9

Tulley bristled. A pang of jealousy speared her heart. Was she destined to spend her internship running into one after the other of Adam's so-called women *friends*?

"Lavinia." Tulley sounded not unlike a growling bear.

At the sound of her name, Lavinia, her arms still clasped around Adam's neck, opened her eyes. Catching sight of Tulley's arm around Erin, Lavinia's smile faded. Her lovely black eyes narrowed and she released her hold on Adam. Straightening, Adam wheeled around. His back stiffened and his lips flatlined.

Her eyes hopscotching back and forth among the three, Erin stepped out of the circle of Tulley's arm. She'd landed in something she didn't quite understand. Something sticky. If she didn't know better she'd swear the look on Lavinia Yow's lovely oval face radiated not just hostility, but jealousy, too. The glower on her face matched only by the glower on Adam's.

Adam? Jealous of Tulley? Did Adam feel about her, Erin, the way she . . . ?

Not possible. For so many reasons.

She moved forward, her hand outstretched. "Lavinia, I'm Erin Dawson. Hard to believe our paths haven't crossed before now."

Lavinia crossed her arms over her chest. "Not so hard to believe."

O—kay. Maybe time to reconsider the sleepover with Lavinia. Erin dropped her hand.

Tulley positioned a hand on his gun belt. "What's wonderful news?" The black baton hanging from the belt dangled at his side.

Adam widened his stance, feet apart, and planted even with his hips.

Lavinia uncrossed her arms and edged between them, forcing space between both men. She slid into a booth with a complete view of Main Street courtesy of a grime-smeared, plate-glass window. "My coffee's getting cold. Sit down, Singer, and we'll tell you." She snared Adam's black Polo shirttail and dragged him in alongside her.

The look Tulley sent Adam's way could've roasted sheep. Hadn't these people been friends since childhood?

Bottom lip protruding, Tulley dropped into the booth on the opposite side. Yanking Erin's arm, he hauled her in beside him so that he faced Lavinia. And she faced a white-lipped Adam.

Lavinia picked up her spoon. "Adam's mom, Hannah, called from Houston. Lydia's had the baby." She reached for the sugar canister, pouring the white crystals into her spoon. "Mother and son are both resting well."

Tulley leaned against the cracked red vinyl upholstery. "Oh." Shooting a glance over to Adam, he wiped both palms down the sides of his uniform pants. "That's great news."

Adam nodded but Erin noticed he, too, relaxed against the cushion. Truce.

Lavinia measured the sugar in her spoon and dumped the contents into the white porcelain coffee mug. The spoon made sharp clunking sounds as she stirred.

Adam took a deep breath. "I already asked Nia about Erin staying over a few days."

Silence.

Lavinia poured, measured, dumped, and stirred—traditional Navajo hospitality and something else war dancing for supremacy across her features.

"Maybe just tonight," Erin offered with a meaningful jerk of her chin over to Tulley at Lavinia's bowed head, rapt over her coffee.

And what a long night it looked to be.

Tulley toyed with a paper napkin. "Thought you'd be with Debra."

She and Adam tensed.

"Haven't found her yet."

Adam fiddled a blue pack of artificial sweetener between his fingers, refusing to meet Tulley's gaze. Or hers.

Tulley handed Erin a menu. "Mind if we share the booth? Looks pretty crowded in here for a Sunday afternoon."

She scanned Lavinia's face for a reaction. But only black eye slits showed beneath her lowered eyelashes.

Adam stuck a leg out into the aisle and slid across the seat. "I'm on my way out."

She swiveled to Tulley. "Would you mind swinging by in the morning and bringing me to the Cultural Center on your way to work?"

Adam plopped onto the cracked vinyl, a huff emanating from the cushion. "Center's closed on Mondays. Why are you going there?"

She felt him move his leg underneath the table and connect with Tulley's shin.

Tulley gasped in sudden pain.

She bit back a smile. She'd managed to stir that pot.

Lavinia raised her head, a peculiar look on her face. Pour, measure, dump. Pour, measure, dump.

Erin gulped. That was going to be the sweetest coffee this side of Texas.

Tulley cleared his throat, shooting a scowl at Adam. "I'd be glad to—"

Lavinia dropped the spoon with a clang against the saucer. "No need to trouble Tulley on his day off. I'm sure I can manage to drop Erin at the Center before I head to Flagstaff."

Tulley leaned his elbows on the chipped Formica tabletop. "What you going to Flagstaff for, Nia?"

She said nothing, her resemblance to the Sphinx growing by the minute. A smile tugged at the corners of Nia's lips.

Adam cut Tulley a look, drumming his fingers in a war beat on the table. "Kind of isolated at the Center with the volunteers and staff gone. Maybe a good day to work on your quest, Erin."

Laying aside the menu, she rested her hands palm down on the sticky table surface. "Best time to get work done is when no one is around. The director went off on a long overdue vacation. He won some kind of sweepstakes out of the blue."

She removed her hands from the table, rubbing her fingertips together to remove the gooey residue. "He'll be gone for two weeks. I promised him I'd inventory and catalogue some items in the storeroom we've never had room to display. Might work up a temporary exhibit."

"You cleared that with Debra?" Adam thrust his jaw forward. "She's in charge with Benallie gone."

She frowned. "Speaking of Debra? Didn't you say you were on your way to find her?"

Eyeballing her this time, he picked up the menu lying on the table between them. "Maybe I do have time for dessert at least."

He flashed the vintage, megawattage smile that was all Adam Silverhorn. "Trying to get rid of me or something?"

Erin's lip curled. "Or something." She flipped her hair over her shoulder.

Lavinia smiled, the effect like a shaft of sun breaking free of the rain. She brought the mug to her lips and took a tiny sip. She slid the mug across the table to Tulley. "Here, you drink it. Too sweet for me, but you might like it."

Tulley pivoted toward Erin. "I'll talk to the old guys on your behalf tomorrow. How 'bout I pick you up at 1:00 and we can get a quick lunch while I fill you in on any info I uncover?"

The smile fled Lavinia's face. A pulse leaped in Adam's neck. Tulley gulped a mouthful of coffee.

He grimaced and shoved the mug in Lavinia's direction. "What are you trying to do, Nia? Send me into a diabetic coma?"

Lavinia wrapped her fingers around the mug, her nose high in the air. "Oh, that's right. You're sweet enough. Just full of . . ." She arched one delicately shaped brow. " . . . sugar, aren't you, Tulley Singer."

Tulley clamped his lips together. He, Lavinia, and Adam glared at each other.

Erin sighed.

It was going to be a long, long night.

Erin laid the duffle bag on the quilt-covered bed in Lavinia's spare bedroom. The pretty Diné woman monitored her from the doorway, her arms folded. Erin glanced around at the red and black checkered blankets hanging from the walls.

She cleared her throat, hoping to make amends. "I'm sure it will be okay for me to return home tomorrow."

Unfolding her arms, Lavinia strolled over to the footboard of the white iron bedstead. "Whatever."

The ride from the cafe to the apartment had been as silent as the grave. Refusing to look in Erin's direction, Lavinia had kept her eyes focused straight ahead on the road to her apartment complex at the edge of town. And Erin realized that in all of the excitement at church and with the break-in, she'd forgotten to tell Adam or Tulley about the Watcher. Or the crushed cigarette she'd found underneath the cottonwood tree.

She sank onto the mattress. Time to clear the air. She had a good notion of what had gone sour between her and the—by all accounts—usually congenial police dispatcher.

"It's not what it looked like between Tulley and me. We're just friends, Lavinia."

A faint smile flickered across Lavinia's features. "On your part maybe." She curled her fingers around the bedrail. "And I got the message loud and clear 'tween you and Adam."

"Adam?" Erin pointed at herself. "And me? That's ridicu—"

Lavinia fluttered a hand. "Whatever you say, but I got eyes in my head and I read something pretty hot and heavy going on between you two."

Erin sniffed and smoothed the blue jean skirt she'd changed into before leaving her violated home. "We're friends. Nothing more."

"Sure. That's your story. You stick with it."

Erin gripped the handles of the bag. "Doesn't matter how I feel or don't feel." She snorted. "Me and every other skirt-wearing person on this reservation. I'm not exactly the kind of girl Adam Silverhorn goes for."

"Why do you say that?"

She shrugged, her lips quivering. "I'm too plain. Too boring. Not a party girl. Too serious. Too . . ." Erin sighed. "We're from different worlds. Different kingdoms really."

Lavinia gave her a measured look. "Adam's been kind of wild since he came back from the army. But Tulley told me not long ago if I and the rest of his friends didn't lose faith in Adam, maybe someday he'd find his own faith again."

Erin struggled to keep tears of bewilderment from welling out of her eyes.

"I've known Adam his whole life and I've never seen him get so flustered around a woman before he met you. I wouldn't be so quick to write off his feelings for you." Lavinia shook her head. "You're everything Hannah Silverhorn has ever prayed for Adam."

Erin flushed. "A *bilágaana* like me?"

"A strong Christian like you." Lavinia's face clouded. "You and I got off on the wrong foot, I think. My jealousy entirely to blame."

Erin tilted her head. "Wrong impression of Tulley and me, you mean?"

"Wrong impression of Adam and me, too." Lavinia stuck out her hand. "Call me Nia like the guys do. And that's part of the trouble. Tulley and Adam think of me as a little sister, only slightly less annoying now than I was at fifteen."

She squeezed Nia's hand. "Oh, I wouldn't be so quick to dismiss Tulley's feelings for you. When we walked in and saw you and Adam . . ." Erin chuckled. "That was one wound tight Indian."

"I'd like to believe that." Nia drifted to the window overlooking a distant red-spired butte. "But to him, I'm just the girl in the hogan next door."

Nia angled. "Police department in Flagstaff has offered me a dispatch job. Better pay and opportunities for promotion, though I'd never envisioned myself leaving the Rez."

The Diné woman squared her shoulders. "But maybe it's time I got on with my life. A life that doesn't include Tulley Singer and stupid dreams."

Joining her at the window, she touched Nia's arm. "Dreams are never stupid. I think God's working on Tulley though you might not see it."

"I've prayed and prayed for Tulley to wake up and notice me." Nia laid a hand over her heart. "Or for God to take these feelings away. But so far, nothing. I'm beginning to think it's me who needs to go away."

She put an arm around Nia as they gazed across the desert expanse stretching toward the horizon. "I'm going to pray for you both and for God to move."

"How about praying for Him to move a little faster?" joked Nia, a self-deprecating tone to her voice.

"God's idea of fast isn't exactly our idea of fast, is it?"

Erin reflected on her search for Olivia, on the years of study and research. She thought of her still unanswered dilemma regarding God's will for her own life.

Nia hugged her back. "Yep. The Creator is definitely not on our timetable. But He's always just in time." She pulled back an arm's length from Erin. "And I certainly see His hand in bringing you to my doorstep. Since my last roomie moved out to get married, it's been lonely. Be nice to have a new one, even a temporary one."

"Even a *bilágaana* one?"

Nia laughed. "A sister in Christ like me suffering the pangs of love."

A hand on her hip, Erin frowned. "I never said I—"

"There's none so deluded as those who delude themselves."

"Shakespeare?" Erin's brow furrowed. "Not the Bible. I'd have recognized that. One of the poets? English or American?"

"From a little-known Diné poet named Nia Yow." She smiled. "Friend."

A friend felt good.

Erin gestured toward the kitchen. "How about showing me how to make a proper Navajo fry bread?"

"I think it's time you got out, Ben." Adam dashed a hand through the top of his short-cropped hair. "It's only a matter of time before you slip up and the homeys know you've been feeding me info on their activities." He leaned against the rough outcropping of the canyon wall.

Ben's fingers fretted at the red do-rag like a noose around his neck. "Not till we drive them out for good. Not till it's safe at school for my little brother, Thommy. Not till no other kid dies from homeys pushing dope." He poked the steel-plated toe of his black boot in the desert sand. "If we don't stop them, they'll finish the job the *bilágaana* started and truly destroy the People for good."

Adam sighed. "I never wanted you involved in the case. You've given us names, locations, and dates. You've done more than anyone could ever expect."

The teenager shook his head and hitched his low-riding black jeans. "Never enough after what I done."

In the dying light of the setting sun, Adam noticed the unshed tears pooling in the boy's eyes.

Ben pushed back the sleeve of his hooded black jacket and brandished his forearm. "You know what they made me do to get this? The old one I—" His voice broke.

The brand on his arm made by a hot knife marked him forever as a member of the RedBloods. Part of the cost of earning his colors.

"I was stupid. Believing these punks were better than my friends and family." He shook his head. "I've wished a thousand times I could go back to those days you coached me in Little League. Life was so simple then."

Ben's face hardened. "But the lure of the power these guys had—all the guns at their disposal—the power of life and death. They were like gods to me."

Adam would give anything, too, for Ben to be that knuckleheaded kid who was the best first baseman he'd ever coached.

He gripped Ben's shoulder. "It's time to quit. We can get you and Thommy and your mom away. You've given me everything I need to tighten the net on these predators and put them in jail for the rest of their lives."

Ben shrugged off his hand. "Still haven't found where the suppliers are making this poison. One last piece to the puzzle. Got to bring back the balance and restore the harmony. One more thing to do to try to wash the blood off my hands and be clean."

Adam knew what Uncle Johnny would say was the only thing to ever make Ben Tso clean again. Adam Silverhorn clean, too. But Adam clenched his jaw, grinding his teeth. The boy needed real help, not some nebulous spiritual platitude from a Jesus Way apple.

Ben held up his thumb and forefinger. "I'm this close to finding out. Just a few more days, Adam. Another delivery for the homeys to sell at the high school has been scheduled for the end of the month. I've managed to earn Rodriguez's trust. He'll lead me to where his cohorts are producing the garbage. We're close, so close to nailing those . . ." He jammed his hands in his front pockets. "Too close to quit now."

Adam sighed, resignation lacing his voice. "Keep me updated as often as you can. I'll be there with backup as soon as you give the signal." He wrapped his arms around the boy, refusing to let go until Ben stopped resisting.

He had to make Ben listen. "Be safe, man. Don't take any crazy chances." He heard the fear in his voice for the boy.

Ben extricated himself from Adam's hold. "It's war, brother. Us or them."

Adam watched him trudge away, his shoulders slumped, through a cleft in the canyon rock and out to the main road. He'd give Ben a good fifteen minutes head start before he followed and retrieved his truck hidden off road behind the protective wall of Monument Butte.

God, please. Keep him safe. Help us end this evil that stalks our children.

Hang on. Had he just prayed?

A picture of Erin floated through his mind. His lips tightened.

No time to think of her. She and her God talk made him weak. Too weak to do what he had to do. Just as Ben had worked months to earn the trust of the gang liaison to the drug dealers, he, too, had worked his way into Debra's trust. Wormed his way.

Bile rose in his throat. Debra—liaison to a Mexican drug cartel. As guilty as any of the homeys she supervised. Killer of old women. Ruination of young men. And somehow, his feelings for Erin had gotten the better of him and Debra had noticed. Jeopardized her trust in him.

If he could only keep Erin out of Debra's vengeful path until Debra or Ben's connections led him and the DEA to the site of the methamphetamine lab hidden somewhere in the vastness of the Navajo Nation. He huddled deeper into his sheepskin-lined jacket. The temps dropped with the sun and winter hadn't yet yielded its grip to Spring on the Rez.

He'd been looking for Debra since he'd left Erin's vandalized home. Unusual for her to take off for hours without contacting him. There were days his cell phone vibrated nonstop with calls from her—calls to ascertain his whereabouts and his loyalty. Something was going down soon and he needed to do major damage control with her if he had a hope of being there to bring the cartel's reign of death to an end.

Adam slipped between the rocky opening as the sun dipped below the horizon, plunging him and the desert into night.

Where was Debra? And what mischief was she up to now?

10

THE CULTURAL CENTER APPEARED DARK AND DESERTED WHEN ERIN ARRIVED promptly at nine the next morning under a brilliant turquoise sky. She waggled her fingers at Nia backing out of the parking lot. Erin slipped her key into the lock and drew back the bolt. Stepping inside the storeroom, she typed in the security code given only to employees and shut off the alarm.

Erin shivered and fastened her jacket closer about her body. She couldn't seem to adjust to what passed for April in Arizona. And the higher elevations predicted to have snow once more before the month was out. Give her heat and humidity any time. April was about tulips and dogwood blossoms. No snow and ice where she came from.

Shrouded shapes and forms loomed out of the darkness of the interior space. Maybe Adam was right. Maybe she shouldn't work alone here today. The Center was a lot more cheerful and bustling with life when the staff and volunteers were around.

Not to mention the infectious enthusiasm of the local dancers, many of whom were still in their teens. But no performances today. No weavers demonstrating their craft. No silversmith artisans, their intricate sterling designs spread out on blankets around the perimeter of the inner courtyard where the dancers performed.

In the storage room, windowless and climate-controlled for preservation of the Diné treasures, she flipped the overhead light switch bringing order and sanity into perspective. If she hadn't already promised Director Benallie she'd take a look at some recently unearthed boxes warehoused on a back shelf since the Depression, this would have been a fine day for joining Tulley in his conversation with the code talkers.

At least she had the remnants of Nia's Navajo fry bread they'd turned into doughnuts. She inhaled. Nothing much beat the smell of fried dough rolled in cinnamon. She lugged the plate over to an adjacent workroom and filled a kettle with water. That and a little hot tea might be the ticket to get her sluggish mind and body hunkered down and ready for serious work. Her dreams had been fragmented and jumbled the night before.

The unfamiliarity of a strange bed? Perhaps she wasn't over her shock at her most intimate belongings slashed and destroyed. The whistle of the teakettle drove her brain free of tortured dream images of knives, war painted hoodlums, Adam bleeding, and of her running, searching endlessly lost through the stark desert night.

Deciding on the full-strength caffeine of English Breakfast, she dunked the tea bag into the steaming water she'd poured into the extra coffee mug she kept at the Center. Allowing the tea to infuse for a few minutes, her mind wandered to Susie's tales of cave paintings. Would they reveal Olivia had indeed returned and found the love of her life?

The idea of a love of her life brought Adam's face to mind. Grimacing, she yanked the tea bag out of the cup, wrapping the bag around a spoon, squeezing the last remains of liquid into her tea wishing she could squeeze thoughts of Adam from her mind as easily. She took a sip.

Brackish.

She'd allowed the tea bag to sit too long when her attention had wandered—as it so often did these days—to one tribal policeman. Fishing around in the overhead cabinet, she located a small packet of stevia and upended the entire contents into her cup. She took another sip.

Better. Not perfect. Nothing like the exquisite cups of tea from her Grandmother Flossie's fine bone china, but drinkable. The tea habit acquired during her adopted family's long sojourn in the remote outposts of the former British empire. Tea somehow tasted better when sipped out of porcelain or perhaps it had been the always encouraging presence of her dear departed Gram, who'd never treated Erin as a disappointment.

Time to get to work.

She carried her mug into the storage facility. A lone desk for visiting university scholars or the Center's staff occupied the middle of the cavernous room lined from floor to sixteen-foot ceiling with row after row of labeled cartons. Leaving her tea, she veered over to a dusty corner of the warehouse to locate the particular boxes Director Benallie wished catalogued.

Heaving the first box off the shelf, she returned to the desk, flopping her load beside her mug with a thud and a puff of dust.

Great. Grit in her beverage now. Just what she needed this morning. She wondered what Adam was doing this morning.

Erin groaned.

Stop it, Dawson. Stupid. Hopeless. Idiot.

Removing the lid, she dove into the box, anything to distract her from unwelcome and intrusive thoughts. She spent the next few hours combing through the contents of one box after another in the section the director had specified. Each item tagged and a description recorded. Every file, document, or artifact logged into the Center's computer database.

With two boxes left to examine, she opened a manila folder to find a collection of quilt photos—some in black and white, others in color—dating from the 1920s to present-day. She smiled remembering the colorful quilts her grandmother and great-aunts had created on the quilting frame they'd set up on the screened porch of the home-place, eager to catch any breeze on hot, lazy dog days of a Southern summer. And, she pictured the room she and Jill shared whenever they returned stateside on furlough, the twin beds draped with the vibrant fruition of those ladies' labor.

Her grandmother, retired from a life of missionary work due to the failing health of Grandpa Dawson, had insisted she and Jill learn to handsew a quilt block. "Every missionary should know how to sew," she'd told them. "Not many Kmarts in bush country." Over the course of several summers during their teenage years, she and Jill had both become adept with a needle and thread. And learned to identify a great many quilt patterns.

To this day, even Todd, influenced to join in by Grandpa—Dr. Grandpa—claimed to sew the finest, most delicate stitches of any person who'd graduated from medical school. He often reminisced how he owed it all to Gram and MK Training 101—Carolina-style.

Sifting through the photos, the bright geometric patterns and hues reminded Erin of the Navajo wall hangings in Nia's spare bedroom as well as the ancient bold designs of the Anasazi pottery that graced the front cases of the cultural center. She was pleased to see how the Diné had captured the essence of their own culture in the traditional *bilágaana* art form of the quilt.

Kind of how Navajo believers like Johnny and Tulley and Nia embraced the Savior of the world and yet colored their distinctly Diné worship of Him with drum and flute accompaniments. If only Adam would realize he could remain completely Navajo without rejecting Christ.

She groaned. Again.

Get out of my head, Adam Silverhorn.

Erin frowned at the sound of a door in the back of the building sighing shut before it nestled into its frame with a soft click. Or had the sound originated from the front? Was she the complete idiot Adam believed her to be? She could've sworn she locked the back door after she'd entered.

She listened, her head tilted to the side like a robin's.

Nothing.

And yes, she was sure she remembered the feel of the cold steel bolt in her hand as she drew it closed after disengaging the alarm.

The fluorescent light fell upon one last quilt photo on the desk. A quilt done in bold tones of black, white, and red. A quilt done in the pattern known as a New York Beauty, its pointed tips altered to resemble—feathers? A quilt with striking similarities—though done in more traditional pastel shades—to the quilt that had adorned her Grandmother Flossie's bedroom at the home-place until her death in the late 1990s.

A pattern also known by another name—Carolina Beauty.

Brought South by a schoolteacher after the Civil War, the pattern had been altered to reflect Southern sensibilities. A pattern copied over and over by a small group of quilters found only in one particular county of North Carolina.

Greene County. A small, rural community. The same community of her adopted parents' forebears and the home-place.

The hairs on the back of her neck prickled and somewhere behind her, a floorboard creaked. Jolting, she whirled. Just as the fluorescent overhead lighting went out, plunging Erin into total pitch darkness.

A shuffling sound. Like feet on linoleum. Close, too close.

The skin on her arms broke out into goose bumps. Her heart pounded. Something or someone touched the sleeve of her blouse.

Erin screamed.

With an instinct born of fear, Erin dropped underneath the desk. Jerking away from the menacing raking fingers on her blouse, her shoulder seam ripped as she scooted under and through the desk to the other side. Light pierced the darkness as the door leading to the parking lot swung open, hinges squeaking in protest.

On her knees, she threw up a hand to shield her eyes. Before the door swung closed again, all she could distinguish was a form silhouetted against the noon brightness of the sun. A man by the build of him.

And now there were two of them.

Had the gang, for whatever reason, tracked her here, alone and vulnerable in the deserted Center? Once again unable to see her hand in front of her face in the cavernous blackness, she scrambled to her feet, primed to run toward the metal shelves and hide.

She took three steps before running smack into the hard mountain of the man's chest. Screaming again, Erin recoiled, but the man captured her in the iron vise of his arms. He whipped her around pinning her spine against him. She heard his ragged, uneven breaths.

"Erin . . ." came the urgent whisper, ruffling the strands of hair dangling against her neck. And with it, a hint of . . .

Before she had time to react, the heavy steel door swung wide again and pounding footsteps sounded across the threshold. She caught a glimpse of another man. With a wide-brimmed hat in his hand. A regulation hat like the tribal police wore.

"Erin?" Tulley's voice rang out in the darkness. "Are you there? Are you all right?"

"Tulley, I'm—" She struggled to free herself.

"I'm here, too," called a voice from the direction of the desk.

The man holding her stiffened. The rapid beating of his heart drummed against her shoulder blades.

"What's happened to the lights?" rasped the disembodied voice at the desk. "The wiring in this old building is so . . ."

The voice of someone who'd spent most of their life smoking cigarettes. Debra. Erin's nose crinkled at the cloying orange blossom perfume Debra wore.

"I know where the breakers are." Tulley fumbled at the wall beside the exit.

The man, his arms wrapped tight around her, took a deep breath. The long mane of her ponytail swayed against his face as he exhaled. Peppermint . . .

Adam.

She nestled into him, her heart pounding from more than just fright.

He leaned his forehead against her head and sighed. "Erin . . . I-I" Regret flashed in his voice. Unwrapping his arms from her torso, he placed his hands on her shoulders.

She'd know his voice anywhere. The way he said her name sent a different kind of shiver through her.

The overhead light blinked on, temporarily blinding her at the suddenness of the brilliance.

His lips grazed her hair. "I-I'm sorry."

Sorry? For wha—?

With a rough shove, he pushed her away. She caught the edge of the desk to keep from falling.

"Thank God that was you." Debra stood on the other side of the desk, breathing heavily. "I came through the front entrance thinking I was the only one here today. I heard a noise in the storage room."

Debra fluttered her hand. "I'd just walked in when the lights went out." She wrapped her arms around herself. "I remembered there was a lamp on the desk. I thought if I reached it . . ." She shuddered. "I groped my way over, but then there was a rustle and I realized someone else was in the room, too."

Erin sagged against the desk. Plausible sounding story, but she couldn't believe she'd imagined the menace in Debra's reaching, grasping hand. Unless since the break-in at her house, she was imagining evil and mayhem wherever she went.

But if Debra had indeed entered through the front door, how had Adam been able to enter through the locked back door?

Tulley moved closer and touched her shoulder, fingering the shredded threads at the top of her lilac-colored sleeve. "You okay, Erin?" He darted his eyes at Debra, his lanky frame gone rigid.

Debra flushed. She drew a shaky hand to her throat. "Did I do that?" She reached across the desk for Erin's hand.

Erin jerked.

"I'm so sorry, Erin. If I'd had any idea that was you . . . But I was so scared." Debra rested one slim, Ann Taylor-clad hip against the desk. "Thank God, you arrived when you did, Adam. Erin and I stumbling around in here could've hurt ourselves and irreparably damaged priceless pieces of the Navajo culture."

Tulley put his arm around Erin's shoulder and eased her away from the desk and Debra's orbit, the police hat still in his hand. Not his hat, she realized. He wasn't on duty today.

Adam's, who was on duty.

Tulley yanked a red do-rag from his pocket. "Found this outside the door."

Adam's eyes narrowed.

Debra tsked-tsked under her breath. "With gang violence on the rise, next time make sure you secure the door, Miss Dawson. The thought of what those vandals could have done to our collection . . ."

This was her fault now?

"Not to mention what they could have done to Erin." Tulley cleared his throat. "Or you," he added as if an afterthought. "Time for our lunch date, Erin."

A smile lighting her Arctic blue orbs, Debra straightened. "How wonderful. I didn't realize you and Tulley were—"

"I've been looking for you since yesterday, Debra." Coming around the table, Adam swung Debra into an embrace. "Came by on the off chance you might be working overtime and I could talk you into lunch. Saw your car out front . . ."

He trained his eyes on Debra, avoiding Erin's probing gaze. A muscle jumped in his cheek.

Debra simpered in the circle of his arms. "How sweet of you." She patted his chest. "I spent the entire day in Flagstaff with an old friend."

"Friend?" Adam curled a tendril of blonde hair around his index finger. "Thought *I* was your friend?" His chest broadened.

Erin cringed at the teasing, flirtatious note in his voice.

Debra laughed, one carmine-tipped finger stroking the outline of his jaw. "No need to be jealous. Just a friend, I promise. But we got to talking and the day flew by. We had so much we had to catch up on."

Adam rocked Debra in a side-step, his voice low and intimate. "Think you'll get together again soon?"

Erin's stomach clenched.

Debra squeezed his arm. "Never can tell, Mr. Navajo Policeman. Not if you give me a good reason not to."

Adam bent his head toward Debra's mouth. "I'll make sure of it."

He planted his lips hard against the red slash of Debra's sensuous mouth. On tiptoe, Debra returned the pressure of his mouth with gusto, snaking her arms around his neck, twining into his frame.

Erin's heart caught, her hands curled into a fist. *Take a breath, you womanizing scumbag . . .*

Giving Tulley and her an excellent view of his back, Adam broke contact with Debra's mouth. "Don't you two have somewhere to be?" His voice tight and husky. "Thought you were headed to lunch?"

Could she just melt into the floor, God, and die right now?

"Dropped your hat in the parking lot, Silverhorn." Tulley sent the tribal police Smokey the Bear hat winding Frisbee style where it landed with a thud on the desk.

Tulley pulled Erin toward the exit. "Let's go, hon."

Her last sight of the two of them, as she followed Tulley stiff-legged out of the building, was of Adam bending Debra over the desk, his lips locked onto hers once more.

The door swung shut.

"Put some more sugar in your tea," Tulley instructed Erin. "Sugar's the best thing in the world for a shock."

She nodded and obeyed, dumping a spoonful worthy of Nia into her glass. Taking a tremendous gulp, she swallowed past the lump in her throat. Sitting here across the table from Tulley at Mamacita's Big Dog Grill, only now did the surreal flash of movement and noise around her morph back into focus. A song blaring from the jukebox by Taylor Swift blathered on and on about some love story.

Her mouth twisted. How ironic. Romeo and Juliet. As star-crossed as . . .

She forced herself to take another swig of iced tea. And her situation promised to end just as nicely as theirs had. She brought her attention back to Tulley's recounting of his conversation with the code talkers in a vain, but kind, attempt to distract her.

". . . none of them knew of an Olivia Thornton or any white woman who'd lived with the Diné in the early part of the last century."

Erin gave him a feeble smile, though her lower lip trembled, but a smile nonetheless. "Is it just me or does the phrase 'last century' sound odd?"

Tulley grinned. Probably relieved she wasn't going to dissolve into hysterics or require the paramedics. "Makes me feel old, too. Anyway, the old gents were fascinated by your story. You may recognize a few from church. They asked to meet you after we had our lunch."

Her eyes widened. "Oh, Tulley. That would be such an honor. That generation of Americans . . ."

He nodded. "I agree. The greatest. These guys were chosen because they spoke Navajo *and* English. They gained the respect of their comrades for their physical and mental toughness as well as their scouting and tracking abilities."

"We could head over now. I'm not that hungry."

Shaking his head, he placed a menu on the tabletop between them. "No dice, Erin Dawson. You've had a scare and a long morning. I'm not having you faint on my watch in this Spring heat wave we're experiencing."

Erin flicked a glance through the slats of the window blinds at the cloudless sky. "Some heat wave. This feels cold to me. And I'm used to heat."

"Wait till July."

Her shoulders slumped. "I probably won't be here in July."

"Drink the whole glass." He nudged the beverage closer. "No need to get dehydrated. Unlike the moisture-laden air I remember from my days at North Carolina State—"

Her head jerked up. "You graduated from NC State?"

"Small world. Basketball scholarship."

Erin fist pumped the air. "Go Pack! I always knew there was something I liked about you, Tulley Singer." She picked up the menu running her finger down the list of items. "And for the record, it's a dry heat here."

Waving over a waitress, he winked. "So's an oven."

11

AFTER FORCING DOWN ONE OF MAMACITA'S WORLD-FAMOUS BIG DOGS, Erin and Tulley strolled the length of Cedar Canyon township—a total of four blocks—to join a group of six old men lounging in metal folding chairs outside the gas station next to the trading post. She'd secured her torn sleeve with a safety pin. Tulley made the introductions. She hoped there wouldn't be a quiz on their names later.

One gentleman leaned back against his chair, placing his hands square with the canvas armrests. "You say this Olivia was a missionary at the original mission school there on the mesa?"

"Yes, sir."

The old gents were Western casual with their denim jackets and faded jeans, long-sleeved flannel shirts, cowboy boots and hats. This gentleman—Joe?—wore a large turquoise ring on his gnarled, arthritic right hand resting on a can of Red Man. A Bic pen rode in one shirt pocket. An eyeglass case in the other.

Another old soldier, wearing a string tie bound at the neck by an oval turquoise clasp, positioned both blue-veined hands on top of his knees and rubbed absently. "Tulley tells us you're a missionary kid yourself. It was the son of a missionary—grew up not far from here—who suggested the United States government ought to look into using Navajo speakers to send and receive messages in the *diné bizaad* to confuse the Japanese."

"Phillip Johnston." Tulley nodded.

The old man jabbed a crooked finger at Tulley. "That's the one."

Joe shook his head. "But the mission schools, Franklin . . ." He scowled. "Tore families apart. Almost drove our language into extinction in the first place."

He speared Erin with a glance. "You know first thing they did when the boys arrived was to cut their hair."

Joe held out a hunk of his long braid, snow white. "Three plaits symbolize the interweaving of the mind, body, and spirit of a person. When they hacked it off . . ." He scanned the desert vista momentarily. "It broke the three-ply balance of beauty and harmony within us. Lot of folks in my generation feel nothing but hatred for all the Anglos and their god."

Tulley shot a warning look at her.

Franklin socked Joe in the muscle of his arm. "Ancient history. Army shaved our heads, too. Mission schools did give us an education. Gave us the chance to better ourselves in the world."

Joe spat a wad of the chewing tobacco at the dirt between his boots. "*Bilágaana* world." A mumbling agreement rumbled among the old ones. "Anybody could speak English."

He sniffed. "It was the complexity of the Diné language that proved important. Meanings change with the inflection of tone."

Didn't she know it. Erin could spend a lifetime studying Navajo and never master it.

Franklin rolled his eyes and gave her a long, slow wink. "Some old coots just set in their ways, Miss Dawson. Pay them no mind. They are . . ." He rubbed his chin. "Iras . . ."

Joe angled. "Irascible?"

Franklin's eyes crinkled. "That's it."

A wry smile twisted Joe's liver-spotted face. "You, old man, ain't the only one who learned big words at the mission school."

"It's such an privilege to meet you all and I want to thank you for your service to this country during the Second World War." She smiled. "If you gentlemen hadn't risked your lives, pushing back the Japanese island by island, I probably wouldn't be here today."

"What do you mean?"

"Come again, young lady?"

"When my adopted grandmother Florence Thornton was eleven," she raised her chin at Joe. "And yes, she was the daughter of a medical missionary in Indonesia, she and her family were rounded up by the Japanese in those early days after they attacked Pearl Harbor. She and her mother were force marched with the Americans, Dutch, and British to an internment camp for prisoners of war."

She swallowed. "They separated the men from the women and children. Gram never saw her father again."

Joe gave her a long measured look as he unfolded himself from his chair. "Have a seat, miss." His hand indicated his chair. "The Diné know all about marches."

Tulley put a hand to the small of her back, leaning over for her ears only. "You had them at the words *rounded up*. Go, do your thing, girl."

Concern shadowed Franklin's eyes. "What happened to your Gram?" Nothing a Navajo—or Southerner—liked better than a good story.

She inclined her head in thanks to Joe and settled herself into his chair. She crossed her feet at the ankles and tucked them underneath. The tangy scent of the Ponderosa pines permeated the air.

"My adopted dad's father Harry Dawson, son of a tea planter in the region, was also rounded up and sent with his mother and sisters to the camp. His dad, a retired British soldier, was decapitated in front of their eyes on the veranda of their home."

Franklin sucked in a breath. "And?" A sense of urgency laced his tone.

"Gram's mother died on the march. Harry's mother adopted Flossie into their band once they reached the camp. Gram used to tell stories about how she and Harry as the oldest would scrounge and trade anything they could barter with sympathetic Japanese soldiers."

Erin shrugged. "Of course, if they'd ever been caught by the commandant . . . ? But it kept a little more food in all their bellies than the meager starvation ration they were fed once a day."

"So they survived?" A reedy thinness had entered Joe's voice.

"Yes. In fact, when it became obvious that American and Australian troops were on the way to liberate the camp, Flossie wove red, white, and blue remnants from the hems of the other prisoners' dresses and made a tiny American flag for her, Harry, and his baby sisters. They were mounted on bamboo shoots to wave when the troops opened the gates to freedom for the first time."

Franklin fidgeted in his chair. "I was with a platoon that liberated one of those camps you speak of." He swung his gray, grizzled head from side to side. "The conditions of those camps? Never seen such filth in my life. And the condition of the women . . ."

He swiped a tear from his high cheekbone. "The children skin and bones."

She patted his hand. "When the Americans poured through the gates—the guards had fled days before—Flossie jumped up and down waving her flag and shouted, 'I'm an American! I'm an American!'"

Joe, Franklin, and the other men let out a collective sigh of relief and chuckled.

"After the war—she and Harry were teenagers by now—though she went back to her Carolina relatives and Harry's mom took him home to England, they kept in touch."

She gave Joe a shining glance. "Once he'd finished medical school and she finished nursing school, they got married, returned to Indonesia to set up a medical mission—not far, mind you, from where the camp once stood," she thumped her chest, "and the rest is history."

The old gentleman gave her a round of applause.

Franklin's lips twitched. "Well, that's about the best thank-you I ever got for my four years of service in the Marines." Several others bobbed their heads in agreement.

She rose, gazing at their weather-beaten faces, each bearing the stamp of honor and integrity. Big difference, she decided, between a weather-beaten face and a life-beaten one. "So you will always be my heroes."

A hitherto silent gentleman shook his head. "We're not the heroes. We speak for those who can no longer speak since Iwo Jima."

"Don't forget Pelieu," Joe added. "On their behalf, we remember so they will not be forgotten."

He extended his wrinkled, weathered hand. She wrapped her hand around his larger one.

Franklin patted her on the shoulder. "You did a fine job leading the music yesterday." The other gentlemen lumbered to their feet. Several clutched carved piñon walking sticks.

One of them leaned over to Franklin. Blue suspenders held up the old man's too loose, tan corduroy pants. "What time you say you folks at the church get started every Sunday?"

Franklin grinned. "'Bout ten every Sunday morning. Wednesday night suppers ain't nothing to joke about, either."

He jerked a gnarled thumb in her direction. "That French silk concoction this girl made last week?" He smacked his lips in remembered pleasure.

As she turned to go, Joe caught her arm. "Seems like I do remember my daddy telling me how the children from Cedar Canyon had a heads up on the rest of the Diné kids shipped off to Flagstaff to the mission school there."

Tulley inched forward. "When was this, Uncle?"

Joe wrinkled his brow doing some quick figuring in his head. "Before the first war—you know the one that was supposed to keep all others from happening."

The men hooted behind him.

"Heads up?" Erin's brows constricted. "How so?"

"Somebody had already taught every one of them to speak, read, and write basic English, set a proper *bilágaana* table with knives, forks, and spoons and . . ." Joe stared straight into her eyes. "Recite from memory whole portions of the book in your Scripture you call the Gospel of John."

A tour bus, a snarling cougar painted on the side, jostled its way off Main Street to the gas pumps. A small flag with a large red dot was taped to the door. An exhaust of air blew the strand of Erin's bangs across her forehead. Billows of steam rose from underneath the hood. Not a good sign in her limited mechanical experience.

She clutched Tulley's arm. "I left an entire box of artifacts out on the desk when we left the Center. I was just so . . ."

Tulley patted her hand. "Distracted? Grossed out? Repulsed?"

She smiled. "You always know what to say to make me feel better. Would you mind—?" She gestured down the block.

Tulley hitched his belt. The large silver concha buckle shimmered in the afternoon light. "Be glad to escort you back into enemy territory."

He paused as the bus doors opened. The Hispanic driver emerged, babbling into his cell phone about a breakdown. "Might be a good idea to stay as much away from Debra as you can, though."

She shook her head. "I'm not sure what I've done exactly to invite such . . . enmity. Do I sound too extreme and paranoid?"

"Not when we're talking about Debra." He bit his lip. "You're on her you-know-what-list due to one thing and one thing only. One person only, I should say."

"Adam."

"Got it on the first try."

"But we're just—"

"Don't try to kid a kidder. But if saying it helps you sleep better at night . . ." Tulley shrugged. "I'm Adam's best friend, but be careful with him. He's not . . . he doesn't . . ." He shook his head.

She frowned and kicked a pebble with the toe of her sneaker. "He's not a believer."

Tulley grimaced. "He's not for you or any other believer. God's words not mine." He held both hands palm up. "Don't shoot the messenger."

Fifty tourists, cameras dangling from their necks, scrambled off the tour bus and past them, headed for the trading post.

"I'm only saying this, Erin, because I—" Tulley swiveled as twenty-five or so old men tourists, accompanied by what looked like their wives and grandchildren, darted and wove around them like salmon headed upstream. The noise level increased in a language that caused him to narrow his eyes.

The code talkers stiffened.

"Are they—?" Tulley gasped. "They're Japanese."

She cocked one ear in their direction. "You're right."

His eyes grew large. "You're sure it's Japanese? Not Chinese? Or—please God—Korean?"

She listened again. "No. It's Japanese. MK Training involved a boarding school in Kyoto."

The rustlings and murmuring among the code talkers grew more agitated.

"And they're old."

She looked at him as if he'd taken leave of his senses. "Well, yeah. So—?"

Tulley grabbed his cell phone, punching in a speed dial number. "Adam?" he barked into the phone. "Pick up, you hear me?"

She grimaced, considering what probably occupied the slimy Adam Silverhorn.

"Adam? Good. We're about to have World War Three erupt out here at the trading post. A bus just broke down loaded with old Japanese soldiers—" He listened a moment. Erin heard squawking from the other end.

She glanced at Joe, Franklin, and the other old Navajos. Their faces set in a grim, straight line, they stood shoulder to shoulder. Blocking the entrance to the trading post.

"Uh, Tulley."

She tugged on his sleeve. "We've got a situation here."

"Get over here now, Silverhorn. I need backup stat." Flipping the phone shut, he swallowed. "Now what are we going to do to prevent the battle for Cedar Canyon?"

She scooted between the old warriors and faced the startled tourists. She bowed deeply from the waist. "Konnichiwa."

Adam raced down the block toward them.

Tulley inserted his body protectively between hers and the code talkers. "You speak Japanese?"

Panting and out of breath, Adam squeezed in on the other side of Erin and faced the code talkers. "Of course she does. MK Training 101." He mocked. "Probably speaks six or seven other languages, too."

"No. Just four." She glared at him. "I'm always the disappointment, remember? It's Jill who speaks seven."

Adam frowned before he cut his eyes at the old warriors. "Now, Joe. Franklin." He held up his hands. "No need to get all riled. The war's been over a long time. We're allies."

The murmuring escalated.

"Good job, Silverhorn." A tinge of sarcasm threaded Tulley's voice. "Rile 'em up some more. Why don't you mention Toyota's latest sales figures compared to good ole American engineering next?"

Adam's hand swept around, indicating the women and children in a vain attempt to restore order. "They're just here touring our great U.S. of A. with their families."

"Just been discussing what they did to some of our women and children, right Miss Dawson?" yelled one of Joe's compatriots.

She winced. Somehow she didn't believe they'd listen to another story right now about how Gram spoke of forgiveness toward her captors.

"I'm sorry." She faced the crowd, forgetting to speak in Japanese. "They were code talkers during—"

"Code talkers?" One elderly tourist pointed a finger at the Navajo tribal elders.

There was a rustle among the Navajo and a stir of appreciation among the other tourists. Erin, with great trepidation, nodded.

"How fortunate." The elderly Japanese man rubbed his hands together with glee.

Not the word she would have chosen. But at least someone spoke English.

Several of the younger generation reached for the cameras strapped to their necks.

"Better tell your Japanese buddies how Navajos' feel about having their picture taken," hissed Adam.

Erin obliged. She then turned toward Joe. "Most hospitable people in the world."

She gestured at the crowd of tourists, their faces wreathed in uncomprehending smiles. "The Japanese."

Erin cocked her head. "Well, maybe the second most. After Southerners, of course."

Adam rolled his eyes. "Your point?"

The old soldiers step by step backed them up against the crowd.

"I'd always heard about Navajo hospitality. Is that a myth, Joe?" She quirked her eyebrows at him. "These men, women, and children are stranded in the desert heat of the Dinétah."

Okay, a stretch. It was April. But she was on a roll.

"Will you disgrace all of us here today by showing less hospitality than your former enemies?"

Franklin yanked Joe's sleeve. "Sorry, Miss Dawson." He shuffled his feet in the dirt. "Got caught up in old wounds. I know better."

He tugged at Joe. "You know better, too. What's Agnes—his wife,"—in an aside to Erin—"going to say about you letting down Navajo pride?"

Joe squinted at Franklin. "You trying to reverse psychobabble me, old man?"

Franklin grinned. "Hey. I watch Oprah, too."

Joe straightened, soldier tall and extended his hand toward the Japanese man. "What'd you say the hello word was again?"

She smiled. Tulley and Adam let out the breath they'd been holding.

Franklin pounded Joe on the back before extending his own hand. "Make love. Not war, man."

She gave into the grin struggling to break free. Tulley had to go behind a gas pump for a moment, laughing himself silly.

With the initial crisis over, Adam slipped without a word back to the station. Tulley and Erin spent the next hour arranging temporary accommodation at a tribal-owned inn and rounded up enough off-duty docents to give the visitors an impromptu tour of the cultural center. She called Sheridan, who hustled over with his entire pit crew of mechanics—three—to assess the broken-down bus.

Sheridan chewed on the end of a piece of tumbleweed. "Take three days at least."

Tulley rubbed his hands together in satisfaction. "No sense in the People not making a profit off this unforeseen opportunity."

Erin laughed. "You're going to make a great tribal chief one day, Tulley Singer, with thinking like that."

She didn't lay eyes on Adam again for the next busy, three days in what became known hereafter in the annals of Cedar Canyon lore as "The Japanese Invasion."

Tulley organized dinner for the visitors at Mamacita's. On Tuesday, Erin, with Tulley's invaluable input, arranged for a fleet of tribal-owned vans from the senior center at Tuba City to take the tourists out to Cedar Canyon's tiny painted desert. Clarence brought his horse that afternoon for mounted, personalized pictures of each man, woman, and child against the backdrop of the rainbow sands.

"No sense in Monument Valley or that bigger, painted sandbox to the west making all the money." Tulley gave an emphatic nod.

Taqueros catered lunch. Joe's wife, Agnes—who also happened to own Kokopelli's, where half the town had pottery, blankets, and jewelry on consignment—was pleased to offer extended shop hours to Cedar Canyon's visitors from the Land of the Rising Sun.

On Wednesday, in an effort to promote harmony and goodwill among the nations, the high school—courtesy of Tulley's teacher mother—opened their classrooms to the younger Japanese visitors and sponsored a symposium with a panel consisting of Joe, Franklin, and three other code talkers plus five Japanese veterans to discuss their shared experiences in fighting for their respective countries.

That afternoon, the mayor called for an informal powwow to share Diné culture with Cedar Canyon's illustrious guests. The church ladies set up a booth and served Indian tacos and Nia's specialty, Indian fry bread doughnuts, to raise money for the youth group's summer mission trip. The aromas of spicy chili—courtesy of the high school booster club—perfumed the air. Doli and her girlfriends manned a Navajo bun booth, winding the dark locks of the Asian women—so like their own—and charging ten dollars a pop.

Teenagers and old ones broke out ceremonial costumes and performed traditional dances in the courtyard of the Center.

The little kids—who learned to ride as soon as they could walk in Navajo culture—decorated their ponies and led a parade down Main Street complete with the local homecoming queen and the lone fire truck from the volunteer fire brigade. Joe, Franklin, and his crew donned—where the waistline allowed— their old Marine uniforms and ended the parade with the high school band playing "The Star Spangled Banner" and a rough, but recognizable version of "Kimigayo," the Japanese national anthem.

Early Thursday morning, Erin joined Joe and his friends as they said their good-byes to their new friends from across the Pacific as they boarded their newly repaired bus. She watched as the code talkers gave their former enemies warm hugs, exchanging addresses and e-mails. She observed the first flowering of a long-distance romance between one of Franklin's grandsons with a sweet-faced granddaughter of a former samurai.

"We were wrong to believe our emperor, a mere man," she overheard the elderly spokesperson of the Japanese contingent say to Franklin, "could have ever been a god. But we will think on what you have told us about this man/God who died for all people for all time."

She smiled. Uncle Johnny and the faithful had been busy, too.

"You get any hits on the fingerprints you lifted at Erin's house?"

Adam shifted in his truck to face Tulley. Parked in the driveway of his mother's house, he'd taken to updating Tulley on the progress of his investigation every week while he checked to make sure the empty house was secure until his mother returned to town.

Tulley sighed. "Not yet. Most of the RedBloods got juvie records, but so far, no matches."

Adam reached under the seat and pulled out a manila envelope. "Got some strands of hair from Debra's brush and I lifted her prints off one of her shot glasses. When we bust her, I want her charged with everything we can throw at her. From Navarro's murder to the vandalism at Erin's."

"We only got the one print off that tube of lipstick the perp used to write the message on the mirror."

Adam grimaced. "See if it matches Debra's. She must have had the gang wear gloves although if she was there, too, why she didn't wear gloves herself . . . ?"

Tulley shook his head. "May not have been Debra."

"Of course, it was Debra. Fits her M.O. to a tee. Venomous. Hateful."

"I'm just saying I've run the prints through the database with no luck on the gang angle."

He rubbed his hand across his face. "Send it to Carson Williams. He has access to databases local law enforcement can't touch. He may have Melendez and his people on file. Or can at least petition Mexico to share their files with him."

A niggling thought tugged at the fringes of Adam's mind. "Check out that low-life Sam Perkins in Holbrook. I've had my suspicions about that loser's connections to Debra and her cartel buddies for awhile."

Tulley stuck the envelope in the inner pocket of his jacket. "Worth looking into." He nudged the small, silver foil-wrapped box on the seat between them. "Gift for Debra? Where do you get the funds to entertain your lady friend on a cop's salary?"

"Bureau coffers. Debra likes baubles." He snorted. "Expensive, gaudy trinkets. Carson and I meet as needed off Rez. Usually at The Wagon Wheel. That's where Erin and I—" He lowered his gaze.

"When's your mother coming back?"

He sighed, grateful for Tulley's change of topic. "In the next week or so. Lydia and the baby are doing fine. Mom's chomping at the bit to get back to her stones. Full of ideas for new designs as usual."

Tulley laughed. "And for her baby boy, too, I bet."

He rolled his eyes. "Uncle Johnny's been shooting off his mouth about my new *bilágaana* friend."

"I take it he doesn't mean Debra Bartelli."

"Hardly. Debra is Uncle Johnny's worst nightmare for me."

Tulley cleared his throat. "Your mom's not the only one chomping at the bit. Erin really wants to go back to her house."

"No way. It's not safe. Not with Debra and her hoodlums on the loose."

Tulley held up his hand. "Maybe you should clue Erin in on the facts of your undercover work. At least, some of it. Like the reasons for your involvement with Debra Bartelli."

He shook his head. "NTK. Need-To-Know. Erin doesn't need to know. Her face is like a mirror. If she knew . . . One little slip in front of Debra could end her life, mine, and a host of others."

"But, man, having her think the worst of you . . ."

He gulped. "Can't be helped. Safer for her and better for me to stay away from her."

Tulley patted his trim waistline. "Well, I got to say it's the best guard dog duty I've ever pulled. She keeps me well supplied with pastry. And sweet tea."

Adam shot a look at his best friend.

Had there been something in his tone when he spoke of Erin? Something more than doing a favor for Adam? Something he should be worried about?

Adam's gut clenched.

Like he had any right to worry or even have an opinion about Erin's love life.

He swallowed past the lump in his throat at the thought of Erin and Tulley together . . .

Couldn't be helped. Tulley was a good man. Exactly the kind of man a girl like Erin Dawson deserved. Steady. Reliable. Dependable. Pure.

Unlike him.

"When do you think this is going to end, my friend?"

Adam dragged his thoughts away from what could never be to what was his reality. "My informant promises soon. The location of the meth lab. And he got wind that a major pow-wow was happening in the next few weeks. Melendez actually setting foot on the Rez to confer with Debra."

"Round 'em all up at once, huh?"

He nodded. "That's the plan. Just got to hold on a little longer."

"Don't know how you keep it up day after day with that woman. Without God as your—"

"Save it." Adam gripped the wheel. "I've got everything under control. Don't need your white God's help. This is a Rez problem and this Rez Indian will deal with it."

Tulley frowned. "What do you mean by that? I see how tightly strung you are. How stressed. Like a bowstring so taut, one little pluck, and I'm afraid you're going to break. If you don't believe the Bible, then believe an English poet. No man is an island, dude. We all need help. You've got some wrong-headed Messiah complex—"

"I can handle Debra. I can handle exposing the drug cartel and stopping the distribution of poison on the People's land. I will bring back the harmony and balance."

"You?" Tulley's nostrils flared. "What makes you think you're so special? Who do you think you are? Superman?

There's already been one Messiah come. And you're." Tulley jabbed his finger in the air. "Not. Him."

Adam bristled. "You. Erin. Johnny. Stop preaching at me."

"We love you, man. Can't you tell? We're concerned you're going to do something that seems right at the time to your mind and to your agenda. But something you'll have to live with the consequences of for the rest of your life. Something there's no going back from. What makes you so sure you can handle Debra?"

Adam narrowed his eyes to slits, fixing Tulley with a steely glare. "Whatever it takes. Whatever I have to do, I will."

Tulley opened the cab door and slid out. He closed it, gently against the frame. "Contrary to the prevalent *bilágaana*"—he spat the word—"worldview, the end never justifies the means."

A resigned sadness shadowed his angular face. "Maybe you're right about Erin. You've got nothing good to offer anyone right now. I won't stop praying for you, brother. But maybe it is better for Erin if you stay away from her. Forever."

12

February, 1907

THE OLD ONE SILVER EAGLE CALLED *SHIMA*, MOTHER, PERCHED CLOSE BY the loom. His orphaned niece, one of the children rescued from the school, stared wide-eyed over the old woman's shoulder at Olivia's vain attempts to master the devilish instrument of torture. Oh, for a piece of cloth, needle, and thread. But no rest for the weary.

She was determined to become as much a part of their culture as she could. Much in the same way Lottie Moon ministered to the Chinese. Much in the same way her brother, Charles, would as he sailed across an ocean to fulfill Miss Moon's call for more laborers for the harvest.

Her awkward, *bilágaana* fingers stiff from the cold, she tried again, inserting the red yarn in the loom. She beat the wool fibers down on the warp, a task even little *Shandiin*— Sunshine they called her—could accomplish easily at her tender age. Whomp. Whomp. Whomp.

On the rim of the mesa that day . . . she'd thought maybe she'd heard God wrong about His call to serve Him among the Navajo. But five months later, she knew she'd heard Him right. She was learning the complex Diné tongue. *Shima* had taught her to make the kneel-down bread spiced with green chiles. She'd taught Silver Eagle and his niece to read and write simple English using the miraculous stories of Jesus from her small testament.

The snow lay in deep drifts across the high country as the isolated family hogan had been pounded week after week with heavy blizzards. Safe from the army and a "rescue" she no longer desired. Safe to do the Lord's work among a people caught in transition between two worlds. A patient, proud people rooted to the earth.

With a crash, the hogan door banged open. In a rush of Arctic air that sent Sunshine scurrying for a blanket to throw around her *shimasani*, Silver Eagle staggered into the octagonal one-room dwelling with an armload of firewood. Kicking the door shut behind him with the heel of his deerskin shoe, he sent Olivia a special smile, a smile reserved just for her.

She cast one more look through the lone window at the hurricane of snow blowing outside. Safe here to love and be loved. But beyond these walls? Theirs—a forbidden love.

And she prayed winter might never end . . .

Present-day, Late April

With the tourists spending so much money at the Center, Debra had grudgingly allowed Erin to act as their unofficial tour guide during their stay in Cedar Canyon. She and Debra had declared an unspoken truce of live and let live. Erin kept her inventorying out of Debra's way. Debra stayed out of Erin's path. By avoiding one another, they managed to keep it civil.

Barely.

Tulley had taken vacation days—"for the good of his people"—and was now playing catch-up at the station. Adam had volunteered to take Tulley's shifts during the days the Japanese were in town. It had been almost a week since she'd last spoken to Adam.

She wasn't sure if she was glad or sad about this. She ought to be glad for the protection of her heart but couldn't quite work up the feeling. Thoughts of Adam floated constantly through her conscious hours. Debra, however, saw plenty of him.

Debra always made sure she 'happened' to mention to another staff member or docent while in Erin's presence about a late-night date or party with Adam. Erin managed to avoid running into Adam on his daily lunch get-togethers with Debra by closeting herself in the storage room. Tulley still wouldn't allow her to return to her vandalized house and so she and Nia continued to cohabit for the time being.

She stopped attending the Little League games, despite disappointing Sani, after one afternoon Debra offered her beverage to Adam who took a sip. Debra then pivoted in the stands toward Erin. Biting the end of the straw with her teeth, Debra smiled her coyote grin like the evil trickster *Maii*. Repulsed, Erin hoisted her purse and left.

The next few weeks flew by. Adam stopped coming to the Wednesday night suppers, though Franklin, a few code talker buddies, and miracle of miracles, Joe Atcitty, came by to sample her pie one night. She was still no closer than she'd been the day she arrived to solving the mystery of Olivia. But the People continued to amaze and astonish her. She'd never felt so much at home anywhere before in her life.

One afternoon, after the last of the docents had gone home and Erin prepared to close the Center for the day, Adam walked in. Cleaned up. Dressed up. His hair still damp from the shower. An enticing aroma of sandalwood preceding him.

"Debra's in her office." Erin retreated behind the safety of the Information Desk. "I can buzz her—"

Adam flicked away her words with his hand as if swatting away an annoying fly. "Sheridan called a week ago. He fixed the windshield and the part he ordered for your car came in, but I," he threw back his head, "haven't had time to deal with it. I told Tulley to take care of it."

His face settled into an expression as hard as the San Carlos. "Which he promised to do this weekend on his next day off."

"Fine." She kept her tone celery crisp, struggling not to allow the tiniest bit of hurt into her voice.

He pursed his lips. "Tulley ought to be able to handle it."

With an effort, she averted her eyes from the vicinity of his mouth.

Adam's jaw tightened. "He's brilliant like you. Got a fancy mechanical engineering degree he's never used."

Something flew right into her. "No doubt he'll make something of himself one day. Already is. Unlike—"

Growling, he bared his teeth. "I don't think you want to finish that thought, Erin Dawson." His tone could've frozen ice cubes on the equator.

"What thought?" Debra slithered into the reception area, swinging her big, Coach purse by the strap. Silver lace rosettes adorned her shimmering, low-cut, cocktail blouse.

He jammed his hands in the pockets of his khaki pants. "Nothing. You ready to go? Meeting friends of yours tonight, right?"

Debra seized him by the lapels of his white oxford shirt, open at the collar. "Yes, we are. And aren't you all cowboy, gone dressed up?" She planted a quick kiss on his lips and gave Erin a wink over her shoulder. "Wouldn't you agree, Erin?"

Erin cleared her throat and tried to swallow past the constriction blocking her lungs. The white shirt was a fitting contrast to his bronzed skin. And the navy wool blazer stretching across his broad shoulders.

"Not cowboy." Adam eased himself out of her grasp, keeping his poker face intact. "More like Indian, remember?"

Debra laughed, shrill and overblown. "Tulley picking you up after work, Erin?" She looped her hand into the crook of Adam's arm.

"Yes."

Adam's eyes went flat. Shadows creased his face.

Debra gave his arm a squeeze, her aubergine claws coiling around his bicep. "Young love, so sweet and pure. But sad." She leered into his face. "Little Erin's internship will be over in a few weeks and it will soon be bye-bye back to Carolina for our golden girl."

Was that a flash of emotion in Adam's eyes, though quickly clamped down? Or just wishful thinking on her part?

She fought the urge to cry. Or, throw the computer monitor at them both.

Debra dragged him toward the door, leaving a pungent trail of orange blossoms in her wake. "Tell Erin good-bye, Adam." She halted on the threshold. "Go ahead, say it."

Adam grabbed the door handle. "Good-bye." And he shoved Debra out onto the sidewalk without bothering to turn around.

Nia was home when Tulley dropped Erin off at the apartment. Noting Nia's long face and fighting her own melancholy, she didn't let Tulley get much beyond the front door before crying off dinner citing a long day and early bedtime for herself.

"Thanks." Nia's bottom lip quavered. "I wasn't up to making polite conversation with him tonight." She plopped on the sofa and patted the seat beside her. "What's wrong?"

Erin filled her in on her run-in with Adam and Debra.

Sighing, Nia cradled a throw pillow to her chest. "I hate to see you go, but I'll be leaving same time as you." She fingered the sage green fringe. "I accepted the job offer in Flagstaff."

Erin drew in a sharp breath. "Oh, Nia. I'm sorry." For Nia to have taken that drastic step meant she'd lost all hope where Tulley was concerned.

"You know there's nothing between him and me. He's my babysitter." Erin made a face. "Assigned to me for the duration of my internship, for some obscure reason known only to the Machiavellian brain of Adam Silverhorn."

"Men." Nia punched the pillow. "Are. Stupid."

"Clueless." Erin nodded. "Tulley Singer is about to lose the best thing—"

Nia grimaced. "The best thing that never happened to him." She gave an unladylike snort. "He'll never even know what he missed."

Erin rested her chin in her hand. "Interesting when you put it like that. I'll have to give that some thought."

"What do you mean?"

The phone rang. Nia unwound her legs and stretched for the side table where she'd laid her mobile. After a brief mostly one-sided conversation from the other end, Nia shut off her phone and rose.

"Dispatcher called in sick." She glanced over to Erin. "There's mutton stew you can reheat in the fridge. All right," as Erin pulled a face, "maybe an acquired taste for your delicate *bilágaana* constitution."

Nia threw her pillow across the length of the sofa. Erin dodged. "Hate to leave you feeling so blue . . ."

Erin scrunched her own pillow missile. Nia's eyes danced, but she backed up a step.

"We'll talk more tomorrow, friend." Erin launched her pillow in Nia's rapidly retreating direction.

After Nia left, the apartment took on the silence of a tomb. Unwilling to face the dark direction of her thoughts, after changing into her comfy gray, stretchy pajama shirt and pink polka dotted bottoms, Erin flipped open her laptop. It'd been a day or two since she'd checked her messages. Mainly because of the message from her mother in her Inbox that she'd been dreading.

"Time to face the music." She worried her upper lip with her teeth as she scanned the message from her mom seven thousand miles away in Papua New Guinea. Her mom wanted to know what she was going to do with her life once the internship was finished.

"Good question," she said to Nia's tabby cat curled into a contented ball at her feet under the kitchen table.

Time was running out. Running out for solving the mystery of Olivia. Running out for deciding what to do with the rest of her life.

Lend an extra pair of hands and hugs at Jill and Fernando's orphanage in Lima? Help Todd organize and operate the administrative portion of his medical clinic in Khartoum?

"What, Lord?" She inspected the ceiling. "I want to serve You with all my heart. Always have since I was little. You know that. Why won't You show me what You want me to do?"

Or, had He already? Through her mother? And Erin just wasn't paying attention?

Her eyes focused on the last paragraph of her mother's e-mail. It read, "A young, handsome Australian surgeon has joined your daddy's staff. I've shown him your picture and he said he couldn't wait to meet you when you come for a visit . . ."

She rolled her eyes.

Really, Mom? Seriously?

She was a grown woman. Twenty-seven come summer. Fully capable of making her own choice for a mate. Adam's face teased at her eyelids.

Okay. Bad example.

" . . . You know we'd love to add you permanently to our staff as well," her mother wrote. "It's time you started taking your part in the Great Commission seriously instead of chasing after ancient history, dead ancestors, and even deader dreams."

Tears winked in her eyes. None of them had ever understood about Olivia. She didn't quite understand the pull of Olivia, either. And she wasn't exactly hiding her believer light under a bushel here. People needed Jesus just as much in Arizona as they did in Papua New Guinea.

She dropped her head onto the table. She was so tired. Sick and tired of the pressure to be like Jill and Todd.

To be perfect. To fulfill the hundred-year legacy of the missionary Dawsons and Thorntons. Her mom hadn't bothered to ask how her search was unfolding, if she was seeing someone, or how her day was going.

"And it's going rotten." She shook her fist at the computer screen.

She missed her sister, Jill, at this moment with an intensity that produced a small ache in her heart. Though their adopted sister, she, Todd, and Jill had always been close. Out in the field as her parents set up one church plant and clinic after another, they'd only had themselves to rely upon.

Her mom had home-schooled them out of necessity during their elementary years, but as soon as each one had turned eleven, they'd been bundled off to the boarding school for MK's in Kyoto. She'd never forget the day she arrived at the school, overwhelmed by the strange language, faces, and smells. Jill demanded her little sister share her dormitory room and had taken Erin under her wing introducing her to all her school friends who hailed from every part of Asia where their parents served in the mission field. She'd also held Erin every night for six weeks as Erin cried herself to sleep missing her parents and the sounds of the rainforest.

At least she'd had Jill. Todd, the oldest, was in the boy's dorm. They'd made a pact to eat meals together and sit together during early morning chapel. When he'd graduated to attend medical school at Duke and Jill had followed to get her teaching degree from the nearby University of North Carolina, Erin had counted down the days and years until she could join them, share the commute from their grandmother's home-place, and complete her education, too.

She needed to talk to Jill. Erin glanced at the time, calculating the hour in Lima. Not wishing to interrupt the routine at the orphanage or any rare, free time between Jill and her native husband, Fernando, she decided to shoot her sister an e-mail.

Dear Jill,

A smile twitched at her lips. Because of her formal, almost British training at the boarding school, it was difficult for her to use the popular, shorthand slang of Facebook, Twitter, and computer users.

She began by recounting her experiences since arriving in Cedar Canyon—the tutoring sessions, the fitness program, her professional duties at the Center. She peppered her narrative with colorful descriptions of her new friends—Pastor Johnny and Iris, Nia and Tulley, Sani, Clarence and Doli. Laughing, she gave Jill a blow-by-blow account of the Japanese Invasion. Her sister would get a kick out of that.

And then, an unfortunate thing happened. Her thoughts flew to a certain tribal policeman.

"Confession is good for the soul," she said out loud to the empty apartment. Jill, a spiritual anchor in her life, would know what to say. Perhaps she'd help Erin know what to do about . . . everything.

She poured out her heart regarding her dilemma and their parents' not-so-subtle pressure to join them. Her sense of failing them. And God. Her never measuring up to their expectations. The grief of always being a disappointment to the family.

. . . And I've been a complete and utter idiot, Sis. There's this man, Adam Silverhorn.

After I tell you what I've gone and done, how I feel, I don't want you to hold back.

Let me have it. Don't pull any punches. I wish you were here . . .

Typing the keys on the keypad madly to finish pouring out her thoughts, she hit Send before she lost her nerve. Before she lost her nerve to unburden her heart of things she'd wished to say to someone for years. She closed her eyes.

Confession *was* good for the soul. It was good to be accountable to another person. But better to cleanse her conscience before her Creator. A wry smile flickered on her lips. She was starting to think like the People, too.

"I'm sorry, God," she whispered, her heart as heavy as the boulders surrounding Cedar Canyon. "Sorry for not obeying the command You put into place for my protection as a believer. Sorry for wasting the opportunity to show Christ to Adam and instead spending most of my time mooning over . . ." She licked her dry lips. In a deep place inside her, a sensation grew God had put her, as well as others, into Adam's life as Scripture said, "for such a time as this."

"I don't know what to do with these feelings for him. Wrong feelings for a believer to have for someone not of Your kingdom." She lifted her hands and her face toward the ceiling. The cat stirred at her feet. "I give my love for him to You. It's Yours now. Do with it what You please." She sighed, deep and long, sorry for the sarcasm and anger she'd launched at Adam earlier. Just because he'd hurt her.

"Forgive me, God?" She closed her laptop and buried her head into the crook of her arm against the table. "I don't deserve another chance. But if in Your grace You see fit to ever let me talk to him again, be my Guide, my Center, my All. Help him to see Jesus in me. Help me to be salt and light for the sake of his eternal soul."

She cried, long convulsive sobs that ended in hiccups for breath. Nia's cat removed himself to the bedroom. Erin followed into the hall bathroom. She winced, taking a quick look in the mirror at her puffy, red face.

What a hopeless case she was. Couldn't even cry pretty.

She dabbed her swollen eyes with the edge of a tissue. Finding the cat on her bed, she scooped him into her arms. She nestled the silky tabby fur against her face as she settled back upon the mattress.

Yet like lancing a rancid wound, the worst hurt was over. Things were right once again between her and her God. A peace filtered through her parched soul like the summer rains on the mesa. But like any serious wound, the consequences of the injury were only now just beginning. The throbbing hurt might stretch into months and years.

She reached for her Bible.

13

I THOUGHT YOU SAID WE WERE GOING TO MEET WITH SOME OF YOUR friends?" Adam pulled back as Debra dragged him through the front door of her small, ranch-style home two blocks off Main.

"All in good time. What's the rush?" She propelled him toward the plush white sofa in the middle of her living room. "You'd think you were more interested in meeting my colleagues than in spending time with me." She headed for her liquor cabinet.

"Of course not, babe." His voice on automatic pilot, he took a quick survey of her ultra-modern, lavishly decorated home. No question where the money had come from to keep up this lifestyle. A lifestyle utterly foreign to most of the inhabitants on the Rez.

A decorating style he found cold and impersonal. The all-white decor as blinding as the noonday desert sun in July. Not the kind of place where you could prop up your feet after a long day's labor—work boots and all—without fear of marring its pristine surface.

Not a comfortable place like Erin's.

He had it bad and he knew it. As bad and as futile as . . . searching for an analogy . . . as the Navajo's last stand against the federal government? Or, visualizing Erin's face, the Confederacy's last stand . . . His mouth curved.

Debra cleared her throat. He blinked, startled to find her staring straight into his face. She held a bottle of whiskey.

A predatory look, like a vulture, gleamed in her eye. "Care to join me?"

"You know I don't drink."

She shrugged her designer clad shoulders. "Don't judge me 'cause you can't hold your liquor."

His face hardened as she sloshed liquid into a small tumbler. He schooled his expression to dutiful devotion as she shifted. She took a sip and flashed him an unnaturally white-toothed caricature of a smile.

Reminded him of something grotesque children wore at Halloween. Something such as the *yeenaldooshi*, Navajo werewolves, were said to resemble. He resisted the chill that rippled along his spine.

He vaguely remembered from the shadows of his earliest memories a quavering voice—the voice his grandfather had called Grandmother—tell him once only one thing protected a body from evil.

"The sign of the cross," the old one had said, "or the name of the One who died upon the crooked tree."

Debra's features sharpened. "I think it's time you and I came to an understanding." A tinge of acid threaded her tone.

He raised his eyebrows to a question mark.

Debra jabbed the glass in his direction. "Before I lay out all my dark, innermost secrets, you need to prove to me I can trust you completely." She slammed the tumbler on a nearby side table, the glass giving off a protesting ping against the chrome.

She sashayed, her hips swaying seductively, over to where he stood, transfixed and uncomfortable in place where she'd left him.

Debra pounced, encircling the back of his neck with her purplish claws. Like coagulated blood. She compelled him downward stopping inches from her mouth, her earthy scent overwhelming. "Full disclosure on my part . . ." She began, in a breathy whisper against his lips.

He smelled the whiskey on her breath and fought his immediate urge to pull away.

". . . will require full disclosure on your part." She toyed with the top button of his shirt, the tip of her claw raking his skin. "It's time to put up or shut up, Injun man."

Hours later, Adam lay flat on his back on the bed in his apartment, counting the cracks in the ceiling plaster, unable to fall asleep. He'd spent a good thirty minutes scrubbing his skin and his mouth, trying to get the taste and the smell of her off his body. He feared the coming of the dawn—the coming of many dawns—when he'd have to live with the ramifications of the choice he'd made tonight.

Adam's soul cringed at the darkness that surrounded Debra. A light breeze ruffled the curtain of the open window. A breeze scented with the clean, pure smell of juniper and sage drifted by his nostrils. A scent that inexplicably also hinted of vanilla.

Or was that his imagination and longing playing tricks?

He rolled over, bunching and punching the pillow underneath his head.

Erin . . . He swallowed hard.

Light to Debra's darkness. Light like the Savior to whom she bowed her knee.

If he lived to be a hundred, he'd never forget the look of disgust on her face that day in the storage room at the Center. A disgust mirrored by the disgust he felt for himself every time he was forced to play his role with Debra. Overplayed that day to protect Erin.

"Oh, God," he moaned into the wind.

But God wouldn't hear a reprobate like him, who'd done nothing but reject Him since he was a boy. The dark of the night weighed heavy against his soul.

He missed Erin more than he thought he'd ever miss anybody. He'd stayed away for her safety. And for the sake of her heart and his.

Tulley and Hershal . . . an incongruous pair . . . were both right. He was nothing but trouble for someone like Erin. Poison to her purity.

But the idea of talking with her one more time tugged at his mind. He didn't want to let things rest the way he'd left it at the Center earlier. The hurt and confusion he'd read in her gentle eyes.

Adam grimaced into the darkness.

Had that happened tonight, too? How long ago and far away that seemed at this point. Maybe if he talked to her once more . . . Tried to explain without involving her too deeply in the sordid mess that was his life?

Adam glanced at the green luminescent glow of the digital clock on the nightstand. Almost midnight. Too late to call?

Too late to confess, relieve himself of the overwhelming guilt?

No, not that. Confessions of that nature would only bring more pain and confusion to someone he'd never wanted to hurt.

Hard to believe he'd only known Erin less than a month in the span of time. His heart felt as if surely he'd known her a century or more. And yet knowing her had changed everything for him. If not for this blasted case . . .

Adam fumbled for his phone.

"Hello?" she said into the phone clasped to his ear.

Adam tried to speak, but nothing came out.

"Hello?" A sudden wariness threaded her voice.

Why couldn't he speak?

"Erin . . ."

She gave a long sigh of recognition, but said nothing.

"Did I wake you? It was stupid to call so late—"

"I wasn't asleep."

He took a breath. "I passed Nia's car in the parking lot of the station on my way home. I couldn't get to sleep. I wondered . . ."

What had he wondered?

He moistened his lips. "I wanted . . ." He sighed.

What he wanted didn't matter a hill of chili beans.

"I couldn't get to sleep, either," she confessed, her voice low.

He searched his mind for something to say to keep her on the phone, something to lead him into forming the words he really wanted to say.

"What have you been doing?"

He winced in the darkness. So lame.

"I got an e-mail from my mom."

Silence reverberated.

He raked his hand over his head.

"She wants to know when I'm going to give up my craziness and join them in New Guinea." Erin laughed, mocking herself. "She informed me she's picked out my future husband—an Australian doctor who just joined the team."

His mouth went dry. He slumped on the bed, his head on the pillow.

"What else you been doing?" His voice croaked.

"I sent a long rambling e-mail to my sister, Jill, about how much I love it here. She probably thinks I've lost my mind." He heard the smile in her voice. "I probably have, truth be told."

"What do you love here, Erin?"

Another lengthy silence.

Then "I also reread Olivia's journal hoping to find any clue I'd missed before. Maybe some mention of a local landmark since now, thanks to our Japanese friends, I'm more familiar with the area."

"Where are you now?"

"I'm in Nia's—oh, I get what you mean. I'm sitting on the bed in her spare room, the journal and my notes spread out."

He heard the rustle of papers and the creak of bed springs. Had she shifted position? Gotten more comfortable?

"Where are you?" She gave a soft gasp. "I'm sorry. None of my business."

He imagined her biting her lip. He resisted a grin. No doubt to her own prim and proper Southern ears, she'd sounded much too forward. A rush of tenderness engulfed him.

Erin Dawson couldn't begin to imagine what constituted forward in his world.

"Same as you." He positioned his free hand underneath the crook of his neck. "But staring at the ceiling having the best conversation I've enjoyed in more days than I want to remember."

She'd smiled at that.

How he knew he wasn't sure, but he was sure enough, he'd have been willing to bet one month's payment on his truck. "I missed you, Erin . . ."

She drew a deep breath. "Oh, Adam, I've—"

179

Her sudden silence screamed Don't Go There. Forbidden Territory.

Adam gripped the phone. A change of topic was necessary if he wanted to keep her on the line. "What were you doing when I called?"

"Praying and reading some Bible passages I needed reminding of."

He chuckled. "Well, if you needed to be reminded of 'em, I most certainly do. Lay them on me."

"You mean you want me to read . . . You actually want me to read them to you?" Puzzlement cloaked her voice.

He laughed. "Out loud and everything."

As she read, he thought he detected a hint of suppressed tears in her voice but shook his head. Surprise? Maybe joy at the opportunity to save a heathen sinner like him?

But tears?

He laid his arm across his eyes as he listened in the darkness of his bedroom. The words of the Scripture, more ancient than the language of the *diné bizaad*, rolled over him like the turquoise sky rolled over the earth.

> Hold on to the confession since we have a great high priest who passed through the heavens, who is Jesus, God's Son; because we don't have a high priest who can't sympathize with our weaknesses but instead one who was tempted in every way that we are, except without sin.

Erin cleared her throat.

> Finally, let's draw near to the throne of favor with confidence, so that we can receive mercy and find grace when we need help.

She stopped.

"Hebrews, isn't it?"

The holiness contained in those ancient words filled the room. Knocked at the door of his heart. Unsettled him.

A gentle laugh, as light as an eagle's feather, tickled his ear across the phone lines. "Something to be said for the benefits of early childhood training, huh?"

He laughed, then sobered, as the full import of the words struck him. "The drawing near business works for you. You belong to Him. You cry out as a child to your father."

Adam shook his head as if she could see him over the phone. "Those words not meant for me. No help to be found for me. Outside the tribe of belonging."

"It could be meant for you, Adam. If you'd allow it to."

"That's always been the crux of my problem with your Savior, Erin Dawson. It's an all-or-nothing proposition. A total bowing of the knee, so to speak."

He laughed again, this time the sound without mirth. "Like my grandfather, I don't do surrender. Never have. Never will. I prefer to be the master of my own destiny."

"And how's that working out for you so far, Adam Silverhorn?"

Recalling himself with Debra earlier, he squeezed his eyes shut. Didn't help. A pulse pounded in his temple. An uneasy silence.

His chest tightened. "Worthy of the Great Evangelist himself. You do your papa proud."

"I didn't mean to preach—"

"You didn't. You were just being Erin. A person I greatly respect and admire. A person . . ." He pursed his lips. "It's late and you and I both need to rest. About Debra, Erin."

Sounds of fidgeting over the wireless. "You don't have to—"

"I want you to understand as much as I'm at liberty to say. Debra is a necessary evil to a group I need to bust for the good of my people. Nothing more."

He waited for her to comment. She didn't.

"In the course of this investigation, I've had to say things . . . do things . . . I deeply regret and am ashamed of."

Why didn't she say something? Anything.

This was killing him . . . hurting her.

Nothing but a tense silence vibrated the space between them.

His guilt. His sin burden. His self-flagellation to bear alone.

"I wish things were different." He grunted. "I wish I was different."

This time, she sighed into the phone. The resignation and sadness robbed him of breath. "I won't stop praying for you, Adam."

"I'm counting on it." He clutched the phone, his fingers turning knuckle-white with the strain. "Good-b—" He couldn't—wouldn't—say those words again. Not to her.

"Goodnight, Erin." He choked.

"*Náá'ahidiiltsééh*," she whispered. "We'll be seeing each other."

If God would only make it so.

14

THE RADIO IN THE NPD BLAZER CRACKLED. ADAM REACHED FOR THE microphone, easing it off the hook. He pressed the mic button and held it to his chin. "Silverhorn. What you need?" He released the button as Nia's voice, crisp and clear, filled the vehicle.

"Drunk and disorderly harassing the patrons of Mamacita's."

He groaned. Not again. Why did it always have to be him?

Adam clicked the transmit button. "Ten-four." He peered out the window. "Cruisin' round the landfill." Shooting a quick look at the dashboard clock, he added, "ETA in fifteen."

"Copy that," Nia responded. "Good luck."

He clipped the mic on the mounted hook on the console. With a sigh, he darted a glance in the rearview mirror and performed a quick U-turn on the deserted county road.

Two miles down the highway, a further burst of static caught his attention. "Pick up, Car Six. That means you, Silverhorn."

Nia again?

One hand on the steering wheel, he grabbed for the mic, tilting his mouth. "Silverhorn here. What's up?"

"Change of assignment. I'm sending Car Eight over to the diner. Got another call, and you're closer to that location."

He reviewed the patrol schedule for today in his mind. "Copy."

Car Eight assigned to Joe's nephew. The drunk was Atcitty's headache now. That brought a smile to his lips.

Nia continued, "Veer off to Dry Gulch Road. Old Mrs. Guileranz says her granddaughter, Elena, chasing one of the sheep, has her foot stuck in a crevice behind the hogan. Little girl's scared and crying. Been stuck for over an hour 'fore her Grandma gave up her own rescue attempts."

"Copy. Silverhorn out."

Adam frowned and switched the transmitter off. A spring breeze breaking the afternoon heat ruffled the short hair over his forehead. But stuck up there in the high country under a blazing sun would scare anybody, much less four-year-old Elena.

When he arrived, he erupted from the Blazer at a run. Spotting a flash of red in the arroyo behind the traditional family hogan, he dashed past the frame of a blue pickup, its engine mounted on cinder blocks, and a rusted metal swing set in the barren, grassless yard. His long strides ate up the distance between the tire-topped roof of the hogan to where the badlands of the canyon began. Climbing the rough deer path upward, sweating with the effort, he skirted jutting outcroppings and stunted Ponderosa pines until he spied the little girl and Mrs. Guileranz.

Elena's face glimmered with tears, her white T-shirt smudged with the red dirt of the canyon. Her blue-jeaned leg disappeared into the cleft of the boulder. Her grandmother, Nessie Guileranz—dressed in the traditional three-tiered skirt and red overblouse with her long gray braid hanging down her back—wasn't far from tears, either.

Nessie's lined face shone with relief at the sight of Adam rounding a steep curve in the path. She spoke to the girl. "Keep drinking, Lena."

"But I already have to go to the bathroom, Granny. Bad."

"Hush up and you do what I tell you." She turned fierce eyes on Adam. "Took you long enough, Silverhorn. Stop for lunch?"

Knowing it was her fear talking, he said nothing, bending over the girl. "Got your foot wedged in there but good, don't you?"

He poked his finger in and around the rocks trapping her small brown shoe. A style his mother would've called a Mary Jane. One of the useless bits of info a guy raised by a single mom and an older sister carried around in his head.

The girl swallowed. "I won't s'pose to go out of the yard. But Lammy . . ." Tears welled in her raisin brown eyes.

Lammy munched nearby on a clump of rabbit grass.

"I want my mommy." Elena's voice quavered.

Nessie clamped her lips together to keep them from trembling. "Already tried butter and grease and everything else I could think of."

She sagged against a hollow in the boulder behind her. "My daughter 'spects me to watch her till she starts kindergarten next year. Maybe I'm too old to take care of a young'un anymore."

He remembered Elena's mother worked in the cafeteria at the high school, her father one of Sheridan's mechanics. "We'll get her out, Nessie, I promise. Everybody take a deep breath and try to relax while I find something to use as leverage and move this rock."

Speeding down the path from whence he'd come, he scouted for a pole of some kind. The tire iron in his car wouldn't do it. He'd need at least six feet of steel to do the job. He heard the bleating of the Guileranz sheep from the sandy basin at the foot of the bluff behind the hogan, tucked safely into their pen.

Getting a sudden idea, he grabbed the tire iron and a hammer. He rounded the corner of the hogan, hanging laundry fluttering like colorful kites in the breeze. He found the sheep in their pen, butted against the bottom of the cliff face. The other three sides were enclosed with mesquite fence posts and barbed wire. He smiled at the sight of the sheep gate to the corral constructed with two long, lovely lengths of steel crossbars.

After a great deal of hammering and brute force, sweat pouring off his face, he wrenched one of the crossbars free. Feeling like an Olympic pole-vaulter, he sprinted up the dusty trail to where Elena waited patiently and Nessie not so much. On his hands and knees, he scraped a small hole in the ground next to one of the boulders trapping Elena. Wedging the pole as far under the rock as he could manage, he rose to his feet, pressing his weight on the other end of the pipe. The rock wobbled.

He grinned over his shoulder at Nessie. "It's working."

She swiped her moist hands down the sides of her skirt. "Put a little muscle into it, Silverhorn." Flinging off the man-size brown Stetson, Nessie cast her considerable bulk on the pole. With her weight added to his strength, the rock gave an inch and then moved another.

"Ease her foot out, Nessie," he whispered, hoarse with the strain. "I got hold of it. I won't let it slip."

Nessie, her arthritic knees creaking in protest, dropped to the ground beside the child. Her fingers fumbled with the silver buckle of Elena's shoe. "Help me, child. The fingers don't work so good anymore."

Elena's small nimble fingers made short work of the shoe clasp. "I learned to buckle my shoes all by myself." Pride of accomplishment shone in her eyes. "Last Christmas."

Holding his breath, Adam tasted blood as he bit his lip with the effort not to allow the boulder to collapse on the old woman and child.

Once the buckle was undone, Nessie quickly slipped the girl's foot out of the shoe and free from the vise of the rock.

"Can't. Hold. Much—"

Grabbing the child around the waist, Nessie scrambled back in an effort worthy of the strength of a much younger woman. The pipe caved in half and the boulder settled once more with a puff of dust in the place God had intended it.

Her backside covered with red dust, Nessie winked at him. "This old woman's still got some moves."

Adam extended a hand to her. "We make a good team."

Back at the hogan, after Elena had made a much needed trip to the bathroom, Nessie handed Adam a tall glass of tea.

He raised his eyebrows. "Sweet?"

"Sun-brewed mint." Nessie's worn face creased into a smile. "Steeped in the sun all day in a gallon jar."

He tried not to grimace as he took the first sip, not wishing to insult the old woman's hospitality. But somehow over the last month, he'd acquired a taste for really sweet tea, Southern-style. Downing the glass in a single chug, he wiped his mouth with the back of one hand smearing red dust across his face.

Nessie frowned, wrinkling her forehead. "You need to wash up."

The cell phone in the front pocket of his regulation trousers vibrated.

As he fished it out, Nessie gave him a curious look. "My daughter can't get that cell contraption of hers to work out here."

He walked a few feet away toward his SUV. "Silverhorn here."

The voice whispered. "Ad—am."

He angled his back to where Nessie watched Elena on the swing—her trauma already forgotten—pump her legs harder and faster as she swung ever higher in her quest to lose gravity and fly.

"Ben?" His heart lodged in the region of his throat. "What's wrong?"

"Followed them . . ."

Adam heard great, heaving gasps of breath as if the boy had just finished running a marathon. "Followed who?"

"Willard." The boy's voice quivered with nerves. "To his meeting with the suppliers. Overheard their plans. I think they made me."

His chest tightened. "Where are you, Ben? I'll get you out of there."

Ben's voice dropped a decibel. "They're close."

Adam placed one hand over his other ear to drown out the raucous call of the red-tailed hawk circling the sky above his head.

"She sent them to eliminate me when I wouldn't—"

"Tell me where you are right now, Ben." His voice rose in urgency.

"I've been running." Ben let the air trickle out slowly, fear lacing his words. "Hiding all night. Figured one place the gang would never look was Old Spotted Horse's death hogan."

Adam sucked in a breath, breaking out into a cold sweat. How terrified the boy must have been to seek refuge in a house where someone had died—taboo according to the Navajo Way—contaminated with the lingering spirits of the dead one, making the house forever unfit for habitation by the living.

Most Diné went out of their way to avoid contact with a dead body. Ralph Spotted Horse had died when Adam was a teenager. A nice man in life, but once dead, not to be trusted. His hogan, a mile over the ridge from Nessie's as the crow flew, had fallen into ruin and was haunted—so said the traditionalists—by his malingering presence.

"I'm close, Ben. I'll be there in less than ten minutes." An engine roared in the background of Ben's phone.

"They're here," hissed Ben. "They've found me. Hurry, Adam, hurry."

"Hang on, Ben. I'm coming. Stay on the—" On Ben's end, a scurrying noise. The call disconnected. Dead air.

Wrenching open the door of the SUV, Adam leaped into the driver's seat revving the engine to life. He pressed his foot to the gas pedal and the SUV shot down the rutted lane toward the highway. Halfway there, he made a sharp swerving turn to the right at nothing more than a barely remembered sheep trail from his youth. Bouncing and jolting, the chassis shuddered and he floored the vehicle, speeding across the rugged terrain for the canyon badlands. A cloud of red dust rolled and billowed in his wake.

Taking up the mic, he relayed his location and the situation to Nia. She promised to send Atcitty and Bridger pronto. He gripped the steering wheel as the SUV momentarily went airborne over a particularly wicked hump in the trail.

His shoulders hunched forward over the wheel, he urged the vehicle to greater speeds. "Come on. Come on." At the top of the last incline, he sighted Spotted Horse's hogan in the valley between two gigantic buttes. A jacked-up black truck sat in front of the dilapidated hogan. A circle of seven teenagers, clad in black baggy jeans hanging butt level and black hoodies, blocked his view from what lay within their coven.

At the sound of his engine, the circle parted revealing Ben on his knees in the middle of them, his fingers locked behind his head. The leader Adam recognized from his snarly expression as Willard Rodriguez, a hard case and bane to the NPD since his elementary years. Willard pointed a .357 Magnum at Ben's head, execution-style. Ben closed his bloodshot eyes. His heart pounding in his chest, Adam yanked his gun from the leather holster.

Barreling in a bone-jarring, teeth chattering descent down the slope, Adam with the press of a button, lowered the window and extended his Glock. "Stop. Don't move—"

The teens scattered like dandelions on the wind. All, except for the stone-faced Willard. Giving Adam the finger, with the other hand he cocked the hammer.

Adam skidded the truck to a stop and threw open the door. "Ben!"

Ben turned his head a fraction.

The gun exploded. Crimson spurted as the bullet penetrated Ben's neck. His body slumped forward face first into the red dust. Willard pointed the gun at Ben's prostrate head, ready to finish the job.

Using the hood of his SUV as a shield, Adam hunkered beside the Blazer. Rising in a two-handed combat stance, his finger squeezed the trigger and he fired straight at Willard's chest. Sensing his intent, Willard lunged for the hogan, the bullet only grazing his arm, but the impact of the shot caused Willard to drop the gun as he ran.

Adam tried to gauge the distance between Ben's wounded body and getting him behind the safety of the NPD police vehicle. With a war cry worthy of his lineage, Willard urged his cohorts to return fire. A hail of bullets issued from the hogan canceling out any ideas of retrieving Ben for the moment. On their hands and knees, two gangbangers crawled scorpion-like out of the hogan and over to the protection of the jacked-up truck.

When one of them made the unfortunate decision to stand and fire, Adam was ready. One shot to the kneecap disabled the gangbanger. Ben's body continued to pour his life's blood into the soil.

If only Adam could reach him. He had to find a way to reach him. The bullet had nicked Ben's carotid artery. He'd bleed out in less than five minutes, if Adam didn't do something. And fast.

Sirens whirred in the distance. Help was on the way.

"Hang in there, buddy," he yelled as he returned fire keeping the gang pinned inside the hogan. Despite the popping retorts of the gunfight, a strange sense of silence ran through Adam's head.

Atcitty's patrol car ground to a halt amid a flurry of sand beside Adam's position. Bridger's vehicle came to rest on the other side. Both men exited their cars with weapons drawn.

"Called in the EMTs," Atcitty shouted. "Figured there might be some business for them."

Bridger squinted his eyes against the glare of the setting sun, training the crosshairs of his rifle on one suspect. Adrenaline running wild, Adam jerked his head toward Ben's sprawled body. "The boy's with us. He's in bad shape. Cover me while I get him. Got to stop that bleeding."

Atcitty gave him a curt nod. Bridger muttered, "Crazy Injun," but with one quick pull of his finger on the trigger put down the other teen at the truck. His heart pumping, Adam crawled his way over to Ben, his head tucked low. With a loud crash, Willard and two gang members smashed through the back of the hogan and bolted toward the desolate expanse of the canyon.

Behind him, Atcitty cursed, but two other gang thugs continued to fire off round after round, keeping the officers pinned down and returning fire.

"Call Tulley," Adam bellowed over his shoulder. "He's off duty and over at Erin Dawson's place where the canyon dead-ends. He and Ortiz can round up the rest of 'em over there."

Sirens of the approaching EMT van blared. But no one could reach Ben until the scene was secured.

Tulley cleaned the engine grease from his hands with a grimy cloth. "Two scoops of vanilla on the side would be just fine."

Erin smiled at the tall policeman filling the archway into her kitchen. "I'll even give you a third scoop since you were nice enough to give up your day off and get my car running again." Cutting a generous wedge of chocolate chess pie, she scooped three liberal dollops of ice cream on the side of the plate.

Sliding the plate across the table to him, she glanced around her home. It was nice to be back in her own home if only temporarily for the afternoon while Tulley installed her new battery. She unwound the apron strings around her waist hugging her amethyst shirt.

As his reward for being a good Samaritan, she'd also fixed that long-awaited dinner she'd promised him weeks ago. Tulley folded himself into the ladder-backed chair, placed his cell phone on the table, and dug into his pie. She busied herself wiping the counter.

"If you don't mind me asking, Tulley . . . ?"

Tulley raised his head, the spoon of ice cream jammed in his mouth at her questioning tone. He swallowed and licked his lips. "I can be bought for a slice of pie and you've already paid the price."

"What made you go into law enforcement with a mechanical engineering degree under your belt?"

He shrugged, sticking his spoon into the chocolate side of his plate. "That was my dad's dream. He loves working those figures and formulas. I'm more like my mother, I guess. Wanted to serve the People. I did an internship with the mining outfit my dad works for. When the job opened with the NPD . . ." His voice trailed off as he loaded his spoon once more.

Erin left off the drying, flinging the towel over her shoulder. "And your dad was okay with that?"

"Sure. I'd tried it his way. He said as long as it wasn't immoral or illegal, it was up to me to decide what I should do with the next forty-plus years of my working life."

If only her mom and dad were as open-minded. "You'll be running the tribal council one day, I bet."

He grinned. "Maybe. Unless Adam's grandfather has Adam there first. In the short term, I'd like a chance at Police Chief Navarro's job."

She pursed her lips. New information about Adam. "I've yet to meet this larger-than-life grandfather Begay."

Tulley shrugged. "A hard man. Hard on Adam. Hard to decipher. Hershal Begay is currently demanding the Council leave the Union."

She arched her brows. "A secessionist? Seriously?"

He nodded, a wry smile on his face.

She laughed. "Take it from a people group who've been there, done that. It didn't work out so well for us. Think the Diné will have a better chance?"

Tulley rolled his eyes. "If Hershal Begay has anything to say about it. Not that the Diné don't have justifiable issues with the government. Native Americans are the poorest

Americans. Not even half of the Diné finish high school, much less graduate from college. And with the gangs, alcohol, suicide rate, and poverty, the average Diné's life expectancy is five years less than his contemporary Caucasian neighbor just over the county line."

"But Hershal has his supporters?"

"After a century of abuse, brutality, and outright lynchings perpetrated against the People," Tulley sighed. "He's preaching a call to action many have waited years to hear. Our land has been exploited by Anglo-owned companies for the mineral resources. Our best and brightest leave the Rez due to lack of economic opportunity here. Many of the People still don't have electricity or plumbing. And this economic crisis has only made life on the Rez harder."

"Hershal's powerful then?"

Tulley stared at her. "Too powerful if you ask me. Like a spark from hell on the powder keg relationship between the People and the U.S. government. And way more influence over Adam than he should. Playing Adam's dysfunctional family and guilt over his father's suicide against what Adam knows is right. But it will take a new generation of men and women like Adam who will commit to making the Rez a better place to live. Who'll fight to create jobs. Improve the schools. Institute responsible policies and steward the sacred land between the four mountains."

"Men like you, Tulley Singer." She nudged the silverware drawer closed with her hip. "I like a man with ambitions. A man with long-term goals for life."

He cocked his head. "Are we talking about me or Adam?"

She flushed. "Don't go there."

He favored her with a knowing smile. "I've got plenty of ambition. Dad and I have been working off and on whenever we get the chance on my first home. An adobe ranch. Warm in the winter. Cool in the summer. Under a pair of hundred-year-old cottonwoods by the creek."

Impressive. "Planning on settling down soon, are you, big fella?"

"Maybe." He gave her a wink. "If the right girl was to come along. And cook me pie every night."

She slugged his arm. None too gently.

"Ow!" He rubbed the spot. "I was only teasin'."

Nia was right. Stupid was a much better word than clueless.

"When a man hasn't got the good sense God gave small animals to see what's right in front of his nose. . . ." She frowned. "Fry bread is a great dessert, too."

He poked his spoon into the pie crust. "Kind of boring after a while. Unless you drip it with lots of agave."

Idiot.

She rolled her eyes. Drastic action would have to be taken on Nia's behalf. But first . . .

An idea had been twisting around in her brain in the wee hours of the night.

"Tulley, do you think you could help me locate GPS coordinates for a certain cave that contains pictographs?"

She wrote the directions on a pad of paper from the kitchen catch-all drawer. The directions she'd memorized from the jotted notes Adam had taken from Susie. If she waited for Adam to take her, she'd be waiting till Judgment Day.

He scrutinized the crude map she'd sketched. "Got your laptop handy? I know this canyon. Haven't been there since I was a boy, though. Well off the beaten path as I remember. A rugged climb in the high country."

After fiddling with the laptop, refining his search three times, Tulley brought up a satellite picture of the remote location. He gave Erin a few visual indicators to watch for.

"Long walk on foot. Adam and I rode out there on our appaloosas when we were about eleven. Easy to get turned around if you're not familiar with the terrain. Johnny or somebody taking you there?" He hit the Print button.

"Uh—"

A familiar tune pealed from Tulley's cell. She raised her eyebrows. From *Bonanza*?

He ducked his head, giving her a sheepish shrug. "Tulley here." A sound, sharp retorts like the sound of firecrackers, emanated from the phone. He sprang to his feet, the chair scraping across the linoleum.

A bad feeling crawled up her spine.

"I'll get ahold of Ortiz," he barked into the mobile. "We'll head them off on this end." He flipped the phone shut, burying it into the back pocket of his jeans.

"What's wrong?" Her hand clutched her throat. "Adam?"

Tulley headed for the door. "Shoot-out. Gang's got Adam and two other officers pinned down. Adam's mole is hurt critically bad. Hate to leave you here. Go back to Nia's. Gotta go!" he called over his shoulder as his feet hit the front stoop.

She followed him outside. "Adam? Is he—?"

He swung into his truck. "Don't know. Details sketchy." He cranked the engine.

She leaned through the open window on the driver's side, her hands palm down on the window frame. "When you find out, will you let me know?"

He thrust the truck into Reverse, jarring her hands loose from the door. "Maybe. Keep your phone handy. And Erin?"

She moistened her dry lips. "Yeah?"

"Pray," he called as he backed out of her driveway, gravel spinning under his tires. "Pray hard."

15

Advancing with their weapons extended and firing, Atcitty and Bridger leapfrogged to Adam's position beside Ben and then gained ground beyond him, storming the hogan. Falling to his knees, Adam gently turned the boy over, face up to the sun. "Ben." He propped Ben's head on his legs.

Ripping off his khaki-colored shirt, Adam wrapped it around the wound and applied pressure. The blood poured out of the hole in his neck, saturating the cloth. His hands grew sticky with Ben's blood in his attempt to stem the tidal flow.

The coppery smell of the boy's blood filled his nostrils. "Please, God. Please."

A heavy hand landed upon his shoulder. Two shadows, large and grotesque, shifted on the sand. Ronnie Tuttweiler and Gloria Chavez, the EMTs, towered over him.

"We got it from here, Adam," he heard as if from a long distance.

Adam blinked at them, his hands clenching protectively around Ben, the blood squishing through his fingers.

"He's not—" Adam choked.

"'Course not, Adam." Chavez pried his fingers off the cloth. "Nicked. Not severed. He's got a chance." She removed a clamp from the black bag at her feet.

Adam's teeth chattered.

He and Chavez, his mind spinning, had gone to the prom together their junior year. But if she didn't let go of Ben, she'd get blood all over that pretty blue dress . . .

"Adam," barked Tuttweiler. "Let us do our job. We need to get the boy to the van."

Tuttweiler, a strawberry blond married to a Diné woman, yanked him to his feet. "You did your job, Adam. You kept him alive till we got here."

He shoved Adam back, bending to help Chavez secure the boy in the gurney. With an effort, Adam refocused his thoughts.

Atcitty and Bridger returned with the prisoners in cuffs. With the toe of his boot, Atcitty nudged the moaning, writhing form of the gang member Adam had taken down. "Got more customers for you over here, Tutti Frutti."

Tuttweiler scowled. He and Atcitty had been going round about that unfortunate nickname since middle school off Rez in Flagstaff.

Bridger tilted his head behind the jacked-up vehicle. "And another over there is beyond your help."

Atcitty deposited one of the delinquents in his car. "Tulley and Ortiz got lucky. Nabbed both runners. They're going to rendezvous here shortly with the prisoners." He wiped the sweat and dust from his brow.

Tuttweiler tended to the other wounded teen, depositing him in the van where handcuffed, he continued to howl. Tuttweiler scooted to assist Chavez.

"Adam?" Chavez called as she worked over Ben. "The boy's trying to say something. Calling for you."

With a rush, Adam came to himself and leaned over Ben's struggling form as the three of them carried the gurney to the EMT van. Ben gripped his hand. The boy's hand already felt clammy to Adam's touch.

"Caught me following them." A trickle of blood oozed out the side of Ben's mouth. "Big deal Mexican connection flying in next few days."

Ben tried to smile but it emerged instead as a grimace. "You've made it too hot for them to stay. Goin' to pack up and relocate their operations."

"Don't try to talk." Adam squeezed his fingers. "Reserve your strength for getting better."

Ben shook his head, fighting Chavez as she injected him with something. "Got to tell you. When they caught me, they said they'd let me live if I did one more deed for them. She—"

He gagged as pain sliced through him, arching his body. Ben shivered uncontrollably. "Cold, Adam. I'm cold. She wanted me to ice your girl, Erin."

Adam's stomach clenched. "Erin?"

Ben shook his head. "Wouldn't do it. Made a break for it. Got enough blood on my . . ." For the first time, Ben noticed the blood staining his shirtfront. His eyes widened in fear.

"Gotta roll," hollered Chavez as they hoisted the gurney inside the van. Refusing to let go of Ben's hand, Adam clambered in with Chavez. Tuttweiler sprinted around to the driver's seat.

"Don't know when the deal's going down, but you can find the meth lab—" Reaching up with a blood-soaked hand, Ben tugged Adam closer. He whispered the location.

"I'll get them," Adam promised.

Ben nodded, the narcotic beginning to take hold. "I'm sorry, Adam. I let you down. I—"

"You did just fine, Ben. Your mom and Thommy are going to be so proud when *we* tell 'em what you've done for the People."

Ben's face slackened.

Adam's gut twisted.

"We're losing him," screamed Chavez, banging on the front of the van. "Get out of the van, Silverhorn, and close the doors." Chavez bent over the gurney, frantically working to stabilize Ben.

Adam vaulted from the vehicle, slamming the doors as she'd asked. With a spray of pebbles, the van lurched toward the ridge and the main road.

Bridger fiddled with the dials of the radio in his car. "Weird," he called out the window. Adam wheeled.

Atcitty stuffed one of the gangsters in the back of Bridger's car. "What?"

"Can't seem to get a signal out here in the boonies."

Atcitty straightened, flipping his mobile open and held it to the air as if searching for a wind direction. "No cell coverage out here, either?"

Bridger frowned, angling toward Adam. "You say, Ben called you at Nessie's on his phone?"

His fear for Ben rolled like tumbleweed over his heart.

Atcitty swiveled to Bridger, his hands on his hips. "How'd you manage to get hold of Tulley?"

"Dunno." Bridger's shoulders rose and fell. "Good thing, Tulley was at the other end of the canyon fixing Erin Dawson's car, too. Coincidence and good luck, I reckon."

Atcitty cast a look over the distant rim of the mesa. The orange blaze of the sun, beginning its descent, set fire to the top of the mesa. "Good for us." He squinted at Adam. "You okay, Silverhorn? Can you drive yourself to the station?"

Mute, Adam stood beside the NPD vehicle, dazed and heartsick. Atcitty shot Bridger a look.

"How 'bout you clean up and go on to the hospital?" Bridger extended his arm out the side of the car door. "We'll take care of the paperwork and get your statement later." He placed a hand to Adam's bare arm.

Adam flinched at his touch. His eyes went skyward at the harsh cry of the red-tailed hawk circling the valley at the mouth of the canyon. "A God thing?"

Disbelief peppered his voice. He swallowed past the boulder lodging in his throat.

Atcitty nodded. "Had to be." He rooted in the trunk of his NPD vehicle and extracted a gray T-shirt. He pressed it to his nose before handing it to Adam. "Barely used." A wry smile lit his thick, blunt features.

Like an automaton, Adam removed his undershirt and slipped the T-shirt over his head, sticking his arms through the sleeves.

The impact of Ben's last words filtered through Adam's consciousness. Failing to secure one hit man to take out Erin didn't guarantee Debra would stop trying to contract another. This little shoot-out provided a perfect distraction for Debra to complete the rest of her plan to eradicate the one person who stood in her way. A light such as Erin's exposed the true darkness of Debra's downward moral spiral.

"Erin." Adam grunted and raced toward the Blazer. "Keep the arrests under the radar as long as you can, guys. We need to arrest Debra Bartelli before she catches wind of this and disappears."

Got to check on Erin.

If anyone could make sense of this day, it would be Erin. Unless it was already too late. Tulley had probably left her alone at the house when he got the call for officer assistance.

His nerves stretched taut.

"Not Erin, God." His voice dropped to a whisper as he twisted the key in the ignition. "Not her, too."

A heaviness settled over Erin's spirit. Grabbing her Bible and cell phone, she exited her small home through the door off the back deck. Her feet turned without conscious thought toward the creek at the bottom of the hill behind her house. Sinking to her knees at the edge of the stream under the shade of the old cottonwood tree, she clutched the comforting bulk of her Bible. Her eyes closed, her lips churned with petitions to her heavenly Father.

She stormed the throne of grace for Tulley and the other officers assigned to Cedar Canyon's police force. Wisdom for them and safety. Calmness for Nia directing and supervising their efforts from afar. Mercy for the wounded "mole." Mercy for those who at this moment sought to do evil.

But most of all, she prayed for Adam.

"Don't let anything happen to him." Her frantic pleas rose to the sky. "Not when he doesn't know You yet."

And as the wind ruffled the budding leaves above her head, an equally gentle presence soothed her mind and heart, quieting the violent turbulence that had rippled across her frame ever since Tulley left.

Her eyes shot open at the sound of tires spinning in the gravel of her driveway. A car door slammed. Her head pivoted in the direction of the house.

"Erin . . ." A familiar and beloved—God help her—voice called.

A pounding on the wooden door. His cries became muffled as he entered her home from the front.

Her legs cramped from sitting too long, she wobbled as she stood. Plodding along the slight climb to the house, her feet, heavy as cement blocks, felt disconnected from her brain. Needlelike prickles stabbed her legs.

"Erin! Where are you?" His voice laced with panic, Adam shot through the back door and onto the deck, his form silhouetted by the golden light of the setting sun.

She lifted a hand and waved. "I'm down here."

His head jerked at the sound of her voice. Relief flooded his face.

She stopped where she stood, her hands clasped to her heart. His face was streaked with dust. His forearms, poking out from under the sleeves of the T-shirt, were covered with the dark crimson stain of dried blood.

His?

She hurried toward him. With three long-legged strides, he bridged the gap between them. Tears streamed down his broad, high-planed cheekbones, leaving gullies of red dirt winding down his face. The desolate look in his dark eyes wrenched her heart.

"Adam?" She stopped breathing. "Are you hurt?"

He shook his head.

She breathed again. *Thank you, God. Not his blood.*

His mouth set in a slash of white, he advanced until he came level to her. She opened her arms and he stepped inside, laying his face upon her shoulder. His arms tightened, convulsing, around her waist.

Adam's body shook, but he made no sound. In a rush of tenderness, she held him, stroking the small of his back and murmuring the inane, nonsensical things one says to comfort a hurting child. She knew as well as she knew her name this was the moment in Adam's life for which she'd been brought to the Rez.

LISA CARTER

For nothing more. For nothing less.

For such a time as this.

God was good. All the time.

Her face peeping over his back, she prayed out loud over him the name of her Savior, giving thanks for God's grace and mercy in preserving Adam's life. Every time she said 'Jesus,' his body uncoiled a little more. Gradually, he stopped shaking.

"Should've never let him do it once he told me what was happening between the gang and the Mexicans." Adam's voice sounded raw.

He didn't let go of her and she didn't let go of him. He told her about what Ben had been forced to do for his gang initiation months earlier and how it had weighed on his conscience.

She frowned, trying to place the name. "Ben Tso?"

"Thommy's older brother."

She gasped. Their plucky little mother worked her fingers to the bone, cleaning *bilágaana* houses in Winslow to make ends meet. This would break her heart.

"And then when he was bleeding out, I—" Adam pushed away so suddenly, she stumbled backward on the uneven slope.

He stuck out an arm to steady her. "Ben was willing to do anything to make himself clean again."

Taking his arm, she drew him toward the chairs on her deck. "Ben wanted to do this. You couldn't have stopped him. Sounds as if he needed to do this."

Adam lowered himself, like an arthritic, old man, into the metal frame chair. He dropped his head into his hands. "Only one way to make that boy clean. Thanks to a lifetime spent under Johnny's teaching, I knew the way. The Jesus Way."

He groaned into the hollow of his palms. "But instead of helping him find absolution and forgiveness, I let him go back to that nest of vipers, exposing himself to danger."

Anger at himself blazed in his eyes. "Let him get information, so we could locate the meth lab they'd set up to manufacture their poison and bust this drug cartel with its corrupt tentacles sucking the life out of our children."

"What's Debra's connection?"

He made a face as if he'd ingested something bile. "She's the American underworld contact to the Mexican cartel running the show." He told her how the DEA, via the Bureau and the FBI, had contacted him after his overseas tour to build a cover story and go deep undercover. He posed as a cop willing to be turned not only to acquire info on the local distributors—the gang members Debra had recruited to sell meth to the students of the Navajo Nation—but also the meth lab production facility.

"The dope and money trail stretches across the canyon country of the Dinétah to the Mexican border."

She drew one of his hands across the table, lacing her fingers through his. "Like a highway."

Adam gave a derisive snort. "A two-lane highway of death."

"How did Debra get mixed up with this bunch?" Her brows constricted. "Her credentials are solid for museum administration."

Adam shrugged. "The cartel needed someone locally placed with a hunger for the finer things like Debra." Exhaustion roughened his voice. "Law enforcement is few and far between here on the Rez. An easy place to set up shop and get away with it. And they have for several years. It's taken me over a year to earn some measure of Debra's confidence. Of course, I hoped they'd hire me on to help Debra run the operation on this end of the border. The FBI believes Debra has drug connections from her days at ASU. One of the Melendez brothers went to school there. We think maybe she's been running small time jobs for him since then. Her degree maybe tailored from the beginning for this project."

He withdrew his hand from hers. "I want you to pack your stuff and move in permanently with Nia." He gave her the condensed version of Debra's abortive attempt to silence her.

She shuddered. The shadows lengthened as the sun dipped below the horizon.

"I had to make sure you were okay. The other guys are tied up at the moment."

He raked a hand through his hair until it stood on end like a mohawk. "If only I had time to go to the hospital and check on Ben . . ." His jaw tightened. "But first, time to settle some unfinished business with Debra." His fists clenched and unclenched on the wrought-iron surface of the table.

At the look in his eyes, she shivered. That scary Adam from the night at the bar was back. Like looking at the wrong end of a gun. Made her glad for more than one reason she wasn't Debra. "I'll stop by the hospital."

He cocked his head, as if thinking out loud, his mind already ahead to the next task. "I need to give the lead agent on the case a heads-up on the latest developments, too." His eyes refocused on her face.

"Erin . . . I want to thank you . . ." He gestured toward the creek, his face flushed. Lowering his eyes, he peered at the wooden planking of the deck.

"Glad to be of service," she joked.

A little levity was needed, she decided. Men had their pride. She thought—and not for the first time—how thankful she was to be a woman for whom society allowed honest expressions of emotion.

He caught her hand. "You almost persuade me, Erin."

Not her. God's Spirit.

A shame a man who knew Scripture as well as Adam did, wouldn't yet believe.

He shook his head. "Don't know I've ever had as good a friend as you in my life."

She squeezed his fingers. "And a *bilágaana* to boot."

A crooked smile broke across his face. "God's mysterious ways."

What that smile did to her insides . . . ? Ought to be licensed. And contain warning labels.

She walked him through the house and to his Blazer out front.

"Keep Ben in your prayers?"

Erin nodded, tears clogging her voice. Would she ever see Adam again? Was God done with her now in Adam's life?

Some sixth sense, some intuition, made her think her time in Cedar Canyon was drawing to a close. Time to go home. Though the whereabouts of "home" eluded her at this moment.

Funny thing about Jesus. Whereas most of the world's religions called for throat-slit, burned sacrifices, He asked for living ones. But the crazy thing about living sacrifices?

Like her, they kept crawling off the altar.

So she laid her desires on the altar.

One more time.

"Bye, Erin Dawson." Adam flung his hand out the window in a salute as he drove away.

He didn't look back.

"Good-bye, Adam Silverhorn," she whispered to the smoky blue haze of the coming night.

What a long—and painful—obedience this was turning out to be.

16

ADAM MADE A SWIRLING MOTION WITH HIS HAND. BRIDGER AND ORTIZ, guns to their chests, scuttled around opposite corners of Debra's darkened dwelling. He leaned against the doorframe. Tulley watched him from the other side, waiting for the signal. Adam nodded.

"Police." Tulley pounded on the door. "Open up!"

Nothing.

"On the count of three." Adam said into the walkie-talkie attached to his shoulder to Ortiz and Bridger. "One—" The search warrant crackled in his shirt pocket.

Easy enough to secure with Judge Keonie sweet on his widowed mother, Hannah Silverhorn.

"Two—"

He lifted his boot. "Three—" And kicked the door, ramming his shoulder against the wooden barrier.

Within minutes, he and Tulley gained access. With the tinkling of smashing glass from Debra's sliding back doors, Ortiz and Bridger timed their entrance to match. A quick search revealed the home was abandoned. Closet and drawers empty. Suitcases gone.

He snatched up a lamp and dashed it to the floor. Remnants of Debra's toxic scent permeated the air. He reholstered his gun and kneaded the back of his neck.

Tulley frowned. "She's done a runner."

Ortiz wrinkled his forehead.

Bridger gave Ortiz a sly wink. "Acting Chief Tulley watches too much BBC."

Tulley elbowed Bridger aside. He took hold of Adam's arm. "She can't have gotten far. It's only been two hours since we brought in the boys."

Adam shook him loose. "She's gone to ground like the vermin she is."

Images of Ben's blood-streaked body surfaced to the front of his mind. And he envisioned Erin's corpse on the sterile steel table of the medical examiner's office if Debra wasn't apprehended soon.

Bridger sighed. "Lot of territory to disappear into."

Tulley sent Adam a pointed look. "You need to go home and get some rest."

He kicked the chrome table at the end of the sofa.

"And calm down, too." Tulley rubbed his jaw. "Cool heads are needed right now."

Ortiz nodded. "I'll call in a BOLO, and we'll find Debra's car pronto."

Adam stalked down the hall to the bedroom. He returned with a pillowcase clenched in his fist. "Once we locate her car, then call out the dogs."

After hearing Debra had fled Cedar Canyon, Erin couldn't be persuaded to return to Nia's. In the two days since the gang had been rounded up, Border Patrol agents found Debra's red Corvette abandoned on a county road that led to the Mexican border. The dogs tracked Debra's movements a few yards but lost the scent. Probably another prearranged vehicle had carried her off to parts unknown. A vehicle pointed south. Mexico's *problema* now.

Erin's intuition about Adam had been sound. He left a message on the station's answering machine saying he was taking the week off and using his comp time. Tulley and the other officers were still trying to locate what they believed to be the now abandoned meth lab. But, in the desolate badlands country, it'd be like trying to find the proverbial needle in the haystack.

Ben had lost lots of blood. She and practically every able-bodied member of Cedar Canyon Community had donated blood and sat with Thommy and his mother at the hospital on rotating shifts. She was with Mrs. Tso when the emergency room attendants handed Ben's mom the tiny red-stained sterling cross they'd found in his clenched fist.

With a sudden intake of breath, Mrs. Tso fingered the silver cross. "I didn't realize he'd kept it all these years." Her voice caught and she buried her face in Iris's bosom.

Iris exchanged glances with Erin, "We give one to each child at the church when they start kindergarten."

Johnny and the other deacons kept a vigil with Mrs. Tso at Ben's bedside. Ben's thin face glowed a translucent white under the florescent lighting of the hospital. Tubes connected his unresponsive body to beeping machines. Every hour one of the deacons led the current group in prayer. The first forty-eight hours were critical, the surgeon had explained.

Ben would either rally to consciousness.

Or, he wouldn't.

Praying without ceasing had come to take on a whole new and more urgent meaning to Erin. Shame how all too often it required great adversity to drive people to their knees. Including her.

Iris had departed with inconsolable Thommy. Mrs. Tso snatched a few winks of uneasy sleep stretched out in the recliner of the hospital room. Erin struggled to keep her head upright, perched on the stool beside Ben's bed. She'd promised Mrs. Tso she'd keep watch while the exhausted mother got some much-needed rest. Johnny and another brother from the church slumped against the door. Her nose wrinkled at the antiseptic smell embedded in the walls of the room.

Funny how the staff had allowed so many visitors from the moment they'd stopped the bleeding and gotten Ben stabilized.

Her gut twisted with the realization the staff didn't think it mattered one way or the other in Ben's recovery. She jerked her eyelids open at what felt like a nudge on her backside.

An inexplicable urge teased at the fringes of her spirit. She shot a glance toward the ceiling. "Really?" she whispered. "Sing? Now? Here? That song?"

She remembered her conversation with Adam on the deck of her home. Blood had covered the visible parts of Adam's torso. The blood spilled out of Ben Tso's veins. She took a deep breath.

"*What can wash away my sin?*" she sang in a half-whisper.

She darted a quick glance over to Mrs. Tso who slept on undisturbed.

"*Nothing but the blood of Jesus.*"

Johnny straightened behind her.

"*What can make me whole again?*" She massaged Ben's cold hand under the sheet. "*Nothing but the blood of Jesus.*"

Her voice rose a notch. "*Oh, precious is the flow that makes me white as snow.*"

The nurse would kick her out any second.

Johnny gripped her shoulder.

"No other fount I know."

The brother came alongside. Mrs. Tso jerked awake.

"Nothing but—" With an almost imperceptible movement, Ben's fingers curled around her own.

She gasped, her eyes wide at Johnny. *"—the blood of Jesus."*

Mrs. Tso rose. "Sing it again, please," she whispered.

"What can wash away my sin?" Johnny and Mrs. Tso blended their voices with hers. "Nothing but the blood of Jesus . . ." The volume of their combined voices filled every corner of the room. A nurse appeared at the door.

The form in the bed stirred. "Mama?" Ben whispered through dry, cracked lips.

Mrs. Tso grabbed Ben's hand. The nurse scurried inside, checking his vital signs.

Erin stopped singing as tears rolled down her cheeks. Johnny clapped the brother on the back. She scooted away as other attendants rushed into the room.

What had just happened here? A miracle?

Johnny's black eyes shone. "Well done, Daughter." He drew Erin into the corridor. "Just as I dreamed. Sent by God to turn the hearts of our children back to their true Father."

And she who'd never fainted in her life—Daddy didn't allow it—collapsed straight into Uncle Johnny's arms.

"Whole town's talking about it." Tulley propped against her kitchen wall. "Uncle Johnny swears it's the start of the great Cedar Canyon revival."

Erin said nothing. She reached inside the plastic grocery sack, withdrawing party plates and napkins.

Tulley chuckled. "Wish Adam was around to hear about it."

"Any word about where Adam is?" Erin strove for a non-chalant tone. She unloaded a set of matching cups and forks from the bag.

Tulley shook his head. "His mom, Hannah, is back. She asked me the same thing yesterday. Bridger said he'd heard Adam was spotted in Tuba City."

He scanned the table littered with paper items. "Hey, you having a party and not inviting me?"

She pulled out a fancy plastic tablecloth, her head bent over the table. "You'll be invited."

He crossed his arms. "What's the occasion?"

She removed a jar of powdered lemonade. "Nia's going-away party."

Tulley straightened, bumping his head on the arch. "What are you talking about?"

He frowned. "Nia's like me. Rez Indian for life."

She made a show of collapsing and folding the plastic bag onto itself. "Apparently not. She's taking a job at the Flagstaff dispatch. She leaves in less than a week."

Panic flared across his face. "That can't be. I'd have known if . . . She'd have told me . . ."

Erin looked at him, her hands stilled. Her green eyes probed his black ones. "Again, apparently not."

"She wouldn't leave me—" His voice cracked. "I mean her family and home." He coughed into his fist.

Careful to keep her face void of expression, she shrugged. "Nothing to keep her here, is there, really?"

She cleared her throat. Delicately. "More opportunities for a beautiful girl like her in the big city."

"It's that Nelson Runningdeer." Tulley's voice rose. "He's been after Nia since high school. He took a job there last year . . ." His voice trailed off. "The trips here lately to Flagstaff . . ." His brow constricted as he put two and two together.

She waited for the explosion.

"Well, I won't let her do it." His finger jabbed the air. "Break her mama's heart. I'll tell that little miss a thing or two."

He spun around and disappeared out her front door. A car door slammed and an engine revved, then the sound of tires wheeling on sand.

"Gotcha."

She smiled at the cloud of dust left in his wake. Erin gave Tulley ten minutes and hit the speed dial button for Nia. When Nia picked up, she spoke into the phone. "I've gone and done something you may not thank me for." She told Nia what she'd said to Tulley.

Nia's laughter across the distance tinkled like wind chimes on a spring day. "I'd have loved to have seen his face."

"I have a feeling you're going to. Any minute now."

"Oh, really?"

Erin heard a banging on Nia's door.

"He's here already." Nia's voice hitched. "Good thing he's a cop or he might have gotten a ticket." Sarcasm tinged Nia's voice.

"I'll hang up now."

"No, no, my dear friend. Let's enjoy the show together."

She heard Nia slide back the dead bolt.

"Why Tulley?" Nia called in an overly loud but straight tone. "Fancy you stopping by. As you can see I'm on the pho—"

"That slimy Nelson Runningdeer on the phone with you?"

Erin suppressed the urge to laugh.

"I thought you had more sense than to be taken in by the likes of him, Lavinia Yow. Hang up. Hang up right now. You ought to be ashamed—"

"I hope you don't think you can tell me what to do, Tulley Singer? Who died and made you the boss of me?" Nia's voice had grown dangerous.

Erin ambled back to her kitchen, returning the party items to the sack. This was better than any reality TV show she'd ever watched.

Tulley sputtered. "I'm only trying to look out for your best interests, Nia."

"'Cause I'm too stupid to know any better? Or, cause you feel like you're the brother I never had?"

A palpable silence. A long, interesting silence.

"Answer that one," Erin whispered. One of those Do-I-Look-Fat-In-This? questions. She smoothed the wisteria knit tunic dress she wore over black leggings.

"I just always thought—" Uncertainty laced his voice. "That you and I . . ." He cleared his throat. "I mean we always fit together . . ."

Bless his shy little heart.

"If you got something important to say to me, Tulley Singer, I suggest you spit it out now or forever hold your peace. I got dreams, you know."

Good for you, Nia. Don't let him off the hook that easily.

"I got dreams, too, Lavinia Yow." His voice had grown softer. "Dad and I have almost got the house finished and I was—"

"You was what?" A note of indignation lined her voice. "Thinking I was waiting around with nothing else better to do than for you to strike the notion to maybe grace my life with your presence? Maybe start with a quick, unobtrusive date through the drive-in at the Dairy Queen?"

Nia was working up to a fine head of steam.

"Lavinia." His voice sounded louder, as if he'd taken a step closer.

"You've had since seventh grade to make a move, Tulley Singer. Give me one good reason why I shouldn't throw you out of my house on your sorry behind this instant?" Nia's breath was ragged as if she found it hard to breathe and fight tears at the same time.

"Because I'm an idiot, but I love you. I've loved you for a long time but thought maybe if I had something worthwhile to offer you first, you'd feel about me the way I feel about you."

"Oh, Tulley. I grew up in a trailer where we had to haul our water from the spring. All you ever needed to offer me was yourself." The sound muffled as if caught between them.

"Don't go," he said. "Or if you'll wait till I can apply for the police department there, we could go together."

"Tulley . . ." Nia breathed. The phone clicked off.

Erin had the feeling there'd be no need for a going-away party. She fingered the long white slip of paper.

Good thing she'd had the foresight to save her receipt.

By the next day, Tulley and Nia's engagement had made the rounds to every corner of the Rez. To allow Tulley and his dad time to finish the small adobe ranch, the nuptials were scheduled for autumn. Nia's mother and Tulley's had also demanded six months to plan and implement the Cedar Canyon Wedding of the Year. Tulley had groaned at the news but knew better than to let anyone, except for Erin, hear him.

She and Nia had just returned from an impulse shopping trip to Tuba City where they'd bought every bride magazine Wal-Mart had on sale.

Nia flipped the pages of *BrideWorld*. "You'll be there for the wedding, right?"

Erin gazed wistfully at a photo display of a garden wedding. "I'd like to and I will if I'm anywhere in the continental United States in October. But at this point, I'm not sure where I'll be."

Nia patted her hand. "You know, I'd love it if you'd be my maid of honor."

She hid her face behind the photo spread. "I could be in Peru. Or the Sudan." Erin sighed. "Or New Guinea."

"You sure God's will is for you to serve Him in one of those places? Or is this you giving in to your mother's will?"

She winced, fingering the cuff of her blouse. "I don't know what God's will is for me. Might as well give into the inevitable, I suppose, and make my mother happy."

"It'd make us happy if you'd stay here in the Navajo Nation." Nia's doe eyes drilled a hole into Erin. "Have you considered that possibility?"

She shuffled over to the kitchen table and rifled through the stack of bridal magazines. "Given the struggle with how I'm feeling about . . ."

Gazing out the window over the arid expanse of desert, Erin blinked back tears. "Better for me to put myself out of temptation's way."

Erin ran a finger under one eye, wiping the moisture away. "What color palette are you thinking of using for the wedding?" She cleared her throat and hoped Nia took the hint.

"Sage green. None of the usual hokey rust and gold themes for autumn." Nia laughed. "I've had some time over the years to ponder my dream wedding, if I could ever get Tulley to the altar. There's a shade of the exact green I'm looking to incorporate into the bridesmaid dresses on the bedspread in my room."

Nia waved a hand toward the hall. "Take a look. See what you think."

Glad to escape so that she could regain her composure, Erin wandered down the hall to Nia's bedroom. Not wishing to intrude on Nia's hospitality, she'd never gone into Nia's private quarters before. Pushing the half-open door with her hip, she first noticed the cream-colored walls and sturdy pieces of pine furniture. Then, her eyes were drawn to the quilt that adorned Nia's bed.

She caught her breath. It was the same quilt from the photo she'd found that day at the Cultural Center. Or, an exact replica. "Nia!" Her voice rose.

Nia padded on bare feet into the room.

"Where did you get this quilt?"

"That old thing? My grandma gave it to me when I moved out of the family home." Nia laughed. "Said it was for my hope chest."

She put a hand on her slim hip. "What a long hope that's turned out to be."

"Did your grandmother make it?"

"No. It was made for my grandmother when she was a young girl. A group of Cedar Canyon quilters met at the church during the war years when so many of our men were overseas. It helped pass the time when the old ones were missing their sons and grandsons."

Erin stuck out a shaky hand. "Could I touch it?"

Nia's eyebrows rose. "Why not? It's just an old quilt. Sat on my grandparents' bed as far back as I can remember."

"Do you think I could talk to your grandmother about it? See what she remembers about the women who made it for her?"

"Sure." Nia frowned. "What's the big deal?"

Erin explained about the unique pattern known as the New York Beauty, brought South to a small rural county in North Carolina where it emerged with changes to be called the Carolina Beauty. And about the photo she'd found in the Cultural Center's archives.

Nia reached for the phone. "Grandma lives with mom now. Let me see if I can catch her before she takes her afternoon nap."

Twenty minutes later, Nia hung up and turned to Erin who sat gingerly upon the quilted treasure, stroking the fabric with the tips of her fingers.

"Grandma says they called it 'Navajo Beauty.' It's not unique. The quilters made one for every war bride during the 1940s."

"Did she remember anything about the quilters? Maybe a white quilter who taught them the pattern or came from somewhere to join their quilt circle?"

Nia shook her head. "Nope. She remembers—'course the quilters are long dead—the old ones told her with every stitch went up a prayer for long life for the young brides and their soldier husbands."

"Any names?" Erin urged.

"One of the Tso family." Nia held up her thumb. "A Yazzie." She raised her forefinger. "Adam's grandmother and her grandmother-in-law. My great-granny Yow."

She continued counting, ticking off the names with the fingers of both hands. "A Singer progenitor. Iris Atcitty's people. The Runningdeers. Old Franklin's mother. And . . ." Nia held up both hands, proud. "Grandma's grandma Nakai."

"Any more of these special quilts still in existence?"

Nia sighed. "Six as far as Grandma knew. You're going to make me call them and get them to invite you over so you can interrogate them, aren't you?"

"Interview them, Nia. You've spent way too much time with cops. In anthropology, we call it a research interview."

Nia rolled her eyes. "Hand me the phone." She punched in a number. "Maybe people are right about you." She tilted the mouthpiece toward her chin. "You are obsessed."

The rage bubbled in his chest. At his helplessness to make things right. At the sacrifices that had been made. The things he'd been forced—no, be honest if nothing else—chosen to do. Adam refused to let Debra and her partners in crime escape justice.

Was it justice he wanted for Ben? Recompense for the giving up of all Adam cherished? The dream of who he desired to cherish?

Or was it revenge he craved? Revenge for how he'd prostituted his soul? What else did he have to lose?

The long arm of the law was only, in reality, so long. Debra and the vermin she spent her time with might just slink, like the cockroaches they were, back to the safety of the border. Until they were ready to prey upon the innocent once again.

He'd spent the week holed up, waiting. Watching the location of the meth lab Ben had given his life's blood to reveal. Nothing. No activity. The lab deserted. Operations suspended. No sign of Melendez.

There had to be a better way to flush out Debra. Another path he'd missed. If only he had insight into their plans, their agenda. But no one had that kind of power.

Or, did they?

As dusk drew its cloak of night across the sky, he parked his truck beside his grandfather's mailbox just off the highway. The graveled lane stretched and curved for a mile to the stone and timber ranch house beyond the wooden fifteen-foot telephone poles bearing his grandfather's ranch moniker, "Begay Cattle Ranch." The wrought iron gates stood open, welcoming. Inviting.

Baiting, a voice in his conscience warned.

In the distance, a cloud of dust billowed his way. His grandfather's truck skidded to a stop underneath the wooden crossbars. Adam glanced around, looking for hidden security cameras. He found none. How had the old man known he was out here? How did the old man ever know anything?

The answer, of course, was power. He, Hershal Begay, had the power. Over his minions of likeminded cronies, spies in every corner of the Rez. A gang of sorts, red-skinned, but as fanatical and dangerous as any Southern skinhead. This ranch, a virtual arsenal of firepower to assist Hershal's political ambitions if necessary.

And what did Hershal require of Adam?

Same thing he'd wanted from his only grandson since Adam was a boy. His allegiance to an unholy greed. A bartering of his soul to achieve the power Hershal craved.

Hershal's insidious words had assured him over and over, the kind of power in Adam's hands, if used for good, to bring down drug cartels and restore harmony and balance to the People. The power to help an entire nation not just survive, but thrive, in the turbulence that belonged to the twenty-first century.

His grandfather had made himself rich by operating under the radar of the law, in a myriad of nefarious means that didn't bear scrutiny. Adam swallowed, reconsidering why he'd come here. Did the end truly justify, as his grandfather oft argued, whatever means?

The old man thrust open the door of his pickup and clambered, stiffly, to the ground. His boots sent up a small puff of dust as his feet made contact with the earth. He withdrew a cigarette from his shirt pocket and stuck it between his dog yellow teeth.

Leaning against his pickup, he propped one leg across the other. Fumbling in his pocket, Hershal drew forth a match and with a flash, he scraped the match against the steel on his boot heel, igniting the blaze. Dropping his leg to the ground, he cupped his hands around the match, holding it close to the Marlboro Man stick of death brand he preferred.

With the cigarette lit, its stubby red end glowing in the shadows of the fading sun, Hershal held the match aloft, still burning, his eyes trained on Adam. Adam watched the flame dance and streak in the wind, burning the tips of Hershal's gnarled thumb and forefinger—as if to say, See me? I can do pain. How about you?—before the match sputtered out. Snuffed out for lack of tinder. Extinguished as it lost its life-giving source of oxygen.

And so, for a long time, as the darkness reestablished its claim on the earth, Adam and Hershal waited and watched each other. Nothing said. No need to. Assessing. Measuring. Counting the cost. The howling of the spring wind, the night's only ballad.

The old man coughed. Smoke wheezing out of his lungs. He flicked the cigarette to the earth and ground it out of existence with the steel-plated toe of his boot. Coughing, beating his chest, Hershal bent double. But then a strange sound.

Adam's arms prickled.

The old man choked up—with laughter. A grin broke the creases in his face as he held one hand up in the air toward Adam and his truck as if Adam might be thinking of coming to his rescue. As if Adam had any intention of setting foot on the crazy old man's property.

Or, did he? Why *had* he come here?

Angry at himself, the old man, at everything, Adam twisted the key in the ignition. The engine roared to life.

Hershal was near cackling now, his hands resting for support upon the patched knees of his faded jeans. He waved a hand. "I'll be waiting for you, son. Whenever you screw up the nerve to take up my operation. I'm ready to teach you everything you'll ever need to know. Things your father was too much of a coward—"

Jamming the gear into Drive, Adam shot back onto the asphalt, a spray of pebbles peppering the grill of the old man's truck. Not yet. Maybe never. Tulley was right. From some paths once taken—there'd be no turning back.

He barreled down the road toward his temporary camp. A strong aroma—vanilla?—perfumed the closed truck cab. His eyes widened.

Not possible. His mind was playing tricks. Couldn't be.

But the scent filled him with the longing to see her once more. To talk with her. To touch her. To . . .

Foolish and impossible, given his present circumstances. She was probably packing to head home any day now. Stupid really, considering how he contemplated giving up everything he valued to follow his grandfather's way. For to embark upon the path with Hershal would be a severing of all ties.

With his family. With his friends. With his career.

He needed—he had to—get Erin Dawson out of his head.

And, yet.

The longing persisted as he drove farther and farther away from the civilization of Cedar Canyon.

A longing for sweet tea.

17

OVER THE NEXT TWENTY-FOUR HOURS, ERIN CONDUCTED TEN INTERVIEWS, managed to track down the six surviving Navajo Beauty quilts, and captured photos of each. A compulsion to find the cave paintings Susie had spoken of—even if she had to find it on her own—began to build until by Thursday morning, she awoke to realize she could repress the urge no longer. Her internship ended on Friday. She had only this one last chance to find Olivia.

Returning posthaste at the reports of Debra's less-than-savory conduct, Director Benallie had assumed the helm of the Cultural Center once more. An elderly docent discovered a priceless black and white piece of ancient Anasazi pottery missing from a display case in the Prehistory section. Another casualty of Debra Bartelli. Tulley and the Bureau put out feelers to contacts in the underground world that trafficked in stolen artifacts. But so far, no luck.

Several additional pieces of late nineteenth century Navajo silversmithing—not currently on display—had also been taken from the storage room. The discrepancies had turned up during Erin's detailed inventory and cataloguing. Maybe another reason for Debra's hostility toward her?

Tulley believed those pieces were long gone and probably financed the oh-so-conveniently-timed sweepstakes win that had sent the Director away from the Center and the Rez in those last critical weeks of the meth lab operation. Still no luck in finding the lab, either.

First thing Thursday morning, Erin walked the director from the parking lot into his office. The director had been more than understanding with her request to take the day off.

"Petroglyphs." Benallie leaned back in his leather desk chair, adjusting the waistband of his navy wool slacks. "At the mouth of the canyon. The cave's halfway up the rock face. A sheer drop to the floor of the canyon."

He laughed. "No place for anything except mountain goats." He'd been a great supporter of Erin's extracurricular quest from the beginning of her internship.

"Be sure and take lots of water. Quite a hike. Only been once when I was a boy. Didn't bother to make the climb myself. Lonely place."

His eyes took on a faraway look. "Not much visited by those among the People who are superstitious." He patted his round belly.

"Or by those of us who were pudgy even as children. I understand the drawings give a rough account of the history of the Cedar Canyon people since the *bilágaana* first set foot on our land."

She nodded.

"Take some pictures for the Center, if you don't mind. And we'll call it a working holiday. Don't know anyone's ever documented those paintings. Be interesting to create a display to include with our Arts and Crafts section." Benallie pushed his reading glasses farther up his nose and reached for a paper on his desk.

She backed away from his office, his attention already drawn to the multitude of tasks he faced on a daily basis.

"And Erin?"

She paused to find him peering over the top of the report in his hand. "It goes without saying you need to secure a competent local guide before venturing into such a wild, desolate place. Who will be—?"

They both jolted as the phone at his right hand rang. As he reached for it, she melted into the hallway.

Least said, soonest mended.

With Tulley on duty, she was glad she hadn't had to lie to the kindly director.

Had to lie?

She frowned.

This Olivia thing had turned into an obsession Erin suddenly couldn't wait to purge herself from.

Erin pulled the car as far into the arroyo as she dared and set the parking brake. Stepping out of the car, she shivered. A chill wind blew downward from the rim of the surrounding cliff walls. Shielding her eyes with her hand, her gaze drifted to the tops of the tallest peaks where drifts of snow still pockmarked the ground. Perhaps winter had decided not to yield its iron grip upon the land just yet.

She reached, as an afterthought, for her jacket and stuffed it with the other articles she'd packed in the backpack. Her 'kit' as Dad called it. She'd included four bottles of water, a first aid kit, a flashlight, extra batteries, a cell phone more than likely useless in this backcountry location, and a couple of granola and chocolate bars thrown in for good measure. Her camera and sketch pad, too.

As she hoisted the strap onto her shoulders, a sharp bulge at the bottom of the pack jabbed into her thigh. A little extra precaution. When facing the unknown, it was best, Daddy had taught her, to pray and hope for the best but to be prepared for the worst. She had no intention of becoming a tasty meal for any predator—animal or human.

The wind whistled among the forested ridge at the top of the rocky slope she had to climb. She took a deep breath. Other than the wind, silence.

No other human for miles. She, out of habit, locked her car. Smiling at her own foolishness, she stuck one booted foot into a crevice, her fingers searching the rough basalt surface for a handhold.

Halfway up the mule deer path that emerged once she'd cleared the first five—or ten—truck-size boulders, she realized this would've been easier with an experienced guide. Unless you happened to be part mountain goat. Once she cleared the topmost ledge, she leaned into the shadow of an overhang and unscrewed the cap of her water bottle. Drinking deeply, she flexed her legs, stretching her calf muscles in the vain hope of working out the kinks. She'd be in for a world of hurt, sore muscles tomorrow.

From her perch high atop the ridge, it was all downhill— literally—from here. Boulders lay strewn across the length of the canyon, like a giant's abandoned playthings. Across the dry canyon floor that opened up below her, she spotted an unusual sandstone formation with chalk white lines— man-made—undulating over the surface of the monolith, resembling the Nazca lines of Peru.

Giant spiraling wheels, stick figures of men, species of animals that no longer roamed the earth. Carved by the Ancient Ones who preceded the Anasazi. And above that rock face, she'd been instructed, lay the cave paintings. The canyon wall itself pockmarked with caves both large and small.

Picking her way down was almost as hard as the uphill climb. As her boots slid and pebbles skidded and clattered to the bottom of the gulch, she concluded downhill was indeed scarier than going up. She blinked rapidly, trying to free her eyes from the grit of the red sandstone.

At the bottom, she paused to catch her breath—and regain control of her tattered nerves. She savored each morsel of one of her chocolate bars as she pondered the best approach to the cave, situated halfway up the rocky face of Petroglyph Canyon. A musky aroma of sage tickled her nose.

Her boots left a track of dusty heel prints in the canyon floor. Clusters of the Apache plume stretched their pinkish feather-like plumes toward the sun arced high overhead. Her forehead prickling with beads of sweat, she glanced at the watch on her wrist and rolled the sleeves of her khaki safari shirt up to her elbows. It'd taken her longer than she'd expected to get to this point.

No more breaks. Time to get moving. Or she and the coyotes would be out here together tonight cavorting their way through the moonlight. After climbing another hour, she reached her destination.

Panting as she stepped into the mouth of the cave, she ground to a halt. The arid sunshine warmed her back. Before her lay . . . inky darkness.

She'd always had a particular aversion to the dark. Erin wrestled with an irrational, primal fear of being buried alive. Of suffocating. She forced herself to inhale deeply and exhale slowly. Erin stood frozen, watching and listening.

No doubt slimy, icky creatures dwelled here under the earth. Maybe a hibernating bear or two. Or had they already awoken from their long winter naps and were now ready to eat?

Fine time, she kicked the ground sending up a clod of dirt, to wish she'd spent more time studying the animals and their behavior before venturing into their habitat and less time with her nose in a book on basket-weaving among the Navajo. "Get a grip, Dawson."

She flinched at the sound of her voice reverberating off the cave walls. And another thought . . .

Could bats actually get entangled in your hair as she'd always heard?

Out of reflex, she ducked and clamped the wide-brimmed felt hat more securely about the crown of her head. She shuddered. How badly did she want to see these cave paintings? Other than thinking to bring a flashlight, she'd deliberately kept her mind from examining too closely the ramifications of what cave exploration would entail, knowing if she did, she'd never force herself to get this far.

Light. That's what she needed. Light always dispelled the darkness.

Unzipping the pack, she fumbled around until her fingers encountered the cold aluminum of the flashlight canister. One flick of the switch and the darkness yielded to the torchlight in her hand. Ahead, a tunnel curved out of sight. She shone the light upward until the light disappeared into the darkness.

Good. The vaulted ceiling high enough so as to be out of sight. She wouldn't have to fight claustrophobia at least. At her feet, the light revealed the ubiquitous red dust of the Dinétah. And the walls were dry.

Maybe no slimy, icky creatures around.

Squaring her shoulders, she tiptoed a few steps forward until she came to the bend in the cave wall. She pressed her back against the stone, the flashlight drawn against her chest and pointed upward below her chin.

For a moment as her face glowed in the light, she was reminded of bonfires at summer camp and ghost stories told when the counselors stepped away. She shook herself. Definitely not the place to think of ghost stories, though this long-forgotten place echoed with atmosphere.

Regretting every supernatural tale she'd ever heard, as she'd seen Adam do when he'd entered her vandalized home, she summoned her courage and whipped around to the other side of the bend. The light bounced off the wall. But not before she caught a glimpse of blue.

Holding her breath, she drew closer, the flashlight scanning every inch of the wall. She advanced step-by-step, awestruck at the still-crisp colors, the delicacy of the lines, feeling like Howard Carter must have when he uncovered the treasure of Tutankhamen.

At the far left, the pictographs began, different from the petroglyphs carved in the canyon below. These drawings were painted onto the surface of the wall with a mixture of crushed mineral substances the artist would've had at hand. Applying the paint first to his fingers, he'd then rub it onto his drawings.

The first drawing, done in white clay and charcoal, depicted the octagonal, dome-shape of the hogan, a few sheep, and the figures of men. The second revealed other men with conical helmets on horseback with lances aimed at a group of hogans. Red and white pigments illustrated this scene.

Spaniards—she wondered—who'd failed so utterly to dominate and control the Navajo unlike their easy conquest of the neighboring Pueblo peoples?

The third panel displayed a fierce battle between many horse soldiers and proud, feather-draped Navajo warriors. The combatants grappled in a life and death struggle against each other. In the background, the square frame of a large building. A figure in a bell-shaped skirt stood beside the building, an interesting blue shape in the place of the head.

A woman? A white woman with a bonnet?

One lone warrior on horseback rode straight for her position. An eagle circled. The Cedar Canyon Massacre?

Erin held her breath and moved to the right along the wall until she came to the next painting. A bonneted woman—that same woman?—in front of a hogan, sheep once again milling about the backdrop of the painting. The eagle flew above the home. Flecks of silver mica reflected in the light Erin held in her trembling hand.

"Silver Eagle," she whispered.

Farther down, jagged streaks of painted lightning sizzled up and down the wall. She gasped, stepping back in alarm. Anger radiated from the wall. And pain?

She was almost afraid to examine the next painting. Was there another painting? Or was this the end of Olivia Thornton's time with Silver Eagle and the People?

Closing her eyes and gripping the light, her feet obeyed her brain and moved sideways a foot. Taking a deep breath, she opened her eyes.

A blue-bonneted woman and a silver-flecked man stood in the doorway of a hogan. Above the hogan, the eagle no longer circled but instead, the sign of the cross hovered above the roof. And the dome-shaped roof?

Tears rolled down her cheeks.

A square had been etched and subdivided into alternating green and blue squares forming triangles and feathered star points.

The Navajo Beauty.

"Olivia," she breathed. She touched a fingertip to the square.

And though she'd never be able to prove it conclusively, in her heart she knew, Olivia had made it home to Silver Eagle and the People of Cedar Canyon.

Olivia's journey—and Erin's—had ended. At last.

18

THE LIGHTING WASN'T IDEAL, BUT ERIN SNAPPED PHOTO AFTER PHOTO OF the images on the cave walls. Drawing out the sketchpad and her colored pencils, she also took the time to do a rough thumbnail sketch of each, documenting the story fully.

At a rumbling outside the cave, she jerked. Thunder? She glanced at the watch on her wrist and squinted at the hands of the dial.

Packing away her supplies, she left her pack with the paintings and rounded the corner to the entrance. Sticking her head out of the cave, she was startled to see the orange afterglow of late afternoon reflecting on the red rock canyon walls. Another rumble of thunder to the north. Over the far mesa, black storm clouds piled high in the sky.

And the temperature had dropped thirty degrees.

Her stomach growled, further reminding Erin of the lateness of the hour. She'd been so caught up in her quest she'd lost track of the time. Which she'd no doubt live to regret as she inched her way down the steep canyon wall in the coming darkness.

Erin frowned. Not a smart thing to do—to try to find her way out of unfamiliar terrain in the dark. But her only other choice?

Spend the night in the cave.

No, thanks.

Hurrying inside, she retrieved her backpack where the tunnel dead-ended. Shivering, she stuffed her arm inside the gray pea coat.

And heard voices on the other side of the stone wall.

On tiptoe and pressing her ear against the rock, she listened but heard nothing else. A faint breath of air ruffled the fine hairs on the nape of her neck. She probed the solid surface and discovered . . . space.

A careful examination revealed the wall to be an actual boulder-size overhang stretching from the ceiling to the floor with a crevice—the width of a man's shoulders—around the side edges. Beyond the crevice, the tunnel continued.

Her mother not having raised any foolish children, she was about to turn around and start for home when she heard it again. Voices. Loud, angry voices echoing through the tunnel. Shouts reverberating off the rock walls.

A bitten-off cry of pain.

Inexplicably, Adam's image popped into her mind.

Her heart thudded. Adam? What would he be doing here?

She dropped her backpack through the cramped tunnel hole before she changed her mind. It landed with a thud. She waited, one ear cocked for its discovery by the voices, but nothing happened. She eased herself through, her feet dangling for an instant in midair before gravity reconnected her with the earth, sending her sprawling on her butt.

Elegant as always, Dawson.

The beam of her flashlight in the outhouse-sized room revealed another cavity in the far wall. Tiptoeing toward the upward slanted opening, she sighted a set of footprints preceding her into the recesses of the cavern.

Not bare feet. Not moccasin feet. The outline of a shoe. A man's shoe.

Cresting the top of the slope, she gazed down at an enormous subterranean chamber—cable lines connected to floodlights zigzagging the perimeter—filled with propane tanks, plastic tubing, rows of mason jars, and empty cans. A stinging, chemical scent assaulted her nose, watering her eyes. Catching sight of three Hispanic men in the sunlit opening at the far end of the chamber, she scooted back the way she'd come to cleanse her lungs.

Glass shattered.

Holding a hand over her nose, she crab-crawled her way back to her hidden perch.

"Cuidado."

In a thick-accented tone, the taller, older man in an open throated white shirt and expensive blue suit urged the other men to caution. An immaculately trimmed black beard, his long black hair was caught up on the back of his head, Diné-style. But he wasn't Diné.

He resembled something more along the lines of a pirate.

The man laughed uneasily. "Careful or you blow us to *el infierno.*"

Lucky her. She'd discovered the back door entry to the meth lab Tulley and Adam had been looking for.

The other two men bustled about unhooking tubing and gathering unused supplies. Through the dying shafts of afternoon light at the wide-mouthed entrance, a feminine silhouette materialized.

"Melendez." She rested one hand on her black-trousered hip. "We need to wrap up our business. *Rápido.*"

Debra Bartelli.

Melendez rolled his eyes at his companions. "Leave it."

He motioned, jerking his head toward the entrance. "Get the plane ready for takeoff. Storm's coming fast."

The men dropped their burdens and skittishly backed out of the cavern giving Debra and their boss a wide berth.

He faced Debra, his lizard-slitted eyes glittering. "Thanks to your shoddy management we've had to suspend operations here in Diablo Canyon." He spat at the ground between them. "And now, once again thanks to you, we also suffer the loss of materials to set up the next lab. You've succeeded in drawing much attention to yourself and jeopardized our entire production and distribution route."

"You're blaming me?" Debra snorted and pointed out the opening. "You can thank that-that—"

A foul expletive erupted from Debra's mouth.

"I am blaming you." Melendez drew himself up to his full height, looking down his long, conquistador nose at the blonde. "You brought that bloody, *rojo* savage into our group. Your responsibility. You assured us he was trustworthy. A new cog in the wheel of justice once Navarro turned chicken-livered on us. My father will not be pleased."

Debra's mouth hardened into a razor-sharp red line.

"And now it is up to me to clean up your mess?" He raised his shoulders to his earlobes and let them drop. Melendez started for the exit.

She grabbed his upper arm, halting him. "I'll take care of Silverhorn myself."

Erin gasped, then covered her hand over her mouth.

Debra's eyes flitted toward Erin's hiding place.

She shrank back, flattening her spine against the rocky wall. But when Melendez shook himself free of her grasp striding out of the cave, Debra spun on her heels and followed.

Counting to twenty backward, Erin climbed from her hidey-hole into the chamber. Sidestepping cans of paint thinner and empty containers of starter fluid, she crept to the cave opening, hugging one side of the entrance. The cave opened onto the floor of another canyon. A chill, stiff wind had picked up in velocity. The storm clouds over the distant mesa had moved closer.

The first thing she noticed was a giant pitchfork-shaped sentinel to her left. A Cessna rested beside the pitchfork, its nose pointed out to where the canyon widened into the barren, scrub expanse of the desert. To her right, a shiny red Jeep. Debra's new wheels probably. Flashy, like her.

Careful to remain hidden from view, she picked her way down toward the canyon.

Melendez leaned against a rocky outcropping, a lit cigarette dangling between his thin lips. A sack of clothing, covered with the red dirt of the canyon, lay between his feet and Debra's booted foot. The sack moved. Debra gave the bundle a vicious kick.

The bundle groaned. Erin dropped close to the ground and scurried behind a boulder within range.

Debra snapped her fingers at Melendez's two men. "Pick him up. It's time to end this." She pivoted toward Melendez. "I'll show you how I handle those who betray me."

"I hope for your sake, Senorita Bartelli," Melendez flicked his cigarette to the sand. "That wasn't meant as a warning for me, too." He ground the glowing tip of the butt with the toe of his Italian leather boot.

The men jerked Adam to his feet. He struggled as they pinned his arms behind him. His shirt torn and his chiseled features bruised and battered, he glared at Debra. "I got a message out on the plane's transmitter before your men caught me."

He thrust his jaw forward. "I radioed my position and law enforcement will be here soon."

Debra sighed. "A liar to the end."

She cupped his jaw in her palm. He attempted to pull away from her touch, but her red-tipped claws dug into his skin. "Such a handsome face. But not so handsome once I've carved my initials into it."

Her face tightened into something less than human. She extracted a grotesque, curved knife from her belt. "I believe being the great bull rider you are, you will recognize what this is used for."

Adam flinched as she brought it inches from his cheekbone.

"That's right." She laughed. "Used for castrating bull calves. Perhaps someone should have taken this to you long ago."

He sucked in a breath and stiffened. Debra smiled and touched the knife to his skin. A tiny pinpoint of blood dotted his jawline.

"A reminder every time you look in the mirror of the one woman who bested you, lover boy."

Dropping behind the closest boulder to him, Erin held her finger on one side of the backpack's zipper to deaden any sound as she slowly opened her pack. Fear for Adam stirred in her body.

Adam kicked a leg out, impacting one of Debra's shins. She dropped to her knees with a whoosh.

"Hold him, I said." With a swift, sudden gesture, she slashed across Adam's blue-jeaned thigh.

Adam grunted, lunging for her.

Debra ripped the knife across his bicep, blood spurting. Adam ceased struggling as trails of red seeped through the green plaid of his shoulder.

Panic flared. Erin's fingers shook. Hurry, Hurry.

She dug her hand inside the backpack, frantic until her fingers wrapped around the muzzle of the 9mm semiautomatic she always carried stateside.

Debra hauled herself to her feet. "Or maybe?" Venom dripped from her lips. "I'll just slit your worthless throat."

One of the men jerked Adam's hair, forcing his head backward and exposing his bronze neck to the dying light of the day.

His arms and ankles crossed, Melendez reposed against the canyon wall, his face a study of boredom. "*Por el amor de Dios, señorita.* Enough with the melodrama. I have a business to run. People to see and dinero to make."

Erin wrapped her shaking hands around the weapon and rested her extended elbows on the surface of the rock. Cocking her head, she closed one eye, drawing a bead on Debra and putting her in the weapon's crosshairs. She took a deep breath and clicked off the safety.

Debra drew back her arm in an arc to strike. A piercing shaft of sunlight glinted off the gunmetal gray weapon in Erin's hand catching Melendez's eye.

"Up there."

His men jerked their heads, and Adam's, toward the direction he pointed. Melendez scrambled behind the protection of a boulder.

Breathing a prayer, she squeezed the trigger. The bullet tore through Debra's upraised hand and ricocheted into the arm of one of the men holding Adam. Debra roared with pain, clutching her bloody appendage.

The wounded man dropped his hold on Adam. Adam wrenched free from his other captor. Kneeing him in the groin, Adam dropped to the ground and rolled away.

With half her head exposed above the rock, she beckoned. "Adam."

His head snapped up at the sound of her voice, disbelief written across his dirt-smeared features. "Erin?"

Melendez emerged from behind the rock, his weapon drawn.

Adam made a motion. "Get down, Erin."

She fired a shot over Melendez's head. As flakes of rock flew into his eyes, he retreated. She shot out two of the Jeep's tires.

Adam crawled behind the safety of the rock with her, his arms shielding his head. "Who are you? Rambo? And what have you done with the real Erin Dawson?"

A bullet whizzed past her ear. She got down as instructed this time.

"What are you doing here?" he hissed between two busted lips.

She started to rise. "I'm rescuing you."

He jerked her coattail back down. "Oh really? Looks to me like you got us boxed in four guns to one."

She sniffed. "No gratitude left in the world, is there?"

He made a grab for the gun. "Give me that thing."

"No way." She jerked free. "I'm doing okay so far. How about 'Thank you, Erin, for saving my life'?"

His lips twitched. "Thanks, Erin." He leaned, planting a rough kiss on her mouth. "Ow." Wincing, he put a finger to his busted lip.

Erin licked her lips. Peppermint. Mmm. "You're welcome." Smirking, she handed the gun, handle over first, to him.

A steady whump-whump filled the canyon air.

He ventured a cautious peek over the top of the rock. Melendez was making a run for the plane, followed by his two injured compatriots. No sign of Debra. "They're leaving, headed for the plane."

She slid her arms through the straps of the backpack, jostling it into position. "You're not going to let them get away?"

He tilted his head to the whirring sound. "Police copter will round 'em up 'fore the plane can get off the ground."

Adam slumped against the rock face. "Let a guy get a breath, why don't you?" He inhaled and then clutched his chest, his brown eyes widening in pain.

"Broken or bruised ribs." She narrowed her eyes, inspecting him. "I can jerry-rig you till we get to the hospital."

He sighed and winced as the air rattled his ribcage. "MK Training 101?"

She rose, offering her arm for support. He reached for her. A shadow loomed, knocking the gun from his grip. The gun clattered with a spray of pebbles down the slope.

A bloodied Debra emerged into the last rays of the setting sun. She aimed a .357 Magnum at Erin's temple.

Shoving Debra's arm away, Adam grabbed Erin's hand. "Run."

Adrenaline pumping, he hoisted himself up the rock face to a ledge, exposing his body to the full fury of the wind. His breath ragged, he extended his hand to Erin and hauled her upward.

With a boom, Debra's gun fired and missed them. At the blast of the gun echoing off the canyon walls, Erin lost her footing, her feet dangling in midair. His heart pounding, he fought the strain in his wounded shoulder, his strength the only thing keeping her from falling to the jagged rocks below.

Another bullet whizzed past a lone Ponderosa pine, splintering the wood, inches from Erin's head. She dug her toes into the rock and scrambled the rest of the way to safety.

Grunting like a maddened bull with the effort to climb with only one working hand, Debra kept coming as certain as Death. And he'd been counting. Still too many unfired rounds left in the chamber of her gun.

He pointed down the trail, snaking in a serpentine route to the floor of the canyon and sanctuary for them, if they made it that far. "Go." He pushed Erin when she refused to budge.

Suspicion darkened her face. "You're coming, too?"

"Please, for once in your life . . ."

"You are coming, aren't you, Adam?"

Stubborn *bilágaana* woman.

"I'll be right behind you," he lied.

She frowned.

He could tell she didn't trust what he said, but with another determined shove in the right direction from him, she took off running. He hobbled a few feet hampered by the Arctic blast of the wind and stopped.

No way with his injured leg could he make a run for it. But there was hope for Erin. He wheeled, facing off against Debra. Despite the wind, Debra's cloying scent—and the rotting, primal stench of hate—assaulted his nostrils.

Puffing with rage, Debra heaved herself over the rim of the rock. He backed up a step. Her shattered hand hanging at her side, Debra advanced, the gun pointed at his chest.

"I'm going to shoot you down like the mangy dog you are and then I'm going to find your girlfriend and carve her up for the crows."

Out of nowhere, flakes of snow began to fall, fast and furious. As if someone had suddenly dumped a truckload of winter upon their bare heads. The howling wind whipped the snow into his eyes, stinging needles of crystal.

When Debra drew her hand up to shield her face, he made a grab for her gun, wrenching it from her hand. With a screech,

Debra wrapped her hands around his throat and breathed profanities.

Adam flung the cold steel over the precipice and Debra, madness glowing from her eyes, dragged him step by step, closer to the edge. He fought to pry her claws from around his throat. With the strength born of drugs or the criminally insane, inch by inch she drove him backward toward the edge of nothingness.

His back arched until he thought his spine would crack. He dug his heels into the loose rock, growing increasingly slippery with the late April snow, fighting to maintain his balance.

Adam gasped as Erin flung herself at Debra, scrabbling for a handhold on the back of Debra's white silk blouse. With her other hand, Erin grabbed for his good arm. Bracing her feet against the rock, she yanked him to the safety of the ledge just as he succeeded in freeing himself from Debra's stranglehold. He teetered. Erin released Debra, wrapping her arms tightly around his waist.

Inertia gave way to momentum as Debra flailed over the drop. Toppling backward, Debra's eyes grew enormous with fear.

"No!" she screamed.

In a viselike grip, she caught the edge of Erin's shirt hanging beneath her coat.

Erin dug her boots into the ground but the pressure of holding him upright and the dead weight of Debra's body drew them inexorably toward the edge.

A satisfied smile wizened Debra's face. "I'll take the both of you with me." She made a sudden lunging move backward. Her rattlesnake eyes glinted.

He threw his entire body against Erin's, pushing, fighting against gravity's pull. "Not today." He gritted his teeth.

With a ripping, shredding sound, a hunk of Erin's shirt-tail came loose in Debra's fist. A gust of wind buffeted the cliff face. Losing her balance, Debra fell backward, unearthly shrieks following her, until her head cracked like a watermelon against the boulders below.

A shiver of revulsion rippled through the length of Erin's body. Averting her face, she let go of him and scuttled back, hugging the relative safety of the canyon wall. He peered over the rim to where Debra's body lay in an unnatural angle, her limbs twisted in a macabre pose of death. Blood from her broken shell of a body stained the snow-covered rocks.

19

Adam's eyes closed for a split-second with relief.

"Is she . . . ?" Erin's voice quavered from behind him.

"Yeah." He dragged himself, painfully, to his feet. "We need to get out of this blizzard."

Her teeth chattered. "Tulley . . ."

"They've got their hands full, I imagine, with the prisoners and the weather."

Sliding her back against the wall, she lurched to her feet. He caught her forearm in time to keep her from toppling forward on her face. "Steady."

And then giving in to his feelings, he swept her into a tight embrace against his chest. "I know a safe place till the storm blows over and the cavalry can rescue us."

"Cavalry?" She stared at him, a funny look on her face. "The snow will cover our prints. How will they track us?"

With the emergency over, he tried putting his weight on his injured leg. The effort, as the pain sliced through him, took his breath. Erin grabbed hold of him.

She placed an arm underneath his shoulder blades. "Lean against me."

Vanilla wafted past his cold nose as he wrapped his good arm around her waist. "Tulley knows where I've been holed up while I waited this week for Debra's associates to fly in and wrap up their business."

She made a face. "And he let us think you'd gone off half-cocked." She sighed in exasperation. "Next time I see that freakishly tall giraffe, I'm going to give him a piece of my mind."

Adam laughed.

His face blanched. "Don't. Make. Me. Laugh." They hobbled forward.

She gazed down the trail. "How far till we get to this place? Can you make it?"

He pointed to where the trail met up with the canyon floor ahead. "There. Another tunnel that leads straight through the mesa to the other side."

"Where?" She craned her neck. "I don't see any—"

"An optical illusion from a distance. Looks like the canyon dead ends." He plodded forward. "Here."

He drew her inside the tunnel, out of the force of the snow. With a soft whinny, a familiar nose buried itself in his shoulder. Erin reeled and yelped.

Adam rubbed the white patch between the horse's eyes. "Just Buttercup."

She stretched a tentative hand to stroke the mare's side. "You left your horse here?"

He motioned toward a wooden trough filled with water and a bucket of hay. "Came in the morning to continue my surveillance and left every evening. Didn't always bring Buttercup but something about the sky this morning made me decide to bring her today."

Adam patted the mare's shoulder. "Glad I did."

With a grunt, he heaved the western-style saddle along Buttercup's broad back and fastened the girth in place. Fighting the salty sting of tears from the effort, he checked and adjusted the stirrups. He dragged his wool-lined sheepskin coat out of the saddlebag, wincing as he slid his hurt arm in the sleeve.

She surveyed the vast, high-ceiling tunnel. Outside, the roaring wind drove pellets of snow into the cavern. At the other end, the milky whiteness of snow cascaded down on the other side of the mesa as well.

"This tunnel?" she whispered. "I wonder . . ."

He stuck his good leg into the stirrup, wrapping the long lengths of the leather bridle around his hands and grabbed for the saddle-horn. With an audible moan, he swung his bad leg over the saddle. "You wonder right."

Adam positioned the horse beside a large rock and reached a hand down to her. "Care to join me?"

She clambered up the rock and eased herself behind him in the saddle, her arms wrapped around his waist. He shifted.

He wheezed. "Don't hold so tight."

"Sorry." She loosened her grip. "What do I wonder right?"

Making a short, clicking motion with his tongue against his teeth, he steered the horse toward the exit. "It's the same tunnel my people have used for several centuries to get away from yours." The horse's hooves clip-clopped over the stones in the dry riverbed.

"You think Silver Eagle and Olivia came this way?"

Leaving the reins looped through his hand on the horn, he placed his other hand over where her hands conjoined at his belly button above the silver rodeo buckle. "Without a doubt. Eons ago this used to be an underground river. Retreating glaciers carved out this crevasse."

Emerging from the protective shield of the tunnel, she buried her face into his back. "I found Olivia in the cave." She shouted in an attempt to be heard above the howling wind and snow.

He caressed her hand. "I saw them, too," he yelled.

Crossing a shallow ravine for several miles, the rugged terrain gradually yielded to a gentle upward slope. "Hang on," he called, leaning his weight back in the saddle as they climbed. They passed under a thick stand of juniper, snow covering the twisted branches.

"Diamondback Ridge." He pointed. "Almost home."

Making straight for the barn, he jumped—make that rolled with excruciating care—out of the saddle and swung the barn doors wide. Once inside, he gave Erin his hand and she shimmied to the ground. Pulling on the bridle, he led Buttercup to her stall and untacked the mare. After giving Buttercup a quick rubdown, extra oats, and water, he stepped out of the stall where Erin hung on the door like a six-year-old watching him work.

The sight of her made him smile.

He shivered in the chill air of the barn. "Come on. Time to get warm."

Adam helped her jump down, her boots landing and sending up a small cloud of dust and hay. It took the both of them to wrestle the barn doors closed again. He wrenched the heavy wooden bar in place.

With his good arm wrapped around Erin, their bodies bowed by the strength of the wind, they stumbled to the hogan across the yard where drifts of snow had begun to accumulate.

He reached for the door and with a flourish, flung it open. "Welcome to the Silverhorn family home place. Make yourself at home."

Erin stepped into the dim interior of the one-room octag-onal structure. The wind sucked the door from Adam's grasp and with a bang, slammed shut behind them. He shuffled over to a wooden three-legged stool and lit the wick of the kerosene lamp. Light cast flickering shadows across the dwelling.

He bent over the half-bellied oil drum stove to open the stove's belly. "Here." A small cherry-red ember glowed in a pile of ash.

Adam stuffed dry piñon branches into the furnace until the flames caught and shot higher, hot orange and bright. A smell of pine and cedar filled the room.

Raising her head, she noted the smoke belching from the top of the connecting pipe out through the square open-ing in the ceiling smoke hole. She joined Adam at the open flames, holding her hands in front of her to warm them. "Thin Southern blood."

"Better?"

She nodded. "Better." She scanned the interior. "You grew up here?"

He shook his head. "The family used it only in summer as a sheep-camp after my great-grandmother died. Where'd you get that gun?"

She grimaced. "Daddy always insists I travel around with it when I'm stateside. I secured all the proper permits to bring it to Arizona."

"I have never—and I repeat *never*—met anyone like you, Erin Dawson. How in the world is target practice part of MK Training?"

"One word." She unbuttoned her coat as her body thawed. "Snakes."

She tossed the garment over to a ladder-back chair. "I was terrified of the creatures in our jungle home. Grandpa Harry taught me one summer in North Carolina. Daddy thought I might need the protection for creatures of a different kind in the states."

"Well . . ." He shook his head.

For once she had Adam at a loss for words. A rare feat.

Time for a little fun at Silverhorn's expense after the week she'd endured due to his disappearing act. "Sorry about my aim."

His eyes narrowed. "Your aim?"

"I'm better with the twelve-gauge shotgun of Grandpa Harry's. I wasn't really aiming for Debra's hand."

His eyes widened and he swayed on the balls of his feet, his knees buckling. "The thought of you with a shotgun makes my blood run cold."

"Sit down. I was joking."

Erin gripped his arm and guided him to an iron bedstead situated against one wall. "We need to take a look at your injuries." The springs of the bed creaked as they sank onto the bare, ticking-striped mattress.

She peeled off the backpack she'd managed to keep attached to herself during the entire ordeal. She removed the first aid kit and helped him slide out of his coat.

"Undo your shirt."

His fingers trembled with fatigue, twisting futilely at the buttons of his green shirt. He looked at her, lifting one corner of his mouth in a crooked smile. "Can't seem to get my fingers to work."

"I'll do it."

She made short work of the buttons and eased the torn, bloody fabric off his shoulder and down his back. The gash looked red and angry, but the bleeding had stopped.

"Probably needs stitches."

She doused a cotton ball with hydrogen peroxide. The muscles of his smooth, hard chest rippled. Her mouth went dry.

He clenched his teeth as she dabbed the wound gently, cleansing away the blood and grime. "Aren't you full of good cheer and optimism?"

"When's the last time you had a tetanus shot?"

She leaned closer to the furrowed row of sliced flesh in a vain attempt to keep her eyes averted from the more exposed portions of his physique. Big mistake. Instead, her nostrils flared with the musky aroma that was all Adam.

"A regular Little Miss Sunshine," he muttered.

Her lips twitched. "Just sayin'." She dotted the wound with Neosporin and pulled out a tube of super glue.

Adam rocked back. "Planning on gluing my mouth shut while we wait for Tulley?"

She brushed a strand of hair behind her ear to see better. "No, though that might be a good idea in your case. I'm going to paint your shoulder with the glue to hold the edges of the wound together till we can get you to the hospital. Good thing Debra didn't cut to the bone."

"Or sever anything vital." He unconsciously brought his knees together.

She laughed.

"Where'd you learn that trick with the glue?" He shook his head in mock despair. "I know. MK Training, right?"

Erin replaced the cap onto the tube and twisted it closed. "Nope." She picked up a pad of gauze from the kit sitting on the bare mattress beside her.

She cut four strips of tape and placed the bandage over his arm. "Who do you think helped Todd study during his EMT training and later for his medical license?" She taped the bandage securely in place.

Erin traced a light fingertip over a scattering of fleshy indentations along his back. "How did you get—?"

He bolted from the bed and over to the stove, fumbling to get the twisted remnants of his shirt to cover his torso.

"Don't do that," he whispered hoarsely, his chest rising and falling in great gulps of air. His black eyes had gone opaque.

Her brows drew together. "Do what? I was just—"

"Don't . . . touch . . . me . . . like . . . that."

She gave him a puzzled look. "Like what? I . . ." At the near-panicked look on his face, she bit back a laugh. "You make it sound like I was trying to molest you, Adam Silverhorn."

Erin gestured toward his leg. "We still have to see what damage has been wrought there."

"Did you just ask me to drop my drawers?" He drew himself up stiffly. "I don't think so, Erin Dawson."

She doubled over, falling sideways on the mattress. "That's a rich one coming from the play-boy of Cedar Canyon." A hurt look flashed across his face.

Erin sat up, the mirth gone. "I'm sorry, Adam. I shouldn't have said that. None of my business—"

"No, I'm sorry for . . ." He shrugged. "Everything."

He sank down beside her. "I've done some things I'm not proud of." His eyes probed the shadows at the corners of the room.

"Things done when I was homesick and lonely while overseas." He shook his head as if to clear his head from the memories. "No excuse."

He drew her hand and cradled it on the back of his shoulder. Her breath stuttered at the warmth of his skin beneath the cotton of his shirt.

"Shrapnel. IED while on patrol in Afghanistan." He released a breath, letting it trickle out. "I wish I could go back and do so many things over again. I wish I could be that pure person someone like you deserves . . ."

"Adam—"

"But life in this case doesn't give any do-overs. Once you've traveled down that path, there's no going back." He gently placed Erin's hand back in her lap. "You of all people can't . . ."

He ran his tongue over his dry, cracked lips and flinched. "I can't have you touch me. Where you're concerned, I know my own weaknesses." His eyes dropped to the dirt floor.

She swallowed. "Oh."

He sighed, the sound floating up like smoke through the hole in the hogan.

She squared her shoulders. "The wound still needs tending to." She glanced at him.

"And your poor face." She rose. "Here are the first aid supplies and a washcloth. I'll keep my back turned while you doctor yourself. I'll see about putting together some food if you think you can eat."

Grinning, he lay back on the mattress, resting his head on a couple of rolled up sleeping bags tied with cord. "Unless I'm dead, Erin Dawson, I can always eat."

Scooting the black duffel bag out from under the bed, she handed it to him and with her back turned, rummaged through the supplies he'd brought with him to the hogan. "Nia taught me to do fried cornbread."

Erin located a bag of Bluebird flour, salt, and baking soda. "Pretty similar to how we bake it back home in the South." She rattled the teakettle on the stove, relieved to find it already filled with water. She'd need hot water to put into the mix and spotting a half-empty bag of coffee, brew an after-dinner beverage.

Heaving an iron skillet from a peg off the wall, she laid it with a clang on the stovetop. "I see you've got some lard I can melt and fry the puppies up with." She heard grunting behind her as he wrestled out of his pants and shirt and into clean ones.

She located a can of pork and beans. "Got a can opener anywhere?" Her fingers happened upon something in a tray on the shelf.

Erin held up the manual opener without turning around. "Found them." She busied herself with the dinner preparations and caught him up on Tulley and Nia's engagement.

"Good for him. 'Bout time that boy got some sense." There was the sound of running water as he poured a pitcher of water into a basin on a stand by the bed. "There's water in the cooler and a pitcher of tea, too."

She retrieved the tea and sniffed. "Sweet?"

"You've ruined me for anything else."

He came up behind her. "I probably didn't mix it right, though. Probably put in too much sugar. Didn't taste the way you make it."

She swiveled to find him tucking a blue-plaid shirt into a fresh pair of jeans. Even battered and bruised, at the sight of his handsome face her heart twisted.

Not everybody could pull off being beaten to a bloody pulp. His face would probably purple an attractive black and blue.

To hide the tears shimmering in her eyes, she pivoted to the stove, stirring the pot of beans and dropping tablespoonsful of batter into the bubbling oil.

"Honey chile." She slipped into the broad, flat intonations of her family's Down Eastern home in North Carolina. "You can't make it too sweet for a Southerner."

She darted a glance at him over her shoulder. "The way my grandmother and great-aunts used to make it? I've seen spoons stand fully upright in the syrupy stuff."

"I also wanted . . ." He put his hand on her shoulder. "I wanted you to know I never . . ."

He dropped his gaze, locking eyes on the scruffy toes of his tan work-boots. "Debra and I, we—"

She whirled back to the stove, closing her eyelids tight against the sting of tears. She so didn't want to hear this. Some things were better left unsaid. "I'm not your Father Confessor, Adam."

He placed his hands on both sides of her face, wheeling her around. His eyes searched hers. "Nothing to confess. That's what I'm trying to tell you."

She stepped away, forcing him to let her go. He wasn't the only weak one.

A muscle ticked in his cheek. "I was assigned to insinuate myself with Debra to gain access to her drug cartel circles. I was told to do whatever it took to win her confidence. That night a few weeks ago when we saw you at the Center and later I called you so late?"

She nodded, bracing herself. She'd suspected as much on the phone with him. But hearing him say the words out loud would hurt. Like an abscessed tooth.

He took hold of both her hands. "You're not listening to me, Erin."

She blinked at him.

"As a test of loyalty, she demanded that I . . ." He cleared his throat and started over. "I couldn't do it."

He shuddered. "Would have been like copulating with a reptile. Maybe if the image of you wasn't always playing in my head . . . But I refused and walked away knowing I'd blown a three-year mission and lost any chance of stopping her crew from destroying the children of my people."

Erin's heart fluttered. "You didn't . . . ? You and she . . ."

Adam's face twisted. "So you see why it's my fault Ben died—"

"Ben didn't die, Adam. He's alive." She touched his sleeve.

"What?" Hope lit his eyes, dawning like the rays of the sun off the Cedar Mesa.

She told him about Ben's miraculous recovery. "And if you don't think it was God, then you're not as intelligent as I gave you credit for being."

Her nose wrinkled and her eyes widened in panic. "You're going to make me burn supper, Adam Silverhorn."

She lunged for the stovetop and stabbed each cornmeal puppy, removing them to drain on a paper-towel lined plate. "Pour the tea." But she favored him with a smile.

Giving her a mock salute, he complied.

Sitting side by side on the bare mattress once more, she and Adam balanced the tin plates on their laps while they ate. "Your mama's back." She stuck a forkful of beans into her mouth.

He groaned.

"Don't tell me a sworn officer of the law like you is scared of that little bitty woman?"

"My mother," Adam arched his eyebrow, "is a formidable person. There'll be hell to pay once she learns everything her baby boy's been up to lately."

"Like getting beaten up." She jabbed the fork in his direction. "And stabbed . . ."

"Remind me not to introduce the two of you."

She slugged him in the arm with her fist.

"Ow," he howled. "See what I mean?"

"Weally?" She mocked him in that singsong voice adults reserved for small children. "Did I hurt the widdle boy?" She poked a finger at his belly.

He veered away from her reach. "Stop."

She cocked her head at him. "Ticklish? Adam Silverhorn, champion bull rider, NPD Native Gang Specialist, is ticklish?" She poked him again.

"Now, Erin." Keeping one eye trained on her, he lowered his plate to the floor. "Don't make me hurt you."

"Hah." She tickled his side, using both hands this time.

Adam squirmed, one arm shooting out, and sent her plate flying across the room. He stilled, shock on his face.

Her eyes narrowed. "I am absolutely *not* cleaning up that mess, Silverhorn."

Something stirred between them.

He gave her a slow grin. Her insides melted and puddled to the tips of her toes.

Adam leaned in closer. "Maybe if you ask me nicely . . ."

She stopped breathing.

His hands cupping her elbows, Adam drew her to her feet and moved himself and her toward the stove and away from the bed. "Best not to tempt fate. Or me, more than I can bear." His hands moved up her arms and cradled her face.

Adam stopped, searching her face. What he found, apparently satisfied. He rested his forehead against hers and closed his eyes.

She listened to the sound of his breaths. Her hand over the region of his heart, she felt its erratic beating, pounding like a drum at the powwow.

"We shouldn't. I shouldn't." He dropped his hands to his sides. "No good for you. Best not to start something we can't finish."

For so many reasons, Erin knew he was right.

But she reached up, circling his neck with her arms. "Just this once," she whispered, her lips close to his ear.

Her heart hammered. "One kiss, Adam."

Just this once. Please, God.

Please . . .

Adam's breath caught.

Had she said that out loud?

"Erin—" he moaned and his lips found her mouth, as hungry as her own.

And if she never had this moment again in her life, she'd die a happy woman. He deepened the kiss and she melted into him as fire ignited places within her she'd never known existed until now. His arms tightened around her.

His lips brushed her cheek and burrowed into the side of her neck. His mouth found the hollow of her throat and trailed across her jawline to recapture her lips once more. She swayed in his arms to a music only they heard, a melody as old as time.

If she could stay here in this primitive hogan with this man for the rest of her life . . . If the world would just cease to exist outside this place? Would God grant such a request—this only request of hers?

Adam wrenched back, leaving her body bereft of him. "I won't compromise y-your—" He struggled to regain his breath. "I respect you too much."

He sighed and his finger traced the curve of her face. He made an attempt at a smile, suddenly sheepish and shy.

Planting a quick peck on her cheek, he pointed to the opposite side of the room. "Nice Diné women stay on the northern end of the hogan."

He winked, taking the sting out of his words. "Diné men who know they need to behave themselves stay to the south."

Moving away toward the one window in the hogan, he drew the calico curtain aside and peered out into the darkness. "Storm's stopped."

She drew a shaky breath. "Didn't notice."

He let the curtain fall into place. "Me, either."

20

"Tell me about what it was like living here in the summer with your family."

She stretched out in front of the stove, cocooned in one of the sleeping bags his family kept in the hogan year-round.

Adam gazed out the window at the moonlit snow. The clouds had departed as fast as the hurricane of snow had begun. He wended his way over to her, wriggling into his own sleeping bag and zipped it to his chest for good measure.

No harm in taking a few precautions. Against himself.

With the temperatures still hovering below freezing, sleeping in front of the stove and not on the bed made the most sense.

In more ways than one.

The two sleeping bags formed a horseshoe around the stove, his head not quite touching hers. On his back, he peered at the tiny points of starlight visible through the smoke hole above. They had just this one night.

The temps would rise come morning. The snow would melt. Tulley'd be here mid-day to rescue them, retrieving Adam's truck from where he stashed it in the canyon.

Not that he ever wanted to be rescued from this place and this moment in time.

"I was scared the first time I remember being here."

She turned on her side, her elbow bent, her head resting on her hand. "Why?"

"I don't remember. Mom brought Lydia and I both here. And this old woman . . ." He heard her raspy, ancient voice in his head again as he had that evening at Debra's. He sat up, blinking.

"She liked purple. I remember now. It was my great-great-grandmother, Grandpa Silverhorn's grandmother. She told me what drove away scary things and said, like her, I was a winter lamb born tougher than those delivered in the spring."

Erin made a face. "I'm sorry I don't like mutton."

He laughed. "Confession time? I don't so much either, but don't tell any Diné I said so. The sheep are everything to the People. Uncle Johnny still keeps a small herd because his parents and their parents before them did."

Adam snuggled into the nylon sleeping bag. "Soon, late spring, it will be time to shear the sheep. My grandparents would come up here to do that and then sell the wool to the trading post at Cedar Canyon where they kept a permanent home near the church. They'd use the money to pay off a year's worth of credit and buy flour, baking soda, salt, sugar, and coffee for the coming year."

"Do you still help with the shearing?"

"Not in a long time." He sighed. "Every August I also used to help Uncle Johnny round up the male lambs to sell so, with my mother's share of the herd, we'd have money to buy clothes and school supplies. I hated leaving those lambs behind at the trading post."

"Excuse me for saying so, but doesn't one sheep look just like another?"

He twisted onto his stomach, leaning his chin on his crossed arms. "To the uninitiated maybe. But you get to know each sheep in the herd. Each one has their own personality. Some lead, some lag behind. One is fearful, another is friendly."

"Sounds like what Jesus said about His sheep. They hear and know the voice of their Master."

His brows drew together. "Yeah, I guess so. Never thought about it before."

"Sorry to be so ignorant." She rotated and plopped onto her stomach as well. "The Dawsons were either missionaries or farmers. How did you remember which sheep belonged to your mother?"

He held up a finger. "One nick in the ear meant it belonged to Grandpa Tom. Two nicks Uncle Johnny." He held up three fingers. "Three for Hannah Silverhorn."

A smile tugged at her lips. "Marked to show ownership. The apostle Paul wrote he bore on his body the brand marks of Who he belonged to."

He frowned. "Brand marks are for gangs."

"I think he meant, due to his allegiance to Christ, his choices and experiences left signs on him. Physically and spiritually. To some extent, whether we realize it or not, all of us are marked by our choices, good and bad, and reveal to whom we've given our devotion."

A flare of anger surged through him. "I mark myself for no man. Not even a tattoo while in the army." The anger had been a part of him so long he almost couldn't remember when it had begun.

But he remembered now. It had begun for him in this very place. When he'd understood his mother meant to separate them permanently from his father. An anger fueled and nurtured over the years by Hershal Begay. "And as far as your

Shepherd, He's allowed His Navajo sheep to be pretty much ravaged by wolves."

She sighed, a note of sadness in her voice. "You bow the knee to no one, you told me once. But after all you've been through these past weeks—"

"Drop it, Erin. There are some things we have to agree to disagree on." He flipped onto his back.

"A huge thing to disagree on, Adam." Her voice sounded small.

Two different cultures. Opposing worldviews. Never work. He clamped his eyes shut. "Go to sleep, Erin."

His dreams were full of strange, distorted images of wolves, the sacred mountains running red with blood and the pure clean water of the snow melting on the mesa in the spring thaw.

And also of sheep.

Erin's words echoed in his sleep, calling from the high ridge of a distant mesa. Beckoning him. Challenging him. Haunting him.

In the dream, Adam tried to save the sheep. But there was no harmony. No beauty. And the wolves devoured them all. Including him. Their jagged teeth ripping and tearing his flesh. The coppery smell of his own blood hung in the air.

When he awoke, he knew what he had to do. What choice he had to make to protect his people. And himself.

When Erin awoke, she knew instantly from the set, hard look on his face, that their moment had passed. She'd waited through the night, longing to hear him say the words that never came. Words of love for her.

And more importantly, for her God.

Without such words—a deal-breaker for them both.

Melting icicles dripped from the roof. Mute and his manner distant, Adam moved about the room, packing his gear.

Relieved when she heard the distant chug-chug of an engine motor, she glanced out the window. An SUV with the NPD logo emblazoned on the side drove into the yard. Followed by Adam's F-150 pulling an empty horse trailer.

"Tulley's here." She let the blue-striped curtain fall in place. "With Ortiz."

Adam handed her the backpack. "Ride with Tulley and Ortiz. I have to load Buttercup in the trailer and haul her to town with my truck." He kept his back to her, stuffing clothing and unused food supplies into his duffel.

"O—okay." She fought to control her voice, hating the telltale quiver.

Save me, God. From myself.

His shoulders slumped. "I have some business to take care of before I put Buttercup in the corral at Mom's place. When are you heading out of town for home?"

Never. If you'd ask me to stay.

But instead, she forced out the words, "Tomorrow after church."

The silence lengthened. Through the window beaded with moisture, she watched Tulley's boots tamping snow against the tire of the SUV. Both he and Ortiz hung back waiting, per Diné custom, for the invitation to approach the house.

Adam strode across the room to open the door. Tulley waved at him and ambled forward. Ortiz stayed put. Tulley grinned at her and clapped Adam on the back.

"Good to see you alive and well, brother."

Adam shrugged him off. "You manage to catch Melendez and his men?"

Tulley leaned against the doorframe. "As easy as pulling ticks off a hound dog."

"Did you find . . . ?" Adam's eyes darted over to her and shied away. "You find Debra's body?"

Tulley straightened and removed his hat. "Yeah. I'll need a complete report from you on everything ASAP. Your buddies from the FBI, the DEA, and the Bureau were chafing at the bit all night to get you back. I told them only a fool tried to go upcountry in a spring blizzard."

Adam grimaced. "Not my buddies for long." He folded his arms across his chest, avoiding looking at either of them.

What did that mean?

She gave Tulley a worried look, cutting her eyes at Adam.

Adam threw open the stove vent and doused the flames with the last of the coffee. "'Preciate it if you'd take Erin to town."

"Maybe you'd like to—"

She grabbed Tulley's arm, swinging her backpack over her shoulder. "Come on, Tulley. You can debrief me on the way into Cedar Canyon."

Tulley's eyes switched to and fro between her and Adam, worry lines etched across his forehead. He put on his hat. "Sure, Erin. I'm ready to go if you're ready to go."

She stalked past him out the door and into the brilliant glare of the desert sun on snow. "I'm ready to go."

Tulley and Erin hadn't been gone ten minutes before the old man drove his Dodge pickup into the yard of the hogan, catching Adam in the task of securing Buttercup inside the horse trailer. He was glad Hershal hadn't arrived while he was still in the house. Out in the open was better. Hershal in his grandmother's hogan seemed somehow, a disloyalty.

No, worse than that. A blasphemy.

The old man eased his way out of the truck cab, stiff with arthritis on the cold May morning. A man like many old men on the Rez, Adam reminded himself. A man unlike any of his Uncle Johnny's friends, however.

His grandfather pushed the white straw hat back on his silver hair, revealing the wide, dark blue headband wrapped around his forehead. "You come to a decision, boy?"

Adam didn't understand how Hershal could possibly know of a decision he reached only in the wee hours of the night before. But Hershal had always known a great many things hidden to the rest of the People.

He nodded. He kept his face like carved stone.

"You and me, boy, we never belonged with that bunch of dumb sheep Jesus people. Deep down, I reckon this day was inevitable. You knew it, too. With my money and your twenty-first-century know-how, we're going to own this land."

Adam bristled. "I'd settle for serving the People. Helping them get their fair share finally of education and employment. Alleviate the poverty and disease."

Hershal shrugged. "Sure, sure. That, too. Main thing is first you got to be in a power position to do good. No more Apples or Navajo wannabes telling us how to run our government, how to manage our own resources. My crew can't wait to meet you at last and usher in this new chapter in Diné history."

Adam swallowed.

The old man clapped his hands with glee. "You got rid of that *bilágaana* girl, I see." He aimed a spittle of tobacco at his tire. "Got enough mongrel mutts here on the Rez as it is."

Adam clenched his lips together.

"Welcome back to the family, Adam Begay. Bring your stuff to my ranch and we'll begin preparing you for the great work for which you were marked long before your birth."

He tried to repress the cold tingle that traveled down his spine at his grandfather's words.

Erin had been right.

Sooner or later, everyone made a choice that marked them.

21

April, 1907

When the messenger from Father Gregory arrived breathless with the news the five Hopi warriors had been captured and strung up by the army in Cedar Canyon, Olivia knew what she must do. Icicles hanging from the eaves of the dome-shaped hogan dripped, the snow tucked only in tiny pockets in the higher elevations. The creek a half-mile from the hogan ran pure, clean, and swift with the heavy snow runoff. The pass was almost clear. The spring thaw had inexorably come. But instead of bringing new life to Olivia, it brought the death of dreams.

She left the leather New Testament on her blanket with a note. She hoped Silver Eagle would read both in the years to come. If she waited for the army to "rescue" her, they'd string him up like they had the Hopis. Thankfully, the messenger had come while Silver Eagle and his friend were away for an overnight hunting trip to bring welcome elk game after the long winter. If he'd been here, he would have never let her go. She recalled the boyish enthusiasm on his face as he'd spoken of venturing to Cedar Canyon when the summer winds blew to enlist Father Gregory's help in uniting them in true Christian marriage. Father Gregory would help her make things right and keep his beloved Navajo safe after the army sent her home.

With her bonnet and calico dress long since disintegrated into rags, she tucked her journal into the pocket of her Navajo-style skirt. She held her breath as she eased between the sleeping forms of *Shima* and Sunshine.

Olivia placed a featherlight kiss on the child's head. Sunshine stirred but did not awaken. How she'd miss her. She glanced around the dark room lit only by the glowing embers of the fire, keeping her eyes averted from the spot on the opposite side of the hogan where Silver Eagle usually slept. Smoke spiraled to the hole in the roof and through it, starlight glistened.

How she'd miss all of this . . . and him.

Would Silver Eagle ever see these same stars in the years to come and think of her?

A sob caught in her throat. Her hand over her mouth stifling the sound, she moved toward the door before she lost her nerve. As she latched onto the door handle, *Shima's* gentle whisper floated out of the darkness.

"Go with God, my daughter. My prayers will follow you until you return to the red earth of the People."

Tears pouring down her cheeks, she dared not turn around but, putting one foot in front of the other, stepped across the threshold and into the night. Pulling the door shut softly, she took one last deep breath of clean mountain air and set off for her own long walk back to—not home—the *bilágaana* world.

Present-day, Early May

Her quest was at an end. In hindsight, perhaps nothing more than an attempt to connect to her adopted family through Olivia Thornton. Time to go home.

Erin spent the rest of the day packing her clothes into suitcases, boxing her books into cardboard cartons. All, except for one. The Narnia book by C.S. Lewis she left on one shelf, Adam's name inscribed on the flyleaf. She'd tell Johnny to give it to Adam when he replaced the vandalized furniture. She drove into Winslow to make copies of her cave painting photographs and delivered a set to Benallie, thanking him for his gracious administration of her internship.

On Sunday, dressed in casual slacks and an orchid-hued knit top, she packed the last of her things in the trunk and gave one last fond farewell to the little house on the mesa. Her eyes ached with unshed tears as she drove down the mesa toward town one last time.

She whispered good-bye to everything and everyone she passed. The Cultural Center. The trading post. Nia's apartment.

Her heart—like Olivia's—forever captive to the People and one man. But she'd learned there were higher obligations of love. She'd learned, like Abraham, a long, slow obedience.

To love Erin Dawson, you must also love her God.

Finally, no longer crawling off the altar, she'd placed Adam on the altar, too.

And left him there.

She parked the heavily laden Camry under the lone shade of a cottonwood. The church pews were packed for once. The curious and new believers drawn to Cedar Canyon Community for the first time since learning of Ben Tso's remarkable testimony. After years of faithful service and little fruit, she rejoiced for Johnny and the Lord's sake.

One final time, she led the People in songs of faith and hope. Her faith remained resolute. Her hope for belonging here extinguished.

Johnny caught her at the door where he stood greeting his flock after the service. "Iris wanted to know if you'd stay for lunch. There's someone I'd like you to meet."

It didn't take a rocket scientist to figure out who the mystery guest was, but Erin, weary in mind and body, didn't have it in her to resist. Thirty minutes later in Johnny's parsonage living room, she found herself staring into the face of Adam's mother. Hannah Silverhorn perched on the sofa, her straight, black hair held to the nape of her neck, chignon-style, with a large squash blossom clasp. Something in Hannah's expression brought Adam's face to mind and with it, a dull pain.

Hannah extended her hand with a warm smile. "My brother tells me, Miss Dawson, what a wonderful addition you have been to our little church. And how much you've meant to my son as well."

Apparently, not so much to Adam.

She took Hannah's long, slim fingers into her own. "I'm afraid I'm on my way out of town. My internship ended Friday, but I was delayed by . . ." A blush mounted in her cheeks at the memory of what she'd been delayed by at the hogan.

Hannah gestured to the couch. "Iris tells me she has dinner under control and I'd love to hear about your latest adventure." She cocked a mocking smile at her brother standing by the mantel. "Haven't yet seen hide nor hair of my illustrious son."

Johnny spoke from across the room. "How exactly did you happen to be in Petroglyph Canyon all by yourself on Friday?" He shook his head. "Not so smart a thing for you to do alone. I'd have taken you . . ."

Erin sighed. "I know you would've. It's a long story that actually started years ago when as a teenager I discovered a journal kept by one of my adopted family's relatives, who taught at the Cedar Canyon Mission School, concerning her six-month captivity with a group of Diné. It became sort of a quest . . ."

She glanced at the stucco ceiling, a niggling feeling at her conscience. "An obsession to find her."

"Find her?" Hannah leaned forward. "Wasn't she rescued?"

Erin nodded. "After being forcibly removed from the Rez, she was sent home to North Carolina. But you see she'd fallen in love with her captor and was determined to rejoin him."

She told them about her interviews and Susie's tale of a cave filled with one Diné artist's rendering of historical events surrounding the Cedar Canyon Diné people. "It probably sounds crazy to you, but I had this inexplicable yearning to discover if she ever made it back to Cedar Canyon and found Silver Eagle again."

"Silver Eagle?" Johnny straightened. "Why, Erin, you never said a word to me about this mission of yours."

A wry look crossed her face. He was right. Somehow her search for Olivia's final whereabouts had never come up with Iris or Johnny.

"You see, Olivia Thornton had a heart to see her adopted people come to know the Christ she loved. So despite the objections of her family who disowned her, she set out across the West to locate her true love and bring to his people the light of the gospel."

Hannah and Johnny swiveled to each other. "Livy," they breathed, wonder in their eyes.

"Livy?"

Hannah grasped Erin's hand. "Johnny get the albums."

She squeezed Erin's fingers as Johnny hurried from the room, calling for Iris. "Livy Thornton Silverhorn was my great-grandmother. Our name Silverhorn . . ."

Hannah reached for the album Johnny extended, Iris on his heels. ". . . was an Anglo combination of Silver Eagle's Diné heritage and 'horn' in Thornton."

Erin sank back against the cushions. "Here all along?"

She turned to Johnny, her eyes shining. "Olivia made it. She really made it. They found each other again?"

Hannah handed her an old photograph of a Navajo woman seated on a wooden ladder-back chair and a child standing next to her. The colors of the photo were fading, the Polaroid kind popular in the 1960s. "She lived to be an old woman. Outlived Silver Eagle by twenty years. They had a son, Jerome . . ."

"Our father, Tom, was Jerome's son," Johnny interjected. "Silver Eagle was quite the artist and drew those paintings in the cave. We always just called our great-grandmother Livy like her husband had every day of their married life."

Erin wasn't sure she was still breathing. "They lived here in Cedar Canyon?"

Iris shook her head. "No, up on Diamondback Ridge in Silver Eagle's clan hogan. Church meetings were held there for years until their son Jerome, with the help of families from town, built the current structure."

The hogan.

Erin closed her eyes to stop the flow of tears. She'd found her. Been in her home. Adam had mentioned a great-great-grandmother.

Her eyes flew open. "Was she happy there?"

Tears ran in rivulets down Hannah's smooth cheeks. "She was the most serene woman I've ever known."

Hannah jabbed at the picture clasped in Erin's hand. "Look for yourself. Here's a picture of me and our beloved Livy."

Erin examined the photo and its subjects. An old woman, her skin as wrinkled as a dried apple and as brown as a nut, clothed in the traditional Navajo blouse of velveteen purple and a sage green calico skirt.

"She liked purple," whispered Erin.

Hannah gave her a funny smile. "How did you know?"

The old woman's silver hair pulled into a bun, large turquoise earrings dangled from her ear lobes, the beaded *heishi* rope of three strands hung about her neck. Large sterling bracelets of turquoise encircled both her wrists and two enormous rings bedecked each hand.

But her eyes . . . ?

Her eyes were blue.

Life and light shone from her face. A resilience. An indomitability matched only by her adopted people, the Diné.

Hannah pointed. "That's me. I was probably six. Livy lived till she was . . . what, Johnny?"

Johnny tilted his head, thinking out loud. "One hundred and . . . five? No one ever thought of her as a *bilágaana*. She'd become one of the People."

The younger version of Hannah curled her fingers trustingly in Livy's hand where it rested on her grandmother's skirt. The little girl, her long shoulder-length black hair pulled back on one side with a barrette and dressed in a pair of denim shorts topped by a pale pink T-shirt that featured Barbie, peeped shyly at the camera.

"She and Silver Eagle are buried in the cemetery on the hill behind the church. Lydia and Adam were young when she died." Hannah bit her lip. "I'm not sure they remember her."

"He remembers."

She told them what Adam had said while at the hogan.

"A bad time." The corners of Hannah's mouth drooped. "I'd gone to the store and left the children with their father. I returned to find him passed out drunk on the couch and the children missing."

Iris settled herself on Hannah's other side and draped her arm around Hannah.

"Something told me to go to Hershal, their grandfather's ranch, a few miles away." Hannah twisted her hands in her lap. "I arrived to find Lydia screaming bloody murder out back and trying to drag her little brother out of the ceremonial hogan Hershal uses for his so-called initiation rites of the Red Brotherhood. They're paramilitary. As racist as any skinhead. When he was unable to get his son to sue for custody, he decided to kidnap my children, thinking I was too weak and powerless to stand up to someone like him." Hannah's voice broke.

Johnny's eyes glinted from his place by the mantel. "There's Rez scuttlebutt he's behind the most notorious of the Navajo street gangs, the RedBloods, too. That he finances them and arms them for his own purposes."

He snorted. "Uses them to line his coffers. Cause he sure didn't get rich off cattle on his ranch. And that's not even half of what rumor has that Hershal's done or plans yet to do."

She knotted her fingers together. "What do you mean?"

Hannah sighed. "Hershal Begay was a prominent leader back in the seventies at the height of the Red Power movement. He's always been slicker than oil and never charged, but he's on FBI watchlists for bombings and . . ." She looked away. "Several unsolved murders of Diné and Anglos who tried to stand in his way."

Johnny clenched his fist. "The Anglos, in particular . . . Their bodies were . . ." He swallowed hard.

Hannah dropped her eyes. "As a teenager, I believed the Begays to be engaged in a righteous cause." Her voice thickened. "For a time, I abandoned everything I'd been taught to believe. Adam's father seemed so exciting. But the pressure Hershal put on his only son broke him. Broke our marriage. And I realized Hershal wasn't about Indian justice so much as he was about vengeance."

Erin shook her head. "But why is Hershal so filled with hate?"

Johnny pursed his lips. "The mission schools."

Her eyes widened. "Like Olivia's school here in Cedar Canyon?"

"The Cedar Canyon School never reopened. But until my generation, the children were sent hours away from family per government policy to be educated and"—his lips twisted—"forcibly Christianized in the name of progress."

Johnny stiffened. "The Shepherd doesn't call His sheep that way. The so-called turn or burn approach. As a boy, far from home, Hershal was beaten and abused by the staff."

He grimaced. "And all in the name of God. That is why Hershal hates the Anglos. And, rejects their God."

"Does Adam know about this? The police?"

"Back then, Hershal had the tribal police under his control. They wouldn't help me rescue my children from his clutches. Told me to let the Navajo Tribal Court settle the issue."

Hannah jutted her chin. "Despite my best efforts to keep them apart, Hershal has been an unhealthy influence. Feeding on Adam's insecurity and his sense of tribal duty. His anger at the injustice with which all of us live with on a day-to-day basis on the Rez. Hershal excels in exploiting the weakness in others for his own gain. He's a master manipulator stoking the collective fear and prejudice of both sides."

Johnny gazed at her. "Hershal's lost all credibility with tribal leadership. Adam is his last hope to one day control the Council through the legitimate political process. He's getting old."

He grimaced. "Old like me. We've been locked in a war over Adam, to whom he would belong in a spiritual sense, from the time he was a boy."

"That day when I found them, Hershal wouldn't let go of his grip on Adam." Hannah shuddered. "I had to . . ."

She gulped, her eyes welling with tears. "I broke his hand prying his fingers off Adam. I put both children in the car and never stopped till I reached my parents and Livy up on Diamondback."

A truck door slammed outside. Johnny craned his head to look out the window. "It's Adam." Relief laced his voice.

Hannah jumped to her feet and had the door open before Adam reached the porch. "Adam." She threw her arms around him. Iris encircled them both with her arms.

Erin stood up, awkwardly fiddling with the hem of her shirt.

His eyes, peering over his mother's shoulder, narrowed at the sight of her. A look of—panic?—then anger. He shoved his mother and Iris away.

"What are you doing here?" He jabbed a finger in Erin's direction. "I hoped you'd left by now."

She flushed and her eyes fell to the floor.

"Adam. That's no way to talk to—"

He did an end run around his mother, leaving her and Iris gaping in the doorway.

"Doesn't matter anyway. Now I'll only have to say it once."

Johnny moved toward the center of the room where Adam glowered.

He reeled back from his uncle's outstretched arm. "I've quit the force. I'm going to live with my grandfather and do everything I can to restore my people to wellness and balance."

"No," Hannah choked out, her hand reaching to steady herself. Iris caught hold of her arm.

"Tell him," Hannah's eyes pleaded to Johnny and Erin. "Tell him the good news about Erin's discovery and our heritage. You can't abandon the faith of your fathers."

His jaw jutted. "I *am* finally finding the true Diné faith of my fathers."

Coldness crawled up Erin's spine at his words. "Olivia turns out to have found Silver Eagle after all. She spent her life at

Diamondback. She's your own great-great-grandmother, Livy Silverhorn."

Erin threaded a note of defiance into her voice. "Guess it makes us cousins, doesn't it, Adam?"

Something flickered for a moment before dying in his hard, flat eyes. "You're adopted. Not a real Dawson or Thornton. And I'm more Begay than Silverhorn."

"You can't tie yourself to that bitter old man." Hannah reached for Adam. "There is no harmony. There is no beauty in him."

He shook her free. "It just shows strong measures have to be taken to purge that *bilágaana* blood from my veins, too," he spat out. "The *bilágaana* way is corrupt and the Jesus Way makes you weak. I need to be strong for the People."

Johnny spoke. "Hatred and anger make you weak. You'll find no true strength there. Only lies, my son."

Adam turned on him. "I'm. Not. Your. Son. And you have kept me from my father's family and heritage long enough."

"Our people are in transition between two worlds." Johnny carefully gentled his tone. "We need a strong leader to show them how to find their way between the shallow materialism of the *bilágaana* world and the spiritually dark old ways. Teach them how to be a true Diné who keeps what is precious and unique from the hand of the Creator and yet follows the only true Shepherd, Jesus Christ."

Adam crossed his arms over his chest. "I knew you'd never understand what I need to do." He stomped to the door. "But I'm done with you and your Jesus."

"No, Adam." Anguish filled his mother's voice. "You're playing with the fire of hell. Hershal—he'll destroy your soul as he did your father's."

Adam let the door slam shut behind him.

Hannah buried her face in her hands. "Johnny, stop him."

Johnny shook his head. "All we can do now is pray for him, Hannah. Like we've never prayed before."

He and Iris led Hannah over to the sofa. He dropped to his knees beside his sister. The three of them bowed their heads and began to storm heaven's gates.

Slinging her purse over her arm, she dashed out the door after Adam.

Erin had a few choice words to say to Adam Silverhorn.

Adam had stopped on the bottom step of the porch, his face constricted. From there, he and Erin both heard his mother's disconsolate sobbing from inside the house.

Maybe God would give her the words to stop Adam from destroying himself and his family forever.

She halted one step behind Adam. His grandfather leaned against the side of Adam's truck, his hands stuffed nonchalantly in the pockets of his blue jeans. The look he sent her way was malevolent.

The eternal battle between darkness and the Light.

A fight for Adam's soul.

She breathed a quick prayer and caught hold of Adam's sleeve. "Don't do this, Adam. Please."

He pivoted so quickly on the step, she shrank back at the look on his face. "Thought you were going home. I *need* for you to go home."

Something flew right into Erin. "Why? Maybe I'll stay and watch you do this abominable thing. Forsaking everything you and your family have ever stood for in this community. Everything that is right and true and good."

Erin tossed her hair over her shoulder. "Maybe I'll stick around and watch the darkness slowly engulf you. Because it will. That kind of hatred always does."

His mouth trembled, but he set his jaw. "Maybe you're not so bright about some things. Don't mistake lust for something else." He laughed, the tone hard.

She flinched.

"That's all this is between you and me. New experience for a church girl like you, I'm sure." Adam shrugged. "Not so much for me. Time to surrender and admit this little mission project of yours, Adam Begay, is unredeemable."

"I don't believe you. Not about you and me. Not about Adam Silverhorn."

"Believe what you want. How clear does a guy have to be?" He snorted. "Can't say it's been fun. It's sure been different with you. But, babe, you're just not my type."

He smirked. "You said it yourself about me once. Can't seem to resist a little white sugar. And sugar is always sweet. While it lasts."

Pain sliced through her, but a voice in her head said to remember he was trying to distract and confuse her from the real issue.

Adam leaned in until she smelled the peppermint on his breath. "You and I are not so different. You have your family's destiny to fulfill. I have mine."

His lips twisted. "Have yourself some fine Aussie pups."

Adam gave her a mocking smile. "Me? Unlike this Silver Eagle hero of yours, I'm not into miscegenation."

She rocked back.

"Already too many *bilágaana* mongrels in my ancestry as it is, thanks to Olivia."

"You're making a mistake, Adam."

Adam laughed in her face. "You don't get it, do you, Erin Dawson? I am the mistake. I'm no good for you. You're no good for me. I'd only contaminate and pollute you. We'd only bring each other to ruin. We belong to different worlds. Different kingdoms."

His eyes glittered. "Different masters."

A power flooded Erin's being and the wisdom of words she didn't possess burst forth. Words for such a time as this.

"The Creator made each of us to long for Him." She jabbed Adam in the chest, punctuating every word. "Drugs."

He backed up.

"Women."

Another step.

"Money. Fame. Power."

His back against the porch railing, he could retreat no further.

"But until you bow your knee and come to Him, nothing—nothing—else will ever satisfy."

He stared at her, unblinking at the force of her words. She dropped her hand.

She stepped aside, giving him room to pass. Without another word, he moved past her and toward the truck where his grandfather waited.

"I'll never stop praying for you, Adam."

He paused mid-stride. "Have yourself a good life, Erin. I mean that."

Adam reached for the handle of the truck cab. Hershal grinned, wolflike, as he made his way around to the passenger side.

She watched until the red taillights of the truck disappeared in a cloud of dust down the lane. And with it, her dreams.

Erin got in her car and headed for Interstate 40, Winslow, and home. She cried all the way to Gallup. Her face streamed with tears, her body convulsed with great wracking sobs.

Afterward, she was never completely sure how she reached the New Mexico border in one piece. She remembered nothing of the journey. Not a town. Not a car. Not a saguaro on the way.

From Gallup to Albuquerque, she prayed as she'd never prayed before, battling the darkness that threatened Adam until her voice grew hoarse in the interior of her car with her beseeching. Her grief gradually gave way to peace.

By the time she crossed the North Carolina state line days later, she was able to hope—she prayed—one day the Lord would allow her to love some other man. And the man would love her back.

That maybe God would bless them with a family.

But she knew beyond a shadow of a doubt—with a sinking feeling verging on despair—that she'd never love any other man as she loved Adam Silverhorn.

When she pulled into the familiar oak-lined driveway of the home-place, Jill stood on the porch as if waiting for her, the sun beginning its molten gold descent into the distant tobacco fields.

With a sob, she sprang from the car. "How did you know? How did you know I needed you here?"

Jill's arms tightened convulsively around her.

The front door of the house creaked.

She looked over Jill's shoulder. Her mother hovered on the threshold. Tears like a fault line cracked the facade of her mother's self-imposed stoicism.

Her strong, unapproachable mother who'd pursued God with a zeal bordering on obsession. Who'd spent a lifetime trying to eradicate any signs of weakness in herself and others.

Who in village after village, armed only with a stethoscope and a Bible, had wrestled cholera to its knees.

Regret—and longing?—shimmered in her hazel eyes. "Erin, honey." She opened her arms. "I'm so sorry. For everything."

And Erin fell into them and came home at last.

22

THE DRUM HAMMERED RELENTLESS IN INTENSITY, POUNDING ITS MONOTO-nous, off-key rhythm into his chest. The cadence mesmerized and compelled. Crescendoing and decrescendoing.

Adam sat cross-legged in front of the fire opposite his grandfather in the ceremonial hogan. The first step into initiation into the Red Brotherhood. Part and parcel of earning his "colors." If he hadn't been so spent—he would have almost found it amusing.

Because, come full circle, Adam found himself forced to prove his allegiance to what amounted to a gang of domestic terrorists. Redskinned terrorists.

Colored quartz chunks, purple and black, and feathers lay in a circle between his body and the fire in a bizarre ritual neither truly Diné nor anything else outside the confines of his grandfather's twisted mind. The grueling tests of loyalty, mental and physical, exacted on Adam by Hershal's thugs over the last few days. Tests designed to break the will and numb the heart. Indoctrination worthy of the Taliban.

His stomach growled with the fierce hunger of a fast begun three days ago. His parched throat ached for a drop of liquid. The smoke rose skyward through the smoke hole. His eyes stung with the harsh fumes created from the bundles of herbs his grandfather continued to throw by the handfuls into the fire.

Adam sensed Hershal's mounting frustration. Adam had failed, so far, to enter the exalted state of altered mind and spirit from the ceremonial rituals. Hershal, himself, had grown hoarse over the course of the last forty-eight hours with the endless, repetitive, obscure chants.

"The white blood is strong in you." Hershal's face contorted. "It must be purged or you will never enter into the power that awaits you. The power that is your destiny. You must renounce all that came before and embrace your new loyalty to the Brotherhood."

He pulled a knife from underneath the mat. The crooked fingers of one hand splayed around the bone handle of the blade. "You must mark yourself, my son, bleed for the vision quest—the quest to restore the land to our people—to come upon you. To ready yourself for the mission to purge the land of the Anglos."

Adam's eyes widened. "W-what mission? What are you planning?"

Hershal held the handle of the knife out to him. "I can tell you nothing until you relinquish the pull of that other Spirit. The Jesus Way of your mother's clan."

Adam frowned, his brow creased, his mind clouded from the never-ending drone of the man's voice. And, the white, hallucinogenic powder Hershal had sprinkled on Adam's tongue two days ago, impatient to hasten his grandson's final surrender.

Hershal growled and thrust the knife at him, forcing Adam to grab it. He spat into the fire. The flames hissed and sparks flew. "They contest for you, even now. You must fight them, my son. Fight them. There is much work, much good, you and

I can do together. Once you've shown me you are done with the past."

Every muscle in Adam's body protested. He was so tired. They'd worn him down, physically, emotionally, and mentally. Yet this . . . this ordeal would never end until he did as the old man asked. Just do it, he told himself.

Get it over with. Then, you can eat platters of food. Sleep. And drink pitchers full of golden liquid.

Sweet tea?

His heart—not yet dead—ached at that memory.

No, never that—or her—again. He'd made the best choice for both of them. Made sure they each walked the path they were meant to walk. Separate destinies.

And this marking his grandfather required? This branding, not so unlike what Ben had done in the name of the RedBloods. This, Adam did, in a more worthy cause for the good of the People.

Wasn't it?

And before he changed his mind, he slashed himself across his abdomen. Not deeply. A flesh wound, but he cried out at the suddenness of the pain.

The blood dripped and pooled onto his buckskin breeches. The fog within the hogan grew. He barely discerned the figure of his grandfather across the fire.

"Again."

He sliced the underside of his forearm. Drops of blood spilled and puddled into the red dirt at his feet. He shrank from his grandfather and the darkness.

"Now with your lips you must curse the Council, the American imperialists, and the Shepherd of the Silverhorn flock."

Adam's breath hitched and he stared at his grandfather.

"I knew you would come to your destiny," Hershal's body writhed, unholy glee distorting his face. "Once I got rid of that *bilágaana* b—"

"You?" Adam's heart pounded. "It was you who ripped apart Erin's home. You who left that obscenity on her mirror."

The old man's face hardened. "She was not meant for you. Nor you for her. She made you weak. You must complete the ceremony to truly become one of us. One with our common aim to rid the land of the Anglo perversion and their Jesus pollution."

Hershal narrowed his eyes. "Curse their Shepherd. Curse Him and be done with their corruption of our homeland."

And then Adam remembered that terrible day when he was a boy.

The knife in his once small hand. His grandfather's urging. His sister's screaming.

Remembered his mother fighting the old man. The coolness of the pines that surrounded his great-great-grandmother's hogan on Diamondback. The pleasing warmth of her gnarled finger as she'd traced the sign of the cross on his forehead that day. The only thing, she told him, that could truly drive away the fear and the darkness.

"Say the words," his grandfather hissed.

Adam's lips tightened. "I-I," he swallowed past the bile clogging his throat. "I will not."

His hand slick with his own blood, he gripped the knife.

"Jesus, help me," he whispered. Gritting his teeth, he made one more small slash across the jagged cut he'd made on his forearm. A bar forming a lower case "t".

And, a cross.

He threw his arm up toward his grandfather's face. Hershal reared.

A strong wind, a cyclone of wind, blew into the hogan, extinguishing the fire, knocking his grandfather onto his face.

"Nooo!" His grandfather howled, spitting sand. "You mustn't fail the People. You mustn't fail me. Or our glorious future."

Adam struggled to his feet, swayed as dizziness overtook him. Hershal coiled his fist around Adam's ankle with the strength of ten men. Digging and rooting in his flesh.

Straining to pull free, Adam called into the wind, "Jesus." And his grandfather retracted his claws, cringing, his wizened bare arms shielding his head.

Johnny had been right. No weakness in this Shepherd Jesus. Only strength. Real strength. True love made His sheep strong.

Adam lunged for the opening.

"Come back," Hershal screamed in unfettered rage. "You are the one marked. You must fulfill the plans that have been made for you."

"I am." Made before the foundation of the world.

Adam stumbled out into the glare of the noonday sun. And he knew that Hershal was the one his uncle had warned him of, the true wolf at the hogan door, preying upon the soul of the People.

"There will be others waiting to take the place that was yours by birthright. This is not over between you and me, Silverhorn. We are many. We will never surrender the fight."

And there would be others. Always others lured, like the youth to gangs, by the promise to be as gods. Drawn to control the power of life and death. Those maimed by bitterness who craved vengeance.

Empty promises. Dreams that became nightmares.

He managed to totter half a mile down the trail back to his grandfather's prosperous-looking ranch house before his knees gave way and he fell into the sand, his blood mixing and mingling with the red dust of the earth.

Adam angled his face to the turquoise sky. "Thank you."

He closed his eyes and drifted for a long space of time.

A clean, fragrant aroma of sage tickled his nostrils. Breathing deeply, he opened his eyes. The sun had moved several paces in its daily trek across the sky.

A phrase Erin had read to him came back to his mind. Something about drawing near to a throne to receive mercy and find grace. But where did one find this throne of grace?

Dragging himself to where he'd parked his truck three days ago, Adam reached for the handle on the door and heaved himself to his feet. He swayed, falling forward against the side of the cab.

Sticky with grit and perspiration, his sunburned chest twinged as his skin rubbed raw against the truck. How long had he lain in the dirt? His head swiveled around, scoping the terrain for any sign of his grandfather. But the desert expanse was empty of any sign of human occupation. The ranch house lay darkened. His grandfather's pickup no longer rested beside the barn.

Hershal had left him to die in the baking sun. Adam was vaguely surprised his grandfather and his would-be anarchists hadn't staked him to the sand, poured agave over him and left him to the ants.

Got to get help. Probably dehydrated, with a touch of sunstroke, too.

Wrenching open the door, he nearly toppled off balance as it swung on its hinges. Clutching his good arm around his belly wound, he hauled himself across the seat. Exhausted with the effort, he laid his head upon the steering wheel as the world refused to stop whirling.

Thank God he'd left the keys in the ignition.

Another prayer? Erin would be so proud.

He let one corner of his mouth tilt up in a smile and winced as the dry, cracked corner of his lips protested. With a twist of his wrist, he cranked the engine. He knew where he had to go first. If God would just grant him the grace to get there.

Somehow, he managed to get himself to Cedar Canyon, the blood coagulating on the steering wheel as he drove half-slumped over the wheel. He passed the Cultural Center and trading post. Tulley and Nia emerged from Mamacita's, recognition followed by concern on their faces as he drove past. He couldn't stop, though. Not until he'd made his peace with the one he'd wronged most of all.

Tires spinning on the gravel, he jolted to a stop at the entrance to Cedar Canyon Community Church. Pushing open the heavy truck door with his shoulder, he thrust first one leg out and then the other. When the soles of his feet impacted tiny pebbles, he realized that he was still barefoot.

Just as well. To come humble. And broken.

Leaving the truck dinging with the door open and the engine running, he hauled himself up the wide adobe steps and turned the knob on the front door, thankful his uncle kept the structure open for all who might need refuge.

And if ever someone needed refuge, it was him today.

The sanctuary deserted, he stumbled forward down the center aisle. Bright shafts of the setting sun created a pool of lasered light directly in front of the offertory table and the large sterling cross resting upon it.

Mercy and grace. Here. At the foot of the cross.

"God?" His voice choked in a sob, his unworthiness spewing from the deep caverns of his being. "Forgive me. Will you cleanse the rotten filthiness in me?"

Filled with loathing for his own pride. His self-sufficiency. The festering anger.

Longing for wholeness, peace, healing.

Tears ran like the snow melt of spring runoff down his cheeks. His hands gripped the edge of the wooden table. The light in a sudden flash from the window blazed against the silver of the cross, blinding him.

A bird's sibilant call echoed from the gnarled piñon tree outside the church. A sound of hope and expectancy. A holy hush fell over the room and Adam.

His hands let go of the table. His eyes closed and his head dropped to his chest.

Flinging his arms wide, Adam Silverhorn fell to his knees, bowing his heart. He received mercy at last.

And found unmerited grace.

His shoulders hunched forward, peering down the long oak-lined driveway, Adam hoped he hadn't taken a wrong turn. GPS and the lady at the corner gas station couldn't both be wrong. Fields of tobacco sweltered in waves of palpable heat. This had to be the right place, though the cashier had given him a funny look when he'd asked for directions to the Dawson place.

The nicotine-stained teeth of the wiry woman behind the counter had grinned at him for a moment. She quirked penciled-in brows. "Weh—ell," she drawled out in the flat intonations he'd almost forgotten from his Fort Bragg days. "I suppose it's better late than never."

Weird. And he hoped—prayed—prophetic.

The August sun beat down upon the gunmetal gray Ford Focus rental. He fiddled with the air conditioning, turning it up one more notch. He ran a finger between the collar of his blue oxford shirt and the sweat around his neck. He had, unfortunately, forgotten until now how humid a Carolina summer could be.

He glimpsed a cluster of green tar-papered tobacco barns. And then ahead, an old, two-story white farmhouse. His foot eased off the accelerator and he looked about for a place to park. At least forty vehicles, sporting license plates from North Carolina and its three surrounding sister states, sat baking in the afternoon sun, parked haphazardly under the oaks and pecan trees on the front lawn. Rusty old pickups, sleek and luxurious BMWs and Mercedes, mid-sized Chrysler sedans.

Great. His timing perfect as always. He'd arrived in the middle of a family party.

Clusters of people—well-dressed, Sunday best people—strolled underneath the shade of the hardwood trees. Pairs grouped on the wide front porch with heaping plates of food. People mingled and mixed, venturing in and out of the house through the screened front door.

No help for it. The urgency mounted in his chest. He swung the vehicle between a black Mercedes E350 and a white Ford Taurus. He sat for a moment, his fingers gripping the wheel, trying to gather his nerve.

He'd sold his truck to buy the airline ticket. He'd turned in his resignation for good this time. Though Tulley, the newly appointed Chief of Police, had merely smiled and stuffed it in a bottom drawer. "I'm going to consider this a long overdue, unpaid sabbatical." Tulley shook his hand. "And if you can, Adam, bring her back to her people."

Adam darted a glance at himself in the rearview mirror, frowned, and tried to smooth his close-cropped hair into a semblance of order. Didn't help he'd spent the last thirty miles raking his hand through it. He sighed.

He looked like some kind of wild—a smile quivered at the word he'd been about to say. A word Erin herself would never have used to describe him. A word that might be the least of what Erin Dawson would say to him today if she was indeed here at the Dawson family home-place. He grimaced, thinking of his last words to her.

Quit stalling, Silverhorn.

He swallowed past a lump in his throat. Better to get it over with one way or the other. The next few minutes—if she was here in Carolina—would change his life forever.

And if she wasn't here?

He patted the envelope of money on the seat beside him that Iris, his mother, and the rest of the church had with typical Diné ingenuity put together to give him the resources he needed to make things right. If she wasn't here—next stop Papua New Guinea.

Get. Out. Of. The. Car. He told his legs. He'd faced down the Taliban, drug cartels, and native gangs. Nothing to be scared of here, he told himself as he forced his hand to grab hold of the door handle. Nothing but a bunch of Southern missionary people. His new brothers and sisters in Christ.

Yeah, right. Erin would probably send him packing.

With her granddaddy's twelve-gauge shotgun.

Exactly what he deserved. What he wanted—needed—was a little grace, undeserved favor he'd learned in the last three months under his uncle's discipleship. And, a lot of mercy from Erin.

He forced his feet onto the narrow, pebbled walk leading to the porch. As he passed, people stopped eating to smile and nod welcome to him. The hum of happy, contented people chowing down on good food surrounded him. Clinking sounds of tall, iced tea beverages in the partygoers' hands. A smoky, succulent aroma of roasted pig floated through the summer air.

Under any other circumstances, his taste buds would have been salivating. Right now all he wanted to do was throw up in the blue snowball bushes that wrapped around the base of the house. Adam wiped his perspiring palms down the length of his jeans. He was so not dressed for this fancy shindig.

Just as well. Better to come humble. And begging.

Mounting the three, wide-planked steps, his heart hammered. If she was here . . . His pulse leaped at the chance of seeing her one more time, even if she sent him away forever.

Screwing up his courage, he raised his fist to knock when the door swung open. A fiftyish lady, with short, salt and pepper hair, stood bedecked in eggshell blue silk on the other side of the screen door. Her back ramrod straight, her agate green eyes sized him up and down.

"Saw you coming." Her patrician face remained expressionless. "Wondered when you'd show."

"Uh . . . Yes, ma'am." His eyes cast about wildly, anywhere and everywhere, for some backup. She'd seemed to know who he was. Of course, he was probably the only Indian around here for miles.

The lady continued to stare at him as if she expected him to say something else.

He floundered. "Mrs. . . . ?"

She sighed. He'd disappointed her somehow, he could tell.

"You want me to go get Erin for you?" She prompted, drawling the words out as if he was slow-witted.

His cue. "Yes, ma'am. Please. I'm—"

She'd already turned her back to him, in the process of walking away. "Oh, I know who you are, young man." She fluttered a hand at him over her shoulder. "Wait here. I'll be right back as soon as I can pull her away from the wedding reception." She disappeared down a hallway toward the back of the house.

He gasped and fell back a step. Wedding reception? Had he arrived in the middle of Erin's—?

Better late than never, he recalled the gas station attendant's words. She'd obviously mistaken him for a wedding guest.

A tall, blond man appeared at the door, dressed in a tuxedo. He pushed the screen door open, stepped through, and let it bang shut behind him. He crossed his arms over a heaving chest, a shiny gold wedding band gleaming in the Carolina sunshine. He planted his feet shoulder width apart in a wide stance. "You've got no business here, Silverhorn. Erin doesn't need to ever lay eyes on the likes of you again."

Was that a trace of a British accent in the man's voice? Somehow, he had expected a more pronounced tone, given the Aussies he'd seen on TV. Adam fell back another step until his back touched one of the half-pillared columns holding up the porch.

And him.

Erin's groom. He'd waited too late to come. Adam struggled to hold back the cry that threatened to erupt from his chest.

He'd lost her. For good. Clamping down his jaw, he turned to go. The hinges of the screen door creaked.

"Adam?"

His gut clenched at the sound of her voice. He closed his eyes. Walk away, he told his feet. Go. Before you humiliate yourself even further.

"That is you, isn't it, Adam?"

Something in her voice. He forced himself to face her.

Erin stood next to her groom, as remote as a glacial peak. Her lovely tea-length lavender dress billowed about her legs in the wafting breeze. For once, she wore her hair long. Tendrils fell in soft waves around her face. Her green eyes round with astonishment, he noticed she wasn't smiling.

Not the Erin he loved. Someone different. Someone else's bride.

He shuffled his feet on the step.

The Aussie's eyes narrowed. "I told him to go, Erin. No point in him . . ."

She curled her fist and punched her new husband in the bicep.

Adam blinked. What sort of marriage had Erin . . . ?

"Stop telling me what to do. I don't care if it is your wedding day. You're not the boss of me, Todd."

That sounded like the old, feisty Erin he remembered. But wait a minute, wasn't Todd her—?

He gulped, his relief so profound he swayed against the column. He pointed a shaky finger at Todd. "He's not your new Aussie doctor husband?"

"My husband?" Frowning, she shook her head. "Whatever made you think I . . . ?"

Todd straightened, rubbing his arm. "I do happen to be a doctor. And I did just become a husband."

He eyed his sister, a note of indignation in his voice. "Just trying to protect you, baby sister. A thankless job as usual." He shot a glance over to Adam.

She placed her hands on her hips. "I'm not a baby who needs protecting, Todd Harold Dawson. I can take care of myself."

Adam commanded his pulse to stop galloping like an out-of-control palomino. She wasn't married. It might not be too late. God had given him a second chance.

Todd sighed. He licked his lips. "Right. Got it." He adjusted his tie, lots of white cuff showing. "Well, then, I leave you two to sort things out."

"So P.O.S.H. Port out, starboard home." She rolled her eyes. "British boarding school," she said in an aside to Adam. Standing on tiptoe, she planted a quick kiss on Todd's cheek.

"I do appreciate the sentiment behind your effort. But go find your bride and cut the cake." She gave Todd a shove toward the door.

He sniffed. "Good luck to you, Silverhorn. You'll need it." Todd wrenched open the door, sticking his head out once more. "And I'll have you remember when my sister does get married, she'll be wearing white." He slammed the door behind him. "Not lavender . . ." His words floated out to them.

The porch had cleared of all other occupants except for him and Erin. She crossed her arms. Her big eyes sandpapered him. "So what *are* you doing here, Silverhorn?"

23

August, 1964

WITH A SWISH, THE OLD WOMAN DIVIDED THE WARP EVENLY, BRINGING HER right hand in a quick, gliding motion across the loom. She lifted the treadle rod and thrust the batten through the warp, holding the place open. In an economy of effort, her dexterity honed through decades of practice, she inserted the red yarn. Beating down the wool on the warp with a whoomp, whoomp, whoomp, her ears cocked at the sound of tires crunching on gravel.

Her son, Jerome, punctual to the minute.

Time to venture down Diamondback Ridge to the trading post in Cedar Canyon. Time to trade the wool from her sheep for winter supplies. But per Diné custom, she knew her visitors would wait outside until she offered the invitation to draw closer to the hogan.

Pushing away from the loom, the old woman placed her wrinkled hands upon the knees of her sage green, three-tiered skirt and heaved herself to her feet. She said a special prayer of thanksgiving, as always, to the memory of her dear *Shima* for her patience in teaching the ways of the People so long ago. Maybe she'd have time for a visit in town this weekend with little Sunshine, an old woman now like herself, a Singer married to the son of Silver Eagle's good friend. Her own hogan overflowing with a swarm of children, grandchildren, and greats.

The old woman smiled as she studied her reflection in the looking glass hanging by its cord on the wall of her earthen hogan home. And who'd have ever guessed she would have lived to be this old? Wrinkled as an old apple. Wrinkled on the outside maybe.

Her blue eyes shone, unfaded by life and time. Full of vim and vigor on the inside. But like the beloved Lottie Moon of her childhood, she knew she'd be immortal until her work for the Lord was finished.

Not one day more. Not one day less.

She reached for the door, swinging it wide and waved at her family waiting in the Jeep. Jerome—now a fine preacher, just like his father, Silver Eagle, before him. She sighed. Jerome waved back from the vehicle. Not a day went by she didn't miss her dearest soul mate, though he'd passed to Glory many years before.

Her granddaughter-in-law waved from the passenger seat. Two small, black heads bobbed from the back of the Jeep. Scrambling from the automobile, a boy and a girl, her great-grandchildren, raced across the yard toward her. Their sneakered feet sprayed gravel.

"Livy! Livy!"

Reaching her at the same time, she wrapped her arms around them both, bending over their tiny frames. She'd had a dream last night about the two of them. The People set great store by their dreams.

Something unique and special the DreamGiver Creator had given to the Navajo. With which He often communed with His Diné flock. As He had with the patriarchs. Something the over-educated *bilágaana* were too enlightened now to heed.

"Brought you some pecans from the trading post." Her granddaughter-in-law, Ruby, arrived more sedately than her offspring, holding aloft a small burlap sack. "Your grandson's meeting us at the post. He's requested you teach me how to make that special pie of yours."

Livy beckoned her visitors inside the hogan. "Come in. Come in."

The children's arms encircled her and the three of them moved as one, Here-We-Go-'Round-the-Mulberry-Bush style.

Livy gestured at her son. "Got some fry bread on the stove." He smacked his lips and headed over.

Something about the shape of his face brought to mind her long dead brother, Charles, and the first of her dreams. While Jerome's son served his *bilágaana* country on a remote Pacific island, she'd dreamed of Charles. Vivid sights. Pungent smells. As real and Technicolor as the moving pictures in Holbrook.

Clad in filthy rags, a wide-brimmed, Chinese coolie hat shading his face, her brother knelt on the ground, his head bowed, his hands clasped in prayer. From his lips she'd heard his prayers for his enemies. His prayers for the preservation of his wife and child. His plea for forgiveness for the sister he'd wronged so long ago.

Then with a whistle, the scythe—wielded by the snarling face of the Enemy in a soldier's uniform—severed her brother's head from his body. His body slumped. His head rolled forward in the mud. Though she'd woken Silver Eagle with her cries, the dream had indeed been the Lord's gift to her, knowing in the end her brother's heart had been reconciled and at peace with hers.

Ruby wandered over to the loom, inspecting her latest project. "This one's going to be beautiful, Grandmother."

Livy shook her head. "Maybe. But I'll never have the gift for it you have. Never produce those works of art the tourists buy from you at the trading post." She shrugged. "It'll keep me warm this winter."

"You're too modest." Ruby moved toward the children who'd discovered the fry bread doughnuts Livy had whipped up as a surprise. "Johnny? Did you ask Grandmother before you helped yourself?"

Johnny's pudgy cheeks bulged, packed with fried dough. His eyebrows arched. "Pwease, may I, Grandmother?"

Livy laughed. "I made them for you. Go ahead." Her dream regarding the boy had been pleasant. He'd become a mighty wielder one day of the Sword.

Ruby ruffled the tousled hair of her son. Already it hung long, braided in the three-ply strength of the Diné. Unlike his grandfather, Jerome, or his parents, he and his sister were safe from being sent far away from home under the federal government's new policy of building schools on the Rez. No more mission schools.

"Y'all wait here. I'll load the bundles for you, *Shima*." Jerome stuffed one last piece of bread into his mouth before darting out the door.

Johnny followed hot on his heels.

Y'all.

The last remaining trace of her Southern heritage spoken now only by herself and her son. She'd endeavored her whole life among the People to borrow the best of the Anglo world and retain the best of the Diné.

Her thoughts drifted to her sister, AnnaBeth. Ten years after she'd dreamed of Charles, the Lord had bestowed His second dream gift upon her.

She'd seen once more the white clapboard farmhouse surrounded by oaks. The powder blue hydrangeas. Smelled the sweet perfume of the Bourbon roses.

One last glimpse of her baby sister wizened by cancer upon her bed. Heard the last words upon her lips. Words of gratitude for the faithful man at her side. Words of inspiration to the children who surrounded her. Words of blessing upon Olivia and her family.

"I promised Tom"—Ruby's husband, Livy's grandson—"I'd get a picture of you here at Diamondback with each of the children."

Livy frowned. "What you want with a picture of an old woman like me?"

"Now Grandmother. Don't be shy." Ruby picked up the chair in front of the loom. "Let's take it outside where the light's better."

Livy threw up her hands. "Just cause that boy got a brand new camera for Christmas doesn't mean he has to document every blessed occasion."

Hannah tugged at her skirt, pulling her out the door after Ruby.

Livy plucked at imaginary threads only she could see on the purple velveteen blouse. "I'm hardly dressed for a picture today."

"You look beautiful as usual in your purple."

"Not exactly fashion model material," Livy grumbled but allowed the small girl to lead her to the chair Ruby had stationed beside the exterior wall of the hogan.

Hannah stroked the intricate curlicues of the oversized ring on Livy's fingers. "Got all your jew-ry on, Grandmother."

Livy plopped her old bones down. "'Cause we're going to town."

She leaned her head toward Hannah. "I'll tell you a secret." She held one finger to her lips.

Hannah's eyes widened.

"I'm going to give that ring to you someday. I know you'll find a good purpose for it."

Hannah touched the wide band of turquoise set in sterling that encircled Livy's wrist. "This, too?"

Ruby frowned, lowering the camera from her face. "Hannah Silverhorn."

Livy chuckled, waving a hand. The silver and the stones glimmered under the cloudless, turquoise sky. "They're all going to her. Hannah's got her own gift with the stones. They speak to the child."

Ruby backed away a few feet, angling the camera for the best shot. "Look at me, Hannah and Grandmother."

Livy placed her hand upon Hannah's small black head. Hannah looked at her, love shining from her face.

"Oh, Hannah," Livy whispered. "What gifts the Lord has for you."

Sudden tears winked from her eyes. In the dream last night, she'd seen the sweet girl turn into a rebellious teenager who'd temporarily departed from the shelter of her faith and parents. Her own heart ached with the pain that followed Hannah's defiant, unequally yoked marriage. But the Shepherd, after breaking Hannah's metaphorical leg so she'd not wander again, had carried this precious lamb back safely to His fold. His Hand would remain upon her Hannah all the days of her life.

And on Hannah's children, yet unborn.

"Hold still," Ruby called.

They faced Ruby and the camera. Livy wrapped her arm around Hannah. Her other hand she rested on her skirt. Nestling closer, Hannah curled her fingers into Livy's. Her brown eyes peeped shyly out at the world.

"Smile," Ruby commanded.

Livy rearranged the wrinkles on her face. The tangy scent of Ponderosa pine perfumed the air. The bleating of the sheep rose from the corral behind the barn.

She smiled at the God-carved red rock sculptures on the horizon. Her world. The Diné world.

A rugged existence. A good life. God's gift to her.

Not one day more. Not one day less.

With a flash, the shutter clicked.

Present-day, August

Erin's eyes drank her fill of him. The blueness of the button oxford shirt, open at the neck. The Wrangler jeans.

Three long, agonizing months since she'd last laid eyes on Adam. A sight she'd never thought to enjoy again. Her arms wrapped protectively about her, she willed herself to not be a fool by lowering her guard.

His face seemed older to her, his eyes more somber. She searched his features for signs of the wickedness he'd given himself to. Losing Adam to the darkness had almost killed her. She couldn't give him the power to maim her today. Not when she was just now getting her life back together.

Adam took a step toward her. Her chest tightening, she stood her ground. Seeing her set face, he halted. "I wanted to let you know since you'd said you were praying for me." He swallowed convulsively. His black eyes dropped to the toes of his brown boots.

Those ubiquitous, cowboy casual boots. She bit her lip. Willing herself not to remember . . .

"I—" His gaze shot to hers. "I left my grandfather after three days."

Adam shook his head at the memory. "I stood on the brink of the Abyss and I saw . . ." His face constricted. "I couldn't go through with it."

He held out his forearm. A pale white scar marred his bronzed skin.

It looked . . . like a cross?

His eyes never left her face. "I remembered your words to me and long ago what Livy had told me."

A humility and a strange vulnerability filled his face. Something she'd never before seen in the arrogant, self-sufficient Adam Silverhorn.

"I did what my mother and Uncle Johnny have been telling me my whole life I needed to do. It's been like you said." His black eyes shone. "A journey. No, more like an adventure."

He smiled. "I bowed my knee to my Redeemer."

She wobbled on the step. Her pulse quickened.

He didn't—Adam's not . . . lost anymore.

She released the deep breath she hadn't realized she'd been holding and threw her arms around him. "Oh, Adam. The answer to my prayers for you to find God's best, most precious gift of salvation."

Adam buried his face into her hair. His breath tickled her neck. Inhaling her.

His arms tightened around her. Tingles like frolicking dragonflies goosebumped her bare arms. The old, not-to-be-trusted chemistry between them.

But then, he stiffened. He released her and retreated so a space opened between them. "Sorry about that." Once again he fixed his gaze on the tips of his boots.

Her heart pounding, she gestured to the top step. "Let's sit down. I want to hear about this great adventure of faith you've started."

Adam sank on the wooden planked step, his back against the column. She joined him, tucking the folds of her filmy lavender bridesmaid dress under her, careful to leave a gulf between their bodies.

For her sake.

Adam had been here all of five minutes and already toppled the three months of defenses she'd managed to erect around her heart. She hugged her knees, shivering at the memory of her unbidden response to his touch moments before.

He cocked his head at her, a question in his eyes. A question he didn't, thankfully, voice. Adam told her quietly about all he had experienced in his grandfather's hogan. How in the end, he'd chosen Light over Hershal's darkness.

Adam related how Johnny had begun discipling him and Ben, serving a short prison sentence for his part in the gang's criminal activities at a minimum-security juvenile detention center. Of all he'd learned. Of all he still hungered to learn from God's holy Word.

How God had stirred his heart as he'd poured himself into Cedar Canyon Community Church. Started a prison ministry with Ben and other former gang members. The online Bible college degree he'd decided to pursue.

Adam jerked his head in the direction of the parked vehicles on the lawn. "Iris, Nia, Sani—I've got at least twenty letters addressed to you in the car."

She smiled. "I've missed them."

Adam's eyes searched hers. "I've missed you."

Her smile faded.

Oh, God . . . Could he really mean what she hoped he meant?

He ran a callused hand through his short-cropped hair, always a sign, with Adam, of extreme frustration. "I tried everything I could think of to get you out of my head and my heart, Erin Dawson. I've run myself ragged 24/7. Yet when I drop into bed at night, yours is the last face I see and the first when I wake up in the morning." He lowered his shaking hand and clenched his fist in his lap.

Nervousness?

"I'm clean." He gave a short, incredulous chuckle. "My heart and mind pure for the first time since I was a boy."

His gaze broke away from hers, flitting toward the sound of the mockingbird perched in the oak that overshadowed the porch. "But I've fought coming to find you all these months because you deserved better than me. You were always meant—chosen—for someone better than me."

"Adam." She laid a hand upon his arm, covering the scar cross. "Me, my dad, Uncle Johnny, and you. We're equal at the foot of the cross. Not perfect people. Just redeemed sinners. That's what grace is all about."

He sighed. "I'm still trying to wrap my head around that one, Erin. Grace . . ."

"Aren't we all?"

He covered her hand with his, absently running his thumb across the back of her hand. "You took off and nobody knew where you'd gone. If I hadn't found you here, I planned on hopping a plane for Guinea, throwing myself on your father's mercy and offering to clean latrines or anything else for the chance to be near you again."

She gasped. "New Guinea? Why would you leave the Rez? It's your home. You love it there."

The raw honesty in his eyes stole her breath. "Because I love you more. Always have. Since you almost stabbed me to death with peanut butter and strawberry jam." A tentative smile lifted one corner of his mouth.

Adam's voice dropped. "You were right that last day. I was lying, trying to convince you there was nothing between us but our flesh . . . "

His eyes darted away. "Trying to lie to myself."

Adam twined his fingers through hers. "Because truth is, I've loved you from the beginning. When I couldn't tell you how I felt because of my undercover work. When you were forbidden to love me while I was an unbeliever. At the hogan when I was afraid of what loving you would cost me."

He snorted. "Some freedom that turned out to be. Chains of a different kind, I forged for myself." He angled toward her.

A shadow of uncertainty darkened his eyes. "If not Guinea, I'd have tried Sudan or Peru next. Anywhere you were is my true home. God kept nudging me until I got on that plane in Phoenix to find you."

He straightened. "I'm willing to do whatever it takes, for however long it takes, to convince your family I am now a man of integrity, of character. A man who can be trusted with their daughter's heart. A second chance with you."

Adam licked his lips. "And I'll volunteer for anything at your family's mission outposts until I can convince their daughter to love me back."

She leaned back. "So that's your plan? The best Diné strategy a warrior like Adam Silverhorn can come up with?"

Her eyebrows arched. "To wear out your welcome until you can wear me down to loving you?"

Adam blinked and his mouth fell open.

She put a finger to his mouth, stalling his attempt to speak. "Don't bother." She laughed.

He flinched. "Erin, I'm sorry for the things I said and did." He gripped her hand. "If you'd let me, I'd spend the rest of my life, showing you how sorry—"

"Don't bother."

He let go of her hand and started to rise, his back scraping the side of the column, a stricken look etched across his beloved chiseled features. She captured his face between her hands.

"Don't bother, because I already love you. Since you walked in all broad-shouldered and handsome in your tribal policeman get-up and sassed me the first day we met at the Cultural Center. *Ayoo aniinish'ni*, Adam Silverhorn. I . . . love—"

Before she could finish, his lips found hers. Peppermint . . .

She wrapped her arms around his neck, her fingers beneath the black hair on the back of his head. The rising crescendo of a Carolina wren broke the silence, filling the August sky with notes of utter rapture.

"*Ayoo aniinish'ni*, Erin," he whispered, his forehead pressed against hers. "I was afraid I'd lost you forever."

His eyes went opaque, his breath ragged and uneven. "God is so good."

Tears welled in her eyes. "Yes, He is."

Her heart swelled with gratitude. For God's faithfulness. For this unexpected blessing after her long obedience.

Adam draped his arm across Erin, tucking her head into the hollow underneath his chin. If she lived to be a hundred, she'd never forget this moment, the scent of her grandmother's late-blooming Bourbons permeating the air, the moment when she and Adam found each other again.

Perhaps a moment echoing through time and space, not unlike the moment when Olivia Thornton had reunited with her beloved Silver Eagle half a world away.

His lips brushed her hair. "So where are *we* going? New Guinea? Peru? Sudan?" A smile stretched across his face.

She cut her eyes at him. "What makes you think I'm going to any of those places?"

His brow furrowed. "But your family? The pressure?"

She traced the sign of the cross on his arm. "Funny thing about families." She told him about the e-mail she'd sent her sister, Jill, while in Cedar Canyon.

"Jill called Mom long distance from Peru and told them how I felt they didn't know or love the real Erin Dawson only the idea of their mission project, adopted daughter of medical missionaries, following in their footsteps."

She smiled at him as tears winked out of her eyelids. "By the time I drove here from Arizona, Jill and her family were here, Todd and his fiancée, and Dad. Mom met me on the porch before I even got into the house. We had a long family meeting. Shed a lot of tears."

Erin laughed. "And that was just Dad's contribution."

She squeezed his hand. "I've never felt so close to either of them before. They told me to make my own decisions about where God was leading me."

He planted a kiss on the top of her head. "Erin, I'm so glad for you."

"Dad also said I have a way with indigenous people. In-dig-e-nous."

Her lips twitched. "I've only begun to look into it. But I hear they could use a good cultural anthropologist in Ute country."

She cocked her head. "Or maybe with the native people in the Dakotas." Her eyes twinkled.

Adam's eyes widened. He inclined his head in a courtly bow. "Well, on behalf of in-dig-e-nous people everywhere, we of the Navajo Nation would respectfully ask you to consider joining our tribe."

He cleared his throat, his heart in his eyes. "Specifically the Silverhorn clan forever."

Adam lifted her hand to his mouth and with the gentlest of kisses, brushed his lips across her fingertips. From out of his front pocket, he drew a silver filigreed ring. A center mounted turquoise surrounded by tiny diamonds.

"The stone came out of the ring Livy wore every day of her married life. The rest my mother designed with you in mind, hoping you'd, and I quote, 'Take her boy out of his misery.' End quote."

A warm glow suffused her being.

Thank you, thank you, God. For Your Son and this new Diné son of Yours.

She smiled. "An offer I plan to take your mother up on, Adam Silverhorn. I do so like your mother."

"And how 'bout me?"

She straightened out her hand. He slid the ring onto her finger. "You're okay, too, I guess." She held the ring up to the dappled light.

"You guess?" he teased. "When? How soon can I start calling you Erin Silverhorn?"

The grin, for which Adam Silverhorn was famous, split across his face.

She sighed.

Dazzling. Mega-wattage. At close range, a person could be fairly blinded. A blindness she'd embrace for the rest of her life.

"As soon as we can decently expect my mother to put on another wedding," she promised. "Would you consider spending the honeymoon . . . ?" A furious blush coated her face from the roots of her hair to her neck.

He shifted closer. "Now you're talking. Anywhere. Anywhere you want to go."

She beckoned with her forefinger.

He bent his head as she whispered.

Adam stared at her. "The hogan? You want to spend our honeymoon at the hogan?"

Blushing again, she nodded. "First, you need to meet my family. Todd and my mother you've already met."

He choked, panic streaking through his eyes. "That was your mother at the door?"

She gave him a peck on the lips. "I've told them about you."

He closed his eyes. "That's what I was afraid of."

She poked him in the chest. "Only good things."

He sniffed. "Yeah. I could tell from my reception committee."

She placed her hand to his cheek. "They are going to love you and your heart for God just like I do."

Adam rose and offered her his hand. "Sure. Introduce me."

He gulped. "But do you think I could get some sweet tea before the Inquisition begins?"

Adam pulled Erin to her feet and drew her into the circle of his arms. "Just one taste?"

Resting her hands on the flat of his shoulders, on tiptoe she leaned her mouth into his. He gave her that lovely, crooked smile. His lips parted as he lowered his head.

"It's going to be sweet," she warned.

And it was.

Discussion Questions

1. What do you find most interesting about the Diné culture? What was the most surprising thing to you in *Beneath a Navajo Moon*?

2. Who is your favorite character? Why?

3. Why did it mean so much to Adam that Erin saw him for himself and not just another Navajo? How do you want to be known?

4. Why is Jesus a hard sell among the People?

5. What can we learn from the Diné culture?

6. What did God desire from Erin? Require of Adam? What does He want from you? What is His calling upon your life?

7. Have you ever had to leave everyone and everything you loved behind for God's sake as did Olivia and Erin? Have you ever faced a dilemma between following your heart or God's will? What did you choose? Why?

8. Like Lottie Moon and Olivia, do you believe you are immortal—not one day more, not one day less—until your work for Him is done? How does that inspire you?

9. What great equalizer did Adam find at the foot of the cross?

10. Adam and Erin testify that "God is so good." How has God shown His goodness to you?

11. How would you answer these three essentials for a happy life?

    Something to look forward to?
    Good work to do?
    Someone to love?

12. Are there areas where obedience is tough for you as a believer? Or are you, like Adam, finding it difficult to surrender, to bow the knee to God?

13. Explain why the conjoined twin of obedience is surrender. How have you experienced this in your life?

14. Has God ever brought you into someone's life or a situation for a specific season or purpose? Brought someone into your situation? What happened?

15. God calls us to be living sacrifices. What things in your life, like Erin's, are difficult to leave on the altar to God?

16. "The Creator made each of us to long for Him and until you bow your knee and come to Him nothing else will ever satisfy." How have you found this to be true in your life?

17. Has God in His mercy and unmerited grace ever given you a second chance? How so? What did you do with it?

18. What work is the Lord today calling you to do for Him? Where do you make a difference?

19. Do you live your life in balance and harmony? Who/what is at the center of your life? In what/whom have you found fulfillment?

20. How does cultural imperialism—past and present—make it harder for other people groups to find the One True God?

21. Are you walking in the beauty of an abundant life with your Creator? What keeps you from embracing the fullness of the life He offers?

22. Is there only one way, one place, for a believer to serve God? Why or why not?

23. What long, painful obedience have you endured in order to pursue holiness?

24. We're marked by our choices, good and bad, which reveal to whom we've given our devotion. What brand marks do you bear on your body or soul?

We hope you enjoyed reading *Beneath a Navajo Moon* and that you will continue to read Abingdon Press fiction books. Here's an excerpt from Lisa Carter's *Under a Turquoise Sky.*

1

As soon as the elevator doors closed behind her, Kailyn knew she'd made a mistake.

Music blared in a mind-numbing, ear-deafening pulse from the penthouse suite stereo. Clutching her beaded purse, she placed her hands over both of her ears. A Latin beat, coupled with a heavy, chest-pounding thumping bass, jangled her nerve endings.

Where was Dex?

Scanning the crowded party, she wrinkled her nose at the pungent odor permeating the room. An aroma once smelled—as any college student could testify—never forgotten. Bodies writhed and gyrated.

Kailyn's lip curled, the lyrics penetrating her consciousness. Gangsta rap.

Spanish gangsta rap.

Couples lounged on the couches, twined into each other. She pursed her lips at the faint lines of a chalk white powder on a coffee table.

Dex had warned her to wait in the car. But she'd refused. No way she wanted to hang out in a deserted parking garage once night fell.

He said he'd be gone only a few minutes. Told her his biggest client wanted him to do a meet-and-greet with an out-of-town business associate. Promised they'd be on their way to the charity ball soon.

She crossed her arms, hugging herself. This was so *not* the charity ball. She tapped her foot on the hardwood floor. Dex better get a move on or her grandmother would have a cow.

Let Golden Boy explain their way out of this one.

It came to her attention of all the occupants in the room, she was the only blond. Probably the only native English speaker, too.

The only woman whose décolletage wasn't cut to her navel and whose hemline wasn't hiked to her thighs. Self-conscious, she smoothed a hand across the ice blue floor-length Vera Wang she wore. She didn't belong here.

Her skin prickled the way it does when you feel someone staring. Someone across the sunken living area. Against the glass-enclosed walls overlooking the twinkling lights of downtown Charlotte, she locked onto the penetrating glare of a thirty-something Latino man. His black hair scraped back from his sharply cut features, a pencil-thin mustache and goatee framed full, sensual lips.

Gold studs glittered in both his ears. He'd been dancing—her brow arched—a euphemistic word for what she'd never describe as dancing. The voluptuous Latina continued to bump and grind. He'd gone stock-still. His dark chocolate eyes narrowed.

She lifted her chin, noting his skintight black pants, the gleam of gold chains against his well-muscled chest. And the smaller silver turquoise cross in the hollow of his throat. His white silk shirt hung open all the way to his—

Her feelings must have shown on her face for he moved around the woman, dodging the other revelers with the grace of a jaguar. Her mouth went dry. Out of her peripheral vision, she noted three other men from the corners of the room advancing.

With a flick of his hand, he motioned the other men away. But he kept coming, his face unreadable. Her chest hammered. She reminded herself this was America, not Columbia. She was an American citizen. She had every right to—

"You don't belong here."

The blond stiffened. She stared for a moment at the cross he wore about his neck. He fought the urge to touch it for reassurance. She cut her eyes at him, the look she gave him derisive.

He folded his arms across his chest. "Go back to where you belong, *chica*."

She squared her shoulders. "I belong where I say I belong."

Defiance sparked from her iris blue eyes. He scowled. "Not here, you don't."

Her nostrils flared. "I'm waiting for my date, Dex Pritchard."

The tension between his shoulder blades eased. He'd spotted her as soon as the elevator doors parted. One look at her designer dress and smooth, flaxen chignon, he'd strode over thinking to provide a lifeline to an innocent who'd wandered into the wrong place at the wrong time.

His bad.

Not an innocent. Not if she kept company with a weasel like Pritchard. Still, the situation was sensitive. Time she got a move on. Perhaps a new tactic was called for.

He broadened his chest and bared his teeth. "Ah." He allowed his shoulders to rise and fall. "Perhaps if I upped your hourly rate."

The woman's eyes widened. Her lips parted, her mouth opening into a round O.

In a reflex move he admired for its swiftness, she raised her hand. He caught it in a hard vise inches before she could make contact with his face. She twisted, yanking her hand free.

He loomed over her. "Such passion, *señorita. Bueno.* I think you and I, we could work out some arrangement."

She took a step backward against the closed elevator doors. With deliberation, he positioned one hand on the space to the right of her head. Trapped, for the first time, fear shone from her eyes.

"Get away from me," she hissed. She pushed at him, her palm cool against his bare chest. Strained with all the consequence of a gnat straining to shift a burro.

Silently, he applauded her courage, her spunk. While he bewailed her stupidity.

He allowed his lips to curve. He leaned into her, her short gasps of breath fluttering against his cheek. "Let me introduce you to Latino-style love. I promise, once you've—"

"Can I never leave you unchained for a moment around the women, *mi amigo?*"

He closed his eyes at the sound of Esteban's smooth tones. He'd hoped to get the woman out of here before his boss emerged from the conference room at the rear of the suite.

"Get your hands off her." The Anglo lawyer, Pritchard, fair and blond like her, shoved his shoulder. To as much avail as the woman.

He planted his left hand on the other side of her head. "Maybe now she's had time to consider the advantages of—"

"Call him off, Esteban," growled Pritchard.

"You should have never brought the *cordera* here." Esteban's voice if anything grew colder.

Pritchard, not as dumb as he looked, managed to catch its glacial chilliness, too. "I—I told her to wait in the car. When I received your urgent text, I came right over."

At Pritchard's words, the woman bristled. Leave it to Pritchard to hang himself by throwing his date under the proverbial bus.

He gave her a slow, menacing smile.

If this woman was half as intelligent as he read in her eyes, she'd realize Pritchard was no friend. In fact, though she didn't know it, he was her only friend in this room. Her only chance.

Esteban snorted. "What? You couldn't have dropped her off at home first? You brought her into our business? *Estupido.*"

With more credit than he'd initially awarded her, the bimbo kept her mouth shut. A shapely, elegant bimbo. High-class. Nothing but the best for the Pritchards of the world.

"She won't be a problem, I promise."

He broke eye contact with the woman, throwing a glance over his shoulder at the near-groveling Anglo. He despised those overprivileged, former frat boy, trust-fund types.

Esteban lifted one eyebrow, stretching the muscles of his face into the semblance of a grin. A caricature of the blending of his Aztec and conquistador heritage. "I will hold you to that." He clapped a manicured hand on Pritchard's shoulder.

The Anglo jumped.

Esteban focused his laserlike attention his way. "Let her go, Rafael."

He made an exaggerated sigh, the air trickling out from his lips. The woman turned her face away. "If you say so, *mi patrón.* I thought she might be part of the entertainment . . ." he licked his lips, ". . . package you provide for your associates." His body pressed hers against the elevator. She trembled.

Esteban laughed, the sound guttural. "Later, my friend, I promise. After our business is concluded. One day, I will introduce you to the keeper of my flocks."

The sound of Esteban's laughter frissoned across Rafe's spine, recalling to his mind his grandmother's tales of the evil *chindi*.

"Rafe . . . " The Latina he'd left on the dance floor called his name.

One of his names.

Esteban chuckled. "I think, *hermano,* you need my help not at all with the chicas."

Time to save this particular *chica*.

He tilted his head, his lips touching the strands of silken hair at her diamond-studded ear. "Run, don't walk, *querida*." She flinched. "And don't ever show your face here again."

To make his point, he raked his hand down the side of the woman's sequined dress. She shrank further against the elevator. His hand trailing down, she tensed expecting him to touch her in a more invasive location, but instead he pressed the elevator button. The doors opened.

Knees buckling, she fell in backward. Sidestepping him, Pritchard caught her arm. Pritchard glared at him, placing a protective arm around the blond's shoulders.

He blew them both a kiss. The doors closed, shuttering them from his view. And he let out an inaudible sigh of relief before turning to face Esteban.

But Esteban lounged halfway across the room in intimate conversation with one of the organization's female groupies. Esteban assumed—rightly—his orders would be obeyed and hadn't bothered to stick around to see them carried out.

Esteban's arrogance and overweening pride would make his job a lot easier in the long run. Be the drug lord's downfall.

Dismissing the Anglos from his mind, he wrapped his persona once more around himself, a second skin. Like her, he didn't belong here, either.

Or he hadn't when he'd first begun this operation. The longer he remained in this slime hole, he worried how much like them he'd become. But this kind of thinking would get him killed. Banishing his doubts, he hardened his heart from the unpleasantness of what he'd have to do to accomplish his mission.

Striding toward the woman he'd temporarily abandoned, he fingered the silver turquoise cross resting among the clanking gold chains. He had his duty to perform. And whatever it took . . . He grimaced before painting the expected leer on his face.

Whatever it took to get the job done, he'd do.

2

Three months later

I'VE GOT A SURPRISE FOR YOU, MI AMIGA."

Amused, Kailyn glanced at her enthusiastic friend. She lounged against the deck chair, sipping her iced tea. "What now?"

She arched her eyebrows at Gaby. "Don't tell me you've ditched my color swatches and gone your own way?"

Gabriella Carmelita Flores Mendoza tossed her sun-streaked mane over a bare shoulder. She spread her coral-painted nails across the surface of the iron-scrolled table at the poolside cabana. "You've found me out."

Her dark brown eyes twinkled. "I've rejected your advice and chosen to paint the master suite—"

"Let me guess..." Kailyn adjusted the brim of her white hat to keep the afternoon sun out of her eyes.

Stalling while she formulated an answer sure to entertain her friend, Kailyn's eyes darted around the perimeter of the Flores's ten-thousand-square-foot mansion. Several months into their budding friendship, Gaby asked Kailyn to redecorate the Flores home. One exquisite room at a time, though the house needed no makeover.

But fledgling interior designers couldn't afford to be choosy. Not in this economy. And what were friends for, Gaby reminded, if they couldn't throw business a friend's way every now and again?

"Black."

Gaby choked on a swallow of water.

"You've chosen, against my advice, to paint the master cavern you call a bedroom black."

Gaby's lips twitched. "You've uncovered my secret."

Kailyn's eyes widened.

Gaby fell over the side of her chair at the expression on Kailyn's face. "Got you. So gullible. So naïve. So . . . "

Kailyn made a move as if to scoot back her chair. "If I'd known I was only coming over here to be insulted . . . "

Gaby patted her arm. Her coral lips widened, revealing perfect white teeth glowing against the brownness of her natural skin tone. "I love you just the way you are, Kailyn."

She squirmed, unsettled by Gaby's praise. "No, I think you were right the first time. All my life I've rushed headlong into situations where—"

"Where *ángeles* fear to tread?" Gaby crossed her legs at the ankle, brushing out a crinkle in her apricot-colored swimsuit.

Kailyn's lips quirked at the way her friend mixed her English with *Español*. Not that she understood much Spanish. Her grandmother had insisted she study French.

Which had proven to be so useful. Like a lot of things her grandmother had insisted she learn.

Not.

"Actually, I was kidding. You have impeccable taste as always. But I do have a gift for you—Wait," Gaby countered at Kailyn's motion of protest.

"You don't have to keep buying me gifts. Your friendship means the world to me."

Gaby's face softened. "Right back at you, my friend. I don't know how I would've survived these months . . . " Her gaze flickered.

They'd been riding bikes next to each other at the gym for a week, same time every morning, before they'd acknowledged the other's presence. But their friendship hadn't blossomed until Kailyn inadvertently followed Gaby into the women's restroom and discovered the Latina leaning against a stall door, sobbing over a soiled tampon in her hand.

"My hopes and dreams died then." Gaby's lips trembled. "I realized the doctors were correct. I'd never conceive without medical intervention."

Gaby's hands fisted in her lap. "And I knew my husband would never agree to invasive procedures calling into question his very manhood."

Kailyn dropped her eyes and traced the condensation down the stem of her glass. She'd never met Gaby's husband. But she long ago realized all was not well in the Flores marriage.

She'd also come to the belated realization Gaby only invited her over when Señor Flores was out of town on another business trip. Her childless friend had been lonely, hence their unlikely friendship when Kailyn offered a tissue and a shoulder to cry upon in the restroom. An unlikely, but mutually satisfying friendship between a pampered, sheltered Southern belle—Kailyn was self-aware if nothing else—and a vivacious, sheltered, convent-educated Latina.

Gaby cleared her throat. "You've given me so much more than sympathy. Your kindness . . . Hope of heaven . . ."

Kailyn shuffled her flip-flops on the concrete, truly uncomfortable now. "I didn't—"

Gaby seized her arm. "Oh yes, you did. More than you know."

"You don't have to shower me with extravagant gifts from Prada and Gucci just because my grandmother cut me off after I ditched Dex."

Gaby's mouth twisted. "You were right to dump that sleaze bucket."

Kailyn nodded. "You and I are in complete agreement there, but Grandmother didn't agree." She bit her lip at the memory of society maven, Carole Eudailey's exact words about Kailyn's choice of friends.

In her grandmother's tunneled worldview, Latinas answered doors and scrubbed kitchen floors.

Gaby scraped her chair back. "You did far more for me. You brought me back to my faith. Come."

She followed Gaby around the pool toward the house. Gaby threw open the glass door on the tiled veranda. "Come see."

"What now? I really don't need any more Bobbi Brown makeup."

"Better, *mi hermana en Cristo*."

Sister in Christ.

Kailyn sighed, resigned to her fate. It was a tough job to be the constant recipient of Gaby's thousand-dollar shopping sprees. But, hey, someone had to do it.

Gaby strolled into the Mexican tiled kitchen. A kitchen she never used. A furious barking greeted their entrance.

Kailyn's eyes rounded. "What the—?" She swung her gaze to her grinning, *loca* friend. "What have you done?"

"Voila!" Gaby swept her arm across the length of the make-shift pen corralling the ugl—One look at Gaby's adoring pet-lover face and Kailyn amended—most unusual-looking dog she'd ever laid eyes on.

Kailyn narrowed her eyes. "You said your husband hated dogs."

Gaby cocked her head. "He does. But this is for you. To greet you when you return to your condo after a long day placating impossible clients like myself." She bowed her chin to her chest. "This, I do for you my friend. To warm your heart. A small token of all you've done for me."

Kailyn planted her hands on her hips. "My heart's less than warmed. I work long hours, Gab. What would I do with a pet?"

Gaby's eyes found hers. "You don't like dogs?"

"I—I didn't say that." Gaby's chin jabbed at the air between them. "You tell me your grandmother no allow pets after you came to live with her. How your parents had promised you a dog but after your mother's death . . . " She raised her shoulders and let them drop in the classic Latino gesture of she'd-done-what-she-could.

"Besides," she stabbed her index finger in Kailyn's direction. "You tell me to find something to expend my energy upon and so I volunteer at the animal shelter like you say."

Kailyn winced. Somehow she already knew how this would end.

"You tell me to lavish the love I have inside on those who need it most."

Kailyn had been thinking the senior center not the SPCA.

"You say I should find the least of these and make their lives better."

Kailyn lifted her eyes to the ceiling.

"Nobody want this dog, Kailyn."

"For obvious reasons," Kailyn smirked, taking a long look at the powder puff-sized mongrel. His hairless body suggested a strong resemblance to an oversized rat.

"This dog going to be executed, if no one take home."

Her lips jerked at Gaby's dramatic turn of phrase.

Gaby laid her hand over her heart as if preparing to recite the Pledge of Allegiance. "I rescue this dog from the path of destruction. I see beneath the . . . " She stumbled, searching for the right words.

"Splotchy gray skin?"

Gaby sniffed.

"Thinning patches of white fur on his head and paws?" Kailyn frowned. "He's not mangy, is he?"

"I see beyond the abuse he's suffered. I see the loyal friend he'll become. I see the special brand of courage he's utilized to survive to this point. I see this dog and I give hope. Just like you give to me."

At the word, "abuse," Kailyn studied the dog more closely. "He's been abused?"

Her heart constricted. As no doubt, Gaby planned.

She hated being so predictable. A sucker for a lost cause.

Triumph glittered in Gaby's eyes. "And so I gift him to you."

Kailyn leaned over the pen. "Yeah, you gift him to *me*."

The dog, all five pounds of him, snarled in her direction.

"A real friendly gift, I see." Kailyn let loose an explosive breath.

The dog jumped half his height into the air.

"No loud noises. You scare our new friend, Kailyn." Gaby sank to her knees on the terra-cotta floor, allowing the dog to see her hand. The growling stopped. The mutt allowed Gaby to place one finger on his head.

"What in the world would I do with a dog?" She hunkered beside Gaby. "Especially a dog who needs so much attention and retraining."

"Love," Gaby corrected, making cooing noises.

"It's not a baby," and Kailyn regretted the words as soon as they left her mouth.

Pain slashed Gaby's face.

"I'm sorry. Forgive my thoughtless words."

Gaby gave her a sad smile. "No, you are correct. And upon reflection, I believe as always *mi Dios* knew best in preventing me from bringing an innocent *bebé* into my situation. I bring the dog home only because Esteban's out of town. It must go home with you or back to the death chamber." She sighed. "At least for now."

Esteban? An uneasy feeling niggled at the edges of her consciousness. Where had she . . . ?

Gaby placed her hands upon her thighs. "I teach you everything I know about how to approach wounded creatures."

"Wait. You said the word, abused, before. Like you, Gaby?"

Gaby's mouth hardened. "Not what you think, *mi hermana*. But abuse comes in all shapes and degrees." She glanced out the window overlooking the side lawn. "I'm finally doing what I should've done the first time I suspected. After seeing you display such courage in throwing off everything you've ever known to do what is right, you've given me the courage—el Cristo has given me the courage—to face what must be faced."

"I don't under—"

"There are more gifts." With the grace of a ballerina, Gaby rose in one fluid motion. She snagged a turquoise leather tote off the kitchen island.

A doggy carrier? A five-hundred-dollar fashion, doggy-accessorized carrier?

Kailyn settled onto her haunches. "More?"

Gaby plucked items from the bag. "Deluxe grooming tools." She laid the brush and comb on the granite countertop. "Gourmet dog treats." Those ended up beside the first items. "A collar worthy of a prince." Gaby laughed. "Even a dog deserves bling."

Kailyn groaned at the sight of the ruby-encrusted dog collar. No way she'd ever appear in public with a canine bedecked in such a thing.

Gaby continued with the canine essentials tour, ignoring Kailyn's weakening protests.

"Exactly what kind of dog is this, Gab?" She tilted her head. "Strains of Chihuahua mixed with a touch of pit bull mixed with Chinese Crested?"

"A dog," Gaby set her jaw. "Who needs love and attention."

"So love me, love my dog, is that it, Gab?" She leveled her gaze at Gaby's oh-so-innocent features. "Just be aware, you're pushing the limits of my tolerance, *friend*."

"A temporary arrangement, I promise." Gaby nodded. "Until I can," she tensed. "Make more permanent arrangements."

Kailyn sighed. "Temporary? You promise?"

Gaby clapped her hands together.

As if the outcome had ever been in doubt.

"What's the dog's name?"

Gaby smiled, a sweet smile. "I sense someone else will name my little darling."

"Darling?" Kailyn took another long gander at the wiggling mass of canine mush. "Huh . . . Some darling." She snorted.

Gaby fastened the collar around the dog's scrawny neck. "I'll teach you everything you need to know."

And for the next hour, Gaby was true to her word. Everything she'd learned from her work at the shelter about dealing with abused animals. At the sound of an engine, Gaby frowned. Glancing out the window, she stuffed the dog's accessories into the oversized purse.

"He still likes you better than me," Kailyn complained. Car doors slammed outside. "I don't see how in the world—"

"*Mi esposo's* supposed to be in Miami this week." Gaby craned her neck as a trio of men exited the black SUV parked in the driveway.

"Here," Gaby scooped the dog from the pen and deposited him inside the super-sized tote. "Why don't you take him upstairs, retrieve those color swatches in the bedroom, and apply more sunscreen to your lily white Anglo skin? You're blinding the neighbors."

She thrust the purse—and the dog—at Kailyn.

"Is this your—?"

"He probably forgot something." Gaby swallowed. "He never stays at home for long during a workday. I'll see what he needs and—"

"I'd like to meet—"

"No." Gaby prodded her toward the hallway. "Best you stay upstairs. He doesn't like strangers in the house. He doesn't know about our friendship, and I think it's best to keep it this way."

"What's going on, Gaby?"

Kailyn strained around her friend, watching the three men. Clad in black business suits with dark polarized sunglasses concealing their features, they entered through the side gate and emerged into the privacy-fenced enclosed backyard.

"Go," Gaby hissed, hustling her to the stairs. "Please, my friend. Do this for me. They can't find you. Whatever happens, whatever you overhear, do not, I beg you, leave the house. I'd hoped to be away before…"

Gaby's voice caught and smothered a sob. "But everything now depends on . . . " She squeezed Kailyn's arm. "Promise me you'll always take care of my dog."

"What's going on? You're scaring me."

"Promise me for the love of *Dios*."

"I promise, but I don't—"

Gaby pushed her backward.

Kailyn stumbled up the staircase. The dog poked out his head, snarling and revealing yellowed fang teeth.

"Gaby . . ."

But Gaby turned her back, squaring her shoulders, lifting her chin when someone bellowed her name.

Kailyn paused at the top of the landing overlooking the cathedral ceiling entryway. Goosebumps scurried up her bare arms. She'd left her wallet and keys in her bag at the cabana. She wished she'd brought her wrap inside. She promised herself as soon as Gaby's husband left, she'd gather her things and leave.

Hurrying into the master suite, she spotted the fabric swatch board where she'd left it on a bedside table. At the sound of angry voices, she sidled over to the Palladian window overlooking the pool. She stuck the swatches inside the bag.

The dog's jaws snapped.

"Hey," she yelped, barely removing her fingers in time from the proximity of the dog's teeth. "Watch it."

". . . What have you done, Gabriella?" the man raged. From this bird's-eye angle, her depth perception was skewed, but she judged him to be a few inches above her own height of 5'6" from how he towered over his more petite wife.

"I've done nothing, Esteban, *mi esposo.*" Gaby's voice had taken on a soothing tone, like one attempting to placate a fractious child. Her hand reached to cup her husband's chin.

He slapped her hand away.

Kailyn jolted.

She'd had about enough of this. She'd not stand by and allow anyone to be abused. Not a dog, much less her friend.

Kailyn considered rushing to Gaby's rescue until . . . Her husband pushed his glasses onto his head, and she recognized him as the same frightening Esteban from the hotel several months ago.

"Where is it, Gabriella? I'll have none of your games."

"Games? I don't know—"

He smacked Gaby so hard her head whipped around. The dog, his eyes bugged to the glass, growled. The two men grabbed Gaby by her forearms to keep her from hitting the ground.

Kailyn's eyes darted around the room, spotting a cell phone. She dialed 911.

A woman's voice answered. "State your emergency."

"I'd like to report a case of domestic violence in progress right now. Hurry. I'm afraid for my friend's life."

A woman's voice on the other end sharpened. "Please tell me your name and your location."

"I don't know the physical address from memory. I've only been here a few times and after typing it into my GPS, I forgot it. Somewhere on Marietta Lane. But I know you can trace this call and the location from the phone. I'm looking out the second-story window, watching this play out in front of my eyes. The other two men have grabbed hold of her—"

"You said this was a case of domestic violence. There are three men? Do you see any weapons? Are they armed?"

"No. Yes. No. Maybe."

Her hand shook. "They're wearing suits in this heat. I can't tell underneath the bulk. Please," she whispered. "Hurry, they're hurting her."

"Miss? Miss?"

"Kailyn," she murmured. "Kailyn Eudailey."

"Ms. Eudailey, I've dispatched two units to your location. Please stay on the line. Don't hang up."

"Oh, God, help us." Kailyn clutched the phone to her ear. "Hurry, hurry," she begged.

Going berserk, the dog launched himself against the glass pane.

"Hush." She stuffed the dog farther into the recesses of the purse, terrified the men would hear.

"You will tell me, Gabriella," Esteban Flores shouted. "One way or the other, you will tell me."

Kailyn tuned out the dispatcher and directed her attention once more to the scene below.

Gaby struggled against the men's hands, holding her like fetters. "I don't know—"

"Two things, *mi esposa*," Flores growled.

He held up two fingers. "Two things I've required from you from the beginning. To beget me a son and to give me your undying loyalty. Both of which you've failed miserably to do thus far."

Lunging against the men restraining her, Gaby spat in his face.

But instead of the explosive reaction she'd expected from Flores, an icy calm settled over his features. Which somehow managed to terrify Kailyn more than his temper.

He flicked his fingers at his men. They released Gaby. She staggered.

"I think a reminder of the punishment for disloyalty is due your way." He unbuttoned the top of his white dress shirt and loosened his silk tie. He shrugged out of his jacket, tossing it to one of his goons.

Unhurried, methodical, he rolled first one sleeve to his elbow and then the other. The expression on his face reminded Kailyn of a snake she'd once seen in the woodpile as it cornered a mouse.

Kailyn shivered.

"I will tell you nothing."

"Oh, yes, you will, Gabriella. Or see me in hell first."

Gaby's laugh rang out over the sultry Southern summer air. His face darkened.

Gaby lifted her eyes to the Carolina blue sky. "One place I can assure you, *gracias a Dios,* I will never be."

Something so evil, so sudden, leaped across the man's countenance, twisting and misshaping his face. Even from a distance Kailyn recoiled, dropping the phone.

Kailyn scrambled, fumbling to retrieve the phone from where it scudded across the Persian carpet. She accidentally punched the power button OFF, severing her connection with Dispatch. She moaned.

"Oh, God. Oh, God." Stupid, so stupid. Why had God made her so clumsy and stupid?

By the time she resumed her watchful position by the window, Flores had grabbed Gaby around the neck. His face convulsed with fury, he dragged her kicking and screaming toward the pool. He shrieked words Kailyn surmised as obscenities in his native Spanish tongue.

Before she had time to think, to react, Flores hurled her friend into the shallow end and plunged after her, the water to his chest. He shoved Gaby face first into the turquoise water and held her down. Gaby's arms flailed, her desperate jabs never making contact with his body.

Kailyn screamed and pounded on the window with her fist. No one glanced up.

Some instinct caused Kailyn to hold the expensive phone to the window and without consciously meaning to, she snapped a photo. And then another. And another.

Gaby went still.

Kailyn couldn't take her finger off the button. She kept pressing, the camera phone clicking and whirring and warming up for yet one more. A sudden beam of light from the descending sun caught the plastic frame of the phone display.

The beam sharpened and fragmented, bouncing off the polar-ized glasses of the men. Momentarily blinding Gaby's psycho husband—

All three jerked up at the same moment. Flores, his hand still cramming his dead wife's head into the water. As one, they shunted toward the house. The water streamed off Flores's ruined business attire as he mounted the pool steps.

Kailyn shrank back. But too late, they'd seen her. Her eyes ping-ponged, seeking a place to hide.

And then, the blessed sound of sirens.

The men froze, exchanging glances. Flores scowled. He motioned for the men to follow him. They disappeared through a gate at the rear of the property.

She wriggled under the massive mahogany desk in the cor-ner, dragging the tote and the whimpering dog in after her. Her knees bunched to her chin, her teeth chattered. Still in her swimsuit, she hugged the tote and the dog to her chest as shock set in while she waited for the police to find her.